MW01178522

To Sleep
with Stones

A Hollystone Mystery

WL HAWKIN

Blue Haven Press

Library and Archives Canada Cataloguing in Publication

Hawkin, W. L., author
        To sleep with stones / W.L. Hawkin.

(Hollystone mysteries ; 2)
Issued in print and electronic formats.
ISBN 978-0-9950184-0-2 (softcover).—
ISBN 978-0-9950184-4-0 (kindle).--
ISBN 978-0-9950184-5-7 (epub)

        I. Title.

PS8615.A8175T67 2017   C813'.6   C2017-900286-4
                                               C2017-900287-2

To Jackie,

Without you, I might never have seen the Ballymeanoch Standing Stones. Thank you for Scotland, much laughter, and a lifetime of friendship

CHAPTER ONE

Summer Solstice

SORCHA FOUND IT IN THE MUD. Pried it from beneath a thin flat stone with tenderness and a trowel—a mud-encrusted, green-tinged, tangled mess. Dylan watched, so entranced he couldn't breathe.

When she popped the trowel back in the faded caddy, she wore tied around her waist, he inhaled at last. Peeling off one glove, and then the other, she let them fall. As she cradled the object in her palm, her green eyes flickered as if it was speaking to her, and his mind flared again. *Did she share his gift? Perhaps, have a talent for psychometry?* Imagine holding a golden torque in your hand and seeing its tale unfold in cinematic brilliance. Imagine knowing whose head it adorned, where all it had travelled, and how many lives it had saved, or snuffed out.

She squatted, dipped her treasure reverently in a bucket of water; then cleansed it with her bare fingers. Sorcha was a renegade archaeologist who didn't always follow procedure or stick to the grid. He usually admired that, but today it gave him shivers.

Kai stamped his foot like a nervous horse, and shone the torch. "Gold," he murmured, with sly elation, and Dylan cringed, knowing he was considering the cash that could be made from the sale of such an artifact on the black market.

"Thank you, god," she whispered, cupping it to her breast. It was just an expression—the only god she worshipped was fame. Sorcha O'Hallorhan was searching for archaeological connections between the Inner Hebrides of Scotland, where they currently stood, and a land twenty-five hundred miles southeast. Egypt. This artifact was quite possibly the connecting cord; the evidence she needed to prove a legend real and grasp that fame.

"Is it—?" asked Dylan.

"Aye lads." She fondled the turquoise beads. *Faience*. Just like the beads that adorned the golden collar of King Tut. "I knew we'd find her." *She* was Meritaten, eldest daughter of Egyptian King Akhenaten and Queen Nefertiti. It was the stuff of story, and to prove it true would change the way the world viewed prehistory.

Kai reached out his large rough hand. He wanted to hold it.

But Sorcha drew back, slipped it in her vest pocket and began climbing the rope ladder.

They'd dug down nearly eighteen feet into a pre-Celtic holy well because Sorcha had a theory. People offered gifts to the guardians of holy wells; and sometimes too, they used them to hide things. At this depth, the team had already travelled back in time three millenniums, and unearthed a scattering of bronze axe heads, obsidian arrowheads, jet beads and pottery shards; the skull of an extinct great auk with its long curved bill still intact; the shed antlers of a stag; and sadly, a malformed infant. But that was nothing compared to this.

Kai followed her up the ladder, his nose way too close for Dylan's liking. Sorcha O'Hallorhan was the site boss, about to claim her PhD in archaeology, but Kai Roskilde was charged with old Viking blood and bent on booty. He'd have her, and anything she found, any way he could.

"Dylan," she called. "Don't you want to see it?" Her voice faded as she skipped towards the artifact tent to legitimize her prize.

"Aye. I'm coming," he said, rubbing his muscles into something pliant. He'd blown his right knee playing rugby, and it was aching something fierce. But when he reached for the rope ladder, it jumped high, right up and out of the pit.

He heard Kai's crazy cackle and glanced up: could see the sneer above the blond frizzled beard, and just make out the long scar that split his right cheek from temple to chin. It was a switchblade; a souvenir from a bar fight in Eastside London. He'd killed the man in revenge and walked away, so he said. Logic told Dylan that was shite, but there was something malevolent lurking beneath those watery blue eyes that gave it perverse possibility, and he did not wish to try the man on.

"Very funny. Now toss her down." Dylan sniffed and rubbed his nose. "Kai, come on."

But Kai was gone, and Dylan was left standing in the cold Argyll muck, cursing his decision to join this summer dig. He leaned back against the mucky shaft and steamed. The faint clatter of camp filtered down as people shuffled and settled into Sunday breakfast. Kai would return, but only when he was damn good and ready; when he'd made his point, and embarrassed him in front of Sorcha. Dylan could wait him out. He'd done it before.

What was he doing here? He could be anywhere in the world. Christ. He'd turned down a field school in Greece to come here…to come *home*.

Argyll sprawls along the south-west coast of Scotland in the Inner Hebrides. Once the prehistoric centre of the region, Kilmartin Glen is rife with chambered cairns, standing stone circles, and mysterious cup and ring marks—over one hundred and fifty documented prehistoric monuments. Dylan spent his youth here, walking the paths of his ancestors and living with his grandfather in Tarbert, a fishing village on the shore of Loch Fyne. Not some boy's cup of tea perhaps, but Dylan was not just *any* boy. It was here he'd first heard the stones speak, and it was *those* voices that called him home.

But, as time wore on, he was aching for a strong cup of tea; something warm to wrap his fingers around. He heard scuffling, and was just about to call out when Kelly Mackeras popped his head over the edge. Fine-featured and clean-shaven, Kelly looked like a kid.

"Dylan McBride. What are you doing down there all by yourself?"

"Kai," replied Dylan.

Knowing only too well the misery that Viking caused around camp, Kelly rolled his eyes. "Heads up," he yelled, and flung down the rope ladder.

"Do you believe in karma?" Dylan asked, as he crawled out of the pit.

"Aye, some days."

"Big lug," he muttered, brushing the dirt from his khaki pants.

"You know *why* he picks on you, don't you, McBride?"

As they followed the bacon and coffee trail, Dylan's belly growled. "Because he's a giant arsehole?"

"Aye, sure, but that's not why. It's because *she* likes you."

"Who?"

"Sorcha, you daftie."

"No way." A woman like her? Sorcha was a stunner. An Irish lioness with bright green eyes flecked in gold, skin like vanilla cream, and a mane of curly red hair that fell past her voluptuous breasts. Just thinking about her made him hard.

"Oh, aye. She wants you and he wants her. So, mind," Kelly said, punching his shoulder. "That bastard could sack a city single-handed."

Dylan rolled his eyes in agreement. "Thanks for this, man. But, how did you know—?"

"Sorcha sent me," he said, elbowing Dylan in the ribs.

Dylan gasped. "Do you really think—?"

Kelly noticed his bulging khakis, and chuckled. "Oh, aye, McBride. She'll soon drain the blood from your sweet apple cheeks."

"But, it's no good," Dylan mumbled, shaking his head. Of course, he wanted her. Who wouldn't? She was bonnie and dead brilliant. But it would never work. Kai Roskilde spent nights in her tent whenever she left the flap ajar. Plus, she was his boss, the kind of archaeologist he dreamed of becoming, and that was not a thing to mess with. Rumour had it, that her mother was an archaeology prof; a lesbian, who'd slept with her most handsome and promising male students, only long enough to conceive a child.

But there were worse things than antagonizing Kai Roskilde or ruining a career. Dylan knew that if he as much as kissed Sorcha O'Hallorhan, he'd fall in love, and that would be the end of him. The only use Sorcha had for men was to feed her lust, and he wanted to be more than mere fodder for a woman; however pleasurable that might be. Hell, he was still recovering from Maggie Taylor, a Canadian girl who'd taken him for her own magical ride last fall.

"Nah. Even if you're right, I couldn't—"

"She's watching you," Kelly said.

Sure enough, when Dylan glanced her way, she waved him over, flashing an open smile of bright white teeth, and he flushed, knowing he'd been bit.

"Just don't fall in love, McBride. And watch your back."

~~~

"Remind you of anyone?" asked Kelly, gesturing to a great jolly Viking statue by the snugs.

"Aye, but that one's a damn site more amiable than his cousin," Dylan replied.

The lads were belly up to the Irish bar in Oban, and the black stuff was flowing freely at Sorcha's expense. She'd taken the whole crew out for a Friday night piss-up to celebrate her dawn discovery. Oban was an hour's drive. They usually ended up somewhere close, but she'd insisted on an Irish night to honour her victory. Murphy's was packed with locals and splattered with summer tourists, as the season was just beginning. A decent Celtic band rocked the stage. Sorcha was tossing back whiskey shots like water, and Dylan figured that he and Kelly would be hoisting her home—that's if Kai didn't get to her first.

She caught him watching, and danced her way across the black and white tiles. Taking this as his cue to disappear, Dylan picked up his pint and bolted up the stairs. He planned to avoid any interactions by taking refuge in the cool quiet of the beer garden. Liquored to the gills, she'd get distracted before she ever made it that far.

Spying an empty table in a far corner that was reasonably concealed by plants, he hunkered down. As he sipped his pint, he stared up at the sky. It was a grand night, June twentieth, the eve of Summer Solstice. He couldn't believe six months had passed since Winter Solstice, when he'd watched the sun rise and gilt the six-thousand-year old burial chamber at Newgrange in Ireland. Estrada had been there with his mate, Michael, and he'd been there with Maggie.

Though they were different in many ways, he missed Estrada more than anyone else. He was a brilliant magician and a good mate. Last year, a maniac turned his life inside out, and Dylan feared he was broken still.

He stared at the stars. Those same stars shone over British Columbia where the coven would celebrate the solstice. He hoped that Estrada was with them at Buntzen Lake. He was their high priest, a key player in their ceremonies, and without him, the magic would not be the same.

He hoped that their high priestess, Sensara, had forgiven him for loving someone else so soon after loving her.

Of course, the folks here didn't know that Dylan was involved in Wicca. It wasn't the kind of thing people shared on a dig. They didn't know that he belonged to a coven in Canada called Hollystone, that he practiced his solitary magic when they were sleeping in their tents, or that he talked with stones.

He must have drifted off staring at the waning moon because he didn't know that Sorcha was there until she draped herself around his shoulders and brushed her whiskey-stained lips across the back of his bare neck.

~~~

Summer Solstice at Buntzen Lake. Inhaling, Estrada absorbed the resinous smoke that swirled from the braziers. Frankincense and myrrh. Fit for a king. Fit for a god. He felt him kick: *The Green Man.* Awakened, the summer god within his soul was desperate to dance.

As Daphne and Raine led him blindfolded into the circle, damp sand clung to the soles of his bare feet and stuck between his toes. He heard their voices blend with the others in a slow chant of syllabic triplets: *Helios, Apollo. Hail our Lord, the Green Man.* Rising in pitch, quickening in rhythm; it drove the witches as they began to dance.

Naked, but for a kilt of ferns, a scarf of hanging ivy, and a crown of oak leaves, he stood before the bonfire; the front of his body toasted by flames, his back prickling in the cool night air. Laughing and chanting, they raced around him, raising power in their passionate frenzy, and filling him with power too—until Sensara signalled a halt, and their panting merged with the sough and songs of the lakeside night.

He felt her move behind him—Sensara, his high priestess—sensed her energy blending with his own, could smell her and taste her: cedar and blood orange, and surprisingly, cinnamon. Had she finally forgiven him enough to wear cinnamon, his favourite spice? The tips of her fingers brushed his hair as she untied the silken blindfold. Did touching him rekindle intimate memories for her, as it did for him? Or had she buried their affair in some cold dark coffin?

As she stood before him and spoke the ritual words, he stared into her dark almond eyes.

"Blessed Be, Green Man. We welcome you. Celebrate with us this Summer Solstice when the sun reigns longest and brightest. It is *your* time."

"The time of the Green Man," echoed Daphne, Sylvia, and Raine.

"We honour you in all your guises." Lifting a large crystal bowl with both hands, she offered it to him. "Join us in drinking the elixir of the sun. We have prepared it especially for you."

Cupping his palms over hers, Estrada held the bowl to his lips and swallowed the sweet fiery elixir. Sparkling wine cut with Cointreau and absinthe, it swirled with strawberry slices and bright yellow blossoms. Protocol demanded he take only a sip, but the Green Man was a passionate god who soaked up liquor like summer rain. And, then there was Sensara. He absorbed her glamour along with the potion.

Draped in a flowing saffron gown, she wore a garland of the same bright yellow flowers around her loose black hair; blossoms of St. John's Wort. He tried to hold her gaze. He wanted her to see him in his godly guise. But she broke away and focussed on the bowl, refusing to share this moment they had shared so many times before. Had her love turned to hate? Or worse still, indifference?

Truly, all he craved was her friendship—a relationship with Sensara was far too constricting for a man like him—but even that door remained closed since their brief entanglement eight months ago.

Behind her, standing in *their* circle, was her new man, Yasu. He caught Estrada's glare, and sneered. Why had she brought *him* here to ridicule their sacred rites? This was no place for skeptics. Did she want him to see what he must accept to be her partner? Or was it something more? Did she intend for Yasu to replace him as her high priest? Estrada tilted the bowl higher and gulped.

"Save some for the rest of us," Sensara said. Having finally caught her attention, he grasped her hands firmly and guzzled half the bowl. Then, he held it to her lips. She feigned a sip. Sensara drank only on rare occasions, hated to let her guard down. He released her hands, and stood watching as she carried the bowl around the circle, offering each witch a sip of the Green Man's nectar.

He appraised Yasu. What did she see in him? A small Japanese man, he looked enough like her to be her brother. When she offered him the elixir, he closed his eyes and shrugged, then turned his face away—an impropriety that revealed his distaste for their rituals. Surely she knew Yasu could never take *his* place?

As the blessed wine had not been completely consumed, she returned to Estrada and held out the bowl. He took it, tipped it, and drained it. After handing her the empty bowl, he wiped his mouth with the back of his arm, and howled at the moon. Hearing giggling behind him, he winked and bowed. Their rituals were not meant to be stern or grim. They conjured for power, but also for pleasure, and he was, after all, the Green Man of the Wood.

Ignoring him, Sensara turned to the altar, where the ritual tools were laid out. Festooned in candles and draped in golden scarves, it shone like summer. She picked up a golden dagger, and turned to face him. Estrada knew what was coming, had played this role a half dozen summer nights; though perhaps not quite so vividly.

"Green Man, we hold this vigil in your honour. For all the plant life growing on our planet we ask healing and sustenance. Without our partners, the plants, we cannot survive. Our forests are in peril. We ask that all humanity take into their hearts and minds the desire to protect our trees, flowers, fungi, and all sentient beings."

"Protect them," came the echo.

Strolling around him, she stroked the knife lightly with her fingertips. "We understand that an offering must be made, for there is no life without death; no resurrection without decay. For all life, we thank you Green Man, and bless you for your sacrifice. The blood you spill this night will nourish the life to come."

"Blessed be the Green Man," came the echo.

"Let my blood nourish the soil," he said.

Then, standing before him, Sensara plunged the knife into his heart. At the faint borders of his consciousness, he heard Yasu cry out. Perhaps she'd prepared him for their theatrics. Perhaps not.

Collapsing to his knees, Estrada clutched the knife at his breast. The stage blood slithered down his belly and pooled in the sand.

"So mote it be," he whispered, and falling sideways, hit the ground hard, as a lone owl cut the silence with her screech.

The women covered him with a sheet. The stage knife and greenery were removed. Then, Daphne knelt by his head. He felt her hands against his scalp as she attached his headdress. Limbs hampered by liquor, he laid there for a very long time, entranced by the sound of the earth's heart beating in his ear.

"All hail the Horned God, Cernunnos. Rise, Dark Lord. Rise, and join us in the dance."

This was his cue. The Green Man was slain, but his twin, the Horned God, who ruled the second half of the year, must rise in his place. And yet, he could not rise.

Leaning down, Sensara whispered: "Going for an Oscar, Estrada?"

In his stupor, he realized that if he did not rise as Cernunnos, the Horned God…if he ruined the ceremony, his fate was sealed. Slowly, he pushed his drunken body up from the sand. He couldn't remember the scripted lines, but it did not matter.

Standing naked before Sensara, he took a deep breath and allowed the god to speak: "I rise from the sleepy darkness of the earth. From this day until Winter Solstice may all sentient beings find love and joy under my reign." Tossing his head, he felt the deer antlers move as if they were part of his skull. "Dance! Celebrate my resurrection with a dance."

"Dance, dance, dance," they chanted, as the sun rose over the mountains like a great golden orb. Daphne and Raine pounded their frame drums to set the beat. Moved by their rhythmic thunder, he jumped into the circle and joined them. It was good to dance with his family on the beach this summer night, and it had been a very long time since he'd felt good.

Cernunnos, Cernunnos. His name resounded as they leapt and twisted around the bonfire. Blood coursed through his body, empowering, hardening, every muscle. *Cernunnos, Cernunnos.* Swaying with the beating drums, he yelled: "I am The Horned God. I am alive."

The women hoisted their long skirts and leapt over the bonfire. Daphne was the first to wrench the flower garland from her hair and toss it into the flames. She held up her fingers stained with the blood of St. John's Wort, whooped, and danced on. Raine followed her, then Sylvia, and finally Sensara.

He regarded the sway of her hips, remembering the slight curves beneath the saffron gown. He wanted to chase her down and throw her to the ground; rip off that flimsy fabric, and remind her how good it feels to love a god. Grasping Sylvia's outstretched hand, he swung her around; then reached out to clutch Sensara. But, in that moment she linked arms with Yasu, and they jumped the fire together.

Ripping off the antler headdress, Estrada yowled; then hurled it into the sand, and ran.

Somehow, he found his Harley on the street. Drunk and desperate, he pulled on a pair of black leather pants and a vest he kept stashed in the panniers. Let her have Yasu. She'd find out soon enough that no one could replace him as high priest. He turned the key and kick-started the bike. Let her feel what it was like to be without him.

CHAPTER TWO

A Fresh Sweet Peach

DYLAN COULD SMELL WHISKEY AND SWEAT—woman's sweat. Sorcha was curled against his back like a ginger cat; her silky hair tickling his bare arms. Reaching up, he clutched the pale hand that caressed his neck to keep from jumping out of his skin.

"Found you," she purred. When her lips brushed his earlobe, her warm breath flooded his body and sent him reeling. She stroked his cheek, then turned his face, and kissed him full on the mouth. He'd never known a kiss like that. Sorcha was no young girl like Maggie. Filling his mouth with her whiskey tongue, she swung down onto his lap, and anchored herself with one leg on either side of his thighs.

When she took his hands, and slipped them up inside her white tank, his breath caught in his throat. Startled by her low moan, he broke away and tried to remember all the reasons this was wrong.

"Relax, McBride," she whispered, holding his hands firmly. "No one can see."

"That's not it." He bit his lip. "You're drunk. Tomorrow you'll—"

"Regret it? Nah, I'm not *that* drunk." She brushed her lips against his as she spoke. "I want you. How could I not want a fresh sweet peach of a lad who looks at me like I'm a goddess."

"Well, you are that. I'll not lie to you, Sorcha."

"Lie *with* me. When we get home, come to my tent. I've need of you, Dylan McBride." She kissed him again, long and deep, and he felt the force of it right to the ends of his shuddering toes.

"But Sorcha—"

"You're about to bust your zipper," she teased. "I'd like a wee taste of what's to come. Wouldn't you?"

Grinning like a Cheshire cat, she slid down between his knees and unfastened his jeans. *Holy Christ.* What could he do? Push her away?

Confess it was his first? He was harder than he'd ever been in his life; watching her red hair spill over his thighs, and the flicker of those dreamy green eyes. He told himself it was just a wee bit of sex; something Estrada enjoyed at least once a day, and likely more. And, then he closed his eyes.

There was nothing but her swirling heat, and his fingers twining in her hair, and for about twenty seconds he was fully Zen, and then he was crying prayers to God. Head rolled back, he blinked to a fleeting shadow, but he did not care for nothing.

Sorcha was aching for a pint after that, but Dylan needed to clear his head, so he promised to take her up on her offer, and staggered towards the street. It was just a wee bit of sex. Nothing more. Like Estrada always said. *Carpe diem.* Seize the day with no regrets—tomorrow may never come. Still his head was humming, and the vision of her hair in his lap haunted him.

Most of the crew had come in the minibus parked out front. Dylan had already offered himself up as designated driver and pocketed the keys, as he had things to do under the solstice moon when they returned to camp. Knowing the pub didn't close until two, he went searching for an all-night coffee shop where he could sober up and think.

He felt different somehow, more a man than a boy he supposed, like he'd experienced some coming of age ritual. And he quivered thinking of what she'd offered. What if he did it wrong or couldn't please her? Would she compare him to Kai? Laugh at him? He craved her something fierce, and knew that even if she broke his heart, he'd crave her still. He was bit bad and swelling with her venom. Perhaps that's why he didn't see the man until he was right up in his face.

"Spill, ya cunt," he spat.

God. The smell: cigar smoke, whiskey, and stale ale. "What did you say?"

Brown eyes leered from behind dark-rimmed glasses. He had a drab moustache, a straggly goatee. Dylan recognized the face, but didn't know why.

"She's a looker. What'd that cost ya?"

He knew he should punch this arsehole square in the face to defend her honour, but he had no fighting skills, and the man was a good head taller and likely more experienced.

"Don't you be calling Sorcha—"

"Ah, come on lad. A burd like that didn't suck a shite like you—"

"Sod off." Dylan tried to push past, but the man caught him by the arm and squeezed. "Look, I've no desire to fight you. Just let me—"

"Don't you want to see your picture?" the man teased. He waved his mobile and for a second, Dylan stood gobsmacked.

"Picture? You took pictures?"

"Oh aye, and a wee video too."

"Give it here." Dylan tried to grab the phone from the moving hand, but the man held it high in the air and snapped more shots.

"Easy, laddie," he sniggered. "I've a proposition."

"A proposition? Not bloody likely. I don't deal with blackmailers."

"I don't deal with blackmailers," the man mimicked. "Fine then. I'm sure Miss Sorcha O'Hallorhan will make a deal. She'll not be wanting her wild Irish curls—"

"How do you know her name?"

The man grinned. "Are you ready to listen, or do I go below?"

"What do you want?"

"Rumour has it, the *lady* found an artifact. Get me the story, and I'll press delete. Get me the treasure, and I'll cut you in."

"I won't tell you shite, and you *will* delete it, and all the bloody rest too." Snatching the phone from his hand, Dylan jumped into the van and hit the auto lock. Ignoring the pounding on the window, he searched for the video.

"Some bleedin' ned nicked my mobile!" the man yelled.

There was tapping on the window and Dylan looked up into the dour face of a policeman. "Mr. Steele would like his phone back. Give it over. Now."

Steele? That's why he knew his face. Alastair Steele was a Glasgow journalist. He wrote a regular column and was known for breaking stories.

After handing the phone to the officer, Dylan was left to stand in the shamefaced position—hands and face against the metal van. It gave him time to cool down, though his temper perked again when he heard the officer snigger. Steele had told him of his public indiscretion, while leaving out his blackmail scheme. After producing his driver's license, Dylan was let off with a warning, and slunk away from Murphy's dogged by their laughter.

Pissed and humiliated, he wandered down close to the sea, dodging scraps around the docks, and remembering why he seldom came to town to socialize. After seeing a couple of drunks get tossed from one of the seedier bars, he grew worried about Sorcha. This was what he'd hoped to avoid; this concern for a woman who had no concern for him. Still it was there, nagging at him, so he hastened back to Murphy's to make sure the bastard was not harassing her.

He found her on the dance floor groping some stranger whose shaved head was dark as stout. Wearing a wife-beater that revealed a bulky set of tattooed arms, the man held Sorcha upright by the cheeks of her arse. She wavered close to comatose, her face buried in his chest.

A shiver careened up his spine. He looked around for Kelly, not that he'd be much help if fists flew, but though his wee red mini was parked outside, he was nowhere to be seen. Then, Kai peered out of a snug looking about as pissed as he'd ever seen him, and just this once, Dylan was glad.

Kai did a double take on Sorcha and the stranger. Then he swaggered over and peeled her off the man, who narrowed his dark eyes, but did not argue with that drunken lug of a Viking. Throwing her over his shoulder like a sack of booty, Kai charged up the stairs.

"Leavin' now," Dylan shouted to the crew. He was relieved that Sorcha was pissed. She likely wouldn't remember their earlier encounter and life could go back to normal.

When they were all tucked away in their tents—Kai in Sorcha's as usual—Dylan set out across the meadow towards the Ballymeanoch Stones. Visible from the highway, the standing stones were a testament to Argyll's past significance. The silvery moon was near round and brightly patched in darkling blue valleys. It was a brilliant night. He'd scarcely experienced one quite like it, and mused that this was what the first people must have experienced: the spirit of the divine in each drop of dew, each fiery star, each stone, and breath of wind.

Summer Solstice was a fire celebration in honour of the sun, so Dylan would wait until dawn to cast his circle in its rising light. Given the clarity of the night sky, morning promised to be spectacular. He checked his mobile. It was just after three, and sunrise would not occur until 4:32. Plenty of time to commune with the stones.

Drawn to one of the central stones in the parallel line of four, he sat on the earth, and leaned back against the cool three-thousand-year old rock. Feeling the indented cup marks against his ribs, he wondered at their significance. For thousands of years, humans had worshipped, as he did now, on this sacred landscape. Would the sun rise above a particular stone in this henge, if it was astronomically aligned as some scholars believed?

Dylan's practice had changed since coming to stay in the camp. He was now a solitary witch, performing rituals alone with no support or comradery, subdued and requisitely silent. Yet, his ability to hear stories from the stones was growing daily. When Dylan McBride laid his palm against a stone it revealed its secrets. Sometimes he heard voices; sometimes he saw visions. Of course, he dared not tell anyone what he heard and saw. They'd think him daft. Gifts such as his used to get people hanged or burned, or both.

He'd discovered this ability just up the road, in the cemetery at Kilmartin Glen, when he was thirteen years old, and laid his hand on a medieval stone slab carved with the effigy of a dead knight. The experience of that moment shocked and changed him.

Gravestones absorb aspects of a person's soul—vivid details of their life and death. If a man was religious, the stone revealed that; similarly, if a man was sadistic or mad or cold-hearted, the stone revealed that too. Though iron plates had saved the knight from being skewered, he'd tumbled from his horse. That day in Kilmartin Glen, Dylan felt the final shudder of the man's body as his neck broke, and it nearly knocked him senseless.

At first, he could touch them for just a moment or two—a man or woman's life was difficult to digest—but gradually his tolerance deepened, and he could sit with his back edged against their solid weight. His visions grew. Sensory images flooded his mind; sometimes accompanied by the music of pipes or drums. And once, when he was confused and asked for clarity, the answer came immediately. That was the day he realized that the stones could read his mind as clearly as he read theirs.

But too often, he was sickened by what he saw men do in the name of God and country. So, he left the carved slabs and worked with natural rock, developing a fondness for megaliths. He could feel each stone's unique energy, see flashes of its sculpting by nature, its weathering over millennia, the people that revered it, and lived and died in its shadow.

Like silent witnesses, these massive stones take on the essence of the land and the memories of its people. Limited by their inability to move; they see, hear, and absorb, yet cannot act. Trapped by inertia, most are eager to converse, even the fiercest of them—those who, like men, have seen too much evil and been turned by it. Also, like men, the stones longed to share their stories. So often, Dylan sat with them in the meadow, conjoined as he did this night; immersed in images, and listening to tongues so ancient he should not comprehend, yet somehow did.

Now, as he leaned back against the stone, Dylan could see a shaman. Dancing amidst decorated bell-shaped beakers brimming with mead, he wore a frayed buckskin breechclout and a red deer antler headdress, fashioned so the skeletal nose of the deer overshadowed his own.

Cernunnos, thought Dylan, and smiled, remembering Estrada's annual portrayal of the resurrected Horned God. *Dylan, he'd say, you can't just act the god, you must be the god.* And Estrada was—just like this dancing shaman.

A body was laid out ready for burning on a wooden pyre in the centre of the circle. Each mourner dipped a hand in a mead pot and sipped its honeyed richness as they passed. When the shaman finished dancing, he lit the pyre, and the sombre crowd stood watching the smoke curl skywards. Fire released the spirit, while ash and bone fell to the earth.

The body on the pyre was an obese male. As the clothes burnt, Dylan grimaced—half his belly had been ripped open. Perhaps, he'd been gored by a wild boar. His weapons lay beside him: a polished copper axe and spear. A young child sat nearby holding a metal object. Slender as a willow, she was tan-skinned, her long brown hair plaited with the stems of plants. She sat apart from the others; looked different from them too, and Dylan felt her bond with the deceased. Perhaps, they were family; travellers come to worship in the glen.

Then, a foreign group entered the stones and a commotion erupted. At its centre was a regal woman perched atop a litter, held aloft by four hefty men. The shaman flew into a rage and shook his rattle menacingly at the intruders.

Dylan stared, mesmerized by her beauty. He could not tell if her skull had been shaped in a peculiar way, or if it was the jewelled headpiece she wore that created such an alien visage. She did not resemble the others gathered in the outer circle, though her enchanting eyes, edged thickly in kohl, were vaguely familiar. The flames from the pyre danced in the gleaming gold crescent-shaped broad collar she wore around her neck and shoulders. Inlaid with precious stones and faïence beads, golden strands hung from the bottom like rays of the sun, and at the end of each was an ankh, the Egyptian hieroglyph for life.

Dylan gasped. Was it possible? Was *this* Meritaten? Could this collar be the same green tangled mess that Sorcha pulled from the muck only hours before? He knew this symbol, knew its history from a course he'd taken on the Golden Age of Egypt. It was the sun disc, the Aten.

Once it was known only as a form of the sun god Ra. Then, around 1350 BC, Meritaten's father banished the entire pantheon of gods and goddesses along with the priests of Amun, and declared that the people could worship only the Aten. Of course, he proclaimed himself Son of the Aten—Akhenaten—so he too must be worshipped. It was a bold political move that infuriated the priests and people of Egypt, angered the gods, and brought down plagues upon the land—a move that sparked the end of the king's reign.

Dylan flinched with the shock of it all, and everything vanished. Wanting more, he edged back against the stone and waited. Seconds, minutes passed, but nothing came. That was the way of his capricious gift.

He wanted to run immediately back to camp, shake Sorcha awake, and tell her what he'd seen. If she shared his ability, she would be thrilled. But, what if she didn't? Then what? Would she think him daft? Besides, she was likely still drunk. And there was Kai to consider.

But this was momentous. Meritaten had walked in this meadow wearing that gold jewelled broad collar. Somehow, he had to tell Sorcha. It was worth the risk. He would wait for sunrise, get her alone, confess his gift, and tell her what he'd seen.

Stretching out on his back in the grass, he covered himself with his cobalt blue cloak, and considered what this could all mean. Surely, if the stones had shared this vision, there was a reason.

~~~

"Christ, man. I've been out here banging for an hour." It was close to six a.m. but Estrada didn't care. He'd driven on autopilot straight to Michael Stryker's flat in the west end of Vancouver. "You never remember to stash the key. You should give me one."

"I believe I have…once or twice," replied Michael. "But, why are you arriving now? And where are your boots? Don't tell me you drove here barefoot on your Harley?"

Estrada shrugged and rolled his eyes.

"You're lucky you weren't pulled over by the cops. And drunk too?"

"Not enough. Not yet."

"Death wish," Michael muttered, glancing around outside. Assured that Estrada was not being followed, he grasped him by the arm and wrenched him in the door. "God, you're freezing. It's a good thing Zoey and Zara are here."

"The dancing twins?" He followed Michael up the creaky stairs to his flat.

"Yes. We were just about to crash." He'd slipped on his black silk kimono to answer the door—still wore the musky scent of love in his messy blond hair. For a moment, Estrada was jealous. Not of his sex life—he'd never hoarded that—but because nothing ever seemed to rattle the man. Believing he was the reincarnation of Lord Byron, Michael Stryker cruised through life on a sybaritic cloud.

"I'll take the couch and a bottle. You can continue—"

"Nonsense. You must join us, compadre." Curling his upper lip, Michael flashed a fang. He'd been playing vampire, as usual. "When I told the girls that sounded like *your* Harley, they perked right up. We can all jump in the tub."

"I'm not really in the mood—"

"You're *never* in the mood."

Turning at the top of the landing, Michael shoved him against the wall and kissed him. Leaning in, Estrada closed his eyes and returned the kiss. It was fierce, deep, and lush.

"Feel how hard you are? I know what you need, compadre." Michael was a tease, but his kisses were real and his instincts usually right.

Hands slid across Estrada's bare back and down his leathers. When their thighs touched, he was tempted. "Christ. It's been six months," Michael whispered. "You've got to let it go. You know, you haven't been the same since *Ireland.*"

Estrada took a deep breath and turned his face away. They had a tacit understanding not to mention names that evoked raw memories, but they both knew what *Ireland* meant. *Primrose.* Her name hovered in the air like the final riff at a rock concert. She'd stripped away layers, leaving him open, vulnerable, and loving her. And then she was gone.

There had been moments like this—Estrada's brush with death had unmasked a tenderness in Michael—but he'd not been able to engage in the sensual parties his friend was famous for hosting. His grief for Primrose could not be cured by casual sex, no matter how good it felt.

Michael stroked his cheek with one long nail, then opened the door.

Estrada tugged off his cold leather vest and flopped on the burgundy couch closest to the window. "Fuck Ireland. And fuck Sensara and her clone."

"Problems in the pack?"

"We're witches, not wolves." Estrada rubbed his eyes. He was exhausted, but knew he'd never fall asleep feeling this way. "I need something. What have you got?" The alcohol was wearing thin, but Michael was a modern-day apothecary who stocked only the best. Known as the E-vamp, his ecstasy was legendary and a prerequisite at his private parties.

"Ah, let me see. Booze. Coke—though I wouldn't recommend *that* right now. Some decent E. Some *unprecedented* pot. Valium—"

"I'll take the E."

"Really? You don't think valium and some weed—"

"You asked me what I wanted."

Michael ran his hands through his hair and sighed. "That I did, but I know you, compadre. I quite enjoy you on E, as do others, but I know how far you plummet on the rebound. Considering how down you've been of late, I'd hate to see you hit the stars and then the skids."

A faint female voice interrupted from the other room, calling Michael by his nickname: "Mandragora? Are you coming back to bed?"

"Don't forget Estrada," said another.

Zoey and her twin sister, Zara, frequented Club Pegasus whenever they were in town. They loved the contrast between rigid discipline and frivolous debauchery. Both were ballerinas, and beautiful, but Estrada didn't want either of them. He wanted something else. He wanted—

"Do you want them gone, compadre?"

He shrugged an inaudible *yes*. Michael lit a joint and passed it over, then went into the bedroom to deliver the verdict. Estrada closed his eyes, sucked back the smoke, and felt like a prick. It was cruel to oust a woman from a warm bed at six a.m. and doubly cruel to oust twins. Add it to his growing list of transgressions.

"This *is* good pot," he said, when Michael returned. Vibrant traces swirled past his eyes.

"I told you. The THC level's close to forty percent." Michael's hands were suddenly on his shoulders squeezing. "Man, you're tight." Running his hands up his neck, Michael scratched his scalp with long nails and ran his fingers through his hair. "Better?"

"Diverting."

"I have some incredible oil here somewhere," said Michael, searching the shelf. "Ah, here it is. Risqué. Vanessa says it's made with licorice, lavender, and ylang ylang. Guaranteed to turn a libido inside out."

"How's that been going for you?"

"No complaints, compadre." He lit another joint, took a few puffs, and passed it to Estrada. "Finish that while I grab a towel."

"Grab the E while you're at it."

"You won't need it. Trust me."

The twins appeared, flashed keen stares, and slammed the door as they left.

"They hate me," Estrada said, when he returned.

"Quite the contrary. They're annoyed because you've been holding out for so long." Spreading a white bath towel over the dancing Persian rug, Michael created an oasis in the geometric sea of sculpted colour.

"I didn't know you were a masseuse, amigo."

"Ah, well. Vanessa is studying Tantric massage and needs a willing subject. She's taught me a few tricks." He caught his hair up in an elastic band and uncorked a bright blue bottle. "Now, drop your leathers and lie face down."

"Listen man—"

"Compadre, smell this oil." After rubbing a few drops into his hands, Michael stood behind him and passed his palms in front of his face. Then he leaned in so close the heat from his lips warmed the back of Estrada's earlobe. "I will only touch what begs touching, and I promise to fill you with nothing but pleasure."

When Estrada awoke, he was still lying face down on the towel, but his naked body was covered with a silky sheet. The quiet clattering of kitchen things merged with the aromas of breakfast. He rolled onto his side and flicked on his cell phone. Christ. It was three p.m. His belly growled.

As if he'd heard it from the other room, Michael appeared carrying a tray. Hair still damp from a shower; he wore faded blue jeans and a black T-shirt, and looked deceptively normal. When you're used to hanging out with an eccentric goth, who likes to pretend he's a vampire named Mandragora, and considers himself the reincarnation of Lord Byron, your perception gets slightly skewed.

"Man, that was the best sleep I've had in weeks. I need that weed."

"What you need is me," said Michael, with a sly grin. And, he was right. What began as sensual massage morphed into carnality in no time at all. After setting down the tray, he squeezed Estrada's shoulders. "Ah, much better. Now you must eat. Feta cheese omelet, toast, black coffee, and a side of piquant salsa, I picked up at Granville Island. Sadie dragged me down there."

"Aren't you having any?"

He shook his head. "I grew ravenous hours ago and indulged in some sushi while I watched you sleep. I enjoy watching you sleep, when I know you're going to wake up." Another veiled reference to Ireland. There, Estrada had fallen into a sleep, so deep, he almost did *not* wake up. Michael had flown over and sat by his bedside for days.

"Thanks man. This is perfect," he said, between mouthfuls. "So was last night."

"Naturally. Now, are you going to tell me what got you so perturbed?" After lighting a joint, Michael leaned back on the sofa and put his feet up.

"Not a what, a who. Yasu. Sensara's new man. She brought him to our ritual last night. There's something about him I don't like. He's cynical. A skeptic."

"So am I, but you accept me."

"Sensara is not grooming *you* to take my place." He smeared the last of his toast through the salsa and shoved it in his mouth. "Daphne says he's an environmental architect. Do you know what *that* means?" Michael shook his head. "He glues fucking Buddhas on rocks."

"And you're sure that Sensara wants this…"

"Yasu. He's Japanese, like her."

Michael shrugged. "So, you're sure that she wants him to become the high priest of your coven? Why? Did you do something to offend?" He paused. "Or, is she in love with him?"

"I don't know. Maybe. She's obviously grooming him. Why else would she bring him to our private ritual?"

"Perhaps, she just wants to introduce him to her world?" Michael lit another joint and passed it over. "I hear that couples—"

"Couples?" Estrada scowled and rolled his eyes, then took a deep hit on the joint and coughed.

"You're not upset because Sensara's got a new boyfriend, are you? I thought you couldn't handle a relationship with Ms. Hetero Monogamy."

"I can't. But, being High Priest of Hollystone Coven means more to me than anything in the world. If that ended…if I couldn't do that anymore…I wouldn't be me." He shook his head. "No, I've lost too much of me already. This is a part I'm not willing to give up: not for anything or anyone."

"God, that's intense. I had no idea—"

"*And* we were partners, Sensara and me."

"Really?"

"Yeah. We used to do everything together. Laugh. Hang out. I could tell her anything. Christ, we were so tight, we could communicate *telepathically*." He shrugged. "She's been my best friend for years."

"Yes, well, it's devastating when you lose your best friend. I used to have one myself; at least, I thought I did. Apparently, I was wrong. He was best friends with someone else all along."

"Oh, don't go all high school on me."

"So, now I'm immature. Well, don't stop. What else is wrong with me?"

"Oh, I don't know. Self-centred? Narcissistic?" Estrada stood up and slipped into his leather pants. The intensity was making him feel awkward. "This isn't about you."

"Of course, it's not. How can it ever be about *me* when everything is always about *you*?"

"Jesus, Michael."

"I'm going to bed. Don't be here when I get up."

"Ah, don't—"

But Michael stomped into his bedroom and slammed the door. Estrada heard furniture being dragged across the hardwood floor.

He banged on the door. "I didn't mean it. I'm sorry," he said. But all Michael did was turn up the tunes. Feeling friendless and misunderstood, Estrada slipped into a pair of Michael's boots, grabbed his vest and keys, and walked out.

CHAPTER THREE

Murder

PERCHED ON THE EDGE OF A WOODEN BENCH in an iron-barred jail cell, Dylan sat with his head in his hands, the most mournful soul that ever lived. He'd driven by the Sheriff's Office in Lochgilphead many times as a teenager. He knew its medieval stonework and distinctive grey turret, but he'd never spent the night locked inside. It was late Sunday afternoon and another night was fast approaching. Biting his lip, he forced back tears.

Murder. They'd arrested him for murder.

Billy Craddock was there, or rather, Constable Will Craddock as he now demanded to be called. Dylan knew him from school. His father was a mean bastard who beat him, so Billy beat other kids. Now he was a cop. It was Craddock that bagged Dylan's cobalt blue cloak after examining the silver elvish embroidery with rolling eyes. And it was Craddock, that dragged him from the field at Ballymeanoch, out through the fenced pathway toward the highway, handcuffed and pleading: "What's happening? Please tell me. What do they think I've done?"

Shut it, you knob, was all he'd say.

When they reached Dunchraigaig Cairn, Dylan saw that it was sealed off with crime scene tape and swarming with police, and he knew something dreadful had happened. The stones were weeping, tearing the air with mournful cries. Still, Craddock refused to talk, to explain what had happened, or why he was cuffed.

An inspector appeared at last, and said it: "Dylan McBride. You are under arrest for suspicion of murder in the death of Alastair Steele." *Murder? Alastair Steele? That bastard journalist from Oban? Christ.*

He'd been stripped, searched, fingerprinted, photographed, and finally given the opportunity to call his grandad. He couldn't do it. How could he call and say he'd been arrested for murder? His grandad was an old man. News like that could kill him. Finally, Craddock called and held out the receiver, smirking as Dylan heard his grandfather's voice. Words were uttered back and forth. The only thing he remembered from the conversation was telling his grandad to call Estrada. He'd rattled off the number.

Dylan didn't know what to do or how to act in a place like this. He wasn't one of the boys who stole, or vandalized, or got drunk and fought, or cracked up their father's cars, or beat up their girlfriends. He didn't do drugs. Christ, until last night, he'd never done more than let himself be kissed. Twenty years old and he'd never made love to a woman—now he could spend the rest of his life locked up with men. Bad men.

He crouched over the toilet and puked. After wiping his mouth, he tried to calm down. It was all a mistake. He was innocent and someone would prove it. The truth will set you free. Isn't that what people always said? Estrada would find Steele's killer and exonerate him. Justice would prevail. If it didn't—

He leaned back against the rock wall and tried to relax. But the stones flooded his brain with the intense despair of a thousand prisoners who, like himself, had crouched behind these bars and wondered what was to come. How had life come to this? Worse than a bloody beating was the despair of loneliness; the knowledge that you might never again be free to walk with those you loved and who loved you. Mental torment far outweighed anything physical that might occur in a place like this.

Whoever said: *if these walls could talk*, had not heard their tales. One man tried to hang himself and failed miserably. Another anguished soul curled up in the corner and bit the stone walls until his teeth broke. Both were innocent. Just like him.

Enough. Pulling back from the stones, he perched on the side of the bench. If he allowed the ghosts of this cell to speak, they would surely drive him mad.

~~~

When Estrada's cell phone rang at noon on Sunday, he hoped it was Michael. He knew he'd hurt him, but he hadn't meant to. Best friends didn't do the things they did. Michael was more than a friend, much more. Something indefinable. A part of him, like a second skin.

But the call was not from Michael. The man's raspy voice betrayed both his age and his nation. Pausing between phrases to catch his breath, he sang his words, and rolled his r's like Billy Connelly.

"This is Dermot McBride, calling from Scotland. I'd like to speak with Mr. Estrada, please."

"This is Estrada."

"Aye. Good. Mr. Estrada, I'm callin' about my grandson, Dylan."

Estrada's belly flipped. "Dylan. Is he hurt? What happened?"

"Well, you see…" He coughed, and then sighed. "Ach, there's no point beatin' about the bush. Dylan's been arrested."

"Arrested?"

"Aye. Arrested." A spasm of coughing erupted on the other end.

"Mr. McBride?"

"Sorry laddie. I'm just…just catchin' my breath."

"Why was Dylan arrested?" Estrada felt suddenly numb. He couldn't imagine Dylan ever doing anything illegal. The boy was pure innocence. He waited for the man to explain, but the pause was so lengthy, he feared he was having a heart attack. "Mr. McBride? Are you still there?"

"Aye, lad."

"Why? Why was he arrested?"

"Murder." The rolling r's sent shivers riveting up his arms.

"Murder? Dylan? That's not possible."

"I'm afraid you're wrong there, laddie. The police arrested him yesterday morning. He's locked up in Lochgilphead."

"But Dylan could never… Who do they think he—?"

"A journalist…Alastair Steele." He took a deep breath and tried to clear his throat, but it did nothing to relieve the hoarseness. "Dylan needs your help. He said that you were the only one who'd understand. I know we're strangers, and I wouldn't ask, except…Ach, I don't know what else to do. Can you help us?"

"Of course. What do you need?"

"Dylan needs you here, lad."

"Here…in Scotland?"

"Aye. We'll reimburse your ticket and any other expenses you incur."

"I'm sorry, but I can't just—"

"I know it's too much to ask, lad, but please think about it. This Steele is a dastardly newshound, the find all, tell all sort. There's likely cheers arising in pubs across the country due to his demise. But, the police arrested *my* grandson and they're determined to convict him. Ach, I know Dylan could never—"

Another coughing spasm seized him. When it subsided, he breathed: "Please, lad. I'm not one to beg. Will you come?"

Why now? The timing couldn't be worse. Sensara was preparing Yasu to take his place in the coven. And Michael…if he left now, the way things were between them, Lord knows what he'd get up to. Still…Dylan arrested for murder?

"Yes. Of course, I'll come. But you know I'm not a private investigator."

"Aye lad, but you're a damn good mate, so Dylan says, and he believes you can help him."

Estrada took a deep breath and exhaled. "I'll call when I've booked a flight."

"Aye, sure, and you can stay here with me. You best write this down: Piper's Dream, Pier Road in Tarbert. That's in Argyll. Everyone in the village knows my cottage. And don't worry about Dylan. He's a Scot and he's a McBride."

Estrada searched for flights. He needed a couple of days to organize his life and make peace with Michael. He chose a direct charter from Vancouver to Glasgow that flew on Wednesday and would allow him to avoid the chaos of Customs and Immigration at London Heathrow. Even with his Canadian passport, he drew constant suspicion from airport security and had been strip-searched more times than he cared to remember while crossing the American border. He wasn't sure if it was his Harley, his penchant for leather, his long black hair and swarthy complexion, or that certain combination, that made him a target. In their eyes, he was either a drug lord or a terrorist.

By Tuesday evening, after several failed attempts at reconciliation, Estrada went to see Michael's grandfather, Nigel Stryker. A successful entrepreneur and owner of Club Pegasus, Nigel had employed him to perform a Friday night magic show for the past four years. A talented magician and escape artist, Estrada performed gothic theatrics; as well as, all the usual sleights and tricks. He drew a large crowd and appreciated the regular gig, which he did whenever he wasn't performing out of town. But Nigel did not just sign his pay cheques: he was the closest thing Estrada had to a father.

So, he told him where he was going and why. Nigel had helped him before, and he knew he'd help him again. He was clever and connected and someone he could count on.

Business aside, he took a deep breath, and told him about Michael. He said they'd had a misunderstanding, and he was very sorry he'd hurt his feelings. He was fishing really, looking for some kind of resolution to a distressing situation. Michael was volatile and he feared leaving things unsettled.

But Nigel knew nothing of the falling-out. Though Michael lived in a turreted tower flat in his grandfather's Queen Anne mansion, he'd been keeping to himself the last few days; wasn't feeling well and hadn't come into the club the last couple of nights.

Nigel patted Estrada on the back. "It takes balls to say you're sorry, Sandolino. I respect that in a man. You know you're like a son to me. The patrons love you, and obviously so does Michael. Don't worry. I'll check in on him. He can be dramatic, but he'll come around."

Estrada wondered if Nigel understood the intricacies of their relationship, or if he assumed they were having a lover's quarrel. He let it lie. Things that could not be explained were best left unsaid.

~~~

As the plane crossed the Atlantic, day morphed into night. Estrada slept fitfully, entombed by bodies, boredom, and bad air. He would rather be cruising down the highway on his Harley with the wind in his face. Then he thought of Dylan locked in a musty old jail cell. Was there no justice in the world? Moments like this made him doubt his belief in karma. Of all the people he knew, Dylan was the least likely to kill a man for any reason. Why would this happen to him?

When the wheels touched the Scottish tarmac, bringing nine hours of cramped confinement to a screeching halt, he was desperate to move. He'd packed light and brought only carry-on luggage, so dashed to the queue. The Customs Centre had recently been upgraded, as had security, but black-suited police from the Anti-Terrorism Squad armed with MP5 submachine guns, did nothing to make him feel secure. He hoped his anxiety would not be apparent in his interview.

Waiting in the non-EU queue, he clutched his landing card and rubbed his chin. Perhaps, he should have run a razor over the twelve-hour stubble. His hair had grown three inches since his head was shaved last fall, and now curled below the collar of his black leather jacket. It would take years to grow back to its former length, but it was a start. He vowed never to cut it again.

He wore a black T-shirt, clean black jeans, and high soft leather boots—none of which was particularly outlandish—and carried his leather jacket folded over his arm. He had multiple ear piercings but no visible tattoos, and he'd washed all traces of eyeliner from his face before leaving home. Men who wear makeup attract undue scrutiny.

He wished that he could conjure a glamour like Merlin did for Uther Pendragon and slip by unseen. Taking a deep breath, he willed himself to ride the grey line between anxious and cocky. There was no cause for concern. He was just a Canadian coming to visit a friend in the U.K.

When he handed the immigration officer his passport, ticket, and landing card, he looked the man in the eye.

"What's the purpose of your visit to Scotland?"

"To see a friend."

"How long will you be staying?"

Estrada swallowed. "Two weeks." At least he'd bought his ticket with a two-week return.

Things were moving along without a glitch, and then the officer read something on the screen, narrowed his eyes, and called over one of the armed police officers. Turning their backs to him, they conferred in dull whispers for several seconds. Then, the cop walked a few feet away and made a call on his cell phone. Estrada broke out in a sweat, as visions of terrorist prisons flooded his brain. He could disappear. It happened. He'd seen it in the movies.

"Follow me, please." It was a wiry cop with an MP5.

Taking a deep breath, Estrada nodded and followed him into a small interview room. An older cop, also carrying a submachine gun, flanked him. Neither of them spoke, and it turned into an awkward staring match: Estrada, seated in a plastic chair behind a table where he'd been placed, and the two of them standing guard by the door. They seemed stalled; were perhaps waiting for instructions.

"Is there a problem, officer?" he asked, anxious to break the tension.

The older cop simply sniffed, while the younger answered a call on his cell. "Aye," he said at last. "Will do. Right away, sir."

He sat down in the chair and stared across the table. "McBride." He waved the landing card in the air. "You've written here that you're staying in Tarbert with a man named Dermot McBride."

"Yeah?"

"What is your relationship with McBride?"

"I've never met the man."

"Yet you're staying at his home?" He pressed his thin lips tightly together and then popped them open as if for emphasis.

"I know his grandson."

His eyebrows rose. "Name?"

"Dylan."

"The Dylan McBride who is being detained on murder charges?"

"Yeah?" Estrada shrugged. What did it matter if he visited a friend in jail?

"What exactly is the purpose of your visit? I mean, considering your mate's in lockup and can't take you on an extended tour of the Highlands." Raising his eyebrows, he looked down his nose and grinned at his own bad joke.

"I came to support him and his family."

"The family you've never met." Another annoying pop was followed by a lengthy pause, as the officer fiddled with his documents. Estrada passed a hand across his forehead. *Cold. Wet. Sweat.*

"I see on your passport that you entered the Republic of Ireland last October and stayed until Christmas. Do you have friends there too?"

"I did, yeah."

"Aye, so we heard," he said, smugly.

"Sorry?" What the hell did that mean? Was he listed on some computer site as an unwelcome guest? *Do not allow this man into your country?*

"Are you Sandolino Estrada?"

"Yeah."

"The same Sandolino Estrada that was involved in two deaths in Ireland: one, a civilian; and the other, a suspect in a serial murder case in Canada?"

"Yeah, but I—"

The cop took a deep breath, puffed out his chest, and launched into a rapid speech. "The Detective Chief Inspector of Police Scotland would like you to know, that if you stick your nose into any murder investigations while you're here in *our* country, you just might lose it. If we suspect you of *anything* you'll be joining your friend Dylan McBride in custody. Do you understand me, Mr. Estrada?"

"Yeah."

"Good. Now, you've been warned. Your name is on our radar and we'll be watching you." He pointed his fingertips to his eyes in the universal gesture. "Comprender?"

Squeezing his fingers tightly into fists, Estrada remembered why he hated cops. If he ever got the chance he'd take that MP5 and shove it right up his tight Scottish ass.

"Make sure you do, or you just might find yourself back in Me-hi-co."

When he flung the passport, Estrada caught it in the air. "I'm a Canadian citizen."

"Aye, for now."

It was almost noon before the taxi driver dropped him off in front of West Coast Harley-Davidson at Charing Cross in Glasgow, but in no time at all, he was ripping up the A82 on a Heritage Classic, the colour of merlot. It took a chunk out of his bank account, but he didn't care. Money could always be made, and that cop had taken a chunk out of his cool—something he intended to get back.

The sun was high in the sky, and with Loch Lomond rippling to his right, he felt like cruising forever. But suddenly, he saw the turnoff for A83, and he was veering left and climbing toward a stunning mountain pass and then all but flying down the other side. Following the rugged shoreline of Loch Fyne, he remembered that Dylan once spoke of his grandfather gazing out over this lake.

He was just ingesting the green lure of the rolling Scottish landscape when he saw a sign for Lochgilphead, and braking abruptly, sent gravel skittering in his wake. This was the place his grandfather had mentioned on the phone. He sat for several minutes, just staring at the sign. The reality of the situation was almost too much to comprehend. *Was Dylan really there? Locked behind iron bars and charged with murder? Jesus Christ. He'd rather die than submit to a sexual encounter with a man. He'll get himself killed.*

No one answered the door at Piper's Dream, so he locked up the bike, and sauntered back down the street to a hotel pub he'd passed on his way through the village. His wolfish soul was crying for a bottle of tequila, but he wasn't fool enough for that. He'd need to restrict any drinking he did to a few pints, at least for now. When he drank tequila, he sometimes lost chunks of time, and he literally had no time to lose.

Tarbert was one of those quaint fishing villages where couples went for a romantic interlude. Fishers sold their fresh catch from boats moored in the harbour. It was late afternoon and the main thoroughfare, which curved around the sea, was bustling with tourists, some with children, most without. He tried to imagine Dylan spending his teen years here, living with his grandfather in the house up the road.

"Out touring?" The bartender struck up a conversation as he sucked back his third pint. Perhaps, the ale had softened his edges.

"Touring?"

"Aye. Saw you cruise by earlier on that Harley. Fine-looking bike. Are you on a motorcycle tour? We get them through here. Tarbert being a ferry port."

"Oh, yeah. A Harley's a great bike for touring."

The man nodded and went to deliver his pints. The place was filling; mostly with locals. A fresh copy of *The Evening Times* (Thursday Edition) sat on a shelf nearby. Remembering what the cops had said about hearing the name McBride, Estrada picked it up. He didn't have far to look. It was right on the front page about mid-way down beside a stock photo of the murdered journalist.

MCBRIDE TRANSPORTED TO GREENOCK

Following his appearance today in Oban, alleged killer, Dylan McBride, having made no plea or declaration, was taken into custody and transported to Greenock prison. McBride, a former resident of Tarbert, is in Argyll working on an archaeological dig with the O'Hallorhan team at Kilmartin Glen. The body of investigative journalist, Alastair Steele, was discovered early Saturday morning, wedged inside Dunchraigaig cairn, mere feet from the A816. Witnesses report seeing the two men argue at Murphy's Irish pub in Oban late Friday evening. Rumour has it that O'Hallorhan unearthed an ancient Egyptian artifact Friday morning. The archaeologist was unavailable for comment.

"Jesus..." Seeing the facts printed in text made it all the more real.

"That's a hell of a mess, yeah?" The bartender was back and wiping down the bar. "I know him...that lad, McBride. Lives up the street with his grandad. Good man. Good lad."

Estrada nodded. "What about this journalist? Is he as dirty as he looks?"

"Oh aye. The last I heard of Steele, a young lass he worked with made accusations...rape."

"Really? Did it go to trial?"

"Nah, they couldn't make a case. Steele claimed it was consensual. Ruined the poor girl's reputation. Too bad. She was just starting out."

"Do you remember her name?"

"Jane is her first name. I remember that cause it's my sister's name. Just hold on a second. Spike will know. He writes for our local rag." Leaning over the bar, he yelled across the patrons to three men conversing at a far table. "Spike. What was the name of that burd Alastair Steele got tangled up with?"

"Janey Marshall," came the reply.

"Aye. Janey Marshall. I'll bet she was fair boiling that Steele got off."

"Enough to kill him?"

"Ah, I don't think she could—not on her own, at least. She's just a wee lass. Still, hell hath no fury like a woman scorned."

Estrada raised his eyebrows. Rape was far from scorn. "This Janey Marshall, does she live around here?"

"In Glasgow, I imagine. Are you a journalist yourself, then?"

"No. Just touring." He smiled. "Could I buy this newspaper?"

"Ah, have it," said the bartender, with a kind wave. Estrada nodded his thanks, slapped several euros on the counter and sauntered out.

The sun was setting over the sea, and he felt guilty for appreciating the quiet beauty of the village. On the crest of a hill stood a grass-covered castle ruin guarded by a brown shaggy-haired goat. The houses looked similar; it was the shade of trim that set them apart. All two-storey and built of grey brick, they rose like sentinels from the harbour. There were no front porches, which seemed odd, considering the ocean was right there on the other side of the road, begging to be admired. Perhaps, fishermen were so wearied by the sea, they did not care to watch it from their homes. Some had pitched roofs and dormer windows, where an anxious wife or mother could scan the waves for signs of her man. Though it was a postcard town, he wondered what secrets hid behind those brick façades.

When he arrived back at Piper's Dream, a white-haired man, much frailer than his voice, stood on the lawn staring at the harbour.

"Let's sit out for a spell and have a wee dram," suggested Dermot after introductions had been made. "I'm done in." He lit a well-worn bentwood pipe and puffed some.

As soon as Estrada breathed the heady tobacco, Michael came to mind. Was he still angry? He downed his whiskey and placed the empty glass on the stone steps.

The sight of a police cruiser on the road below interrupted his thoughts. "I don't want to alarm you, Mr. McBride, but that's the second time I've seen the police drive by and glance in. Are you under surveillance?"

"Call me Dermot, lad. Ach, no. The press, though…Damn fools camped here for days." He puffed on his pipe as he spoke. "That lad in the cruiser is Billy Craddock. He'll keep an eye on Dylan. They were schoolmates. The police here are fair and honest and protect them that need protecting."

Estrada nodded. His introduction to the Scottish police force had not left him with that impression, but then, he was an outsider. They were intent on protecting Scotland from him.

"The people here know that Dylan is no killer."

"Yeah, I heard that said in the pub." Estrada sniffed the damp sea air. "I need to talk to him."

"Aye, sure. If you don't mind waiting a day or two, I'll take you myself. I went today…to court, and then to the prison…wanted him to know he was not alone. Takes eight hours, there and back again, what with two ferry crossings. I only just arrived twenty minutes before they closed the visits room. Managed to leave £50 with the officer, though, so he can get what he needs."

Eight hours of travel for a twenty-minute visit? No wonder the old man was worn out.

"You should rest this weekend. There are things I can do here." He was curious about the Egyptian artifact mentioned in the paper; the one found by O'Hallorhan, the archaeologist at Kilmartin Glen. It was likely connected and seemed a good place to start.

"I wrote down the visiting times," said Dermot, pulling a scrap of paper from his pocket. "If we arrive by half-two on Monday, you can see him for thirty minutes. Tuesday and Wednesday, they only allow visits in the evenings."

"Let's go Monday then." The old man pulled a flask from his pocket and filled Estrada's glass. He nodded and sipped…felt comforted. A sense of peace in the harbour town eclipsed the chaos, and he sunk inside it. "Can he make phone calls?" he asked at last.

"I don't know. I brought his mobile home." He fished around in his pocket, pulled it out, and stared at it. "You might as well use it. Then I can reach you if I need to." He handed Estrada the slim phone and smiled sadly. "You needn't report in, or anything like that. Back door is always unlocked and you're free to come and go as you please. But if you need anything, my number's in there under grandad."

"Thanks Dermot. I appreciate that."

The old man downed his whiskey and then hung his head in silence for several minutes. Estrada gazed out at the lights reflected in the water, and allowed him his time. When at last he looked up, the old man's greyish eyes were thick with tears. "Ach, my lad's locked inside a prison cell. I still can't believe it." He wiped them and sniffed. "Thank God his gran's not here to see this day. It would break her heart."

It's broken yours, thought Estrada. "I'll get him out," he said. "I promise."

When the cruiser drove by the third time, Estrada considered what the cops had threatened at the airport, and vowed to do whatever it took to free Dylan from that prison. Even if it meant ending up in there himself.

CHAPTER FOUR

Fire & Ice

THE SUN BEATING DOWN against Sorcha's eyelids veiled the world in red. Red like the blood of kings. Red like a Galway sunset. The archaeologist was a little sun drunk that morning. It was the first hour she'd had to herself in weeks. Sick of the muck and the damp and the cold war that raged within her camp at Kilmartin Glen, she'd stolen away to the western pasture. If they needed her, they'd call.

Stretched out on a vibrant Turkish sarong, she felt the hot sun caress her thighs. God, what she wouldn't do for more of that. Reaching behind her back, she unhooked her halter and slipped it off. Sorcha believed that a woman's body was beautiful, especially her own. At university, she'd explored the female form with other girls; learned what a woman liked and what *she* liked, learned the value of her body, and how it could be used to her advantage. Halters had their place, could accentuate and deepen, making mounds into mountains, but they'd surely been invented by men—to tie down their women like their horses. And Sorcha was no horse, which was why she let her breasts run wild.

She had to be mindful though during this heatwave. Bliss could quickly turn to pain with skin so pale. Sometimes, she wished her mother had chosen a man without the Celtic gene; someone swarthy like the man she'd danced with at Murphy's. *My Black Spaniard.* She sighed. What a sexy devil he'd been. She mused for a moment what could have happened that night…remembered the heat of his breath against her neck, his lips lingering on her flesh. Spanish and Egyptian, he'd said. Skin like smooth dark chocolate. His people must have come from somewhere south near the Sudan. She wished *he'd* taken her home that night, instead of Kai. How grand it would have been to make love to an Egyptian with Meritaten's collar only a breath away. Ah, but so much for romance. That night ended in disaster.

Feeling the sun's fire intensify, she rolled onto her belly and laid with her cheek against her arm. It had been a crazy fucking week. She felt responsible for Dylan's predicament. Her plan to liberate his puritan soul with a little casual sex had backfired and cost him his freedom. She'd found and lost the Egyptian collar, and that *must* be connected. She'd even dragged them all to Murphy's that night. If they'd gone somewhere else, anywhere else—

She flinched when her mobile rang and then realized it was just someone from the Kilmartin Museum. Likely another journalist was snooping around looking for dirt. Fucking press had been like flies on a corpse all week.

"O'Hallorhan."

"There's someone here asking to speak with you." It was Emma, a sweet girl who sometimes came to dig.

"Paparazzi?"

"Doubtful. His name's Estrada." A flush swept through her body. *Estrada? Could it be him? My Black Spaniard?*

Emma paused, and then whispered, "I think you'll really want to meet this one."

Holy Mary Mother of God. "Did he say what he wants?"

"Aye. He's a friend of Dylan McBride's. Just flown in from Canada."

Ah. Couldn't be him. Damn. "Right so. I'll be along."

"Sure, Mr. O'Hallorhan. I'll let him know."

"Ah, another one who assumes I'm Indiana Jones, is he?"

"Aye sir." She giggled.

"Ah, Emma, I owe you a pint."

She combed out her crazy hair with her fingers and pinned it up, tied the sarong over her khaki shorts, and positioned the halter for maximum effect. Lord, it was hot. Not even a faint sea breeze. An hour before noon and the sheep were slow-grazing under the shade trees. Hiking up through the fields, sweat seeped between her breasts. Damn climate change. Northerners had lived without tropical adaptations for millennia. They weren't cut out for this.

Early Friday morning the museum had few visitors which made Estrada from Canada rather obvious. Crouched in the graveyard by the church, he was examining tombstones. He'd a lighter complexion than the Black Spaniard, but was just as striking. Sorcha was suddenly glad that Kai had left yesterday to dive in the islands. Though he held no claim on her, Kai Roskilde could be intimidating. He said, he was adding underwater archaeology to his repertoire, but Kai was a born pirate and the Hebridean coastline rich in sunken treasure.

She crept up behind him. "Good morning. I'm Sorcha O'Hallorhan," she said, extending her hand.

"Oh," he said, and stood to his full height, easily six foot two. Tilting his tanned face, he grinned. "Estrada."

A Latin lilt and a voice like honey. When he took her hand in his, a twinge rippled through her belly and down her thighs. *Ancient genes.*

"I'm sorry to disturb you, but I wonder if I could have a word."

You can have more than a word, she thought; *take the friggin dictionary.* Egyptian eyes nearly black, lined in kohl pencil, and thickly lashed. No, not Egyptian, closer to Spanish, and something else, something…indigenous? Black hair hanging in his eyes; ears riveted with turquoise studs. His nose was long and angular, but had been broken and reset, at least twice. *Was he a scrapper, then?* He'd shaved recently— she caught a whiff of musk mixed with sweat—but a scruff of beard crept like a sexy shadow across his chin and dimpled cheeks. Dark nipples pierced his pale blue tank. He had smooth brown shoulders and was well-muscled, athletic even, and well-packed into snug blue jeans. But, what intrigued her most in all this perfection were his lips—thick and heart-shaped, they were the most kissable lips she'd ever seen.

The looking continued for several seconds and then his gaze dropped to the significant cleavage that threatened her halter-top.

"They're real," she said, with a little cheek. "Want to touch them?"

"Just one," he replied, and reaching out, he cupped her left breast in his palm and stroked the taut edge of her nipple with his thumb.

A quick gasp escaped before she could contain it. "Grand," she said, stepping back, beyond his reach. "Shall we chat in the café? I need some *real* coffee." What she needed was to take control. It was rare that a man unnerved Sorcha O'Hallorhan.

From the outside, the café looked like an old barn, but the interior was all stonework and oak timbers. She watched him take it in, and liked that he admired the rustic beauty. When he pulled out the chair for her, his hand brushed hers, and sent a jolt up her arm. He laughed, had felt it too.

"I sing the body electric," he murmured.

"Are you a poet?"

"No. Whitman's a poet. But, who can ignore the charge of the soul?"

"Ah, you *are* a poet." Settling into the chair, she lost herself in those dark eyes. *Swarthy*, she thought, and smiled at the awkward sounding word that rocked her senses.

"Actually, I'm a magician." His belly growled. "And hungry."

"Well, order lunch then. It's half eleven and I can vouch for the food." She passed him a menu. "A magician? Can you make a living at that?"

"I do about as well as an archaeologist," he replied, and pulled those delicious lips into a half-smile that nearly unseated her. How the hell was a man like this, friends with a lad like Dylan? Perhaps, he was an investigator sent by the McBride family.

"How is it that you know Dylan?" she asked.

"We met through friends in Canada."

"Dylan's interested in magic, is he?"

"Actually…yes."

"Well, perhaps you can spirit him away from that blasted prison."

"The thought crossed my mind." She'd been flirting, but his response was genuine.

When his smoked salmon baguette came, he all but inhaled it. Then he polished off a bowl of chunky minestrone soup. "Much better. I didn't realize I was—"

"Ravenous…like a wolf." He cocked his head curiously. "I don't know why I said that."

"Well, I *am* following a trail. I promised Dylan's grandfather that I'd get him out of that prison and I intend to do it. I thought perhaps you could help. You don't have to tag along for the jailbreak, but anything you can tell me—"

"Aye, of course."

"I figure the only way to vindicate Dylan is to find the real killer. It could be dangerous."

"Ah, bring it on. Dylan didn't kill that cunt or have anything to do with stealing the artifact." His eyes widened. Perhaps, Canadians weren't used to such terms. Well, if he was going to hang around with her, he'd have to let loose a little.

"Right. I read something about that in the local paper. You found some treasure? Was it really stolen?"

"Aye, and not just *some* treasure. *Her* treasure."

"Her?"

"Meritaten, the daughter of Akhenaten and Nefertiti." He furrowed his brow. Was it concentration or confusion? Perhaps he needed educating. "What I found confirms that an Egyptian Princess came to Scotland, just as the legend says."

"Legend?"

"Aye. In 1435, Walter Bower, the Abbot of Inchcolm Abbey, wrote what's now considered a historical document—the *Scotichronicon*. In it, he tells the story of an Egyptian princess who arrived with her entourage in Scotland around the year 1350 BC. Generally, we accept what religious people write as—"

"Gospel?" His smile was compelling.

"Aye, they wrote what had been passed down through the oral tradition…along with Christian embellishments." He nodded. "Bower called her Scotti." She sipped her coffee.

"As in Scotland."

"I believe he was referring to her as a foreigner or raider."

"But Egypt's got to be a couple of thousand miles south—"

"Aye, but she did not leave Egypt bound for Scotland. Bower claims that her ships followed the River Constantine through Africa, and they stayed for some time in present-day Algeria. I've travelled her route. It's possible."

As she explained, she traced the route on the table as if it were an invisible map. "He says that from Africa, they sailed to the island of Cadiz in Spain, and then to the northeast Spanish mainland, where they settled by the mouth of the River Ebro. The indigenous people of Iberia didn't like being ruled by an Egyptian Queen, so they were forced to flee again. With bridges burned in Egypt and Spain, they sailed northward, past Cornwall, and on through the Irish Sea. After crossing the channel, they ventured into the sound."

"But, how would they know where to go?"

"Ah, well. During the Bronze Age, traders from several nations were sailing through the channel regularly, trading goods from the Mediterranean and France with the people of Ireland and Scotland, even as far north as Skara Brae in Orkney. Everyone needed tin to smelt copper, and the best place for tin was Cornwall. Three thousand years ago, the sea due west of us was a bustling thoroughfare, and this valley, a religious and cultural Mecca." She sipped her coffee. "But, I think she came here for the stones."

"The stones?"

"Aye, the standing stones." He cocked his head. "The megaliths," she said.

He still did not seem to understand and paused with the thought. Had he not seen them? The Ballymeanoch stones stood in a field along the highway and were visible to everyone driving by.

"So, what did you find?" he asked at last.

"Her broad collar." He narrowed his eyes. "A neck and shoulder piece," she explained, using her hands to illustrate how it sat against her clavicle. "It was crafted in gold and decorated with precious stones and faience beads; just like the ones Carter discovered when he unearthed the tomb of her cousin, Tutankhamun. You've heard of him, I presume. King Tut?" When he pursed his lips, his cheeks hollowed out in shadow.

He nodded. "Of course."

"Well, if *she* hadn't left Egypt, Meritaten would have ruled in his stead. Some say she didn't leave, but I know she did. And I'm sure that what I found was hers."

"How can you be sure?"

She snorted. "Trust me. I'm sure." She wasn't about to tell him what she'd seen when she held that collar in her hand. He'd think she was mad. But her visions were revealing and they never lied. She'd picked up images from metal objects since she was a little girl. "In 1955, O'Riordain found a similar collar in Ireland at Tara with a corresponding date. The legend says, Meritaten's people fled there after the people of Scotland cast her out."

Sipping her coffee, she watched him process what was second nature to her.

"Egyptians in Scotland," he said, and shrugged. *Was it meaningless to him?* "So, who do you think stole—?"

"The collar? Honestly, I'm baffled. I do have a lead on where it might surface though. There's a healthy black market for antiquities in Europe if you know where to look. I'm heading to Glasgow tomorrow to do a little digging, pardon the pun. I know a wee fella—"

"I have a Harley out front," he teased, his eyes brightening, "and I'm headed that way myself. There's a woman there with a grudge against Steele. I'd like to talk to her. Any enemy of Steele's—"

"It's a date," she said. Her mobile rang then and she slid it open. "Sorcha."

"Sharesies?"

"What's the craic, Emma?"

"There's a Detective Erskine-Steele headed your way."

"Steele? As in Alastair Steele?" she whispered.

"Aye, as in Mrs."

~~~

Estrada finally understood why Dylan had volunteered to dig in the dirt of the Scottish countryside all summer long. Sorcha O'Hallorhan was sexy, sagacious, and charming. He liked her spirit. And, on a more practical level, realized his need for an ally. As partners, they stood a greater chance of liberating Dylan. She had a keen wit, and knew her way around Scotland; something he did not. She also knew the people who worked at her camp. He was about to suggest forging a pact when a tall, willowy blonde flashed a police badge before his eyes.

"Detective Erskine-Steele. I have a few questions."

"Steele," said Sorcha, with narrowed eyes. "You're not related to Alastair Steele, are you? The man who was murdered just up the road?"

"Neither a matter of consequence, nor your business."

Estrada wondered if the detective's eyes, masked behind dark mirrored glasses, were as soulless as her voice. He wished to see them. Her platinum hair was bound severely in a low ponytail just above her collar. Having slipped her badge back in the pocket of her grey trousers, she stood stiffly; pale hands braced against a thick leather belt from which were tethered several leather-cased items: a phone, a radio that emitted a dull hissing sound, what appeared to be a semi-automatic pistol, and an extra magazine. *How fast could this bitch shoot?*

"I think it is," said Sorcha, recovering from the sergeant's curt response. "Both of consequence *and* my business. A friend of mine is in jail for Steele's murder. If you're related, I consider that a conflict of interest."

Cocking her head, the detective stared down the archaeologist. "Noted," she said, at last.

Sorcha took a deep breath and exhaled loudly. "Bloody cunt," she hissed. The pejorative caused the right side of the detective's lips to rise in a slight sneer. She was a woman who revelled in her power.

If the archaeologist was fire; the detective was ice. Turning her back to Sorcha, she faced Estrada. He gazed up at the lithe leaden form and wondered what it was she *really* wanted. Everyone has a personal agenda, no matter what they say. If she *was* the victim's wife, perhaps it was justice; possibly vengeance. Then again, if the man was as nasty as he seemed, she could be relieved, grateful even.

"Let's walk, Mr. Estrada." It was not a suggestion.

Recalling his experience at the airport, he stood obediently, withdrew a few euros from his wallet, and tossed them on the table. "I'll be right back," he promised Sorcha, then smiled and winked. He hoped to mollify the woman. There was no point arguing with a grieving widow, especially one that was armed.

When he stood beside the detective, her height surprised him. He was six foot two, and she was slightly taller. "After you," he said, and flashed his most captivating smile.

Though sinewy, she floated as fluidly as a dancer, her posture perfect. No panty lines, yet through the pale grey tailored blouse he perceived a lacy outline. A villain, yet oddly angelic. His mind reeled in the contradiction.

At her car, she turned, and stood stiffly. With a sudden breeze came the faint scent of feral sweat, and he breathed it in like a tonic. When she removed her glasses, her eyes, as icy grey as the North Sea, caught his and held them.

"Fuck," he breathed.

"Fuck you," she said. "We're watching. We know what happened in Ireland last fall, and we know about your connection with the Stryker family in Vancouver. We know they're dirty, and we know you're dirty. So, if you so much as breathe wrong, we'll jail you first and investigate later. If you value your freedom, Mr. Estrada, you'll catch the next plane back to Canada."

"Wait a—"

"Dylan McBride is a killer and will be convicted. This is the last *courtesy* you'll get."

He wanted to protest, to scream corruption, or threaten to expose her to the press, but as her hand strayed near the pistol, he felt a cold caress against his flesh. Nodding in acquiescence, he turned and padded into the restaurant where he'd left Sorcha. When he glanced back, Detective Erskine-Steele was sliding into her Prius.

"Did you give her a piece of your mind?"

Estrada shrugged. "She wants me gone. I don't get it. Why the intimidation? If *my* partner was murdered, I'd appreciate any help I could get. I'd want to know what happened."

"Ah, she's just a skinny bitch." Firmly planted in the chair, she'd crossed her arms beneath her breasts. A warrior queen poised and ready for battle.

"Steele's body was found nearby, right?"

"Just down the road."

"Are you keen to solve a crime, Sorcha O'Hallorhan?"

"Aye, that I am, Estrada."

"Let's go then." He sauntered out of the restaurant with Sorcha following behind. If the Scottish police were going to threaten him, he'd find out why.

"We could walk."

"I'd rather keep the bike close," he said, walking toward the Harley.

"How's about I drive, then? I know the way."

"You're legal?" The detective's threat harried him.

"Aye, sure." He wondered where her licence was. It wasn't in the pocket of those tiny khakis or tucked into that halter. He handed her the extra helmet and waited. As she settled and started the engine, he slid up close behind her and wrapped his arms around her waist. She took off fast, sending a spray of gravel sideways and mounted the pavement. Minutes later, she pulled off the A816 into a car park.

"It's just there," she said, pointing to the other side of the highway where the remains of yellow police tape littered a grassy rock-strewn hump.

"Is this the kind of thing you excavate?"

"I know it doesn't look like much, but even Dunchraigaig Cairn can provide a stunning view into the past." Standing amidst the rocks, he watched her anger deflate like a balloon. "The earliest burial we've found here occurred three thousand years ago. They laid a body on the ground and built a stone coffin over it. Must have been someone important; someone they admired. Later, they left decorated pots with the ashes of people they'd cremated. Do you not find that the least bit intriguing?"

He shrugged. "What can you really tell about people from bits of bone and broken pots?"

"We can tell that they cared about each other; that they believed in an afterlife. They were as human as us. Maybe more so."

Estrada nodded. He couldn't argue with that. People caring for people was what life was all about.

One side of the large mound looked as if it had been pried open. A thick square stone hung over like a lip. Inside the gravel strewn floor was darkened by shadow.

"Where was Steele's body?"

"Just there," she said, pointing into the darkness. "He was lying on his right side."

"I suppose it's ironic that his body was left in a burial cairn."

"Sardonic, I'd say. Skull bashed in with a rock. At least, that's what Kai said. He was up early that morning, heard the commotion, and came to investigate."

"Who's Kai?"

"One of my crew. He saw them arrest Dylan. The poor lad was down in the other field asleep by the standing stones when the police arrived."

"You're kidding. They believe that Dylan bashed in Steele's head with a rock, and then went to sleep in an adjacent field?" He shook his head. "That's ludicrous. When did this murder take place?"

"Last Friday night…a week ago today."

Summer Solstice. That explained what Dylan was doing out in the field by the stones. Without the coven, he was living as a solitary. Estrada knelt and peered inside. "Not much room in here. Do they think Steele was struck while he was underneath this thing? Or was the body placed here after he was killed?"

"Killed right there." Squatting down, she pointed inside the cairn. "A bloody rock was discovered beside his head."

"A rock with Dylan's prints on it?" She shrugged. "So the killer somehow got Steele to crawl inside the cairn, bashed in his head with a rock, and then left everything there for the police to find."

"What are you thinking, man?" Sorcha collapsed on the grass beside the cairn. The sun was scorching her pale Irish skin a warm shade of pink. He sat down beside her.

"Someone lured him in there. Perhaps used your Egyptian collar as bait?"

"High-priced bait."

"Yeah, and why Steele? What's the personal connection?" asked Estrada. These things were rarely random.

"From what I hear, Steele was a successful cunt with a slew of enemies. He had a penchant for antiquities…collected artifacts and stories, and sold to magazines worldwide."

"I can't see Dylan getting involved with someone like that. What have they got on him? Other than finding him sleeping in an adjoining field."

"Motive." Sorcha smiled "And, I'm afraid that's *my* fault."

He cocked his head. "Oh?"

"I had a little too much whiskey that night. Kai's been giving Dylan a hard time lately, and the fellas in camp tease him about being a virgin. So, I gave him a little *head* start, if you get my meaning. Liked it too, he did. Caught him alone in the beer garden at Murphy's and had my way with him."

"Really?" Estrada laughed. Dylan had no experience with women. This bawdy Irish woman *and* out in public. He couldn't imagine.

"Ah, it was all innocent…sweet to see his eyes roll. I think it was his first. Steele—the slimy bastard—took photos and teased him. You can imagine how embarrassed he was. Dylan's so straight-laced. Anyway, he grabbed Steele's mobile and tried to delete the photos. I think he was protecting my honour. But the police intervened. Kai heard them talking about it. They think that Dylan lured Steele down here using the artifact to get his hands on that mobile. When things got rough, he killed him."

"Bashed his head in with a rock, and then went to sleep in the next field?" He scoffed. "Where's this phone now?"

"You want to see the photos?"

"It could be useful."

"Ah right. Taken into evidence? Or, perhaps with the grieving widow?"

"There's a girl named Janey Marshall that accused Steele of rape. Apparently, the case got thrown out and it ruined her career. I think she might be more comfortable sharing her story with a woman." She nodded. "How about I pick you up at the museum around nine tomorrow morning and we cruise into Glasgow?"

"Grand, but only if I get to drive in the city. We should see the Wee Pict first, and you'll never find his shop, even *with* directions. It's a hole in the wall."

"Deal. Just be sure to bring your licence. I've already been targeted by the cops."

She stood and stretched. "Hey, there's another one of my crew," she said, suddenly. Estrada looked across the rocky outcropping that topped the cairn and saw a slim young man perched on a rock beneath some strange looking trees. "Hey Kelly," she yelled, and waved.

He touched his sunken cheeks, smiled forlornly, and waved back.

"He looks upset."

"Aye. Kelly's a good lad, but emo. He's Dylan's mate from Tarbert and he's taken it hard. I'd introduce you, but I think it's best to leave him be."

"He reminds me of someone," said Estrada, thinking of Michael. "Someone I need to call." He'd left it long enough.

CHAPTER FIVE

The Wee Pict

"I LOVE THIS BEACH," said Daphne. She stood in the sun, towel-drying her chopped burgundy hair. It had been a long rainy spring and British Columbia hadn't had many days like this: turquoise sky, sun-kissed ripples, and a hint of promise in the air. She smoothed out her towel and collapsed on her belly. After swimming across the lake and back again, she was feeling delightfully exhausted.

"Me too," said Sensara, dreamily. Stretched out on her back on a blanket, she was soaking up rays after a leisurely float in the lake. "What's it called again?"

"White Pine. We only just discovered it. Raine and I love living near Belcarra. There are so many places to play, and this lake is much warmer than Buntzen. It's too bad we can't use it for ceremonies."

"Why can't we? There must be a way in at night."

"Oh yeah. There are trails from a road over there," she said, pointing across the water, "but it's not secluded. We might end up scaring someone."

Sensara smiled. "We've done *that* already."

"You're terrible," said Daphne, flicking her arm.

"I know, but it was a brilliant plan. Yasu has vanished from my life and my mother will never set me up with one of her friends' sons again." She giggled. "Did you see his face? I thought he was going to faint."

"Obviously never met the Green Man before."

"I think Cernunnos pushed him over the edge." Daphne's snort sent Sensara into hysterics. She had to lean up on her elbows to catch her breath. "When I grabbed his hand to jump the fire, he was vibrating."

Daphne opened her flask and gulped some water. "Have you talked to Estrada yet?" She was suddenly serious. "Have you told him—?"

Sensara shook her head, and faint droplets flew from her long dark hair.

"You're not still mad at him for what happened last fall? You know you'll never stop him from freestyling."

"I know."

"Besides, he was enchanted. We *all* were."

"We may have been reacting to a charm at first, but later it was real— at least it was for me."

You still love him, thought Daphne, *that's why you can't let it go.* "Forgive him, Sensara. You saw how he acted at the ceremony. He acts tough, but he's fragile."

"He's also damn unpredictable." Sensara sat up, squeezed some sunscreen on her palm, and spread it on her arms. "I can't believe he left his clothes on the beach. His new leather jacket and his boots. Do you think he drove home naked?"

"Naked and bootless? I wouldn't put it past him." Daphne's giggle sent them into another reel of laughter. "At least he took the antlers off. Cernunnos naked on a Harley—that would be something to see coming at you in the middle of the night on the freeway." She turned onto her back. "Perhaps you should have warned him."

"My love life is none of his business."

And yet, you judge him for his, thought Daphne.

"Why should he care anyway?" Sensara pulled a brush from her bag and jerked it through her hair. When she was annoyed, she could be just as intense as Estrada. "I don't comment on *his* love life."

Not now, thought Daphne. But when they were a couple, she had plenty to say. Estrada's sexual escapades were legendary. He was a romantic, who fell in love hard, fast, and frequently. Sensara was no prude, but she believed in monogamy. If he was going to be *her* man, he couldn't be lusting after other people. Especially that friend of his, Michael Stryker, who she detested and blamed for Estrada's lascivious shortcomings.

"No, but he doesn't bring his lovers to ceremonies either," said Daphne. She'd always had a soft spot for Estrada, and hated to see him suffer.

"Good thing. They wouldn't all fit on the beach," she said, rolling her eyes. "Besides, Yasu was *not* my lover."

"A point Estrada apparently missed. You know he still cares for you, Sensara."

"I know." She sighed. "But, you don't know him like I do. Estrada's all about the drama: drinking, drugs, sex—" She'd finished brushing her hair and was weaving it into a fishtail. "Anyway, he's not even here. He'll be in Scotland for god knows how long."

"I hope he can do something for Dylan. Sometimes, just before I drift off to sleep, I hear him playing the bagpipes. Remember the tune Dylan played last Mabon? It's still stuck in my head."

"Yeah." Sensara reached out and rubbed her shoulder. "I've been sending him blessings, but maybe we should gather for a ceremony. Create some positive energy and send it out?"

"Sylvia would be into that. And Raine. And our high priest, if he were here." She reached into her bag, pulled out an apple and handed it to Sensara. "Estrada may have his vices, but he's one of the good guys. Remember that."

~~~

Sorcha O'Hallorhan was deep in conversation with a brawny dwarf, she affectionately called The Wee Pict. His name was Magus Dubh—the last of which she pronounced *dove*. He'd welcomed her with a kiss on each cheek, and was now perched atop a cluttered desk. Cuddled up close to her cleavage, he whispered and giggled. Sorcha really was a clever woman. The wee man was melting from the heat.

Working in a goth bar, Estrada had seen his share of freaks, but Dubh was something else. He wondered how he survived in a city like Glasgow. Perhaps, no one saw him, and mingling amongst the invisible hoard, he wandered the streets alone. Or perhaps, he was more than he appeared. Fully bearded, his long bronze hair was drawn up in a high ponytail. Nothing outlandish about that; however, there was no air-conditioning in the shop, so he'd stripped off his shirt. All his exposed skin, including his face right down to the eyelids and earlobes, was tattooed in royal blue symbols—a beastly menagerie, interwoven with vines, spirals, crescents, and other abstract shapes.

Estrada scrutinized the tats, wondering how far the ink extended beneath the worn leather kilt, and just how painful it would be to have your genitals tattooed. He knew about ink—wore the black lacy wings of an angel on his back. Her feathers extended across his shoulders and down his glutes. That ink had broken more than his skin.

It was strange how memories were triggered by the oddest things. He'd seen plenty of tats and not thought of Alessandra. She was seventeen and extraordinary—he was thirteen and insatiable. They'd fallen in love, however crazy that seemed, and she'd refused to accept payment for her work. It was an act of adoration. She wanted to immortalize him by painting his body in pictures, words, and love knots. Only she hadn't had the chance.

Alessandra was not just his first lover; she was his first love. And, when he heard she'd been killed in a revenge shooting for something her younger brother had done, Estrada discovered that he truly *was* a black angel. She was the first girl to teach him that attachment causes the kind of pain that exacts vengeance. And, he carried that corpse for years in the cracks of his soul. Until last fall, when Primrose—

Catching himself wallowing in the past, Estrada turned away from the strange pair, and wandered around Dubh's shop. Sorcha said the wee man was a Druid, who worshipped Nature, particularly trees. Estrada felt a similar connection to the forest, and assumed that Druidry must be something akin to Wicca. *Dubh*, she said, was a Gaelic word meaning dark—Estrada wondered what dark charms the wee man could spin.

The shop was dark too, eerily lit by the odd bare bulb, and cast its own enchantment. Just a blue door in a wall; it had no windows and no sign. No one would guess it ran deep, and was crammed with antiquities. It was a sword and sorcerer's dream, but Dubh also stored shamanic relics from several continents, and a full catalogue of treasures from the British Isles and Scandinavia.

The patrons at Club Pegasus revealed their fascination with Estrada's guillotine—a replica Sixteenth Century Scottish Maiden—by screaming madly or booing; sometimes even crying, when the steel bar slammed down to slice off his head. So to speak. Whenever life got stale, people yearned for the past. Medieval romance was in vogue and suited him, so he searched for paraphernalia he could weave into his act—escape artistry and illusion wrapped in a gothic cloak.

He'd just discovered a cache of torture devices from the witch craze and was considering how he might adapt a rack to illustrate the horror of the time, when he saw a crack of light. The shop door had opened.

Sorcha saw it too. She took one look at the customer, and slipped behind a large wooden throne. Following her cue, Estrada ducked behind an Iron Maiden and peered around to see who had prompted such stealth.

Detective Rachel Erskine-Steele. What was *she* doing here? Stalking him? Or had the woman drawn her own conclusion about the connection between the Egyptian broad collar and her husband's murder?

Dubh crossed his painted arms across his chest and braced himself—he obviously knew the woman, or at least who she represented.

Conservatively dressed, in tight trousers and a short-sleeved tailored shirt the colour of smoke, she masked her considerable sexuality. He wondered if she preferred women. Possibly, and yet she emanated an alluring pheromone that induced arousal, even at this distance. After pushing her sunglasses over her smooth platinum hair, her hands came to rest on that well-equipped leather belt. She sized up the shop and the wee man.

"Good day Mr. Dubh." She flashed her badge officially.

"Detective."

"I expect you've heard that an Egyptian artifact unearthed in Argyll has disappeared."

"Is that so?"

"Aye, it is."

"Huh," breathed Dubh from his desktop perch.

In one graceful movement, the detective slipped into a chair and swung her feet up on the desk beside him. To his credit, the wee man didn't flinch; even when her stiletto heel nearly punctured his thigh. Chic black heels with a thin ankle strap—expensive, sexy, and not police issue.

"This particular artifact is possibly a neckpiece from the time of King Tut—a broad collar, I believe it's called. It hasn't been authenticated yet, but it could be the real thing."

Her neck was long and slender, her flesh as pale as swan feathers. Estrada's skin prickled as he imagined her naked and draped in Egyptian jewels, a pearly Nefertiti. Catching himself, he wondered what the hell he was thinking. She was a spiteful cop—the widow of the man his friend was imprisoned for murdering.

"The real thing you say?"

"Correct. Which makes it the property of the Crown and subject to the law of Treasure Trove."

"I am aware of that law, detective."

She nodded. "You wouldn't want to defraud the Queen and Lord Treasurer's Remembrancer."

"Heavens no. That would be treasonous."

"Criminal. Especially with the abundance of antiquities you have here." She glanced around the shop. "You wouldn't want me to suspect you of hoarding treasure, concealing artifacts belonging to the Crown, or arranging the sale of such relics, would you Mr. Dubh?"

"I most certainly would not want *that*, detective. We dwarves gave up hoarding treasure when we crawled out of our caves. If it wasn't for Professor Tolkien—"

"It doesn't look that way to me." Drawing up one side of her mouth in a sly smile, her cheek flushed slightly. "So, Mr. Dubh, what do you know about this Egyptian broad collar? Are you arranging a deal? Has it shipped? Or is it still around?" As tenacious as she was beautiful, Estrada wondered what secrets hid beneath that prim demeanour.

"May I first extend my condolences, detective, on the loss of your husband. It's a tragedy when a man is murdered in his prime. I pray that you discover the identity of the perpetrator and bring the cunt to justice."

"I appreciate your candour, Mr. Dubh. Now, about the artifact."

"In that regard, detective, I swear on my father's grave, I cannot help you. I'd be lying if I said, I wouldn't like to see this piece myself. I am partial to Egyptian antiquities. But, I've not heard a word as to its current whereabouts. I will call, however, if I do."

"You do that sir, or when I return I'll bring an army and a search warrant, and we'll have a good look around your shop." She smiled sweetly, then stood and stomped a floorboard—the opposite end popped up to reveal a tidy stash. "Even in those *secret* places." Releasing it with a slap, she smirked, and sauntered out the door.

When Sorcha and Estrada emerged from their respective hiding places, her cheeks were crimson.

"You handled that magnificently Magus. Don't let that bitch get to you."

Smiling, the dwarf touched his palm to her cheek. "Don't let her get to *you*, my lovely Irish queen."

"Ah, I won't. She's just—"

The sound of the front door cut Sorcha's sentence short. Estrada grasped her arm and yanked her behind the throne, in case the detective was returning. Anger wafted in scarlet streaks around Sorcha and he was in no mood for a cat fight. Dubh skipped towards the front of the shop to put some space between them and whoever had entered. He was one protective son of a bitch.

"Jesus," breathed Sorcha, and clapped her hands across her mouth as a dark-skinned man swaggered towards Dubh.

"Can I help you?"

A few mumbled words from the man, and then Dubh said emphatically: "No. I *really* don't."

Triggered by the distinctive click of a switchblade, Estrada leapt from behind the throne. When his elbow caught the edge of a suit of armour and sent it crashing to the ground, he tripped and fell forward, landing on his hands and knees. "Damn!"

"Smooth," said Sorcha, sarcastically.

The man cast him a death glance, then turned to Dubh, whispered something, and slashed the open blade in an upstroke across his naked blue belly. Dubh's cry ended in a gurgling groan as he buckled and hit the floor. The man smirked and bolted.

The spurting blood sent Estrada reeling back to Primrose and that night she laid in his arms with a knife in her chest. Paralyzed, he relived the fear and grief he'd felt in that moment. *Don't leave me, Primrose. I love you.* He saw her angel face. She'd opened his heart, and then—

Sorcha shoved him as she ran by: "Estrada! Get him!" Crouching over Dubh, she pressed a scarf to his belly to staunch the blood. "What's wrong with you, man? Move!"

He shook his head to erase the vision. Feeling compassion for Primrose's killer, he'd let him escape. This time he would show no mercy.

He raced after the man and grasped the edge of his jacket in his fist just as he opened the door. The switchblade skittered up the back of his hand, slicing the flesh between thumb and first finger all the way to his wrist, and spraying blood up his arm. Surprised, he released his grip, and as he did, the man jerked free and lurched out the door.

"Go after him!" yelled Sorcha.

When Estrada caught sight of the assailant less than a block away, he was running toward the river. And then, he was gone. Vanished. A narrow overgrown trail led to a blond sandstone tenement, but he couldn't have made it into the building. He likely knew the city and was hiding somewhere close.

For a moment, Estrada stood still, caught his breath, and assessed his hand. The bastard had cut a vein—it ran deep and was bleeding profusely. He stripped off his leather jacket, then his T-shirt, and ripped it into strips. After rapping it hastily and tying it off, he pressed the wound for several seconds to staunch the bleeding.

"I know you're here and I *will* find you." Scanning each surface, he listened for sounds in the weeds. He knew he was ramped up on adrenalin. He also knew he couldn't think straight in that condition. If he was to find this bastard, running blind and angry into the tenement would do him no good. He needed to calm himself and think past the panic.

Why had he suddenly thought of Primrose and the night she died? It was the blood. They'd been covered in her blood. It was all he could see; and then she'd shown him the faeries. That night she'd taught him to see them, and then she'd walked between him and the man with the knife. Like she knew… She'd saved his life, and then—

He sighed. He knew what she would say. *Calm yourself, Sorcerer. Focus on a peaceful thought.*

Perching on a step, he took long deep breaths until his pulse slowed. *You are my most peaceful thought, Primrose. But, I need to find this man. You told me, if I ever needed you, you'd come. I need you now. Please, help me.*

As he huddled in the alley, the sounds of the city night dimmed, and his eyes welled up with tears. Grief squeezed his chest: grief for her, and for Dylan, and even for the stranger who lay bleeding on the shop floor. It threatened to disable him, and there was nothing he could do, but feel it. He snorted and cried, let it out, and then sniffed and wiped his face.

When her lilting voice rose like a song on the wind, he caught it, and held it. *Close your eyes and breathe. Find your own sweet heartbeat. I can feel it in my hand.* As if in a dream, he felt her fingers drum lightly against his breast as she kept the pulsing rhythm. *Now open your eyes just a flutter, just enough to let in the light. I'm with you, sorcerer. Accept this gift with love.*

The world slowed to a hush. The tenement, the laneway, even the bushes, appeared in varying shades of grey—a silent film of blurring lines and shifting mists. *Light and shadow. Illusion.* He scanned the passage. Flushes of colour emanated from the concrete like the dust of a Tibetan sand painting. One red footprint, and then another, moving down the sidewalk—a trail of heat prints left by the attacker. No need for night goggles when a man could see with faerie eyes. *Thermal imagining,* he thought, and smiled. *Thank you, my love.*

Following the trail, he approached a rusted metal platform half-buried in the earth. It was cool bluish grey, but a smattering of red handprints clung to one hinged section. Carefully, he grasped the metal lid and lifted. A rush of stale air burst from the hole below. Somewhere, in that darkness, hid a knife-wielding killer. He had met such a man only a few months before, and that time the man had—

No. He must stay present lest his grief take hold and strike him impotent again. He couldn't go there now. Now, he must crawl down the red-edged metal ladder and descend into this subterranean world. Now, he must find a weapon.

He bundled up his leather jacket, and stashed it behind a swath of weeds. No encumbrances. He wished he had the knife he always carried in his boot back home. He'd had a leather sheath sewn into the inside of his right boot for just this purpose. Not to worry. The bastard had a switchblade, and that would do.

After easing backwards down the ladder, he turned to find himself in what appeared to be an abandoned subway tunnel. The malingering odour of earth assaulted his senses, and something else—the unmistakable stench of death. Some rotting animal; a rat perhaps? He was in no mood to discover a body in the Glasgow underground.

Though dimly lit, he could make out a deep crack in the mouldering tiles along the wall above the old train track, where trees thrust gnarly roots into the void. Unable to find an anchor, they twisted precariously and clung. Judging by the graffiti, this was a meeting place, possibly home to a Glasgow gang. Sorcha had warned him to ignore the neds— *non-educated delinquents*—that gathered in groups and harassed the tourists. Was this their place? If so, where were they? And, where was the man who'd cut Dubh? He was no ned.

He heard water dripping and the odd clanging of pipes, but saw nothing to betray the man's whereabouts. Focussing on his breath, he waited until he could see the scattered patch of red that confirmed he'd been there. His tracks ran along the platform and disappeared over the side. Senses alert to enemies in the shadows, Estrada dropped onto the rocks that surrounded the abandoned track.

~~~

Sorcha was sure that tight-assed detective was involved in this—maybe not directly, but she had led the Black Spaniard to the Wee Pict's shop. Why else would he suddenly appear wielding a switchblade? And why was he in Oban the night she discovered the artifact? She shivered, remembering how much she desired him, drunk or not.

Placing her ear close to the Wee Pict's mouth, she listened to his ragged breathing. His skin was cold and clammy. He was in shock. Where was the fucking ambulance? She'd called ages ago. Lifting the scarf, she peered beneath. Poor wee Magus. His guts were bulging out. What kind of man disembowels another? She pressed her hand against the wound, and cried, but it was not enough.

"If he dies," she screamed, "I'll hunt you down and kill you my fucking self!"

~~~

The underground tunnel was a shadowy maze that ran nowhere—at least nowhere Estrada could see from where he stood on the platform below the ladder. Searching the ashen ground, he'd lost sight of the heat imprints left by the man. He'd simply vanished…again.

Then, a slight sough overhead, and he sprang like a panther.

Landing on his back, the man caught his neck in the crook of his arm and squeezed to choke him out. Unbalanced, they fell forward, and Estrada sunk his teeth into the soft flesh and bone below the elbow. Shaking the arm viciously, he bit off a chunk of flesh, and spat it out.

"Animal," the man seethed.

An involuntarily jerk provided just enough space for Estrada to crawl out from beneath him, and spring up. The man leapt up too, shook his bleeding arm, and spit, as Estrada rammed his fist into the jaw with an uppercut. Groaning, the man drew back, then careened forward fists flying. He caught Estrada with a succession of jabs to the gut. Curled over to catch his breath, he heard the click, and leapt back.

The blade reappeared. Right hand. Low. Estrada had seen plenty of this in L.A. and mirrored his opponent's movements. Seething, the man searched for a way in. Estrada kicked for the hand, and missed. Taking swift advantage, the man drew up, going for his hamstring, but caught it low. The blade slashed across Estrada's calf, ripped through his jeans, and drew blood. Feeling its bite, he leaned down. He'd been passive too long, was out of practice, and anger was impeding his skills. Leaping, the man lashed out again, slicing into his left shoulder and clean across his chest in a wide arc. Dizzy, Estrada swayed. Then, catching sight of the blood streaming down his bare breast, he felt a surge of adrenalin.

The man glared. "You want more, *muchacho*? Maybe I'll cut your heart out."

"Fuck you." Estrada's lips twisted into a sneer, as the man lunged again.

This time he was ready, and with all his energy focussed on his right foot, he kicked up and out, grinding it into the bastard's gut. Spiralling backwards, the body hit the tile wall with a thump and hung there, breathless. Leaping, he kicked the blade from the hand and crushed his knuckles into the astonished face. As he felt the bones in the nose break, he raised his palm for one last shot—a fatal smash to the bridge of the nose that would ram the bastard's nasal bones up into his brain.

The steely barrel of a pistol kissed the back of his neck.

"Don't move Mr. Estrada."

His stomach flipped. *Rachel Erskine-Steele.*

Holding his hand to his nose, the man spit bloody snot, then turned, and limped through a dark hole in the wall like a rat.

"He's getting away." The muzzle of the pistol bruised the base of his brain.

"He won't get far."

"He sliced Dubh."

"It appears he sliced you too."

He felt her step back though the pistol did not move.

"Now, raise your hands and turn around." He hesitated. "Do it," she threatened, and cocked the trigger.

With no choice, he turned. Both hands were wrapped around a Glock aimed at his heart. "Aren't you supposed to protect the innocent, detective?"

"Do you see someone innocent? I just stopped you from murdering a man." She rolled her eyes. "Vigilante. I knew you couldn't leave it alone. Now move," she said, motioning towards the ladder with her gun.

"Listen. That bastard assaulted Dubh and he just tried to kill me. Christ, he probably killed your husband." His breath was fast and shallow.

"Don't talk."

"At least call someone to—"

"The police and ambulance are there. It's under control."

Feeling suddenly lightheaded, he swayed into the wall. Reaching out, she touched two fingers to his carotid.

"You need medical attention, Mr. Estrada."

"Stop calling me that."

"It's your name."

"Estrada. It's *just* Estrada."

She nodded. "Fine. Let's climb out of this hole, Estrada. It's too dark in here to see the extent of your injuries."

Holstering her pistol, she hooked her arm around his waist. Stronger than she looked, she took his weight on her shoulder, and together they shuffled along the track. "Watch your—"

"Christ. It's just a graze. Why are you—?"

"It's more than a graze. You've lost a great deal of blood and you're in shock. Now, up you go."

Grasping the rungs of the rusted ladder in his hands, he climbed out of the darkness into sunlight that was near blinding. Feeling suddenly nauseous, he turned and puked, then dropped onto a cement step and wiped his mouth with his fist.

She emerged into the sunlit passage unruffled and peered at his chest wound. "Needs sutures. Your leg and hand does too."

"Nothing Crazy Glue can't fix."

"Perhaps, if we were camping in the Canadian wilderness, but we're not. Glasgow has hospital emergency rooms. Come on, I'll take you."

"Nope. Not into it." She'd ruined his chance at redemption and now she was holding him hostage. First, she'd take him to the hospital and then to the airport. He wouldn't go willingly.

"Desperado." For several seconds, she stood and stared at him, calculating her next move. Then she shook her head. "How about a deal?"

"A deal?"

"Yes. I have sutures and bandages in my flat."

"Your flat?" Why the sudden change of heart? Looking quizzically into those deep grey eyes, he saw a spark of something perilous. "Then what? The airport? Jail?"

"Is *that* what you're afraid of? You can relax. I'm just concerned for your welfare. Trust me."

"*Trust* you?" Trusting police was out of his comfort zone; especially this one.

"I warned you to stay out of it." She picked up his jacket and threw it at him. He shrugged as he caught it. "Well, now you've involved yourself in a complex issue."

"Just how complex? International incident? Police corruption? The Mob?"

"You'll just have to trust me."

Again, those words. He knew he had no option. She was a Glock-wielding detective in a foreign country, whose husband had been killed *allegedly* by his friend. But, it was an intriguing game and he felt like playing. Hell, he'd even play by her rules for a while. She knew things. Had connections.

He stared into her eyes until she flipped her shades down and he saw his pale face reflected in the black mirrors. "What's the rest of this deal?"

"Either you come with me to my flat, or I call for a patrol car."

"That's not a deal."

She holstered her gun, then held out her hand. "It's the only one I'm offering."

CHAPTER SIX

Byron & Brandy

MICHAEL COULD NOT SLEEP. *How many nights had passed? Six? Seven?* Estrada *still* had not contacted him. Of course, that was nothing new. Once, he'd disappeared for weeks and not returned his calls. Michael was, it would seem, as superfluous as last night's wine.

He rolled the small wooden ball between his fingers, then held it to his nose and inhaled the pungent cedar scent. Estrada had slipped it into his pocket when they were in Ireland last December. It was supposed to bring him luck. *Bullshit.* All he felt was empty. Desolate. Abandoned. Again. As usual, he was stuck in Vancouver, while Estrada flew off to Scotland to play hero. *Fuck him and his witchy friends.* He flicked the cedar ball across the bedroom, watched it ricochet off a crystal bong, and fall to the carpet.

After gulping another mouthful of wine, he lit a cigarette, and gazed down at the young man sprawled on the bed beside him. Raven tresses spilled across a white pillow. Exquisite bone structure, sharpness and shadow in perfect proportion, and not a line or crease. Of course, Christophe was years younger than Estrada, closer to the age he'd been when they first met.

He took another drag and blew a smoke ring while he watched him sleep. *So young and beautiful.* If he'd been an artist, Michael would have painted him. At the very least, he must write a poem to immortalize his flawless symmetry, as Byron would have done.

Sensing Michael's gaze, Christophe reached over and stroked his belly with long sharp fingernails. Whitened tips from a French manicure; a faint trail of cocaine was trapped in the creases. "What do you need, Mandragora?"

He loved being called by his nickname; it made him feel distinctly dangerous.

"Nothing you can provide, I'm afraid." He blew another smoke ring and punctured the circle with his finger. "Can you cure this anguish? Quell this madness of the heart?"

"So dramatic. You come from another time, n'est-ce pas?" The fingers danced, reawakening a sensual hunger in Michael's weary body. "But, perhaps I *can* cure your madness, chéri."

"How?" Michael scoffed.

"With love."

"Love?" His tone carried a certain contempt disregarded by the young man.

"Oui, *amour*."

Michael sighed. "What do you have in mind?"

"Whatever you desire. I live only to please you."

"Ah, Christophe." His lover was a budding actor, a sought-after model, and almost as beautiful as Estrada. "Whatever I desire? Anything?" Raising his upper lip, Michael exposed one of his fangs.

Propping himself up on his elbow, the young man held out his hand and took the cigarette from his fingers. "Anything and everything." He paused for an elaborate French inhale, then dropped the cigarette into the ashtray. "It is whispered that Mandragora has developed an exotic taste of late."

"Is it?"

"In circles as intimate as ours there are few secrets, mon ami, and *you* are a legend."

Michael ran a fingertip down the sculpted cheek and across the lips. "Anything and everything," he echoed. They kissed feverishly for several moments. And then, catching an edge of the swollen lip between his teeth, Michael bit down hard with his sharpened fang; so hard, he could taste Christophe's coppery blood. The boy inhaled sharply. "Even if it hurts?"

"Can there be pleasure without pain?"

Picking up a small mirror, Michael offered his lover another long line of the precious white powder. Dipping his fingertip into the cocaine, he dabbed it on the puncture. Then, with a razor blade, he cut out a portion for himself and snorted it all. He set the mirror back down on the dark glass table beside his bed and held out the dusty blade. "This is an instrument of both pain and pleasure. Would you agree, Christophe?"

"Both the pleasure and pain are mine, chéri, but you must sip from somewhere the camera cannot see." Tossing the pure white sheet to the floor, he offered his inner thigh.

"Ah Christophe. I hate to mar your beauty, but I do so want to hear you moan."

~~~

Lions perched menacingly above the arched entrance to the Steele's ornate Victorian apartment building; though the flat itself was a showcase for contemporary Scandinavian design. A blatant contradiction, like the woman.

If Alastair Steele *had* lived here, there was no trace of him now. Was this the way they lived? Or had she obliterated every vestige of the man since his death nine days before? He leaned towards the latter. The tart scent of lemon and bleach lingered in the silence as if he'd been scrubbed from her life.

"Chic," he observed. White walls, polished wooden floors, lush grey leather sofas, and gleaming French doors that led onto a private terrace.

Rachel shrugged. She'd dropped the first line of her defence, and seemed hospitable. He was betting her curt exterior was something she'd cultivated to survive the Scottish police force. To make detective at such a young age—she couldn't be over thirty—showed ambition. He could imagine the woman fighting off a hoard of sexist pigs. Any women in the force would hate her just on principle. Her beauty was daunting. But, why go through that? Why police work when Rachel Erskine-Steele could easily be a model? A cover girl.

"You're bleeding on my floor," she said. For a moment, they both stared at the red drops by his feet.

"Sorry." He readjusted the balled-up towel she'd pulled from her gym bag in the car, and pressed it harder against his shoulder.

"It's coming from your calf. The shower room is downstairs to the right," she said, gesturing to a spiral staircase. "Can you manage?"

Estrada nodded, but then, feeling suddenly faint, literally bounced off the wall. Catching him by the shoulders, she settled him on a bench. "You're still in shock." He watched her easy sway as she walked to an oak cabinet in the dining area. He'd never seen a woman move like that.

She returned with a bottle of Cognac, half-filled a brandy snifter, and offered it to him. "Here, sip this."

He cupped his hand around its warm belly and sniffed the heady nectar, then tipped it to his lips and downed it all, exhaling with a shiver as the heavenly liquid surged through his body. He loved Cognac. It was something he savoured with Michael on damp winter nights by the fire during the Vancouver rains. It made him remarkably poetic.

He sighed aloud. "Refill?"

She shook her head. "That was a good four ounces."

"Ah, come on. I'm injured."

"There's a seat in the shower room. I'll join you in a minute."

"Join me?" Her stern look said it all. He'd overstepped some invisible boundary. He glanced again at that pistol packaged so neatly around her slender waist. "Sorry detective. It's post-traumatic stress."

"Aye, of course it is." Tipping the bottle, she sent another splash that filled the glass.

"Why, detective…"

"Just sip it," she commanded. "I'll get my kit."

He gulped half of it. Ironically, the brandy made him feel grounded; leastways, his feet felt extraordinarily heavy. Balancing the snifter in his left hand, he grasped the wooden bannister and staggered downstairs. The doors to all but one room were slightly ajar, and he peered inside each of them.

The largest bedroom—he assumed it was the master—adjoined the shower room and was decorated in the same contemporary style as the rest of the suite. An immense bed with slate grey leather headboard and footboard dominated the room. Apart from a crisp white duvet and pillows, there were no *things*: no photos, plants, books, or keepsakes, nothing to reveal the woman's story. Was this how she lived? With all details trapped behind stiff white walls? Another set of French doors led from the bedroom onto the terrace, and he stood for a moment relishing the sunlight that streamed through the greenery.

"Lost?"

He stirred at the sound of her voice. "No. Just thinking how wonderful it must be to have a terrace off the bedroom; a place to relax on warm moonlit nights and—"

"I've never used it," she said curtly, then disappeared into a large walk-in closet and shut the door.

Taking this as his cue to hit the shower, he sucked back the brandy, set the empty snifter down carefully on the vanity, and turned on the faucet. The shower stall was twice the size of his bathroom at home. Hot water beat down on his hand, beckoning, and so he stepped inside and stood beneath the stream. When his legs felt weak, he slumped to the wooden bench and leaned against the wall, closing his eyes to curb the spin.

"You're drunk," she said.

"You did feed me liquor."

"You didn't even take your socks off." He opened his eyes and took a quick breath. She'd changed into a white sleeveless mini-dress. Her long legs and feet were bare, her toenails pearlescent. What kind of game was she playing?

"Jesus, woman. I could fall in love with you." When she smiled, the shower stall glowed. "Did I say that out loud?"

"You should have gone to hospital, Estrada. I'm going to check your vitals." She turned off the water, then gripped his left wrist and stood silently for several seconds.

"Will I live, detective?"

"Perhaps." Her pale hair was still upswept, but caught water droplets like dew in a spider's web, while the steam curled tendrils round her ears. "A silver swan caught in winter's ice."

"What?" She laughed.

"When you laugh, I hear bells."

"No more brandy for you. At least, until you've regained your senses."

"My senses are perfect." Everything about her appealed. Grasping the handheld shower, she rinsed his shoulders and chest with warm clear water. It felt divine. She was divine. "You pretend you're tough, but you're really an angel."

She laughed again. "I see you have wings of your own. This is quite the tattoo."

Her fingers danced on his skin. Then she squirted soap on the wound, and he gasped. "Fuck! That stings."

"Come now, Estrada. It's only antibacterial soap. I can see from your scars you've endured far worse."

"You're a sadist."

Smiling again, she rinsed it clear and placed a clean linen towel over the wound. Taking his right hand, she held it against the towel. It too was bleeding, so she wrapped another towel around his hand. "Hold this. I need to stop the bleeding. Keep pressing until it's sutured." She pulled a pair of silver scissors from her kit. "Can you stand? I need to cut off your jeans."

"You can't cut off my jeans. I need my jeans. Unless you're planning to hold me hostage." He winked to no response. "Come on. I'm attached to these."

"Aye, you are. I suppose they can be mended, if you can get them off, that is. They're skin-tight and now that they're wet—"

He coughed to clear his throat. "Don't talk like *that*, detective, or I'll never get them off."

She flashed him one of her scathing looks. He winked, then stood, and unzipped his jeans. He was ready for love. Hadn't been with a woman for months—not since Primrose. Had lost the hunger. But, now it was back. Months of apathy caught in one shameless erection. A pink cloud rose on her cheeks.

"If you hold the towel, detective, I'll just—" He shimmied out of his jeans and dropped them in a heap on the floor.

Kicking them aside, he placed his good hand over hers and caressed the soft flesh between her fingers. When their eyes met, her pupils dilated. She too was aroused. Acting on impulse, he leaned in for a kiss, then felt suddenly weak, and wavered.

"Here, sit down. What blood you had left in your brain all rushed south." She pushed him down on the bench and covered him with a towel. Crouching, she washed his leg with the hand shower, and then stared at his calf. "This looks bad. You're fortunate nothing vital was nicked."

"They'd better catch that bastard. If they don't, I will."

"I called in. Ms. O'Hallorhan gave a detailed description and a bulletin's been issued, so there's no need for more vigilante threats." Standing abruptly, she dried her hands and slipped on a pair of latex gloves. He feared he'd pushed an invisible button.

"You don't need gloves. I've been tested. I'm clean." He wanted that made clear.

"Perhaps you are. But, I don't know you well enough to take your word for it. Besides, I'd get a retest, if I were you."

"Why?"

"Well, even if *you're* clean, how clean is Mr. Dubh?"

"Why does *he* matter?" He shook his head. "I don't—"

"The assailant cut you right *after* he cut Dubh, yeah? Did he clean and sterilize the knife in between?" Estrada glanced at his right hand and remembered how the bastard had slashed up his thumb with the blood-soaked blade while he held him at the door. Was it possible to transfer a virus like that? She'd opened a package of butterfly sutures and was applying them to the wound on his calf. "From what I hear, Magus Dubh has a penchant for boys—the kind that don't always look after themselves."

"Dubh's a pedophile?"

"Perhaps, not *that* young."

"You mean he's gay?" Estrada didn't believe that for a second, not the way he was fawning over Sorcha. Perhaps like himself, Dubh didn't discriminate.

Pausing in her work, she looked him in the eye. "Scotland is a conservative country."

"I see."

She stood and began applying sutures to the long diagonal slash along his chest and shoulder. He'd suddenly lost his buzz. What kind of information travelled beyond borders? *Warning: bisexual magician. Admit at your own risk.* Was that written in a file as well?

"Of course, it happens here. We even allow same sex marriages now. Things are just done…discretely—"

"Like in closets." She was either naïve or in denial. He was sure that Glasgow was as proud of its queer community as any other European city.

She finished off by suturing the slash across his hand. "There. Now all you need is a sling."

"No sling, detective. I need my arms. I'm riding a Harley, remember?"

"Suit yourself, but you won't heal right." She shrugged. "Pig-headed too."

"As long as it's only the one part."

She snapped off her gloves and tossed them in the wastebasket. This was the most emotion he'd seen her display since he met her. He wondered why. What had triggered this irritation? Was she homophobic or just cautious? Then, as she slipped through the door, he caught the mumbled invitation. "Coffee's in the kitchen."

Wrapping a white towel around his waist, he glanced at the spiral staircase. Perhaps, he needed to show Rachel Erskine-Steele just how much he could enjoy a woman.

When the Proclaimers sang from the pocket of his leather jacket, he recognized the ring tone, but not as something he should be answering. He'd forgotten that Dermot had given him Dylan's cell phone.

He slid it open. "Yeah."

"Estrada? What happened to you? Where the hell are you?"

"Sorcha." He'd forgotten all about her.

"Who were you expecting? The bloody queen?"

"How's Dubh?"

"Still in surgery. Look, if you're wondering where your bike is, I drove it to the hospital—the Royal Infirmary on Castle Street. Where are you?"

"I'm…I'm at a walk-in clinic," he stammered. He hoped there were such things in Glasgow and paused. When she didn't object, he continued. "I caught up with the bastard, but he cut me and took off."

"Jesus, Estrada! How bad is it? Where are you? I'll come get you."

"It's my turn soon. I'll call you after I've seen the doctor."

"Grand."

And that was that. He slipped the phone back in his jacket pocket and crept up the stairs. The only doctor he wanted to see was the one who'd just sutured his wounds.

Rachel stood facing the stainless-steel counter in her white kitchen. She'd strapped some high silvery heels on those slender ankles. Her tight white dress was backless, the shoulder straps merging into a long V at the base of her spine. Hugging the curves of her ass, it ended about two inches later; an effect that made her legs seem about six feet long. With her hair pinned up in a French roll, she looked exquisite. High class. Perfection. A woman did not dress like this for herself.

He dropped the towel, and edging in close behind her, laid his hands over hers on the counter. She took a quick breath, though she must have heard him coming. He could hear the throbbing of her heart from the other side of the room. She was leaning slightly forward, her weight on her palms, gazing through the window at the terrace. Her scent was intoxicating; an indescribable blend of everything he loved. For several seconds, they stood locked in this embrace. Flesh to flesh. His bare chest edging her bare back, his fingers caressing the sensitive flesh of her hands, his breath warming the back of her ear. And like a drug, he breathed her in.

"You found me," she said, at last. Merging into her silhouette, he nuzzled against her neck, smelling almonds and summer flowers, as the tiny hairs at the base of her neck prickled under his lips. Then, reaching up, he pulled the pins from her hair, let it spill, and ran his fingers through it. Her sigh was barely audible, but she leaned back and the weight of her head filled his hands.

"Can't do this wearing a sling," he said.

"Can't do a lot of things."

He kissed her long pale neck and then meandered slowly down her back; tasting her, savouring her, tracing her form with his fingers. At the bottom of her spine, he unzipped the dress, and slipped it off her naked hips, burying his face in her flesh, inhaling her musky scent. God, she was perfect. But, he mustn't rush. Needed to take his time, to savour every moment.

Rising, he swept her hair aside, and kissed the soft flesh behind her ear. She had not moved, yet he could sense the blood rushing through her veins.

"This is why you brought me here, isn't it, Rachel?" he growled. "You want me." He caught her cheek in his hand and turned her face, stared into her grey eyes. "I want you too. I want to kiss you…every inch of you—"

"No. I can't." Breaking away, she caught her dress and used it for cover as she darted across the room. "I just can't."

"I know you feel it…this thing between us. It's real. It's—"

"You should go to the hospital. Get them to redress your wounds. You're bleeding—"

"Rachel, I—"

"No, Estrada," she whispered emphatically. "No. This never happened."

~~~

Sorcha was furious by the time she hopped off the back of the bike in front of the Kilmartin Hotel. Estrada insisted on driving the Harley all the way back, and he was surly too, in one hell of a mood. Didn't want to talk. Didn't want to eat. Didn't even want a pint.

She'd hoped to spend some quality time with him, get to know him better, maybe even get him in the sack. She craved tangibles like food and flesh, after spending hours in the infirmary worrying about whether the Wee Pict would live or die. Ah hell. A woman on her own in a pub never stayed alone long.

Several pints later, she stumbled home through the sheep trails using a torch to find her way. Almost midnight, and the sky above Kilmartin

Glen was studded with stars. She wondered what the ancient ones, whose shattered bones and shards she painstakingly dug from the earth, thought of these glittering diamonds in the sky; if their cup and ring marks in the rocks were maps of constellations or something else. She'd give anything to understand them; to go back in time and live among them. It was one thing to imagine; quite another to know it, to live it.

The broad collar had revealed some of its owner's secrets when she placed it around her own neck that day in the privacy of her tent. Meritaten *had* walked these fields, had lived here and loved here, and almost died here. But, the damn thief had stolen it before she'd seen it all. That's why she needed it back; not for money or fame—those were just perks—but to know its secrets.

She slipped inside her tent and stripped off. After downing one last shot of whiskey, she opened her bed chamber and knelt. She couldn't wait to stretch out inside her down bag. And that's when she heard it. Breathing. She wasn't alone.

"Who's here?"

"Who were you expecting?" The voice was deep and rough and tinged with northern timbre.

"Kai? Not you. You said you'd be gone all weekend."

"Did I spoil your plans, boss?"

"No. I just had one cunt-of-a-day and wasn't expecting a Viking in my sack."

"We were never expected. That's how we took this land."

"Right so."

She felt his large rough hand touch her shoulder; imagined him running wild…raping and killing…women, monks, anyone that was too weak to escape those long violent strides. Yet, Kai had a tender side that brought her comfort; and that was why, on nights like this, she laid in his arms, spooned against his chest, and slept soundly with his breath warming her neck.

"Come on, Irish, lie back and tell me all about your cunt-of-a-day."

There was no point resisting. Half-drunk and exhausted, Sorcha melted into his flesh.

"I went to Glasgow this morning to see if the Wee Pict had heard anything of the collar."

"And?"

"And while I was talking to him, a man burst in. Slashed his belly wide open. Jesus! I knew the bastard."

"Did he—"

"Kill him? He's not dead yet. But Christ! The poor wee man. His guts were hanging out, Kai. It was fucking horrible." She shivered, and he rubbed the bumps from her bare arms. "He was still in surgery when I left."

"And this man…you knew him?"

"Oh aye. I danced with him at Murphy's…a dark-skinned bugger, shaved head. Did *you* see him?" Though she didn't remember coming home that night, she'd never forget the Black Spaniard.

She felt him tense just for a second. Then he took a deep breath and sniffed. "Sounds like the man you were dancing with just before I carried you out."

"Aye. That's him. A black Spaniard. Half Egyptian, so he said."

"I don't remember his face. Do you?"

"Oh aye." She'd never forget those eyes. The way he stared into her soul when he plucked her off the bar stool.

"Did they catch the cunt?"

"Estrada went after him, but the bastard cut him too, and then he vanished."

"Estrada?"

"Oh right. You haven't met him yet. Estrada's from Canada. He's a friend of Dylan's come here to help."

"Help how?"

"He intends to exonerate Dylan by finding out who really killed Steele."

"So you went to Glasgow with this Estrada?"

"Aye. We both had business in the city, so we went together. Drove in on his Harley, went to see Magus, and then that bastard walked in and just sliced him. Gutted him like a fish." By then she was ranting, needing to vent. "Something's going on and Meritaten's collar is involved.

Estrada will figure it out. He's a smart cunt and he knows more than he's telling. You know, if Magus Dubh dies that bastard can be charged with murder."

"Your man won't die, Irish. He's a tough wee prick."

"Aye. Well, if he does, it's cold-blooded murder, and I saw it all. I can identify him."

"Jesus boss. You did have a cunt-of-a-day." She felt him shift and lean over her in the dark, felt the brush of his whiskers against her cheek, smelled the faint odour of whiskey on his breath. "Shall I put you to sleep?" Kai Roskilde was rugged, like the land of his ancestors, a man of mountains and fjords, a real man's man, but he never took without asking and often gave without taking.

"Aye, Kai. Put me to sleep." Reaching out, she caught him behind the neck and brought his mouth to hers. It was this remarkable mouth that gained him passage night after night.

"Lie back and close your eyes, Irish. I'll take you where you need to go."

CHAPTER SEVEN

Cinnamon Toast

CONFESS YOU ARE A WITCH. Cruel voices. Searing steel. *Do not speak. Do not confess. To show weakness is to die.* The putrid stench of burning hair, burning meat—

Estrada gasped and awoke to darkness; throat parched, shoulder throbbing. Another one of *those* dreams, likely triggered by Dubh's torture chamber and the trauma of his injury. Somehow in the night, he'd turned over on his injured shoulder and wedged it beneath him. After easing onto his back, he took a deep breath and rubbed his eyes. Then, he grasped Dylan's cell phone. 10:10. Sunday, June 29. He *could* smell burning meat, but there were other aromas too: coffee, potatoes frying in butter, toast, and eggs. Breakfast. He was in Tarbert, Scotland and Dermot McBride was in the kitchen cooking his traditional fry-up. Hallelujah.

After turning on the bedside light, he assessed the damage. There was a dark red stain on the sheet. Damn. He'd have to clean that somehow. Blood seeped through the gauze that crazy Rachel had used to swath his chest and arm. An eight-inch gash ran almost to his heart. Had the bastard struck any lower or any deeper, he would be dead.

And Rachel *was* crazy. Unstable. Volatile. Why bring him to her home, seduce him, and then reject him?

Getting that close to a desirable woman had triggered all kinds of stuff—stuff he'd locked away. It suffused his mind all night, merging with memories of Primrose and Michael.

She had once told him that she would always be there to help him—*in every breath of wind*—and she *had* helped in the alley. She'd gifted him with fey sight. It was a strange comfort to know that she was only a sigh away, even if she'd transformed into something beyond human.

And Michael. He couldn't stop thinking about him and that meant something was very wrong. As Michael, the world was relatively safe, but as Mandragora, his deviant nature intensified to the detriment of himself and anyone else he might beguile.

Estrada didn't want to come off like a stalker, but if that bastard had caught him at a different angle, like across the throat, he could have bled out in that dark hole without ever having said what he needed to say. This quest could very well get him killed and there was no backing out, not until Dylan was free.

Somehow, he needed to connect with Michael. He could phone, but Michael would likely not pick up. Email was best. He should have brought his cell phone. Would have, but the roaming charges were fierce, and he'd been caught in that trap before. Besides, most places had an internet café.

After pulling on a pair of black jeans, he splashed water on his face and fixed the bandages. He'd need to get fresh ones today and redress the wound. He slipped on a black cotton shirt and descended the carpeted stairs. There was no point telling Dermot what happened in Dubh's shop, or in the abandoned tunnel. The poor man was stressed enough. The bandaged hand he couldn't hide, but he could say that he'd stumbled at the archaeology site and smashed it against a rock. And that's exactly what he did.

Later, they sat on the front steps sipping coffee. Though his belly was full of fry-up, Estrada had a pain in his gut. His concern for Michael was gnawing at him.

"I need to check my email. Is there an internet café in this town?"

"Not that I've heard," said Dermot. "The wee library across the bay has a few computers, but it's closed until Tuesday. I don't know if anyone else has a computer you can use. B&Bs might. I don't use the damn thing myself but Dylan frequents the library. You can see it just there," he said, pointing across the water.

As Estrada walked through town he relaxed into a sense of calm that gave him hope. Sunshine glittered off the white masts of sailboats in the harbour and transformed the small sleepy village into a postcard. Idyllic.

Magical. Surely, they would find a way to prove Dylan's innocence and bring him safely home.

The library was indeed closed, but the pharmacy opened at noon. After picking up some gauze and antibiotic ointment, he asked the pharmacist if he knew of any place with internet access.

"You're that lad that's staying with Dermot McBride. That friend of Dylan's from Canada," said the man behind the counter. There were no secrets in a place the size of Tarbert.

"Yes I am. I need to do some business."

"Aye, sure. There's the library just there, but it's Sunday—"

"Sorry to interrupt Mr. Brechin," said a gaunt young man who stood next to him at the counter. He held out his hand to Estrada. "I'm Kelly Mackeras. Dylan is my mate." Estrada clasped his hand and shook it. *Kelly*. This was the guy Sorcha pointed out yesterday by the cairn where they'd discovered Steele's body. *Emo*, she'd called him. "I work at the Kilmartin dig along with Dylan, at least I did until—"

"He got arrested. Yeah, I'm trying to remedy that."

"Dylan could never murder someone. He's cheap," Kelly quipped. "The cheapest lad I know. But he's no killer."

"Too cheap to buy a data plan?"

Kelly grinned. "Aye. Exactly."

It was good to see him smile. Sometimes, Estrada could pick up colours around people, energy that flowed through their aura in differing hues, depending on their feelings and state of mind. Anger was often bright red, as was passion. Kelly was swathed in a dreary blue haze slightly deeper than the shade of his eyes. He was thin, fragile, pretty, and wounded. Shaggy brown hair edged his gaunt face, highlighting strong bones over hollow cheeks, long lashes, and pouty lips. If Michael had been there, he would have seduced Kelly Mackeras in a second. Estrada thought back to what Rachel had said about homosexuality in Scotland. What would it be like for a gay boy growing up in a village like this?

"Hey," he said, and the shadowy veil around his face lifted slightly. "Since we're both mates of Dylan's, why don't you come to *my* flat? You can use my laptop."

"Yeah?"

"Aye, sure. If you don't mind waiting a minute. I just have to get mum's pills."

"That would be great, but if your mother's sick—"

"Oh, mum won't mind. She keeps to her room." He lowered his voice to a whisper and glanced around the shop. "Mr. Brechin knows, but she doesn't want everyone in town taking pity on us." He gave Estrada a knowing look which he did not understand. "Cancer," he breathed at last.

"Oh. I'm sorry."

His eyes glassed over. A mother sick with cancer. That explained a lot. Sorcha must not know. If she did, she surely would have mentioned it, when they saw him at the cairn. Sometimes, it was easier to confide in a stranger than someone you must face every day. "She fought it a few years back. I just keep praying she'll do it again."

"Well, maybe I shouldn't—"

"Oh, aye, you should. Once mum's had her pills, she'll rest easy for a while, and she'll be glad to know I have a visitor. She says I keep to myself too much. She worries. You know how mothers are."

Twenty minutes later, Estrada stood in an old Victorian house by the sea, where Kelly and his mother shared an upstairs flat. Though tiny, it had snug dormer window seats, comfy armchairs, and walls lined with books.

"Man, it smells good in here."

"I baked this morning."

"Yeah? You baked?"

"Oh aye. I lived for a wee while in Edinburgh and worked part-time in a bakery while I was in acting school. I came home when mum got sick." He shrugged.

"You're a good son."

"An only son. There's just the two of us."

"That makes it hard."

"It's been that way forever." He walked into the kitchen, and then popped his head around the corner. "So, Estrada, can I offer you coffee and cinnamon toast?"

"Cinnamon toast. Are you serious, man? I love cinnamon."

"It's mum's favourite too. Even the smell of it cheers her up."

His sad smile was a heartbreaker, and for a moment, Estrada considered seducing Kelly himself. What if he never knew, never experienced—? No, he'd been to acting school in Edinburgh. Regardless of what Rachel said, the capital of Scotland was a vibrant modern city. Surely, he'd had lovers.

When he finally got logged on, Estrada was surprised to see an email from Michael. It was brief:

Forget me. I've found someone who loves me and will not abandon me. Someone who will do anything I desire. I don't care if you ever come back.

Christ. When Michael was in one of his moods, he was so melodramatic. Though he'd never been diagnosed, Estrada believed that Michael was bipolar; something of a Jekyll and Hyde. And, he spent a considerable amount of time playing the equalizer. Self-medicating did little to stabilize his erratic mood shifts. Once, he'd had one of the new Sentries—the club's version of bouncers—publicly flogged on the stage at Club Pegasus until he begged for mercy. Then, he took him to bed. Dell still worked for him, and that, Michael said, was loyalty. Estrada could only imagine what he'd get up to with this new lover. Male or female, it wouldn't matter.

Words could be interpreted in so many ways. He didn't know what to say or how to say it now that he had the opportunity. Still, he had to say something. Finally, he hit reply and typed:

Dylan is in prison for murder. If it was you, you know I'd do anything to free you. Please understand and be careful. I'll be home soon. E

"I don't mean to pry, but you look upset. Girl trouble?"

"More like *boy* trouble."

"Really?"

Estrada felt a kinship with Kelly. He imagined that if he returned to Edinburgh, he could be himself, but here in this village, he'd never be able to come out.

"Yeah, my friend Michael is pissed at me."

"Are you a couple, then?"

"No. We're solid though, you know?" He shrugged. "It's complicated."

Kelly sighed, as if he could never imagine having a solid relationship with a man. "Ach, I'm sure things will be all right now that you've written and explained. Sometimes we just need to know we're loved. We need to hear it."

I hope someday you hear it, thought Estrada, *and from somebody decent, who means it.*

~~~

The trip to Greenock Prison took over three hours and involved the crossing of two lochs by ferry. Estrada was relieved that, for once, he wasn't driving. Despite fresh dressings, his shoulder throbbed. He'd need to chill for a couple of days and let it heal, or he'd end up having to see a doctor. He couldn't risk an infection with so much at stake. The charming scenery he'd marvelled at on his way into Argyll, took on a dull tarnish as Dermot described Her Majesty's Prison.

With over two hundred and fifty inmates, the crowded prison was famous for having once housed a Libyan terrorist dubbed "The Lockerbie Bomber". Megrahi was convicted in the bombing of Pan Am Flight 103. The bomb exploded over the Scottish town of Lockerbie on December 21, 1988, killing everyone on board and several people on the ground. Total fatalities: 270. Megrahi was sentenced to life, but granted a transfer to Libya on compassionate grounds in August 2009. Diagnosed with terminal prostate cancer, he'd been given three months to live. Dermot knew all the details and was still furious. Three months had stretched into two and half years.

"The man *never* should have been released. Ach, my grandson is locked in that damn Ailsa Hall with murderers and terrorists."

"We'll get him out, sir."

"The Crown has one hundred and one days to prepare their case. They'll hold him until his trial in the high court."

"What about bail?"

"Doubtful. We'd need to give them a damn good reason—the real killer, or at the very least, a name and evidence that points to him."

Or her, thought Estrada. He hadn't pursued Janey Marshall after what happened to Dubh, but there could be several women angry enough to kill Steele. Perhaps even his crazy wife.

The prison complex was a mass of brown bricks, concrete, and barbed wire. Estrada made it through the ID screening with his passport and driving licence, and was allocated a table in the visits room. Then he had to pass through a metal detector and endure a pat down. He sat in the waiting area for what seemed like ages wondering how Dylan could cope in this place.

When he was finally allowed into the room, he sat nervously at the table, remembering the warnings he'd been issued by the police at the airport. At last, Dylan was escorted into the room. When he began to talk, Estrada was more concerned about his headspace than legalities. Normally even-tempered, the kid had spoken with his lawyer earlier and was frantic.

"He wants to plea bargain with my life—wants me to plead guilty to culpable homicide!"

"Manslaughter?"

"Aye. He wants me to stand up in court and confess that I killed the man *accidentally*. Says it will reduce the sentence. I'll only get five years and be out in three. Three years! This is his fucking *good* news. Tell me you've got better news than that, Estrada. Tell me you've got some way to prove my innocence and get me the fuck out of this place."

An officer hovered in the visiting room but seemed oblivious to their conversation. "Is he listening?"

Dylan shrugged. "Nothing we can do about it if he is." After his outburst, he looked defeated.

"Tell me what happened."

"I apologize, man. Here, you've come all this way to help me and I'm acting mental. I wish I smoked. Most of the men smoke. It seems to help."

"Trust me. It doesn't," Estrada said, thinking of Michael and his chain smoking. "You remember what we do back home to calm down and focus, right?"

"Aye. Breathe. Meditate."

"Better than smoking." He was worried about Dylan. Had never seen him quite this agitated. "Maybe if you could tell me what you remember? Like why they picked on you?"

"I scuffled with Steele in Oban. That's the only time I ever saw the man. I swear."

"I believe you. What else happened that night?"

Sorcha took us all to Murphy's to celebrate. She'd found a three-thousand-year old Egyptian collar." He smiled at the memory that lagged in his brain. "She got drunk, really drunk, and she...she..."

"Gave you a blow job?" Estrada grinned, and Dylan turned scarlet.

"How do you know that?"

"She told me."

"*She* told you? Christ! She *told* you? What did she say?"

"Just that."

Dylan covered his face with his hands, but Estrada could still see the red blaze that painted the tips of his ears. He could imagine how embarrassed he'd been when Steele told him about the pictures.

"Is nothing private?" he whispered at last.

"Not when you do it in public." Estrada winked to lessen the tension. "What happened after?"

"After...aye." He took a deep breath. "She went downstairs to the bar, and I went for a walk to clear my head."

"And..."

"That's when I ran into Alastair Steele. I didn't know who he was. Just some wanker. He said filthy things about Sorcha. He'd taken a video and photos of us...I told him to delete it all. He agreed to, *if* I told him about the collar. He said that he'd cut me in, if I got it for him. I couldn't believe it. I was so pissed, I grabbed his phone and locked myself in the van. Then the polis appeared and made me give it back."

"And then?"

"I went walking."

"Anywhere special?"

Dylan shook his head. "Just around the docks…sobering up. When I got back to Murphy's, it was near closing time, and Sorcha was dancing—" He rolled his eyes. "She was near comatose—draped over some black man, a hard man, I'd say." He cleared his throat. "Kai carried her to the van."

A black man. He'd seen very few black men since he left Glasgow, and none that he considered tough. He thought of Dubh's assailant and Sorcha's reaction when he first appeared in the shop. Could it be the same man? Had she recognized him from the pub that night? He'd been so upset by his experience with Rachel; they hadn't talked afterwards. Nor had they since.

He glanced at Dylan. "You ended up sleeping in a field, I hear?"

"Aye, by the Ballymeanoch Stones. It was solstice, and well, you know… I miss being with you all."

"Yeah, it's hard to be on your own, especially for Sabbats." He'd lowered his voice, didn't want the guard to hear anything about their activities. Though times had changed, witches were still suspect. Estrada eyed the guard. "Did you hear anything? See anything?"

"I saw—" He stopped talking.

"What?"

"Ach, it had nothing to do with the killing. Just a vision." He reached up and rubbed his neck and shoulders to relax the taut muscles. "I never saw the sunrise. I fell asleep with the stones. That's where Craddock found me in the morning."

"So, what have they got on you? Your lawyer must know."

"My lawyer thinks I'm guilty. I'm sure of it. They're saying that I lured Steele down to the cairn with offers of the collar, and then cracked his head open with a rock when he refused to delete the photos of Sorcha. That police officer from Oban is a witness."

"Sexy photos? So what? Neither of you are married."

"Opportunity? They found me sleeping in a field a few hundred feet from Steele's body."

"Which makes *no* sense. You don't bash a man's head in with a rock and then go to sleep in the adjoining field. Do they have any *evidence*?"

"One of my hankies…smeared with Steele's blood."

"What? How do they know it's yours?"

"My granddad gives me a box every Christmas. He gets them monogrammed…*DDM*."

Estrada sighed. "Where'd they find it?"

"Just outside the cairn. They think I used it to clean up—"

"And tossed it?"

"No, it was stuffed in a hole behind a rock. They brought in a dog."

"Did you lend a hanky to someone?" Dylan shook his head. "You know what this means?"

"Aye, sure. Someone is framing me…someone from the dig."

"Look Dylan. Something else is going on here. I don't know what yet, but it involves that Egyptian collar."

Estrada rubbed the stubble on his chin. He wanted to tell him about Magus Dubh and the bastard who'd cut him. And, he wanted to warn him that if Dubh died, that bastard could be charged with murder. If it was the same man Sorcha danced with in Oban, all three of them could be in danger because they could *all* identify him. But, he was leery of the guard who'd just glanced over and pointed to the clock.

"He just gave me the five-minute sign. So…how are you doing in here?"

"Surviving. It's not so bad. My cellmate is decent enough. He's innocent too."

Sure he is, thought Estrada, *as innocent as every other guy in prison*. Knowing how awkward Dylan could be around the subject of sex, he wasn't sure how to bring it up, but he needed to say something.

"Listen Dylan, if your cellmate, or anybody else, tries to get *friendly* with you—"

"Ah jeez, don't talk about *that*."

"Listen to me." Dylan hung his head, couldn't look him in the eye. "I know how you feel about *that*, but it's not worth dying over. You hear me? If someone corners you, it's best not to fight, just relax and—"

"Take it up the arse?" His voice was low, emphatic, muffled by his hand. "Is that what you're saying? I should take it up the arse?"

"If you get caught, the more you resist—" Dylan shaded his eyes. "There are worse things—"

"Worse than being buggered?"

"Yes. You could get the shit kicked out of you, or get cut, or maimed...or *killed*. If you don't fight back, they don't have to show their power."

"*They?* Jesus Christ." Dylan crossed his arms over his chest and stared at the floor.

"I'm going to get you out of here, but I need you to stay alive."

"I'm done talking about this."

"You want to see Sorcha again, right?" He winked and Dylan's cheeks flushed crimson again. "Christ, man. You've got it bad for her, don't you? Are you *in love* with her?" He said it in a teasing tone, to lighten things up, but Dylan's expression revealed the truth. "Shit. You are. You're in love with Sorcha."

Dylan shrugged. "What if I am?"

"Hey, she's a gorgeous sexy woman. I understand—"

"Estrada, please don't tell her. She'll laugh at me."

"No, she won't." Dylan seethed through clenched teeth. "Okay. I won't say a word."

"And, *don't sleep with her*. I can't think about you out there with her, while I'm locked up in here."

"Listen man, I flew across the fucking ocean to get you out of this. Trust me."

"I do. I trust you...at least, to set me free."

"Oh, but not when it comes to Sorcha." He shrugged. "Fine. I'll say it: I will not sleep with the woman you love. You have my word."

Dylan seemed content with that and they both glanced up at the clock. Time to change the subject.

"Listen, I've been thinking about something." Dylan lowered his voice to a whisper and the guard shuffled a step closer. "You told me once that you connected with Sensara telepathically."

"Sort of."

"Do you think you could—"

"Connect with you?"

"Aye. Try it now. Tell me what I'm thinking."

Estrada rested his forehead in his hand and closed his eyes. Immediately shapes appeared in the darkness. The speed and clarity surprised him. He was shocked they shared such a strong connection. Perhaps it was because they'd played out so many rituals together with the coven.

"Tree branch?"

"Aye."

"Letters. O A K. Oak."

"Magic," said Dylan. The guard moved in and signalled for Dylan to stand. "I go to sleep early…ten o'clock. Can we try it then?"

"Absolutely," said Estrada. "Stay safe." His eyes stung as he watched the guard lead Dylan back into the prison.

That night, Estrada excused himself early and went upstairs. Dermot seemed relieved. After the long drive and stressful news from the lawyer, he'd spent the evening quietly clutching his heart. Dylan's incarceration was weighing on the poor old man. Estrada needed to fix this before anything else occurred. The bloody hanky bothered him. Knowing that someone from Sorcha's camp was intent on framing Dylan, narrowed his list of suspects, but also raised the stakes. He needed intervention of the divine kind.

Now, sitting in a steaming bath, he carefully removed all the dressings and examined the wounds. His hand and calf were healing rapidly but his shoulder looked grim. The sutures held it closed, but the skin around the edge was raw and oozing pus. Infected. Damn. He had no time for injuries. He laid a compress against the wound. *Draw out the infection and give it air.* That was what his abuela had always told the kids.

Back in Mexico she used leaves and roots to heal. He had nothing but antibiotic ointment. He left the bandages off. He'd have to cover the wounds again before he went to bed. Dermot had discovered the blood stain and changed the sheets. He hadn't asked and Estrada hadn't offered. Some things were best left unsaid.

After gathering his tools, Estrada stood naked in the centre of the room, and cast a circle around himself by chanting the ritual words:

I conjure this circle as sacred space
I conjure containment within this place
Thrice do I conjure the Sacred Divine
Powerful goodness and mystery mine
From East to West, and from South to North
I cast this circle and call magic forth.

Then, beginning in the East, he raised his hands to the sky and thanked the gods and goddesses of all creation for the element of air that sustains life through breath.

Turning to the South, he imagined the sun, and blessed the element of fire for its light and heat and protection, even from the earliest times.

Facing the West, he stared into a basin of water until he could envision a waterfall. Cupping the water in his hands, he sipped and touched it to his face, and whispered: "Blessed be the precious water that cleanses and heals us."

Turning North, he sipped from a glass of deep red wine, and imagined Dionysus walking barefoot through a warm vineyard. He thanked the earth for nurturing such bountiful grapes, and drank again.

Finally, he stood in the centre and said: "Blessed be the sacred spirit within and around me. I am grateful for the ability to move and bend and shape energy. For this is Wicca."

Then he sat and observed his breath. For breath was life. Man could survive being buried beneath the earth, or trapped underwater, or even in fire, if he had air. Oxygen. Watching his breath flow into his nose and lungs, and out again, he calmed and focussed his mind. Thoughts slipped away. There was nothing but breath—a pale pink mist surrounding his body, flowing in and out, warming every cell.

Dylan's unexpected entrance into the circle startled him. Appearing as a swift shadow, he swooped in, hovered in the air for several seconds, as if ascertaining that he was in the right location, and then settled into a similar seated position across the circle. With Sensara, it had been different. They'd passed images between them while still both in corporeal form, and once he'd entered her mind and body; even felt what she was feeling. But it had never been like this. Dylan was there in spirit—a shimmering astral traveller—having left his body behind in prison. "Stone walls do not a prison make," wrote Lovelace. Perhaps, he too, had learned to free his soul.

Dylan did not even need to speak: his thoughts appeared directly in Estrada's mind.

We need to cast a spell.

The last time we did that, it didn't turn out so well, Dylan.

It stopped the man.

And four people died.

This time we're more aware. I know what to do. I dreamed it.

Tell me.

There is an oak forest at a nature reserve called Taynish. You must go there and cut a wand. You'll know the branch when you see it. Best go alone and…well, do it right. Bring an offering.

And then?

One week from tonight, at midnight, cast a circle among the Standing Stones at Ballymeanoch. Call on the Oak King.

The Oak King? I don't know…

The Celtic Oak King. This is his territory. Ask for protection and aid in unveiling the true killer. I will come too, as I am now, but you must be there in body. You must bring the tools, cast the circle, and raise the power. Find out everything you can about the Oak King, and bring him something precious; something to please him.

I can do that.

And Estrada. Taynish is an unusual place. You might see things you've never seen before. If you do, don't be afraid.

CHAPTER EIGHT

Off with the Faeries

CHRISTOPHE HEARD THE FAINT PING of Mandragora's laptop as he dozed on the soft leather couch. Curious, he flicked the long dark hair from across his eyes. His lover was such a trusting soul. As usual, he'd left his email open. Even as he focussed on the print, Christophe knew he was breaking some tacit boyfriend agreement. He didn't care. This Estrada was a stalker. Some ex that could not let go. Some ex that Mandragora fretted over incessantly.

Before the magician had left for Scotland, he'd left several emails. Christophe had deleted them all. Finally, out of sheer frustration, he'd responded; told Estrada he'd found someone else and they were done.

Now, as he read the man's response, he thought of a harsh reply, something that would end it completely. He typed a few letters, then reconsidered. What if he got it wrong? Added too little or too much? Used words Mandragora never would? He stared at the words: *if it was you I'd do anything*, bit a nail, and exhaled. Then, just as he had done with all the others, he hit *delete*.

Mandragora was still soaking in the tub, had likely passed out. He opened the delete folder. There it was again. *Permanently delete?* Yes. There were no more precise words in the English language for what he wished for this magician.

Rising from the couch, he slipped off his silk robe and slunk into the bathroom. It was time to up the ante.

~~~

The tiny Tarbert library was open only two days out of seven: Tuesday and Thursday. Perhaps that was a good thing. Estrada's shoulder was inflamed, the slash line crusted with pus. He slathered the wound with antibiotic ointment and popped some pain pills, then covered it with clean gauze. He'd do anything but go to the hospital. They'd want to know things, like how it happened.

He sauntered into the library mid-afternoon. There were only two other people there; a young woman and her daughter, so he was given the remaining laptop. The first thing he did was scan his email for a message from Michael. Nothing. A wave of nausea passed through his gut, and he swallowed to choke back his trepidation. Who the hell was this new lover? And what could they offer Michael that would turn his head so completely?

When Estrada closed his eyes and conjured Michael, he saw a nebulous silhouette shrouded in darkness. He hoped that he did not return to find him obsessed with some junkie. Addiction took many guises, but what he felt inside Michael was the languid stasis of opium, and it pissed him off, because there was nothing he could do about it. If Michael chose to morph permanently into Mandragora and dwell only on the dark side, he would walk that road alone. Still, he grieved.

Realizing that he was slipping into a black place of his own, Estrada determined to focus on the task at hand. Dylan wanted him to find a wand for the Oak King, and that meant they would invoke him. Appealing to gods and goddesses was integral to their ritual magic.

Cernunnos was a fearless and lusty hunter, the quintessential fertility god. With his killing spear, he provided protection and meat for the tribe; while with his fleshy spear, he fertilized the goddess. Wearing the horns and skins of his freshly killed stag, Cernunnos was bloody, erotic, violent, and ecstatically charged. But, the Oak King? This was someone Estrada had never encountered.

After scrolling through a few pagan websites, he gleaned a cursory understanding of the mythology surrounding the Celtic Oak King. He was engaged in a life and death struggle with his shadow aspect, the Holly King, over the affection of the goddess. It was a love triangle. Nothing new. And followed a yearly ritual. At Winter Solstice, the Oak King killed the Holly King, usurped his power, and began his reign over the waxing year. At his peak on May first, he mated with the fertile

Goddess at the Beltane fire. Then, at Midsummer—the time that had just past—the Holly King killed the Oak King...burned him alive. The Holly King then ruled the waning year. He, too, mated with the Goddess before the Oak King regenerated to slay him. And so, the circle of life, sex, and death continued eternally.

Though it sounded complex, it was no different from the ritual drama the coven had just performed at Summer Solstice when the Goddess (played by Sensara) sacrificed the Green Man (played by him) and he revived as Cernunnos. They too were twin aspects: one symbolizing the plant world; and the other, the animal kingdom.

When the librarian placed a large book on the desk in front of him, Estrada was startled. The white cover was embossed in a triad of gold oak leaves.

"*The White Goddess?*"

"Aye. I noticed you've been searching the Internet for knowledge of the Oak King. The web serves its purpose, but to appreciate the old ways a book is what you need; a divinely inspired book. Robert Graves. He's the one. Mind, I've read this tome several times myself and cannot grasp all the man is saying. It's akin to the Bible in that regard. But, there's parts that might help you, especially if you've the heart of a poet, which I think you have. You have the broodiness." She rolled her r comically and winked. "I'm closing the library for today, but you can take it with you, if you promise to bring it back."

"Thank you. My name's Estrada. Do I need a card or something? I'm staying—"

"I know who you are, lad. And I know Dylan. Take it and help him and blessed be."

"Blessed be," he repeated, surprised that this tiny silver-haired woman was spouting Wiccan phrases.

Back at Piper's Dream, Estrada sipped coffee and leafed through the book. Wicca followed a yearly round of Sabbats tied to the seasonal landscape, but Robert Graves revealed a calendar based on thirteen lunar months. Like all indigenous people, the Celts understood that nature pulsed with spiritual energy. Each calendar month was dedicated to a sacred tree, for the energy of trees was a source of divine healing. Still more amazing—each tree stood for a letter in the ancient Druidic alphabet. Graves theorized that the tree alphabet was a secret code created by the Druids to preserve pagan culture during the onslaught of Christianity, when witches and oak groves had been burned alive.

The seventh tree in the calendar was *Duir*—the Oak. *Duir* meant door in many languages. People built doors from oak because of its strength and endurance. Estrada believed a door was a portal and he wondered what awaited him on the other side. The moon began June 10 and ended July 7, which was, coincidentally, the day Dylan had chosen for their midnight rendezvous with the Oak King. He smiled. Had the librarian introduced Dylan to *The White Goddess* too?

Cernunnos was closely related to the Oak King though these two wore different masks: one animal, the other botanical. Still, the storyline was universal: birth, regeneration through the sexual act, and finally death—three elements spiralling in a continuous cycle. The land must be fertilized to ensure a harvest, just as the goddess must be impregnated to ensure the continuation of the tribe.

There is no life without death, no death without life, and no perpetuation of life without sex. This was the sacred dance of the god and goddess, and *this* he understood.

~~~

Perhaps it was the remnants of the circle he'd cast with Dylan, or perhaps it was the land itself, but the trees at Taynish whispered at every turn, their voices merging into a mesmerizing chant the farther on he walked. Estrada loved the fecund odour of the forest, the primeval scent of damp earth, especially after a rain. Elemental and enchanting, it was something he relished about the Pacific northwest, and this was like that, only different. This was ancient deciduous woodland; whereas, most of the Pacific forest was densely evergreen. Ash, holly, hawthorn, rowan, birch, and oak—all the trees in the Celtic calendar grew here, their skins shrouded with mosses, lichens, liverworts, and ferns. Gnarly wooden faces noted his passing, as did dragonflies and tawny saffron butterflies that danced on slight sea breezes like Shakespeare's faeries.

For hours, he wandered entranced. Passing the shoreline of Loch Sween and the salt marshes, on and on through woodland trails; watching, as Dylan had said, for a sign from the tree that would offer its branch for a wand. Before leaving Tarbert, he'd stopped at the shop of the Ironmonger and picked out a new hunting knife. It was safely sheathed in his boot. He wouldn't be caught short again. Ironically, its first taste of blood would be his own, for only a blood offering would make this right.

Sorcerer. The voice was faint at first, evanescent, a lilting on the breeze, and he thought he'd imagined it. *Sorcerer.* He heard it again: higher, louder, clearer, the tone teasing, and he whirled around, searching for *her.* There was only one woman who called him by that name, whose cadences were flecked with old Irish. But, where was she?

Later, he realized he'd walked past her several times without recognizing her. With skin so summer-tanned, and draped in verdant gossamer rags, she merged into the bush; her tiny nut brown face concealed by shadowy bark. It was her eyes that finally gave her away. Golden yellow, they glittered like cat's eyes when she smiled.

"Primrose."

"Ah sorcerer. You found me." Her cinnamon voice sent a shiver through his soul.

Remembering the feel of her faerie flesh, he held out his hands. "Can I touch you?"

"Only if I can touch you back." He smiled, had missed her wit.

"I thought I'd never see you again." Grasping her hands, he kissed them, and touched them to his cheek. "You feel so real. I thought I'd never feel you again, or hear your voice. Never—"

"Make love to me again?"

"Again? But, we never—"

"Ah," she sighed. "You did not bring back your memories. More's the pity. But, no matter. You *will* remember this." Running her fingers along his jaw, she caught his lips with hers and kissed him, filling his mouth with the taste of spiced apples. Stepping back, she eyed him curiously, her shaved and tattooed head cocked to one side like a songbird. The tattoo had always amazed him. A Celtic mandala—three intertwining violet trees infused with emerald green spirals and lightning bolts—it ran from forehead to spine.

"You've changed, sure, though I can't fathom how."

"You changed me," he said.

"All I did was free you from your burdens. But, this is something else. Something in your essence, in your cells, in your—" Running her tongue along his throat and neck, she tasted his flesh. "In your *blood*."

"My blood?"

"No matter," she said, and wrapping her hands around the back of his neck, she stretched up on her bare toes and kissed him again. Wanting nothing else, he swept her up and cradled her in his arms, their bodies dancing with memories. When at last he broke away, it was only to whisper I *love you* with his eyes, staggering as if an arrow had pierced his heart.

"And I love you," she echoed aloud. "Now take me to some mossy bank and ravage me."

"Primrose," he whispered, feeling Cernunnos stir within, "you are a goddess."

"Have you only just figured that out?"

He walked a while with her in his arms, searching for a bed fitting for his fey lover, and when at last he laid her down, it was beside a rivulet swathed in wildflowers. Standing over her, he tugged off his jacket and shirt.

"What's this now?" she asked, sitting up and gazing at the bandages. "Are you hurt?"

"It's nothing…just a cut."

"Ah, go on. Let me judge for myself."

He sat down beside her and watched as she unwrapped the yards of gauze. Her eyes narrowed as she examined the gash in his shoulder.

"How did you get this?"

He winched when she touched it. "Asshole with a switchblade."

"Tell me now, and tell me all."

"Can't it wait?"

"No."

He sighed, clutched and kissed her hands again. It felt like a lifetime since he'd been near her.

"It happened in a weird little shop in Glasgow. I was with an Irish woman, like yourself, an archaeologist. An Egyptian collar that she dug up in Kilmartin Glen was stolen. She thought this antiquities dealer might know something."

"Did this lad have a name?"

"Sorcha calls him The Wee Pict. He's a dwarf, all tattooed in blue symbols—"

"Magus Dubh."

"Yeah. You know him?"

"Aye. I know him. What earned you this?"

"While we were talking, some bastard barged in and gutted Dubh. I went after him. Chased him into an abandoned tunnel—"

"Underground, like?"

"Yeah…some old subway system." He cupped her cheek and kissed her lightly on the mouth. "You came to me. You helped me."

"Did I?"

"You know you did." When she giggled, her eyes twinkled.

"Lie back, sorcerer. Rest against the earth and let me heal you."

Remembering her skill as a healer, he closed his eyes and hoped it would not hurt too much. The last time was agonizing. But, the soft moss cradled him like a cool velvet blanket as her warm hands moved over the wound.

When he felt her fingers unclasping his jeans, he opened his eyes only to discover her kneeling naked beside him.

"Did you drift off?"

"Off with the faeries." Smiling, he slid out of his jeans and caught her in his arms. In the late afternoon stillness, he made love to her slowly with his entire body and soul. It was the first time he'd loved a woman since her death last December, and he did not want the moment to end.

"In the old days, *that* would have made us a baby," he said, afterwards, surprised by his own thought. She nuzzled beside him, her head tucked under his chin, soft lips brushing his throat.

"Aye," she breathed, "in the old days." There was a sadness in her voice that rent his heart in two.

"Can *we* be together, Primrose?" He'd never imagined himself as a married man with a family. Not until her. And now, that was all he wanted. The woman had unleashed some desire in his soul that eclipsed sex.

"Like married, you mean?"

He nodded and kissed her. "Yeah, like married, like a family."

"Ah, sorcerer. You can love me till the cows come home, but you're a flesh and blood man with a hefty desire for physical pleasure. I'd never hold you to loving only me. You need your freedom, always have."

"Since I met you, I've thought about marriage and children. Maybe it's time. Maybe we can find a way—"

"Hush now," she said, and sitting up, she stared deep into his eyes. "You must let me go. Pledging your life to me will only bring you pain; keep you locked in a kind of limbo. And I love you too much to see you suffer like that." Touching his cheek, she said the words he did not want to hear. "Sorcerer, I'm dead. I died there on that faerie rath in Ireland."

"Don't say that."

"I must. You need to hear it, and you need to accept it. I'm dead as a doornail dead. I'll never be human again. I'm not the one for you. Not now. Not like this. You've got to let me go, and move on."

His eyes burned and he turned his face away. "Ah, don't cry, beloved. You'll be a father one day."

"I will?"

"Aye sure."

"But how do you know?"

She waved her hand and shrugged. "Trust me. You'll be a father and a grand one. But it won't be me by your side. We fey can't conceive, you know that."

"Right. Faeries steal a baby from the human world and leave a changeling in its place." He rolled on his side. Even in his grief; perhaps because of it, he was desperate to make love to her again.

"That's one tale. But sorcerer, what's that on the back of your leg?"

"Just another gash. The son of a bitch tried to hamstring me."

"You're fortunate he missed. Show me." When he peeled off the adhesive bandage, she ran her fingers over the wound. He watched her face. "What's wrong? Is it infected? It doesn't hurt."

"Have a look yourself."

Sitting up, he crossed his legs and pulled the skin of his calf forward. "It's healed."

"Look closer."

"Looks like a thin line of shiny gold dots, kind of like the chrysalis of a monarch butterfly."

"Aye."

"What does *that* mean?"

"You remember when I said you'd changed, like there was something different in your blood?"

"Yeah?"

"Have you felt strange or experienced anything weird since this happened?"

"Besides making love to a faerie in the woods?" He winked and she looked annoyed. "I had a weird experience with my friend Dylan in our circle the night before last. He's locked up in prison, and yet it was like he was right there in the room talking with me. It was Dylan who sent me here." He wondered if he would have met Primrose at all if he hadn't come to this place.

"Well, sorcerer, I think you may have a few more of *those* experiences."

"Because?" He waited, barely breathing, while she gathered her words.

"Your leg was cut with the same knife that cut Magus Dubh, is that right?"

"Yeah?"

"Well, that wee lad is as fey as he is human. His mother was born in the Highlands, but his father is fey."

"That happens?"

"Oh aye. Not so much now, but in the old days ofttimes a fey man would steal himself a bride if he wanted children of his own."

"So, making love to faeries in the woods isn't particularly weird?"

"It happens." She shrugged. "It happened to Moira. Her ancestors were Picts, that's true, but her lover was of Danu...of the *sidhe*."

"The Tuatha de Danaan," he said, remembering what she'd told him months ago. The tribes of the goddess Danu were Neolithic farmers defeated by the invading Milesians in Ireland. Only they didn't die. They fled underground and survived as faeries, the *sidhe*. Primrose was now one of them. "Does Dubh know?"

She nodded. "Oh aye, and uses his powers, sure, and not always for good. Magus Dubh is not his real name. It's a moniker he gave himself when he became a Druid. Magus means priest in the ancient tongue, and he is a priest, of sorts, something like yourself."

"Dark priest."

"Aye. Now this gold dust embedded in your scar tells me that you've been touched by the fey. The dark priest's blood runs through your veins. By the time that man cut your shoulder, the magic must have been spent. But, that healing I just gave you will amplify it."

"Jesus."

"Sorcerer, you're walking between the veils now, straddling the edge of two worlds. My own entry into living with the fey was years long, and I had my ma and gran to help me understand. I waded in slow-like. But, you've jumped in hard and fast. I haven't had that experience but I can tell you this: you will need to keep your balance lest you trip. A fall, when you've a foot in two worlds, can land you in the breach."

"What do you mean? Like purgatory? Oblivion?"

"Hush now. Make love to me again." Catching his mouth with hers, she climbed on top of him, and danced a sultry dance that left him spent. As darkness fell on the forest at Taynish, Estrada fell into a dreamless sleep cradled in her arms. It was the deep sleep of a man who fights a long hard battle and lives; and then, for one moment feels utterly safe. Her healer's hands could do that to him.

"Sorcerer, wake up." Her voice, as soft as milkweed silk, played at the edges of his awareness and he feigned sleep just to hear her speak again. Only Primrose could get away with calling him sorcerer—a term with evil connotations—and he loved it, like he loved her. "Wake up!" Loud and insistent, she shook him vigorously.

"Kiss me and tell me this is no dream," he whispered. "Tell me you are real." Stubborn as she was, he felt her refusal in the silence and reluctantly opened one eye to her sweet, sombre face. "What's the matter?"

"You may be touched by the fey, but your human belly is growling like a hungry bear. It's dusk. It's time—"

"No, not yet. Please. I don't care about food. We can stay here forever and live on love."

"Or, on that cheese you're spouting. Romantic poets…holy god."

Smiling, he leaned on his elbows. "Well, I *am* thirsty. Is there a faerie well about?"

"Aye, but you know better than to eat and drink in the company of faeries, I presume?"

"Yeats mentioned that. But, does it matter now that I'm—?"

"Sorcerer. You're not invincible. That blood may enhance and fine tune your senses. And, it will help your body heal quickly, but you're not one of us. You're still human as we both can see by that sabre you're sporting between your legs. Holy god, man. You're insatiable."

He rolled on top of her. "It's you, Primrose. You do this to me. I'm going to keep you captive here forever."

But when his cell phone sang he jumped and reached out automatically to retrieve it from his jacket pocket.

"Ah, saved from another ravaging by modern technology."

"Not yet you're not." He checked the screen. "It's only Sorcha. I won't take it."

"Ah, go one with you," she said, and vanished in a kind of rushing mist.

"Primrose!" He stood and searched the trees to no avail. *And what seemed corporal melted as breath into the wind.* The phone continued to sing— insistent and demanding like Sorcha, until finally, he slid it open.

"Estrada. Is that you?"

"Yep."

"Are you busy? Did I catch you in the middle of something?"

"Yep."

"Well, I'm sorry. But I've just spoken with the hospital in Glasgow. It's bad news."

"Tell me."

"Magus is dying." Her voice caught. She was crying.

"I'm sorry, Sorcha."

"Sorry? Is that all you can say? He's been moved to Intensive Care. The poor Wee Pict is in critical condition."

Rachel's threat of AIDS sprang to mind and he grew suddenly wary. If Dubh's faerie blood had filtered through, what else now percolated beneath his skin? "What happened? Infection? What?"

"Ah, the buggers won't tell me. They only talk to family."

"So, say you're family."

"They'll want proof. The only way we're going to find out anything is if we sneak into the hospital and—"

"We?"

"Aye, you and me. You've got to help me, Estrada. I'm sure Magus knows something about Steele's murder—something he's not even aware of. Why else would that bastard from the bar in Oban try to kill him? The Wee Pict is the only lead we've got."

So, there it was. Dubh's assailant was in the bar in Oban the night Sorcha found the artifact and Steele was murdered. It was all connected.

"Let me think about this. I'll get back to you tomorrow."

"Promise?"

"What?"

"Promise that you'll call tomorrow morning."

"I'll call." Damn her. She'd interrupted his time with Primrose and that was precious time he could never reclaim. Who knew when she'd suddenly reappear, if ever? Estrada ended the call.

Sorcha was right about Magus Dubh though. He knew something—something worth his life. And whatever it was, it was tied to Steele's murder.

Saving Dylan was reason enough to sneak into a Glasgow hospital. He dressed, and then sat on a log, ensconced in dusky shadows, willing Primrose to return. She did not. Even when he called her name. Apparently, this was no scenario in which he could invoke her or command her to appear. The woman was no genie. She was, he decided, something akin to a ghost. Though no ghost had ever pleased him like she just did.

Cold and hungry, he finally accepted that she was not returning, and began the long trudge back to the car park. About halfway there, he paused. Off towards the east, one tree glowed with a radiant mist. When he got up close he realized it was an oak tree. *An Oak Tree.* Bemused by Primrose, he'd forgotten the very reason he'd come to Taynish.

Kneeling by the base of the tree, he bowed his head and took several deep breaths. Finally, feeling calm and centred, he reached out to touch the tree's trunk. Several inches away, he could feel its energy, a kind of sweet heat that emanated in deep pulses from its core. He'd always known trees were alive, but *this* was something miraculous—life vibrating in the palm of his hand.

"I am Estrada, High Priest of Hollystone Coven. I've come to you for help. My friend, Dylan McBride, is imprisoned. Please give me one of your branches to use as a wand. Your power would aid us in our quest for truth and justice. I offer my blood."

Pulling the knife from his boot, he cut across his left palm and drizzled the blood on the earth beside the tree's roots. For several moments, he kneeled and listened to the creaking song of the wind in the treetops, the owl's cry, and the rustle of small creatures in the grasses. When rain began to fall, he raised his face, and tasted its freshness against his parched tongue, and when he lowered his head again, he saw it. Lying on the ground beside him was a solid oak branch twisted at the end in the shape of a serpent, and it was shining gold.

"Thank you. I will use it well."

As he rose and backed away, the storm worsened. After picking up the golden branch, he held it to his side and loped along the path. He was perhaps a mile from the car park when he realized that he was following a trail no human ever could. Though stratus clouds concealed the waxing moon, he could see everything. He could see in the dark.

CHAPTER NINE

Vixen

ESTRADA WAS PERCHED ON THE FRONT STEPS of Piper's Dream, sipping coffee with Dermot in the Friday morning sunshine, when the grey Prius pulled up. *Detective Rachel Erskine-Steele.*

When she stepped out, the first thing he noticed was her missing belt. Minus her battle gear, Rachel looked deceptively casual, benign even. In tight white capris and a skinny tank, she aroused more than his interest. Whatever unseen force drove his libido had multiplied exponentially since their last meeting; something he attributed to the infusion of faerie blood. Rather than climb the steps to join them, she leaned against the car and motioned for him to come down. He admired her audacity, but held his ground, refusing to be summoned.

"Do you have a date, son?" asked Dermot.

"No, I do not," Estrada replied, and set down his coffee.

"She's a beauty," the old man muttered as he stroked his chin.

"She's a cop, and a little crazy." Estrada stood and ran his fingers through his hair. "I suppose I should find out what she wants."

"Aye, lad. I'm curious myself."

As he approached the car, Rachel retrieved a parcel wrapped in plain brown paper from the passenger seat.

"Detective."

"Good morning, Estrada. I brought your jeans. The laundry patched them." She'd drawn her platinum hair up into a high ponytail and he grew transfixed watching an ivory vein throb in the soft flesh of her neck. The woman was mesmerizing, and he caught himself wondering if she'd somehow cast a spell of her own. "I know you're attached to them," she added with a sly smile.

He nodded, then stepped closer and accepted the package. "Well, thank you, detective. I'll just go and get the pair I borrowed from you."

"No, don't worry about that. Not now." They stared at each other until it felt awkward, and she glanced away.

"I'm impressed that you took the time to find out where I was staying, and then drove all the way from Glasgow," he said, facetiously. They both knew he'd been flagged in the police system. "Was there something else you wanted?"

Her lip trembled, and settled into a half-smile. "It's a beautiful day."

"It is that, detective."

"Call me Rachel."

"If you insist."

She shrugged. "Since the weather's so grand…I wondered…Would you come for a wee drive with me?"

"A drive?"

"Aye, our last meeting ended abruptly. I'd like a chance to make it up to you; perhaps explain—"

"No need, detective. You just lost your husband. I understand."

"I'd consider it a personal favour if you'd come." Leaning back against the car, she smiled and crossed her arms. "I promise to be… pleasant."

He could smell the almond-scented soap she'd used that morning, and beneath it, all the subtle odours of a woman's body on a warm day. As he breathed her in, his wolfish senses quivered and he realized she was ovulating. *Was this another effect of faerie blood?*

"Pleasant," he repeated, caught up in his thoughts.

"Aye." She slid into the driver's seat and pushed up her shades, a sense of desperation creeping into her smoky eyes. "Will you come?"

"Give me a minute." He turned, and sprinted up the steps.

Dermot was in the kitchen pouring his second cup of coffee. He raised his eyebrows when Estrada bounded through the door.

"That, sir, is Rachel Erskine-Steele. Alastair Steele's widow. She's a police detective."

Dermot furled his eyebrows. "Aye?"

"She wants me to go for a drive with her."

"She's not arresting you?"

"No, I think she has…other ideas."

"Oh. Oh, aye," he said, with sudden understanding. "Well, surely you're not asking my permission, lad?"

"No, but I'd like your opinion."

"I see." He stroked his whiskers and sniffed. "Well, first off, I want you to know how much I appreciate all you've done for my grandson. I know it's not been easy. You've put yourself in harm's way and you're a good friend."

"It's nothing Dylan wouldn't do for me."

He nodded. "Aye. So, I'll tell you the truth, laddie. That one: she's the look of a vixen. Whatever you do, be careful." He sipped his coffee. "Do you think a woman like that could help or hinder my boy?"

Estrada shrugged. "That's the question I asked myself. She knows things that we don't, has access to police records, and frankly, I'd rather work with her than against her. She could be a bridge to the other side."

"Bridges can be dangerous. Some water's deceptively deep and some's an undertow."

And some harbour trolls, thought Estrada. He nodded. Dylan had been lucky to wind up living with his grandad. The more time he spent with Dermot, the more he saw their similarities and was determined to reunite them, whatever it cost.

As he closed the kitchen door he heard Dermot quip: "And, make sure she buys you a respectable breakfast, laddie."

"Where are you taking me, detective?" A few miles south of Tarbert, she'd turned east off the main highway onto a single-track road that wound around steep green hills and haphazard rocks by way of treacherous hairpin turns. She drove like a maniac, and after just missing a couple of straggling sheep, that crossed the narrow paved path right in front of the car, he was gripping the edges of the seat.

"The beach," she replied.

"The beach? There's a beach?" A truck appeared on the road directly ahead, and as the track was simply too narrow to accommodate two vehicles, she swerved into the closest pull-off, braked, and waited for it to pass. The driver sped by without so much as a nod.

"Aye, sure. We used to come here when I was a child," she explained, as she pulled the car back onto the road.

"You and your family?"

She nodded. "This part of Scotland reminded my mother of her childhood home in Sweden."

It was pastoral, picturesque, and largely untouched by progress. Estrada felt as if they were travelling back through time. As they turned south, the verdant hills and valleys gave way to ocean cliffs and sparkling blue vistas. She rolled down the window and took a deep breath.

"Your mother was Swedish." That explained the platinum blonde hair blowing back from her shoulders like a silken veil.

"My mother *is* Swedish and quite famous in Scandinavia. She was a dancer and model when she was younger. Now she's an actor. Perhaps you've heard of her. Her name is Magdalena."

"Sorry, no. But, if you look anything like her, I can imagine why she's a star." He bit his bottom lip, wishing he could take that back. Sitting next to her was unnerving. The sea breeze wafting through the open window washed him in her scent and set his body tingling. It was indescribable—a sensual picnic that galvanized his heart.

Reaching her left hand across the seat, she stroked the inside of his thigh. "You don't have to romance me, Estrada. You were naked in my shower. Remember?"

And you were naked in your kitchen, he thought. *Right before you threw me out.*

There was something about Rachel that left him unhinged. Whether it was her bravado, or the fact that she was a police detective, or something else entirely, he didn't know, but when he was with her, he felt like she was driving him the way she drove her car. Her fingers had found their way to his zipper. Any second now, she'd be gearing down.

"How much farther to this beach?" he asked, jamming his hand on top of hers to halt its roaming.

Truthfully, he was conflicted. Rachel Erskine-Steele was the first woman in months he'd been sexually attracted to, and yet, his heart ached for Primrose. A woman who existed in another realm. A woman who could never be human again. A woman who'd told him to forget her, and move on. Still, their lovemaking in the forest at Taynish was so real, so vibrant, he felt guilty to be careening down a seaside highway on a drive that would undoubtedly end in sex.

Stranger still: what if *this* woman was *the* woman Primrose alluded to? *You'll be a father*, she'd said. That line haunted him still.

When he glanced at Rachel, she smiled and bit her bottom lip. "There's nothing *but* beaches along this coastline." She moved her roaming hand to the wheel as they sped around another curve. "And there's a gorgeous little hotel in Port Righ at the road's end. It's about nine miles. I thought I'd treat you to lunch there."

"You don't have to—"

"Oh, but I do. It's the least I can do after what you've been through. You only came here to help your mate, yeah?"

My mate. Exactly. He remembered what she'd said the first day they met at Kilmartin Glen: the day she was ready to hang Dylan from the nearest tree.

"Do you still think he's guilty?"

She shrugged. "It doesn't matter what I think."

"Of course it does."

"Guilt is a matter for the court to decide."

"But, don't you want to know the truth? Don't you want the real killer brought to justice? If it was me…if someone killed my partner—"

"You'd track them down and skin them alive." She glanced at him and grinned. "We're similar in that regard."

"Then you need to know the truth."

"The truth?"

"Yes. Dylan had nothing to do with this. Your husband's death is linked to the theft of the Egyptian collar."

She stiffened, and her eyes narrowed behind the shades. "Why do you say that?"

"Why else would Magus Dubh be attacked?"

"You're making assumptions. There's no evidence to suggest that the two incidents are related. Dubh's been involved in illicit activities for years. Anything could have precipitated that attack. A deal gone wrong…a vengeful client. He deals in black market antiquities."

"Except…the bastard that cut Dubh was in the Irish bar in Oban the night Sorcha found the collar—the same night your husband was there, and ended up dead just down the road."

"How do you know that?" She geared down, braking so hard the tires squealed.

He gasped, and fought to keep his cool. "Sorcha remembers dancing with him at the—"

"*Sorcha?* Ah Christ! I thought you had something *real*. Not O'Hallorhan. She was hammered." Regaining her equilibrium, she eased the car onto the shoulder beside a pale sandy beach. "I'm a detective, remember? I've interviewed countless witnesses. And the one thing I know is that the stories drunks tell are not credible. They don't hold up: in court or out of court."

She mumbled something incomprehensible and shut off the engine; then opened the door, and stepped out.

He sat staring at the sign ahead. *Grogport*. Rachel was right. Sorcha liked her grog, and she *was* wasted that night. She'd been carried out of the bar and remembered nothing except the man. And, she'd only glimpsed him for a second or two before he'd run out of Dubh's shop. She was an unreliable witness. He hung his head, feeling suddenly defeated, like all his investigating had come to nought.

When he glanced up again, Rachel was standing by the edge of the road, gazing out over the sea. Against the sparkling cerulean water, strands of her silvery hair caught in the morning breeze like the filaments of a spider's web.

Finally, she leaned in the window and flashed an apologetic smile. "I'm sorry, Estrada. I've been stressed lately, and I've no right to take it out on you." The hollows of her cheeks flushed pink with emotion. "Can we take a break from all this? Just for a wee while? Will you walk with me by the sea?"

Dermot's comment echoed in his head. He didn't much like deep water anymore. When he was a boy, they used to visit his father's home near Mérida, Mexico, and swim in a deep cenoté the colour of cyan. An underground river exposed by the collapsing limestone shelf, blood red stalactites hung like spears from the ceiling amid slick tree roots, and caught the sunlight that filtered through a hole in the ceiling. He remembered diving, splashing, and laughing in the warm water. It was a good memory; one he'd not recalled in years. They were happy then, and life was simple. Perhaps, like Rachel had been when she'd come to this place with her family.

He opened the door and stepped out.

"I feel somewhat disadvantaged," he said. "You know all about me, and I know nothing about you." She'd slipped off her high-heels and was strolling through the wet sand in bare feet. Against the blue of the sky, her skin glowed like alabaster. Even her toenails were ivory.

"I don't know *all* about you."

"You know where I work, what I do for a living, and who my friends are. You've searched my criminal record. Christ, you probably know how much I paid in income tax last year."

"Negative. I don't care about your finances." She turned and stroked his cheek. "You're incredibly sexy. I like that."

He caught her hand and held it firmly in his fist. "What do you want from me, Rachel?"

Breaking his grip, she picked up a handful of smooth stones and tossed them into the waves one by one. "Let's play truth or dare," she said, at last.

"Truth or dare? How old are you?"

"Come on. Can't we just have some fun?"

He shrugged. It seemed like a long time since he'd had fun.

"I'll start," she said. "I dare you—"

"Wait a second. You can't start with a dare."

"Aye, sure you can. I dare you to wade into the sea with me."

"*No es problema,*" he said. "The sea and I are old friends." Leaning against a rock, he pulled off his boots and socks, and rolled up his jeans.

"Your wound healed quickly," she said, running her fingers over the pale gold threads that wove through his flesh. "How's your shoulder?"

"Is that one of your questions, detective? Because I believe it's my turn," he said, stepping into the waves. He'd forgotten all about his shoulder. Primrose had healed it completely with her faerie hands only yesterday; drawn out the infection and closed the wound. Not even a scar remained. He would need to keep this inexplicable phenomenon hidden. "What do you want from me?"

"This," she said, and caught his mouth with hers. Her kiss was titillating and slightly wicked, as he imagined it would be. Not like Primrose, or Michael. Something altogether new, and it left him breathless. He flung his boots across the sand and stroked the back of her neck, let loose her hair, and tangled his fingers in the silken strands. As her lips brushed his ear, he heard her answer: "I want to make love with you. No commitments, no promises, no complications."

"No complications?" Releasing her, he stepped back. "I'm here to free the man accused of murdering your husband—"

"Christ, Estrada! Can't we just live in the moment. I thought you wanted me. Last week, you—"

"Last week, I made a mistake, and I'm sorry for that. I was drunk and you were vulnerable. I shouldn't have taken advantage of that."

"Did you ever lose someone, Estrada?" A tear slipped down her cheek. Taking off her dark glasses, she wiped her eyes, and his heart shuddered.

"Yes." He touched her face, then wrapped her in his arms and held her, feeling the beating of her heart against his. "Yes, I have."

"I lost my baby," she said, suddenly. "Two years ago. And Alastair never forgave me."

"What a bastard," he said. "But, that wasn't your fault."

They strolled in silence, her arm pressed against his, waves lapping at their feet. He thought of all the things he could say, but nothing seemed right. At least, she'd stopped crying.

"How *do* you feel about me?" she asked, at last. "I know I can be cold. I don't mean to be."

He stopped walking and took her in his arms. "I don't think you're cold." He smiled. "I think you're beautiful...and sexy...and I could tear up this beach making love to you. But if I did, I'd fall in love. I know I would. And, that *would* be complicated because I'd want more than sex. Promises...commitment. I'd want it all." He touched her cheek with his finger, and felt the pale skin as soft as a flower petal. Then stepping back, he stood amazed by the string of sentiment that had flown from his mouth.

"Really?" she asked, clutching her chest. "Thank God." Like a delighted child, she danced around, the water swirling beneath her feet. "I was lying."

"Lying?"

"Yes, your reputation. I—"

"My reputation? How the hell did you hear—?"

"The Pegasus chat room. They're quite explicit."

"What?"

"Estrada: I want to fall in love with you too."

He was still reeling from the idea that people were describing his sexual exploits in a chat room. "Well, if that's true…if we're contemplating some kind of relationship, we can't start with sex."

"But, last week—"

"Last week was different. If we want something beyond sex, we need to learn to trust each other. With our clothes on."

Taking his hand, she kissed it tenderly. "If that's what you want."

Nodding, he brushed his thumb across her lips. "I want to do it right." Leaning in, he kissed her gently in a way that said, *I want you bad—just not here and now.* And it was no lie. "If we're going to trust each other, we must be open and honest. We must be *allies.*"

"Allies, sure." She locked her arm in his as they began to walk.

He chewed his bottom lip, decided to take a risk. "I don't want to get you in trouble, but perhaps, we could help each other by sharing information about the case." He figured that calling it *the case* made it sound more benign. It wasn't about Dylan or about Steele. It was just something they were both entangled in.

"What do you need to know?" They'd come to the end of the beach, turned around, and were ambling back towards the car, their bare feet catching the edge of the surf. He waited for her to say something more. Her eyes were fixed on the horizon.

"Sorcha's worried about Dubh. He's in intensive care, and she thinks he's dying."

She nodded. "She's right. His condition is deteriorating."

"Do you know why?"

"Blood. He lost too much blood."

"Can't they give him a transfusion?"

"They've tried. All the blood is incompatible. He has some rare blood type."

"So, it's not AIDS complications—?"

"Oh. No. I shouldn't have said that. It wasn't fair. It's just when I heard about you and Michael Stryker—"

"Fuck."

"Exactly," she said, smugly.

He let that one go, and they walked in silence. He didn't intend to defend his bisexual nature or his need for freedom. Until recently, he'd indulged in sex whenever, and with whomever, he felt a mutual attraction. Gender did not matter to him. It never had. Nor had love or romance, though both could enhance the experience. He'd lived that way for years and could easily revive his libertine passions. If things got serious between them, then he'd share everything: his dreams, fantasies, preferences, proclivities. She likely had a few of her own. Everyone does.

She unlocked the Prius and they both slid inside. He watched her fiddle with the seatbelt and put the key in the ignition, then touched her hand to stop her from turning on the engine.

"You said that Dubh has some rare blood type. Does that mean they can't find a match?"

"They've tried. That's what the report said."

Two thoughts struck him at once. The first was logical. If Rachel was reading hospital reports on the condition of Magus Dubh, she was definitely working the case. The second was incredible. He'd had an infusion of Dubh's faerie blood. He might not be fully fey but his own healing had been miraculous due to this potent fluid. He could save Dubh's life.

"How much time do they think...?"

She shook her head. "It would take a miracle."

Pulling her close, he kissed her hair. "Miracles happen, detective. Just look at us."

~~~

Sorcha didn't hear a word from Estrada until Friday evening when he called her mobile and requested that she meet him across the street from the museum at the Kilmartin Hotel. When she walked into the pub, she could tell right off that something was different about him. He'd been with someone. She suspected a woman. Softened like butter when you leave it sitting out on the counter in a warm pantry, his smile lit up the dark contours beneath his cheekbones. She was infinitely jealous.

"Listen Sorcha. I'm sorry I didn't call you earlier, but I know what to do about Dubh." He shoved a pint across the table in her direction.

"Well, out with it."

He glanced around the room surreptitiously and lowered his voice. "You're an archaeologist. You must have read and seen some bizarre things on your travels, right? Things that most people would consider impossible simply because they're so incredible?"

"Aye, sure. Humanity is bursting with peculiarities. That's what makes my work so fascinating." She took a long haul on her pint and leaned forward. His eyes were brighter too. She was curious who the lucky cunt might be.

"What I'm about to tell you, Sorcha, you can't tell anyone else. Understand? I'm trusting you with this information because it might save your friend's life."

She nodded. "Go on, then. Cut the drama."

"I know what's wrong with Dubh."

"How did you—?"

He shook his head. "That's not important. It's his blood. The doctors gave him several transfusions but nothing's working." He paused a moment. "They can't find the right match."

"You're saying that Magus has some rare blood type?"

"The rarest. Now, this is the incredible part." He took a deep breath and leaned in close to her ear. "Dubh is half human and half...faerie."

"Faerie?" she whispered, and then she giggled. "Ah, now you're having me on, man."

"No, I'm not." His face was dead serious. "His mother's name was Moira and she was a Pict, but his father...his father is fey. I know it's hard to believe but—"

"You do remember I'm Irish?"

"How could I forget?"

"Well, we Irish are faerie spawn. Why wouldn't I believe?"

"That makes it so much easier." While he tipped his glass, and finished his pint, she signalled the server for another round.

"So, the Wee Pict's half faerie," she mused. "I can't say I'm surprised. It's fey blood, he's needing then."

"Exactly." When the server came by to drop off two fresh pints, he hushed up.

"So, where the hell are we supposed to get—"

"Me," he whispered. "Remember when I fought with that bastard that slashed Dubh?"

She nodded. "How could I forget?"

"Well, he cut my hand and the wound healed overnight because Dubh's blood was still on the knife. And when he tried to hamstring me and ended up slicing open the back of my calf, that wound healed in two days." He pulled up his pant leg and showed her the faint line of gold dots. "My shoulder needed a little more magic, but it's healed now too."

"So you—"

"Yeah, me. My blood will work."

Oh, she thought suddenly, *perhaps it wasn't a woman who'd transformed Estrada at all. Perhaps this fey blood was the catalyst. What effect would it have on the human mind and body? Could it heighten his senses? Fine tune his powers of perception? Enable him to appear and disappear at will?*

Faeries were known for sudden appearances and just as sudden vanishings. As a child, she'd seen a horse drawn carriage driven by faeries in the forest near Galway where her grannie lived. The woman was dressed in a beautiful violet gown and the man wore a crown. The woman smiled and gave her a wild rose. But when she told her mother, she didn't believe her. She even mocked her: said they were travellers playing a prank on a gullible child. Sorcha squashed that rose with her boot and never mentioned them again. She'd stopped believing and made science her god, just like her mam. But Jesus…now he was saying they were real.

"Sorcha?"

"Aye?"

"What are you thinking?"

"I'm thinking we need to get some of your blood into Magus." When he reached across the table, took her hand and kissed it, the shiver ran right up her arm. "Drink up," she said, and took a big swig of her ale.

"You've seen them, haven't you?"

"Aye. Once upon a time in a land far away. Now, how are we going to go about this caper? I mean, do you know *how* to get your blood into his veins?"

"I haven't quite figured that out yet. You don't know a doctor or nurse you can trust, do you?"

"No. But I have taken several forensic archaeology classes and carved my way through a few cadavers. I know my way around a body, more or less."

"That'll have to do. We can do a direct transfusion. I looked some stuff up online this afternoon."

"Internet directions? Christ, man!"

"Why not? Between the two of us, we can do this, Sorcha."

"Aye. We'll do it for Magus." She raised her glass, as he raised his.

"For Dubh," he chimed, as they struck their glasses together.

CHAPTER TEN

How Precious the Peat

IT WAS HALF TEN when Estrada parked the Harley outside the Glasgow infirmary. Sorcha waited outside while he swaggered in and engaged in a flirtatious conversation with the night receptionist. In tight black jeans and leather, he looked like a rock star. He'd lined his eyes in black and was emitting sexual energy she attributed to his new fey blood. She'd not seen him quite like this before and the whole package sent lusty shivers down her spine. When he came back out he was whistling.

"I gather you found out where the ICU is."

"Yes, ma'am."

"And what did you tell her to make her smile so?"

"I'm planning to surprise my girlfriend with a proposal after she finishes work. She's new here, an ICU nurse. I need to know when she'll be off and what door she'll exit from, so I can be out front on my knees when she does."

"And she bought that?" He winked. "Of course, she did."

"Shift change is at 10:50 p.m. They'll be coming out that door right over there."

"Exactly how does this help us?"

"I figure there'll be fewer nurses on the floor after eleven, and if we wait until midnight, most of the patients will be asleep. They'll all have had their bedtime meds. Don't you agree?"

"Actually, I think we should enter just before eleven. When they do their shift change, they'll chat for a while at the main station, to pass on anything vital and catch up on the craic. Those leaving will be tired or thinking of the evening ahead, and those coming won't quite have settled in yet. They'll all be preoccupied. If we're stealthy, they won't notice us at all."

"Brilliant."

While they waited, he explained to her what he'd read about the procedure for a direct transfusion. It made some sense. Then they slipped in, as planned, and split up to search for Dubh.

Sorcha couldn't find him in the ICU. At first, she panicked, thinking that he'd passed on and been taken to the morgue. Frantically, she searched nearby rooms. Finally, she found him, sleeping like a baby; in fact, they had him in a child-size bed. Fortunately, it was a semi-private room and the other bed was empty. The poor Wee Pict was hooked up to several machines and an IV.

She texted Estrada the room number and then assessed the equipment. She could leave the syringe attached to the vein in his arm, but they'd have to connect the other end to Estrada's artery. What they needed was another syringe to attach to the tube. They were apparently thinking on the same wavelength because when Estrada appeared in Dubh's room he pulled one out of his pocket along with a handful of other instruments.

"Stealthy," she said.

"Naturally," he said, with a wink.

She motioned for him to help her move the other bed, so it was adjacent to Dubh's. The two fellas would need to lie side by side for this to work. They set everything up, and he'd just stepped into the bathroom, when a custodian popped his head into the room. A rather large bald man carrying a broom, the name *Marek* was written on a badge attached to his uniform.

"What are you doing here?" he asked, with a thick Polish accent.

Too late, Sorcha thought: *we should have grabbed some scrubs.* Standing there in a pair of faded blue jeans and tight T-shirt, she was obviously no one remotely connected to the hospital. Momentarily stunned, she couldn't concoct an appropriate response.

"He's my father—" she said at last.

"Your father?" That threw him. Perhaps, he was trying to comprehend how a dwarf could have a daughter anything like her. Since a mutated gene causes dwarfism, it was entirely possible. Should she try to explain?

"What? You don't think—?"

"You go," he stated. He leaned his broom against the wall and pointed at his watch. "No visit now." She was suddenly afraid that he was either going to accost her, or call for a nurse.

"But, Marek," she whispered, all pouty and seductive. Leaning forward on the side of the bed, she pushed up her breasts with her arms. It was an exaggerated move, an invitation that no man could mistake. "*Please*, let me stay. He's dying."

His gaze fell to the deep cleft between her breasts and he took a step forward, a slight smile stretching across his face. Estrada opened the bathroom door, but Marek didn't notice. He was much too focussed on the midnight opportunity that had befallen him. She watched Estrada take something from the pocket of his jeans and raise his hand into the air. A twirling crystal suspended from a silver chain dangled from his fingertips.

"Hey man," he growled.

When Marek turned, Estrada held the crystal directly in front of his eyes, where he couldn't help but see it.

"Watch it now. Watch it turn. This crystal is your whole world, turning and shining like a night star. It's making you sleepy. Your eyelids are so heavy; you can't keep them open. You must sleep. Lie down on the floor and sleep. Sleep until I awaken you."

Sorcha watched in amazement as Marek laid down on the floor and closed his eyes.

"How did you—?"

"I'm a magician," he replied. "Hypnosis is part of my shtick."

"You've got to teach me how to do that."

"You have your own mesmerizing tricks," he said, thrusting out his chest. She punched him in the arm and giggled. It helped to ease the tension. He winked, and then closed the door to the hallway before anyone else could wander in. "Help me drag him over here. If we're lucky, no one will notice he's missing."

"Are we ready to do this?"

"I am," he said.

"Grand. Lie here," she said, gesturing to the bed, "and relax your right arm. I'll need to make an incision to expose the artery. How are you with blood?"

He shook his head. "Doesn't bother me. Do it."

She put several gauze pads underneath his arm to absorb any blood spill. Then, she disconnected the cord that ran from the IV down to the Wee Pict's vein, and quickly attached one of the fresh syringes from the tray. Following the line of the thumb on the underside of Estrada's wrist, she felt the area where she believed the radial artery to be. After swabbing the skin with a gauze pad and disinfectant, she picked up a small scalpel and made a tiny lengthwise incision, being careful not to cut so deep as to nick the artery. With a sharp intake of breath, he grimaced, but made no sound. Blood leached from the wound and she covered it with a fresh gauze pad.

"Christ," she muttered. "I can see the artery, but I need another hand. Can you hold the incision open while I insert the syringe?"

Leaning over, he spread the incision. "Piece o' cake."

"Right." But just as she was about to insert the needle, Marek moaned, and she flinched at the unexpected sound.

"Steady woman. He's probably just dreaming about nuzzling some buxom damosel."

"Be careful, Estrada. You're in no position to make any lascivious remarks." By the time she'd finished her sentence she'd inserted the syringe. "There, it's in."

"It doesn't feel like it's in."

"Be still, mad man. If indeed you have a heart, it should pump your faerie blood right into the Wee Pict's vein." Straight away, she could see blood moving through the tubing. *How amazing,* she thought, *that in this moment we are saving a life—and not just any life, but the life of a half-fey dwarf.*

"How do you know when to stop?"

"Good question. I'd say, either when *he* perks up or *you* pass out. Whichever happens first."

When Estrada closed his eyes, Sorcha sat on the edge of the bed and stared at him. He was exceptionally beautiful, and she wondered again if someone had melted his heart. She hadn't seen him for a few days. Perhaps he *had* met someone.

Minutes passed. She probably should have been timing the procedure, but she just hadn't thought to do that. She glanced over at Magus. If his skin grew pinker, surely that would be a sign. But through all the blue ink it was difficult to see any colour change. There must be at least one part of the Wee Pict that was not tattooed. Smiling, she casually drew the sheet to one side and gasped: his penis was tattooed in turquoise snake scales. The artist had added some silver to the dye to give it the appearance of armour.

"Eager to meet the mighty dragon?" With a voice like sandpaper Magus spoke. "Like what you see, my Irish queen?"

"I like what I hear," she replied, letting go the sheet. "Are you better? Have you had enough?"

"Enough what?" he asked, and turned his head towards Estrada. "Is he? Is he giving me his blood?"

Sorcha nodded.

"Why?"

"Just lie still now, Magus. I'm going to remove this syringe and ligature Estrada's artery. I think he's passed out."

Indeed, he had. After cleaning his incision with saline, she closed it with butterfly sutures, and finally wrapped it in gauze. He slept through the whole thing.

"Magus, I'm going to reattach your IV. I think you'll rally now."

"How long have I been here?" he asked.

"Seven days." He looked amazed. "You were cut across the belly. It was bad."

"I remember," he said. "Did they catch the bugger?"

"Not yet. Your belly is stitched up and swathed in bandages. But, they couldn't find a donor to match your blood. You were dying until Estrada discovered that he was a match. You owe the man your life."

"Saints alive."

"Aye. He's that." Sorcha cleaned up everything as best she could; then went into the bathroom and washed her hands. When she returned, Magus was staring at Estrada.

"He must have extraordinary blood. I feel fantastic, like I could dance a jig."

"Aye, he's extraordinary, and so are you." She got him a glass of water and set in a bendy straw. "Sip it now, and no jigging."

Then she got a cool cloth and wiped Estrada's face. When the water touched his lips, he opened his eyes.

"Hello, beautiful man."

"Hey. How'd it go?"

"See for yourself."

He glanced over at Magus, who nodded. "Much obliged kind sir. I am indebted, and a Pict always pays his debts."

Estrada smiled. "Once we're both feeling better, I'll be coming to collect on that. We have a few things to discuss."

"Aye, you've made me most curious."

The custodian groaned.

"Estrada, if you can walk, I think we'd best be off. We've been here over an hour. Our luck must be running thin."

~~~

With Sorcha driving the Harley, they cruised from Glasgow to Kilmartin Glen in just under three hours.

"Damn. The pub's closed. We should have stopped at Murphy's in Oban," he said. "I need a nightcap."

"Ah, well. I've a fine old bottle of Irish whiskey in my tent," said Sorcha. "Come back to camp, and we'll hoist a few to the Wee Pict."

"Only if you promise *not* to seduce me," he said, in as grave a tone as he could muster. Something had unleashed his wolfish soul. Whether it was the faerie blood that stirred in his veins, his magical meeting with Primrose, or the possibility of romance with Rachel, he did not know. But he felt alive and free and potent, despite the blood loss.

"I *can't* promise that, you being a handsome hero, and all. Whiskey's after waking my inner harlot. It's both a blessing and a curse."

"Then I can't come," he said, in all seriousness. "I made a promise to a friend, and I can't break it."

"A promise concerning me?"

They were parked in front of the Kilmartin Hotel. Sorcha was stretching after the long drive and he was leaning heavily against the bike. The woman was growing on him. He was impressed by the way she'd handled herself at the hospital, and the more secrets they shared, the more he admired her.

"Yes, a promise concerning you. And since I also promised *not* to discuss it with you, the subject is now closed."

"Dylan McBride," she said, shaking her head. "Holy Mary, Mother of God. Why do they always have to fall in love? Can a man not just enjoy a woman and let it go at that?"

Estrada shrugged. "I agree." He'd enjoyed countless men and women without falling in love. "But a promise is a promise."

"Fine then. I'll *try* not to seduce you." Tossing back her head, she ran her fingers through her long curls. "In the condition you're in, I don't think you could take it."

"Taunting me will get you nowhere."

"I'm serious, man. You look as if you're going to keel over."

"I am feeling a little lightheaded."

"Ah, it was only blood and you saved a man's life tonight—"

"*We* saved a man's life. I couldn't have done it without you."

"Aye. We're a good team, you and me. So, shall we celebrate our victory over Death?"

Estrada nodded. "I can almost taste that whiskey now."

After Sorcha nudged the Harley in behind the museum, they headed out across the field on foot. Wisps of cloud partially covered the silvery half-moon that hung in the sky and the earthy smell of dew-stained soil was thick. As he ambled through the grassy fields, he breathed in the wet salt-rich air and felt energized. She walked ahead of him as regal as an Irish queen.

"It must be well after two. Won't everyone be asleep?"

"On a night like this?" She took a deep breath. "Who wants to sleep? Ah, it's grand here—reminds me of home." She took off her leather jacket and slung it over her arm. "Don't worry about my crew.

Archaeologists are a special breed. Only a handful stay here, and most of them are locals that go home on weekends."

As they drew near the camp, Estrada could smell the distinctive odours of wood smoke and pot. In the distance, people lounged on blankets and deck chairs in front of a blazing bonfire. He watched a banjo player pick a tune, his fingers a blur, while two girls tried to keep up with guitars.

"Ah see. They're having a wee session. Joel there is from the States. He's been teaching Tina and Shelly how to play his style of bluegrass."

"Bluegrass? In Scotland?"

"Ah sure. Down Home America is all the rage here. You know, *this* is one of the best parts of a camp like this. People come from all over the world and the craic is ninety." He looked at her curiously. "The camaraderie," she explained. "Join them if you like. I'll just nip into my tent and fill a couple of glasses with the good stuff."

"That's a tent?" She was walking towards a huge green fabric structure that looked more like a space capsule. He estimated it to be four metres long. It had windows and even a front porch. Sorcha unzipped the door and turned to him.

"Curious? Come in, then. I'll give you the official tour."

He slipped off his boots, following her lead, and stepped inside. He expected to see sleeping bags on the floor. He'd camped once with friends in British Columbia, and they'd all piled into one crammed square like a crate of drunk puppies. But, when she turned on the lamp, he saw a scene from *Arabian Nights*. Patterned fabric hung from the walls and rich Persian rugs covered a floor strewn with large sleeping mats, vibrant pillows, and blankets. An engraved brass table served as a central gathering area, and several shelves along the far wall housed books, maps, pottery pieces, and various other treasures.

"Very cool," he said, strolling towards the shelves.

"Welcome to my home," she said, and winked. "When you spend your life living at a dig, comfort is key." Kneeling before a heavy metal trunk, she fiddled with a combination lock.

"Treasure chest?" he asked.

"Aye. Some things can't be left lying around. Great craic, but not everyone can be trusted." He wondered how valuable an item had to be to make it into the chest.

"Was your Egyptian collar locked in there the night it went missing?"

"No, I kept her close to me that night. That was my mistake." She'd lowered her voice, so he crouched down beside her to hear. "You see, sometimes I see images in my mind when I touch certain artifacts. Where they've been and who they were with...like a play. Wood, not at all, but there's something about bronze, copper, silver, especially gold."

"That must be helpful to an archaeologist," he mused.

"Aye. It's one of the reasons I went into this field."

He cocked his head, wanting to know her story. "Go on."

"Well, when I was fourteen, a body was unearthed in a bog near Dublin. It was the second they'd dug from the peat in three months. Both were noblemen during the Celtic Iron Age, and both had been ritually killed."

"Really?"

"Aye. My mother had friends on the team at the National Museum, so she took me to see it...or I should say...*him*. He was wearing a leather braided armband with a bronze amulet covered in copper mounts. Even through surgical gloves, the moment I touched the metal, I saw him, and he was *beautiful*...a tall beautiful man. I'll never forget his face."

"Psychometry."

"Aye. I've heard it called that before. I nearly fell on my arse when it happened." She shrugged. "I can't explain it, and I don't even know why I'm telling you this, except I think you'll understand, and we're sharing secrets tonight. But, that was the moment I knew I had to know them...our ancestors...how they lived and how they died. And that need to know has never left me."

Estrada thought of Dylan's ability to commune with stones. These two *really* should talk. They had more in common than they could imagine. But that was not his secret to share.

"That's quite a boon for an archaeologist. It must be incredible, like travelling back through time."

"Aye, and that's why I need her collar back. There's a wealth of knowledge trapped inside that artifact I've yet to tap."

"One more reason to solve this. And don't worry, your secret's safe with me."

"Good. You see those bones there on the shelf? That's all that remains of the last man who crossed me." He glanced at what appeared to be the skeleton of some reptilian bird flanked by several spiked antlers and cattle horns. "Now then. That's enough confessing for one night." She stood up and brushed her hand over the green bottle as if it were made of diamond, then presented it to him.

"Connemara Peated Single Malt Irish Whiskey," he read aloud. "Sounds serious."

"Sixty percent serious and twelve years old. The barley's dried over peat fires in Connemara, my childhood home. Tastes like the smoke of heaven."

"You continue to impress me, Ms. O'Hallorhan."

She smiled and winked. "I've been saving it for a special occasion." Taking it from him, she opened the bottle, then sniffed and groaned. "Go on then. Have a sniff yourself."

He breathed it in. "Gorgeous. May I do the honours?"

"You may," she replied, setting two glasses on the table. He poured both, and then handed her a glass. "To Magus Dubh, a ballsy wee man with a heart of gold. And to you, Estrada who could charm the knickers off a nun—" The look on his face confirmed her suspicions. "Ah, you have, haven't you?"

"What?"

"Charmed the knickers off a nun."

"Maybe one or two, when I was younger. I *was* Roman Catholic. But you've forgotten to toast the most important person here and that's you, Sorcha O'Hallorhan, because you care about people."

"Oh that's it? That's all I get? I care about people? How about Sorcha O'Hallorhan for her bravery in the face of eejits, her surgical audacity, and her incredible breasts?"

"They are beautiful," he said, and they clinked glasses.

"Sláinte."

The first swallow rushed through his body like a stream of liquid gold. She refilled their glasses and each downed a second shot.

"Jesus," he breathed, collapsing into a heap of pillows. What was wrong with him lately? He used to party all night. This whiskey went straight to his head and kicked out his legs.

Laughing, she set another full glass on the table in front of him. "Ah, we're just warming up, my man." When she flopped down beside him and brushed out her long auburn curls, he suddenly wished he hadn't made that promise to Dylan. Sorcha O'Hallorhan was brave, beautiful, intelligent, tough, sexy, and charming. And he was a free man.

"I can see why Dylan's fallen in love with you." He feigned a gasp. "Ah shit. I wasn't supposed to say that."

"Too late, and I must advise you to be careful, Estrada." She threw back her head and drained the glass, then set it down on the table. "Saying things like that could get you into trouble."

"What kind of trouble?"

"You could wake up naked and spent in my bed wondering what transpired."

"I promised not to sleep with you," he said, in all seriousness.

"Ah, well, there'd be no sleeping." Leaning in close to his face, she whispered, "I've been wanting to kiss those perfect lips since I met you. Would it break your promise to share a kiss?" He touched her cheek with his palm and she moved her mouth against the soft flesh of his hand. "Just a kiss, to celebrate our victory," she murmured. "No dishonour in that."

Estrada drew in close and caught her other cheek in his hand. "I think a kiss would be—"

Before he'd finished speaking, she'd covered his lips with hers and pushed him back into the pillows. Their tongues joined in a sensual dance that travelled the length of their merging forms. Then, catching his hands in hers, she held his arms back against the blankets and rocked against him. The alluring rhythm sent his senses reeling. Somewhere in the recesses of his whiskey-stained mind, he wondered just how far he could push the promise line. *It's still just a kiss,* he told himself.

"Who the fuck are you?" A man was suddenly in the doorway. Ducking his head, he sauntered into the room emitting a stench of sweat and alcohol.

Releasing Estrada, Sorcha sat up, swung around, and yelled, "Jesus, Kai. Get out of my tent."

"Shut up, bitch." He spat the word so vehemently his saliva flew.

Estrada sat up, downed the rest of his whiskey, and tossed the glass into the pillows. The pair rose simultaneously and he shoved her behind him, just in time to catch a sucker punch to the gut.

Winded, he reeled back to catch his breath and assess his opponent. *So, this was Kai Roskilde.* He was only slightly taller, but a good fifty pounds heavier. Ginger beard and blond hair that fell long and loose around his face—something he could use to his advantage. Estrada could fight dirty when he needed to: no rules, no mercy. A long scar ran down the man's cheek, which meant that he didn't know how to protect his face. And, he was stumbling drunk.

Grasping Sorcha by the shoulders, Kai shook her. "Everything I do for you, Irish, and you're going to fuck this asshole right in my camp?"

"It's not *your* camp, Kai. It's mine, and this is *my* tent. Now, get out before I fire your arse."

"Ungrateful bitch," he spat, and backhanded her across the face.

When a man gets mean with a woman, there's nothing to do but take him down. Estrada approached from behind, grabbed a handful of Kai's frizzled hair and yanked. Cursing, the man leaned backwards, then turned to grapple him. Before he could, Estrada brought his knee up and caught him in the nose. Heard the bones break. Saw the blood.

Letting go of his hair, he pushed off, took a couple of deep breaths and waited to see the result. The man had no moves. He'd likely bullied his way through life using intimidation to avoid any real physical altercations, except for perhaps the man or woman who'd wielded the knife. Emitting a stream of foreign curses, he lurched forward. Estrada blocked his punch and countered with a hard, quick kick to the groin. Down he went, gibbering over his aching balls.

"Enough," yelled Sorcha. She stood in a corner holding her cheek.

Maybe, Estrada thought, *but maybe not.*

Kai stood up grimacing, and staggered around like a wounded bull. Had he left it there, Estrada would have too. But he didn't. Turning to Sorcha, he spat a bloody gob that landed on her breast. "Fucking slag. You'll pay for this."

Estrada set up his kick and deftly lifted the man's kneecap. Kai went down then, threats and blood flying from his face. Just to be sure, he hoisted the brass table and bashed the bastard over the head until the noise stopped.

Sorcha stepped in front of him. "Jesus Christ, Estrada. Don't kill him." The man was still breathing, but had no fight left. Throwing down the table, Estrada wiped his hand across his face.

"Kai," she said. "I know you can hear me. I'm calling 999, and I'll get you out to the highway, so the ambulance can pick you up. But after that you're on your own. Don't come back here. Ever."

Then, pivoting, she turned to Estrada. "And you—" She shook her finger in his face. "You are going to help me."

The rest of her crew peered in through the tent door, some petrified, some shocked, but most with broad smiles on their faces. "Somebody get the tractor and cart," she said.

Then, turning to Estrada, she shook her head. "You realize you've just made yourself one fuck of an enemy."

"I was defending your honour."

"My honour?" Stepping outside the tent, she pulled on her shoes. "Jesus Christ, man. Is that what you call it now?"

CHAPTER ELEVEN

The Old Celtic Gods

DYLAN WAS RELIEVED TO SEE Estrada sitting in the prison visiting area on Sunday afternoon. He needed that protection ritual and he needed it now. His *innocent* cellmate had offered him a deal: he'd shield him from other men in the prison, but in return he wanted favours—sexual favours that Dylan was not prepared to give. It was only a matter of time before he stopped asking and started taking. This was what his life had come to: deals with the devil. He lived in a world of men…bad men, whose lust for power knew no bounds, and the only power he knew lay in magic.

"Did you get to Taynish?"

"Yeah, a couple of days ago, and Dylan, you won't believe who I saw out there."

Dylan shrugged, then rubbed his eyes. He hadn't slept in days and was feeling woozy.

Estrada's eyes lit up. "Primrose."

"Primrose?" Dylan thought back to Estrada's experience in Ireland. When he slipped into a coma, Maggie's gran said he was *off with the faeries*. Was it possible? Were faeries real? Had Estrada somehow slipped between the veils again?

"I mean it, man. Primrose was there, and as real as you or me. I could feel her, smell her. We made love. It was amazing."

"And you were awake? It wasn't a dream?" Dylan played the bagpipes at her funeral. Saw her laid out in a casket festooned in flowers.

"It was real, man. I was walking through the woods, and she called out to me. She was there."

"I'm gobsmacked. How did you—?"

"I don't know. But thank you for sending me there. If I hadn't gone to that place, maybe it never would have happened." He reached across the table, grasped Dylan's hand and squeezed it. "It helped me to sort things out. I feel like I can move on now."

Dylan could see from his friend's face that he was telling the truth, not that he ever considered for a moment that Estrada would lie to him about anything.

"But, enough about me. You look—"

"Yeah. You need to do it right away. *Tonight.*" He'd hoped his trepidation wouldn't show, but he'd forgotten that Estrada could read other things beside facial expressions.

"Did someone—?"

Dylan shook his head. Had no words for it. "Are you ready? Did you get what you need?"

"Yeah, and I'm making progress. A friend of Sorcha's finally remembered something…something that almost got him killed. A woman came to his shop looking to sell the broad collar."

"A woman?"

"A young woman, good looking. She didn't have the piece on her, but she described it, so was likely sent by the thief. Now, this dealer owes me, so I'm going to get him to give the police that information, and maybe, that will be enough to get you out on bail. It's worth a try, right? Your grandad says that if we can give them enough evidence you can be released."

Dylan shrugged. Hearsay was not evidence. It wouldn't be enough. His lips felt dry and tight like they were stretched over his teeth. "How's Sorcha?" He didn't want to mention her, but couldn't help himself.

"She's good. She's helping me."

"Is she." It wasn't a question.

"Look. I need someone who knows their way around here, someone I can trust. I'm positive that whoever killed Steele is connected to the dig and those are *her* people."

Dylan hoped Estrada had kept his promise. But, it didn't matter now. Sorcha was just an image he conjured at night when he lay stiff in his bunk.

"Oh. I met your friend Kai last night."

Dylan snorted. "Kai Roskilde is no friend of mine."

"Yeah, I thought you'd like to know: he took a beating. Terrible fighter, and he's suffering: dislocated kneecap, broken nose…"

Dylan glanced down at Estrada's bruised knuckles. "Jesus."

"And, he no longer works at the dig. Sorcha fired him. So, when you get out of here, no more Kai. That's good news, right?"

"Oh, aye." He forced a smile. He was thrilled to hear that Estrada had taken a piece out of Kai, but was beginning to think that the only way he'd get out of Greenock was in a body bag. "Aye. That's the best news I've heard since…Jesus, I don't even know how long it's been…" He'd seen scratches on the stone walls in Lochgilphead. Now he knew why. The days just blended.

"Since?"

"Since the Solstice." His last night of freedom.

"Two weeks and two days," said Estrada.

"Sixteen days. It feels like years."

"Don't give up, Dylan. After tonight, things will accelerate, and in no time at all you'll be out of here. The guard's giving me the nod. I'll go and get things ready, but I'll catch *you* later, right?"

"Aye. Later."

He couldn't explain this latest threat to Estrada. Speaking it aloud would make it all too real and he knew what the response would be. It was Wiley's thirtieth birthday next Friday, and Dylan was to give him a very special gift. If he didn't agree, Wiley was going to trade him to Ezekiel. This *Big Zeke*, as they called him, was not just a rapist, he was a sadistic killer.

Estrada would say: *give your cellmate what he wants.*

Only Dylan couldn't do that. He would rather die.

~~~

When Estrada left Greenock Prison that afternoon, he knew that if he didn't get Dylan out soon, he would not survive. If he could trade places with him, he would. He knew Dylan had been threatened. He could smell his fear. But, there was fuck all he could do about what went on inside a prison. He considered calling Rachel to ask if there was anything she could do, but decided that a Glasgow detective would be just as powerless inside one of Her Majesty's prisons as anyone else. If he'd given him something concrete, perhaps, but Dylan wasn't talking. And he never would. It wasn't something Dylan *could* talk about. He knew his friend would fight to the death before he'd allow a man to molest him. All Estrada could do was spin as strong a protective cocoon around him as possible and find the killer. If he failed in his quest, Dylan would die.

~~~

Leaning over the railing of the yacht, Michael surveyed myriad flickering lights in the distance.

They'd embarked from Vancouver four nights before. The first two days were heaven; the last two, hell. The boys rigged the sails, and under sun and turquoise skies, they skittered up the coast as far as Lund. Michael partied hard those first two days, relishing the freedom and novelty of sailing. Christophe, high as a soaring eagle, surprised him with delicacies, old champagne, and a plethora of good drugs. But, after a romantic supper on a cedar-shaked patio facing the sunset, he was satiated...ready for home.

Christophe smiled in agreement, but when he awoke the next afternoon, they were headed northwest across the strait, fighting the westerlies. A grey rain sunk into his bones and curdled his soul. *I want to go home*, he cried like a child. And when he felt in his pocket for his cell phone, found it gone. *Where's my phone? What have you done?* he yelled, in between bouts of puking. But Christophe only held back his hair as the boat surged on, and whispered. *It must have slipped overboard, chéri.*

When the boys tucked them into a marina somewhere on the west side of the strait that night, Michael stayed below, surly and dank, his belly heaving with each quaking wave.

The next morning, the sky was clear, and they chugged up a blind channel. Trees, rocks, and sea. Lonely desolate islands. And always Christophe, beside him and whispering. *Trust me, chéri. We are almost there. And then...you will know the joy of the ultimate gift.* Michael smoked his pot and drank his wine and sprawled on a deck chair in the sun, longing for escape.

And now, at last, they were here.

As their yacht docked in the tiny marina, Michael noticed others: monstrous white powerboats that reeked of corporate money, several sailboats, and two antique vessels trimmed in wood. Most bore American tags, and all had been emptied by the raging bash whose beats eclipsed the silent night.

"You are so grave, chéri. Laugh. Enjoy the party." Catching him against the railing, Christophe grasped and kissed him. "I give you this gift because I love you, Mandragora."

Love. That word was bandied about much too casually. Michael gazed into eyes craving praise with canine desperation, and when they kissed again, he closed his eyes, and saw a pretty black spaniel. His stomach lurched.

Club Pegasus was his domain, and he rarely ventured outside those walls. It was one thing to frolic in fantasy; reality was another matter completely. No one understood this, but Estrada. The two men shared an uncommon intimacy that could not be duplicated, which was why it hurt so much to be abandoned and ignored at the magician's whim yet again.

"What is this ultimate gift?" Michael asked. Christophe was completely in control of this escapade, and he did not like it.

"Come. I will show you."

"Just tell me."

"It cannot be said. It must be experienced. But, you will love it, Mandragora. Trust me."

A full moon cast silvery shadows through the trees lending the whole scene an ethereal atmosphere; and always in the distance, the tumultuous beats throbbed as if the island itself was alive.

"How on earth did you find this place?"

"The earth has much magnificence. A man need only ask the right questions," said Christophe.

"A man must also know the right people to ask," replied Michael, lighting a cigarette. "Was this place built as a movie set?"

"No. It was a gift from a nobleman to his lover long ago."

"A nobleman? How long ago?"

"It is said, the builder sailed these waters in 1775 aboard *La Sonora* with Juan Francisco de la Bodega y Quadra." Michael scoffed. "It's true. We passed Quadra's island this morning when you were ill."

Michael mulled this over, as they left the dock and followed a crushed stone pathway. Lit by flickering lamps, it meandered through dense pine and cedar forests.

"Are you really trying to tell me that this resort has been here, hidden away on an island for over three centuries?" he said, at last.

"There are many resorts in these waters." Christophe shrugged. "Le Chateau is not really a resort—although people do come here to play."

"I dislike your riddles." Michael disliked much of what was happening, however glamorous it sounded. Days of imprisonment, a lack of control, a lover who tried too desperately to please. Yet, a sense of nervous excitement mingled with trepidation and made him tremble.

When at last they turned a corner, Michael stopped and stared. An exotic palace from another time and place loomed before him.

"Impressive." Michael knew little of architecture, but he could appreciate antique symmetry. Floodlights emphasized the deep carmine walls and polished mahogany double doors ensconced in their carved stone façade. Byron journeyed to palaces such as this in the Mediterranean Sea.

"I feel like I'm about to enter another century."

Christophe exhaled. "Ah, chéri, I knew you would love it. And this is just the hors-d'oeuvre." Michael had never seen him smile like this. The pleasure, erupting from somewhere deep inside, illuminated his entire face.

But, there was something infinitely dark about the scene Michael encountered when he walked through those double doors. A magnificent gold cathedral, whose lavishly frescoed walls rose into a soaring coffered ceiling, played host to a writhing debauchery of bodies engaged in deviant play, most of which had a sado-masochistic bend. Beats blasted from hanging speakers in the panelled dome, as strobe lights flashed slices of live porn through a smouldering dope haze. Is this what Christophe thought he wanted?

"Come," mouthed Christophe, and taking his hand, led him through the throng. Stopping before a stone archway, words were exchanged with two burly guards, and then the thick oak doors swung wide. They stepped through into a cool tiled passageway that ran a few metres before ending in another oak door. For the first time since arriving on the island, Michael could not hear the beats.

"That looked like a scene from the Spanish Inquisition," whispered Michael. "Just to be clear: that is *not* what I want."

"Of course, chéri. I know you are not like *them*. This is an antechamber," explained the young Frenchman, "to cut off *this* from *that*. Those ones back there are mere beasts who revel in baser pleasures. But someone must pay the bills, no?" He grimaced and shrugged. "S & M. Vulgaire."

Yes, thought Michael, *vulgar unless vital.*

They stopped beside a candle in the stone wall and Christophe used its light to assess Michael. He smiled as he combed out his long blond hair with his fingers, and then glancing down, he frowned. "You are not dressed quite right, I think. Take off your shirt."

"My shirt?"

"The black trousers are chic. But, you must reveal your perfect neck and chest." With quick fingers, he unbuttoned Michael's shirt and slipped it from his shoulders. Running his hand across the smooth breast, he smiled. "Your flesh is like alabaster. Pale and perfect."

"Christophe," Michael said, grasping his hand. "Who are these people you are taking me to meet?"

"Do not be afraid. They are the ones you revere. Authentique. *Real.*"

"Real what?" Michael breathed. "What do you mean? Where are we?"

"Le Château de Vampire, chéri. I have arranged it all."

~~~

Passing through a fine mist, Estrada skirted Dunchraigaig Cairn, the tomb where Steele's body was discovered. He followed the fence line and opened the gate into the narrow green pathway that separated field from field.

The six remaining Ballymeanoch Stones stood in two parallel lines in a grassy sheep pasture to the southwest. It was the first time that he'd stood amid the towering stones. Feeling humbled, he marvelled at their stature, and the men who'd erected them as if they were children's blocks. Running the beam from his flashlight over the cool grey surface, and then his hand, he examined the lichen and engraved rings that signified, he knew not what.

The one thing he did know, was that this is where Dylan slept that night, where he'd been apprehended the next morning and dragged off to jail, and this is where he must endeavour to set him free.

From his pack, he pulled a purple scarf, unfolded it, and set it on the grass in the middle of the stones. On it, he placed candles, creek water, a quartz crystal, and an eagle feather; each object symbolizing a different element, and all necessary to achieve a sense of unified balance. Then he held the oak wand that he'd created from the Taynish branch. Drawing it close, he inhaled the sweet fragrance of the wood. Tipped in an amethyst dragon's tooth, it was a simple, yet potent, tool for directing energy and, he prayed, enough to invoke Dylan's mysterious Oak King.

After stripping off his clothing, he walked toward the stones in the east. The moist night breeze swept across his skin stirring his tactile senses. He was just about to cast the sacred circle when he heard a cry.

"Wait! Estrada, wait for us."

Coming out of the north, a jagged beam of light skittered haphazardly from the hand of Sorcha.

"What are you doing here?" he asked, when she arrived, panting, her chest heaving.

"We're here to help."

"We?" And from out of her shadow emerged a winded Magus Dubh. "How did you—?"

"You have powerful blood, Estrada. I healed almost straightaway, and when I did, I knew what you were up to here tonight. Don't be distressed, but I seem to have gained some knowledge of your thoughts along with your blood. It's rather amusing. We are now blood brothers in the most intimate of ways."

This confession left Estrada speechless. He stared into Dubh's eyes and thought loudly: *if you ever fuck with me, Dubh, I'll kill you.*

"Don't be alarmed. I'm sure it will fade," replied the wee man. "I am discrete and trustworthy, and I'm aware of the importance of what we are about to do here. Please, don't fret, my friend." He reached out a hand, which Estrada accepted and shook. "I've conducted many of my own rituals over the years, and I'd be honoured if you'd allow me to lend my power to the proceedings."

"Me too," said Sorcha. "Better three than one, yeah?"

"Magnifies the power," Estrada replied. "That's why we work as a coven." He glanced again at the dwarf. Just how many of *his* thoughts traversed Dubh's mind? "Well, I was just about to cast the circle, so…"

"Do I need to—?" She appraised Estrada's naked body with a grin, and then pointed at her clothes.

"Oh yes. Everything, my Irish Queen" said Dubh. Then, turning to Estrada, he remarked: "That's the real reason I came tonight. Ah, to glimpse the breasts of the goddess."

Estrada rolled his eyes. "Get it over with now Dubh, cause once we begin, I need your complete concentration on the task at hand."

"And you will have it," said Dubh, doffing his clothes to reveal the full extent of his tattoos.

"The same goes for you," he said to Sorcha. "This is business."

"My appraisal is complete," she replied, with a wink.

Estrada held the oak wand aloft with both hands. It shimmered with a golden glow, as he called down the gods of protection and light in the East. Then, walking clockwise, he continued casting a gigantic circle that encompassed the standing stones; invoking and summoning at each compass point, and asking for aid in their endeavour.

Dubh stood in the centre with a blackthorn wand that cast a light from a quartz crystal embedded in its tip. Estrada heard him banish all negative energy, and with it, he called for the spirits of the ancient Druids and Fey to join the circle.

When Estrada walked into the centre again, he was thrilled to see Primrose standing skyclad between them.

"You're really needing four. Right, Sorcerer?"

"Four is perfect," Estrada said, taking her in his arms. "As are you."

"Ah," muttered Sorcha. "Here's the butter. Is she…?"

"Primrose is one of the Fey," stated Dubh, and nodded his greetings.

Estrada glanced at Sorcha and furled his brow. "Butter?"

But, the archaeologist just shook her head and grinned at them both. And so, introductions aside, Estrada took a deep breath, and began.

"Our circle is cast. In this protected space, we raise our power." He opened a bottle of absinthe, and poured several ounces into a deep brandy snifter. Then, he held a sugar cube over the mouth and drizzled cold water over it. A few swirls with his wand, and the greenish liquid transformed into a creamy white louche.

He offered the concoction to Sorcha, who looked hesitant for the first time since he'd met her. "It's absinthe," he explained. "Seventy percent alcohol, but diluted. The main herbs are fennel, anise, lemon balm, and wormwood, and none of them will harm you. I promise."

She sipped, and passed it to Dubh, who took a couple of swallows, and offered it to Primrose. Clutching the snifter with both hands, she took a long drink, and then handed it to him. Estrada finished it off, and set the glass back with the rest of his tools.

"Join hands to seal the energy," he said. Dubh and Estrada stood across from each other with Sorcha and Primrose between them. The second they all clasped hands, his fingers tingled. He'd never experienced a circle with anyone who wasn't human, let alone a faerie and a half-fey Druid priest, so he wasn't sure what to expect.

When he glanced again across the circle, a shadowy Dylan sat cross-legged in the centre. Eyes half-closed, he'd come in spirit, leaving his dense body back in Greenock. Estrada smiled and nodded; then took a deep breath. Where he first stood alone, now there were five.

"This night, here among these sacred stones, we call upon the ancient Oak King to aid us in our quest. Known by some in his animal guise as the ancient horned god Cernunnos, the Oak King holds sway in this land over life and death. He is the god of endurance and triumph, and bestows protection on those in need. And so, we bid the Oak King join us in our circle. Hail Oak King. Hail Cernunnos. Hail Oak King. Hail Cernunnos…"

As they continued to chant, he bent his knees in the pose of the mountain, for the earth quaked beneath his feet. Releasing hands, they all took a few steps back. Then the winds picked up, swirling through the treetops, scuttling the clouds, and exposing the half moon, as the sound of the shifting leaves and branches grew to a near-deafening roar.

Estrada didn't know what he expected to see really, but when the Oak King appeared it was like nothing he could have imagined. Towering above them, he filled the circle, an enormous tree creature like Tolkien's Ent. Birds flitted around the oak leaves and mistletoe that garlanded his gnarly face. Primrose leapt to embrace him, then clung to his bark like a tree frog. Sorcha stood stunned and speechless. He'd lost sight of Dubh and Dylan entirely.

"Hail Oak King. We welcome you to our circle."

The wind died down and a sudden eerie silence descended. Estrada held his breath. And then great booming laughter filled the air.

"Hah. It's been a long time, a very long time."

"Gracious Lord," he said, relieved. "We call you tonight to right a wrong. Our friend, Dylan, is in danger. A man was killed nearby and he was blamed and imprisoned. But he is innocent. We ask for justice and protection in his name. And we ask that you aid us in our quest to find the true killer."

"That is much to ask. Where is this Dylan now?"

"I am here," said Dylan.

"Ah, I see," he said, glancing at the shifting image to his right. "You fall to shadow, as do I. A prison is a horrible place. There is neither earth, nor sun, nor rain, nor wind. Without freedom, we live in a state of dormancy. It is a living death." He shivered and the rustling leaves echoed like a wind chime. "So much of this land is dead. Desecrated. It began when they felled and burned my sacred groves. I feel your innocence, human. I will honour your request for protection and justice."

Dylan eyes glazed with tears. "Thank you, my lord."

"Do you require recompense?" Estrada asked.

When one of his branches descended beside Primrose, she climbed on, and he raised her gently to his face. "Your embrace pleases me, fey child." As she touched his cheek, her hand shimmered gold and he laughed joyously.

He glanced down at Estrada. "People have forgotten the old gods. It is enough that you remember. I am honoured by your calling. I wonder though…you summoned my brother, the Horned One. His visceral nature may require something more substantial."

"We will give whatever he desires," Estrada said, wondering if a blood sacrifice would be demanded. If it was, of course he would comply. He'd done so in the past and bore the scars proudly.

"The earth reeks of blood." This was a new voice, a sultry voice, and it flowed from lips like ripe mulberries, from a face that could only be described as something merging man and deer. Above the elongated nose, his eyes were vibrant and human, the colour of ripe chestnuts. His moustache and feathery beard were amber, a shade darker than his long loose hair. Tall, youthful, and well-muscled, animal skins adorned his body, and he wore the rack of a red deer on his head.

"Once a sacrifice came willingly to show reverence and devotion. Now blood is drawn only in greed. It sickens me."

He sashayed around them on cloven hooves, until his eyes settled on Sorcha. "You *will* need my help," he said, not shifting his gaze from her. Reaching out, he touched her forehead and cocked his head as if listening to her thoughts; then he ran his fingers slowly down her cheek, her neck, her breast, her belly, finally settling on her hip. "And you will have it. But for this, I exact…a mate."

"A mate?" asked Estrada.

"When the earth turns, and the streams run wild with spring rain and life rekindles. Then, I will come." Taking Sorcha's hand in his, he brought it to his dark lips and kissed it. "I will come for *you*," he crooned.

Beguiled, she appraised him in much the same way as he did her. Then, taking a step closer, he inhaled her scent and danced around her body, touching her hair and her soft pale skin. When the hide that hung from his hips rose and parted, exposing his erection, she gasped.

"You're on," she murmured.

"Sorcha, are you sure?" Estrada did not understand the terms. Did he want her only for a night, say for Beltane? Or did he intend to take her away with him somewhere?

"I've never been more sure. I'm honoured to be chosen as your mate," she said. "Whatever that entails."

"Then it is settled. I will come here on Beltane…for you. We will walk together, and we will merge."

"Hah. Splendid," said the Oak King. "There was a time long ago when we worked alongside the humans and the fey. Perhaps, that time will come again. It is sorely needed." And with that the wind grew blustery, the earth quivered and quaked, and they all fell to the ground. When Estrada glanced up, they had both disappeared.

"Close the circle," said Primrose. "Trouble's coming. Pack up and hide yourselves."

In the distance, Estrada saw headlights in the lot across the road from Dunchraigaig Cairn. He couldn't make out who it was, but that mystery was solved when two cops sauntered down the passageway between the cairn and the Ballymeanoch Stones. He recognized their white and black checkered hatbands in the swinging beam of their flashlights. Trees ran along the hedgerow where they all hunkered down. As they drew closer, he could hear their conversation.

"Ach, there's no one here. It was probably just kids again. Since that damn reporter was killed, this place has become *the* place to hang out."

"Aye, everyone wants to find a body. It's the new drug. If they *were* here, they probably saw us coming and lit out."

"I hear they do fertility rituals here."

"What'd you mean?"

"You know…" And with that he feigned some rutting gestures. Estrada heard Dubh suppress a giggle with a kind of soft snort.

"Well, that would be something to catch them at, wouldn't it?"

"Aye, well they're not at it now, so we might as well go back. This place gives me the willies. All those stones standing here for aeons."

"Ah, piss on it. The sheep do it all the time," he said. And then, he did. Having just experienced the power of the gods, it was all Estrada could do to remain ensconced in the shadows while the sniggering idiot desecrated the stone. When he'd finished, the two of them buggered off.

Sorcha laid her hand on his shoulder. "It's no different than sheep's piss, Estrada, and the rain will wash it away."

He acquiesced. The stones had been standing for six thousand years. It would take more than cop piss to diminish their power. Of that he was certain.

"I thought they were both aspects of one entity, but they're more like sidekicks: one plant, one animal," said Estrada. "I didn't expect that."

"Well, now you know," said Sorcha. "And, you've met them."

"All I know is that I owe you my life," said Dubh, swallowing another mouthful of absinthe. "Whatever happens now, I'm in."

The three of them were huddled around the brass table in Sorcha's tent. It was near daybreak and her tapers had melted into tepid wax pools. Whether it was his fey blood, or the absinthe, or sheer exhaustion, he did not know, but the shadowy world was etched in trails of shooting stars. Magic was energy. To create it, to resist it, to use its power, all demanded a price. Together, they had experienced something new and precious; something they were not ready to part with for mere sleep.

"Me too," said Sorcha. She sprawled among the pillows, her head wrapped in gypsy scarves.

Estrada smiled and toasted them both, then wondered again what Cernunnos would demand of her at the fertility festival of Beltane.

"Aren't you afraid?"

"Of him?" She shook her head. "I'm an anthropological archaeologist. I live my life sifting through ancient waste because I need to know and understand prehistoric cultures. It's my vocation...and something of an obsession. A find like Meritaten's collar is rare. Most of the time, I'm picking through middens, man. Trying to imagine what life was like from bone fragments and refuse. And now, along comes this stunning mythic god, who wants to *merge* with me—"

"What if he wants more than sex?"

"Hell, man. You're in love with a faerie. And *you* are half-faerie," she said, turning to Dubh. "So, let me have my moment. Whether it's sex or something else entirely, I don't care. I want it. I want to *know* him."

Estrada raised his hands in the gesture of surrender. Sorcha could take care of herself. Dylan might not be pleased that the woman he loved was planning to *merge* with a god, but Estrada felt comforted that they'd at least secured him some spiritual muscle; though he had no idea what the Oak King or Cernunnos could do to help.

"We should go over what we know, and make a plan. Truthfully, I'm not sure how to proceed from here," he admitted. They had yet to find Steele's killer or the artifact thief, if by some chance they were not the same person.

"Well, I told you about the woman that visited my shop. Not everyone knows its location, so this lovely must have been sent by someone familiar with Glasgow and antiquities."

"I wish you'd had the chance to tell us about her that morning we came to Glasgow. We might be one step closer," said Estrada.

"Yeah, well that fucking detective interrupted our plans, didn't she?" Sorcha took another swig from the bottle of absinthe, was still carrying a grudge. Whatever it was he'd started with Rachel Erskine-Steele must remain *his* secret.

"And, you'd never seen this woman before?" asked Estrada.

"Nor have I since," Dubh replied, shaking his head.

"Too bad you didn't take her picture," said Sorcha. "What did she look like?"

"Well, she was *slightly* taller than me," he said, sarcastically, and she smacked him.

Magus Dubh was growing on Estrada. He was savvy and charismatic, and so far, had not revealed anything that resembled a dark side.

Dubh was grinning, conjuring the woman behind closed eyelids. "Aye, I remember now. Five nine or ten, and stacked, much like yourself, Miss O'Hallorhan. She was wearing a skin-tight mini dress with a high neckline, scarlet, I believe. It hugged her firm bottom. Long bare legs. Oh, and fancy brown cowboy boots, high heeled with a pointed toe and burnished floral pattern."

"Apparently, he did take her picture," Estrada remarked to Sorcha.

"At least from the neck down. What about her face, her hair?" she asked.

"Long, straight, shiny black, with a blunt fringe. Cleopatra style. Could have been a wig, I suppose."

"A Cleo wig to sell an Egyptian artifact? Someone has a sense of humour," said Estrada. "And her eyes?"

"Sunglasses."

"Naturally. Can you remember anything else about her?" Estrada asked. "Tattoos? Piercings? Jewellery? A particular way of speaking?"

"Sorry."

"Ah well, you've done well, Magus," said Sorcha. "That's more than we had before."

Estrada nodded. "True enough." He crossed his hands behind his head and leaned back against a stack of pillows. The adrenalin was wearing thin. His body craved sleep, but his soul longed to solve this murder. "So, two days after the theft, a mysterious woman…let's call her Cleo…calls on Dubh at… Does your shop have a name?"

"Certainly. It's The Blue Door."

"Of course it is," he said, remembering the blue door in the wall.

Sorcha laughed. "Aye, it is. I've seen receipts. The man's legit. Even does paperwork."

"So, how did you leave things with Cleo?"

"I told her that I could move anything she could produce."

"And—"

"And I assumed she'd return with the merchandise, if she had it."

"But she didn't," said Estrada. "I wonder why not."

"Perhaps the thief's plans changed. I doubt our Cleo is working alone," said Dubh.

It has to be someone connected with this camp," said Estrada. "Whoever killed Steele had one of Dylan's handkerchiefs. They wiped some of Steele's blood on it, and stuck it where it would be found.

Whoever framed Dylan likely knew he was sleeping in the field that night too. How many women work here?"

"Three full-time, and a handful who help out occasionally," said Sorcha. "They're all volunteers, in it for the experience and the craic. The full-time girls are all at uni studying archaeology. But, I can't imagine any of them doing something like this." She shrugged. "Kai, though. He could have enlisted some woman to help him."

Enlisted was too kind a word for Kai's methods. Coerced, blackmailed, forced, paid, all came to mind.

"Was he with you that night? Here, in your tent, I mean?" Estrada was a little surprised that Sorcha was involved with Kai Roskilde, but then again, he'd never understood why women chose the men they did.

She shook her head. "I honestly don't know. I passed out in the van and don't remember a thing."

Rachel was right about that. Sorcha *was* an unreliable witness. Dubh's assailant might have been in Oban that night, and she might have danced with him, but it would never stand up in court. Too many witnesses could testify to her drunken state.

"One thing that stands out," she said, "is that Kai was at the cairn early Saturday morning right after Dylan was arrested."

"Like maybe he knew it was going to happen?" asked Estrada.

"Kai's a bastard. I can't defend him." Sorcha shrugged. "It all leads back to the broad collar."

"Steele tried to bribe Dylan for information about the artifact. Perhaps, someone else took the payoff and things escalated." He thought of Janey Marshall. "Did he talk to any women at the pub? Perhaps Cleo?"

"Sorry," shrugged Sorcha. "I don't remember seeing Steele that night at all."

"Ah, but you remember that bastard that tried to disembowel me."

"Well, *he* was hard to forget. We danced." She cleared her throat. "I'll tell you another thing that bothers me. This woman comes into The Blue Door on Monday afternoon looking to barter, and then it's a full five days before the Black Spaniard appears and accuses Magus of being the fence. Why so long?"

Estrada shrugged. "Who knows?"

"Just before he cut you, he said something, didn't he, Magus?"

"Aye," replied Dubh. "I'd forgotten that. It was something like: *If you've brokered a deal, kill it. The piece is not for sale.* He paused and looked at me like he was debating something. Then Estrada tripped, and he said, *what the hell*, and cut me."

Sorcha wrapped her arms around Dubh and hugged him.

"*What the hell*, like, why not eviscerate the dwarf?"

"Why wouldn't he want you to sell it?" asked Estrada.

Dubh shook his head. "In this business, you hear bizarre things. Artifacts have more than monetary value. Some people consider them objects of status and power."

"We need to find that woman," said Sorcha. "Maybe these two aren't working together at all. Maybe, The Black Spaniard was just trying to stop you from selling the broad collar because he wanted it himself."

"By killing me?"

"That *would* stop you," said Estrada. "I agree with Sorcha. We need to find that woman—find out who sent her and how they are connected. She must know something."

"Oban is an out of the way place. I mean, a Glaswegian wouldn't go to Oban just to drink. So, if Cleo, or her accomplice, met up with Steele at the Irish bar in Oban two weeks ago, there's a good chance she's local. Perhaps even a regular," suggested Dubh. "If we described her to the bartender?"

"Murphy's *is* the place where all these people intersect," said Sorcha. "The scene of the crime, so to speak."

"Well, what do you say to hoisting a few pints at the Irish bar?" asked Estrada.

"Aye," said Dubh. "It can't do any harm."

CHAPTER TWELVE

The Ultimate Love

ESTRADA AWOKE WITH A WICCAN HANGOVER: parched, queasy, and peevish. He heard music. The cell phone was singing. It might have been the absinthe. Sorcha had wanted him to stay with her and Dubh in the tent, but he needed time alone to think, so he'd cruised back to Tarbert on the bike.

He checked the screen. *Rachel.* He recalled their conversation three days past on the beach. They'd agreed to meet for dinner on Tuesday night in Glasgow. It was Monday 7 July, 3:52 p.m. Perhaps, she'd changed her mind and wanted to cancel. He flipped it to silent.

What did she want from him? *Love?* The word conjured only pain. He'd loved three women so far in his short twenty-eight-year life, and each brought only grief. Whenever he opened his heart to a woman, it closed in tragedy.

Alessandra, his first love: murdered in a vendetta, he'd been honour-bound to avenge.

Sensara, first his friend, then his spiritual partner, and finally his lover. Now, he feared, hating him with the same passion she once loved him.

And Primrose, so sweet and precious: dead because of him. Or at least, forever fey.

Love was a villain that could not be trusted.

~~~

"Le Chateau de Vampire?" asked Michael, incredulously.

"You must trust me, chéri." As Christophe pushed open the heavy door, Michael felt his hand at the small of his back, steadying him, and pressing him on. And then he whispered: "Behold."

Vampire? Behind-the-scenes at a risqué Euro fashion show—that's what Michael saw. Gorgeous young men, in varying states of dress and arousal, lounged on rugs, cushions, and couches: touching, embracing, talking and drinking, flirting and pouting, smoking and imbibing. Some were sombre-faced, some elated, and others wasted. A pungent hashish haze drifted through the scarlet and gold chamber, and clung in the hollows of its lobed Moorish arches, along with the salty scent of love. Michael breathed deeply of the ethers, and sighed. It was not the horror show he feared, though tension hung in the fog like a fiend.

"I need a cigarette," he said, reaching for the gunmetal case in his trouser pocket. After extracting a thin gold-banded cigarette, he lit it with a flick of his monogrammed lighter, inhaled the Turkish smoke, and leaned back against the young Frenchman.

Christophe brushed his hair to one side and kissed the back of his neck. "You see? Here, there is only love." Fingers whispered down his belly and into his trousers. "Ah, it excites you. I knew it would. Come, we must mingle and meet the others."

Before any introductions had been made, however, the two men settled into a swank crimson couch in the central courtyard. Tiled in terracotta, ivory, and sapphire, a coffered ceiling protected guests from the elements. Gilt-edged paintings stood out from deep scarlet walls. A dense wooden balcony ran around the square; its many closed doors offering a haven to those guests preferring seclusion.

"Was it worth the journey?" asked Christophe.

Michael cocked his head, assessing his surroundings. "I haven't decided yet. But, if we ever come here again, we're taking a float plane."

Christophe sighed. "I thought you would enjoy the yacht. I'm sorry you were so ill, chéri."

"I'm sure we can find an airport on the mainland. I'm not spending another four days on that bloody boat."

"Of course, chéri."

A vintage bottle of red wine was proffered by an alluring young man in a tuxedo, and a smoking hookah by another. As the wine and hashish found their mark in Michael's brain, he sank into the opulence and gazed at Christophe.

"It *was* worth it, non?"

Michael grinned. "Le Château de Vampire. You're playing with me, my charming boy. There are no vampires here. They do not exist."

Christophe's eyes were so dark brown, there was no difference between iris and pupil save a faint circle of flecked gold. With a soft smile, he winked. "Do you like my play, chéri?"

"It's unorthodox and extravagant. Of course, I do."

"Such a scene would enhance Club Pegasus, no? A private room for artful play?"

"Perhaps. It's rather like an elite gay club for only the young and beautiful. Very *Dorian Gray*. I'm curious though. Why are there no women here?" Michael had seen several in the outer chamber; the one where the *beasts* played.

"Women are mere fodder to Don Diego. He lost interest in them long ago."

"Don Diego?"

"Oui, this is his home. All of this belongs to him, and yet, he is gracious and shares his good fortune. But, I must tell you his story, chéri, for soon he comes."

Michael shrugged, then took several long hauls on the hookah. He didn't care to hear the man's story, even if he was rich and powerful. As the smoke billowed, he sank into the cushions, his imagination soaring. Was this Mecca anything like Lord Byron encountered when he journeyed through Ottoman Turkey? Exotic and carnal, it was a pleasure palace straight out of *Arabian Nights*. He must write about it as Byron did with "Childe Harold." What would Estrada think of it? He must exaggerate his homoerotic adventure just to make him jealous.

He glanced at the couple lounging on the couch across the way. A black man, whose long hair twisted into a mass of beaded dreadlocks, kissed his lover's neck; then, a trickle of blood escaped and dripped down the pale flesh. Sensing eyes on him, the man turned, curled back his upper lip and exposed a fang, as Michael often did himself. A shiver rippled through his flesh. He'd been entombed with Christophe for days and was bored. A man needed variety and could only endure so much bootlicking. When every hunger is fed, there is nothing to crave but freedom. Aroused, he ran his tongue across his lips flirtatiously.

"Mandragora? Are you listening?" Christophe motioned to the man with the hookah. "Indulge, chéri. You must let go."

"Let go of what?" asked Michael. His body felt like stone. He could barely lift his hand to grasp the pipe stem. Exhaling a cloud of smoke, his eyelids fluttered, and the spectral patterns in the carpet wavered and danced. The hashish was potent, headier than anything he'd ever smoked before. Close to passing out, he leaned into Christophe.

"Let go of your beliefs; of everything you judge real or unreal." Christophe found his mouth and kissed him. As he closed his eyes, time and space merged into a swirling ocean of colour. When at last, their lips parted, his lover's eyes remained locked on his. "Listen, Mandragora. Listen and believe."

"Very well, Christophe. If that is what you want."

"It *is* what I want." He poured a tall glass of red wine and placed it in Michael's hand. "Drink, and listen." Michael drank.

"Don Diego was born in Madrid. He became a Spanish naval officer when he was young, crossed the ocean, and married a woman in Peru."

"Don Diego. The man who sailed with Quadra in the late 1700s?"

"Don't mock, Mandragora. Believe. If only for me."

"Fine. For you, I will suspend disbelief."

"Come, lie down." Grateful for the invitation, Michael swung his legs up on the couch, and dropped his head in the young man's lap.

"Where was I? said Christophe. "Ah, oui. Don Diego sired a son and named him Salvador…*saviour*. But, on his many sea voyages, he missed his son. And so, when Salvador reached the age of twelve, Don Diego took him on his first voyage."

Sprawled on the couch with his head in Christophe's lap, Michael closed his eyes and imagined the tableaus. Fingertips lightly massaged his temples. He opened his mouth to speak, and then closed it again, luxuriating at last, in a moment of total abandon.

"Salvador voyaged with his father for three years, and then, one night, while they were exploring the Alaska coast, a tempest struck. The sea covered the deck, and in the midst of it, Don Diego found his only son clinging to the railing. Crying out, he raced toward him through the sleet, but his boot caught in a rope that had blown free of the mast. Entangled, he fell to the deck. Impotent."

"And then?"

"The boat dipped and a great wave swept over the railing. When it receded, Salvador was gone."

"Gone." Michael sighed.

"Don't look so sad, Mandragora. There is a happy ending to this tale."

"How can there be? The man's son drowned."

"True. Don Diego grieved for many years. But then, one night, he met a man who offered him a means to salvation, a way to immortalize his Salvador, to make him the saviour he was meant to be."

Michael's confusion must have shown on his face, for Christophe touched his pursed lips with his fingertip, and leaning over, kissed him again, slowly and deeply, as his fingers slipped inside his trousers.

"I want to make love to you very much, Mandragora. These sharp bones in your face, these dark hollows in your cheeks, they thicken my blood. Each scarlet drop belongs only to you." His wandering hand had found its mark. Each kiss, each rhythmic caress, brought Michael closer to the edge. "Ah, but, we must wait, for soon he comes."

"God, Christophe, you're a tease," Michael breathed. "Don't leave me aching."

"Chéri, there will be time for play."

"You don't play fair."

Christophe sighed, and then slipping to his knees, he undid Michael's trousers and engulfed him. Michael gave the dreadlocked man a lingering glance, and to his delight, he dropped his lover on the couch, and appeared above him. Kneeling beside Christophe, he gave Michael a slow deep coppery kiss. His heart pounded. And when the man pierced his neck and sucked his blood, he came in a violent crush of sighs.

Christophe shoved the man away, while Michael fought to catch his breath. "I felt the sharp kiss of the blade in my neck. How did he—?"

"You make me jealous, chéri. Am I not enough?"

Basking in the lingering glow, he did not reply. Of course, Christophe was not enough. Michael was a libertine who satiated his appetites with whomever he desired. Surely, the boy knew their relationship was not exclusive. They had never discussed such things, but *this* was not the time and place for melodrama.

He touched his neck and felt the warm stickiness of blood. How had the man punctured his neck? More authentic than razor blades, it felt real. Scanning the room, he searched for him.

In the ensuing silence, Christophe sipped wine from a golden goblet, and pouted. "These scars you have given me. I cherish each one."

"As do I." Catching Christophe in his arms, he pulled him close and kissed him. "Don't be jealous. I came here with you, didn't I? Though I still don't understand your ultimate love."

"That is because I did not finish the tale." He refilled their wineglasses, and sipped. "The young men who come here, those you see all around you, they are waiting."

"Waiting for what?"

"They wait for Don Diego to make his selection." Michael squinted in confusion. "Each hopes to become El Salvador, the chosen son. When it happens, they are filled with such joy, they renounce their old life, and give everything they own to their new father—their inheritances, their businesses, their yachts. What need have they for these things when every desire is met? It is a great honour to become one of Les Vampire."

Smiling, Michael slowly applauded. "Vampire Paradise. Great story. I suppose you're waiting to be chosen too."

Christophe frowned. "Once, that was my hope. But I came to accept that I would never be chosen. To be Vampire is not *my* destiny."

Michael looked at the young Frenchman quizzically as his dulled awareness grew. "Then we are here—"

"For you, chéri. I am the procurer."

"Procurer? As in pimp? You're a vampire pimp?"

"Do not be base. It is an honour to discover the man who will become the next Salvador. It is a joy beyond imagining to *be* the next Salvador. Don Diego pours all his love into the creation of his sons."

"Listen, Christophe—"

"He comes." Excitedly he hauled Michael to his feet.

Throughout the room, the young men stopped whatever they were doing and stood respectfully for Don Diego. Short, slender and middle-aged; a high, starched, white collar sprung from his waist-length black jacket. His dark hair was combed straight back and a widow's peak emphasized sharp cheekbones, a handlebar moustache and goatee. Michael followed his gaze around the room, as he appraised the young men gathered in his courtyard. When it fell on him, the dark eyes melted into gold. No breath, no motion, shook the silent room. Then smiling, he raised his hands in welcome and the young men bowed in deference.

"He likes you," whispered Christophe. "I think you will be—"

"I think I will *not* be," stated Michael. "My God, man. How could you?"

~~~

"Come on Estrada, tell me your secrets. I told you mine." Rachel was back to playing games.

"I've none to tell."

"No past? No family? Everyone comes from somewhere."

He fondled the strands of flaxen hair that veiled her pale breast. Talking was the last thing on his mind. Ducking under the silky sheet that lay askew across their bodies, he searched for the one thing that could avert conversation.

"You can't get out of it *that* easily," she said, rolling onto her side.

"Really?" he asked, cuddling up behind her. So far, it had worked perfectly. No more talk of love or relationships had sullied their tryst.

She sprang irately from the bed and disappeared into the bathroom. A few moments later, she appeared in a short white robe, rubbing her hands with lotion.

"Rachel—"

"I want to *know* you Estrada. *Sex* is not enough."

He had to concede that there had been little talk since they arrived at her flat, after a Chinese feast in downtown Glasgow. He possessed unusual stamina. Perhaps, it was the faerie blood that brewed in his veins and heightened his senses. It was now nearing morning, and he feared their date was about to end with showers and coffee. Having not yet segued into his current challenge—that of securing police files—he reasoned that revealing a few of his less dangerous secrets might prove opportune, perhaps even sway her fidelity.

"Will you accept an abridged version?"

"Only if it's true."

"As true as I remember." Satisfied, she uncorked another bottle of wine and refilled their glasses; then, cuddled facing him on the bed, still wrapped in her robe. Clutching her hand, he brushed his swollen lips across her almond-scented flesh. "I never tell my story. I don't believe in dredging up the past. But, this one time, and only because you asked, I will. Then we won't speak of it again. Deal, detective?"

She nodded her head, and stared into his eyes. "Deal."

He took a deep breath, wasn't playing up the pain. It hurt to speak of such things. "What do you want to know?"

"Tell me about your parents. Where did they come from?"

"You want a genealogy?"

She shrugged. "I'm curious, that's all."

"My mother is Mayan and my father is Mestizo—"

"Mestizo?"

"Mixed blood. Somewhere along the line, one of my father's Spanish grandfathers married an indigenous woman."

"Ah." She placed her pale hand beside his dark hand. "Go on."

"Is this how you conduct your police interviews?"

She smiled. "Estrada, I want to *know* you—"

"Yeah, yeah…but—"

"Where were you born?"

"God, woman." He breathed deeply and exhaled. "You know the answer to that." The past was the past. Why did it matter? Michael always said: *to live a life of pleasure, one must revel only in the moment.* Even *he* did not know all of Estrada's secrets.

"Mexico's a big place."

"Mérida…in the Yucatán."

"And you grew up there?"

"No. First, we moved to Mexico City, so my father could work in commercials. Then, when I was nine, he landed a movie deal, so we moved to L.A."

"Wow. I was *not* expecting that."

He shook his head. "You wanted the story."

"A movie deal in L.A. Your father must be a handsome man…like his son." He shrugged, wanted to do anything but talk about his family. "What happened? I can tell by your face—"

"Yeah, well. A few years later my handsome dad disappeared. Just didn't come home one day…the same day my baby sister Maria was hit by a car." There. He'd said it.

"Oh my god. Did she—?"

"Yes."

"I'm so sorry. Two tragedies in one day? Were they connected?"

"How could they not be?"

"Your poor mother. What happened to her?"

"She lost it…couldn't cope."

"That's understandable."

"Uncle Eduardo and his wife had immigrated to Canada. He felt bad that his little brother's family was messed up, so he came to L.A. and offered to take us all back to Vancouver. My mother refused. She took my sister, Ana, and went home to her village."

"And you?"

"Me? Me, she sent to Canada…figured I needed my uncle's strong arm. At thirteen, I was already too much for her to handle."

"Were you?"

"I'd been recruited by a street gang."

"At thirteen? I don't believe it."

"You're a Glasgow detective. How can you *not* believe it?"

"Oh, I know it happens. It's just hard to believe it happened to you."

"Well, it did. One minute, I'm the son of a celebrity living in paradise, and the next, *poof*, I'm a kid running dope to stay alive. Then, with another wave of the wand, I've lost my family and I'm living in another country with a Roman Catholic tyrant who believes in corporal punishment. I picked up the wand and learned how to use it."

"You became a magician." She kissed him with a fierce intensity. After, there were tears in her eyes.

"I understand pain and anger. I lost my parents too."

"Tell me," he said, and kissed her gently, keen to shift the focus from himself. There were too many things he couldn't say.

"When I was about the same age you were, my mother left us to live in Sweden. It's weird that we both had celebrity parents that abandoned us." He nodded, and she cuddled into the crook of his arm where he couldn't see her face. "My dad looked after me as best he could until he was—" She paused, and he waited in silence for her to find the words and the courage to say them. "My father was shot in the line of duty."

"Your old man was a cop? So, that's why."

"Why what?"

"Why you're a cop. When I first saw you, I wondered why a woman with your grace and beauty hadn't become a model."

"A model? That's why she left us. She didn't want me ruining her career. After my dad died, I ended up in the system."

"I'm sorry. So, you're righting wrongs like your dad?"

"He was amazing. I'm not half the man he was."

"You're perfect just the way you are." Pulling her close, he held her face between his hands. "Though if you *were* a man, I'd still seduce you." He winked, and she slapped him, just hard enough to provoke a wrestling match. When they calmed down again, it was like they'd passed through a portal into some new level of intimacy. Sharing secrets had that kind of power. When she kissed him, his heart heaved with her breath, and he felt himself falling.

"I know we live oceans apart, but perhaps there's a way we can work this out, Estrada. People do it all the time."

"*This* as in…*this relationship?*"

"If that's what you want."

"You know I have to see this through, Rachel. I made a promise to a friend."

"Of course. I understand that's your priority."

"Will you help me?"

She paused a moment, perhaps considering how much of a conflict of interest she could dodge. "I said, I'd be your ally, and I meant it."

He shrugged. "There are things I need to know."

"Like?"

"Like the evidence the Crown has against Dylan. Other leads the police are following. Details in the files."

"His solicitor should have all that information."

He shook his head. "He wants Dylan to cop a plea."

"I see. Well, tell me what you know, and I'll try to fill in the blanks."

"I know that a bloody handkerchief was found near the body." As soon as he said it, he froze. It was her husband's body. How insensitive.

"It's in evidence. I haven't seen the findings, but I can locate them," she said, with surprising detachment. He supposed that was how a cop stayed sane.

"And, I know that Sorcha's stolen artifact is connected. It disappeared that night, and a woman came into Dubh's shop a few days later asking about buyers."

"That's news to me."

"Yeah. Dubh forgot about her when he was attacked." He took a deep breath. "And Sorcha still maintains that The Black Spaniard—"

"The Black Spaniard?"

"Sorcha calls him that. We don't know his name." She cocked her head. "You remember the man who attacked Dubh?" She nodded. "Well, before he gutted him, the man told him *not* to sell the artifact."

"Perhaps, he was looking to buy, or had a buyer of his own?"

"But why kill the broker?"

"Maybe he didn't intend to kill him. Maybe he was just warning him to stay out of it."

"Some warning." Estrada sipped his wine and thought for a moment. "I also know that Kai Roskilde had access to the artifact that night. He put Sorcha to bed in her tent. What I *don't* know is why the Crown has Dylan McBride locked up in prison when none of this has anything to do with him."

"They have enough to hold him. You know, I think you know more than I do. My leave is almost over. When I go back to work next week, I can do some exploring…discretely. Would that help?"

He kissed her. "Absolutely."

"You know a part of me doesn't want to help you."

"I understand. I keep forgetting that it was *your* husband that was killed. It must be so hard for you to be involved in this."

She shrugged. "Alastair and I were finished long ago." She took his hand. "What I'm afraid of, is losing *you*. When this is over you'll go back to Canada, to your work, your friends."

"Rachel. All we can do is take one day at a time. I'm here now and this thing between us, whatever it is, feels good…really good. You were right. Talking helps."

Sharing his story and hearing her own had opened his heart and deepened his understanding. The woman was just trying to cope: mother a star who didn't want her, father killed, time in the foster system, husband a brute, workmates that were cops. She had plenty to deal with. He felt like he'd cracked her hard shell and freed the angel inside. He was afraid to say the words, *I'm falling in love with you*, but surely she could feel what was simmering between them.

From behind her ear, he produced a white rosebud. "A gift for a white goddess."

"Blimey. Where did that come from?"

He answered with a kiss that propelled them halfway through Thursday.

CHAPTER THIRTEEN

Taken

MICHAEL'S THOUGHTS RACED as he bolted from the room. To exist forever enslaved to bloodlust and this Don Diego? Did Christophe really think *this* was his ultimate desire? Had their dalliance been nothing but a ruse to ensnare him—another victim for this crazed fiend who exploited young men for their assets? It was nothing but a cult.

He touched his neck and felt two holes. Twin punctures. Blood drizzled down his skin. He thought of the dreadlocked man, his fangs, that thrilling bite, and the sensations that sucking caused in his body. Was it possible? Could vampires *really* exist? What had Christophe said? *The women are mere fodder?* Was this all an elaborate ruse to lure potential victims to a vampire nest?

After clearing the candlelit hallway and the S&M gallery, he ran. There was only one way to escape this freak show: find his way back to the dock, and steal a boat. He'd never been physical, and with a body tempered by too much wine, hashish, and tobacco, could barely walk. Still, his life depended on it. And so, he ran. Eight, perhaps twelve steps, and then his stomach revolted. Slipping behind some shrubs, he sank to his knees and puked. The vile liquid burned and fumes caught in his nose. Coughing and gasping, he wiped his mouth, then peered through the trees. Had they seen him? Were they following?

The boat they'd arrived on had been chartered by Christophe. Even if the crew remained on board, he had little cash to buy them, and they could not be trusted. But, tied to the dock some nine metres distant was a power yacht. Sleek, white, luxurious—pale foam gurgled in the dark water at her stern. She was off on her own, and she was running. Standing nearby, smoking a fat joint, was a kid—not one of the pretty boys, just a regular sun-bleached tanned-skinned beach bum wearing a white T-shirt and shorts. Mostly likely, a deckhand left to guard the boat, while his rich employer slipped inside for some novel entertainment.

The kid's feet were bare. Michael remembered this detail because when he charged the wasted deckhand and rammed him off the dock, a pale foot flipping through the air was the last thing he saw. He untied the lines and slipped them from their rings, then pushed the boat as far from the dock as possible, and leapt aboard. He could only hope that no one was downstairs snorting blow, or fucking, or doing any of the other things that rich people do on yachts.

The kid, foolishly zealous, grasped a dangling line and attempted to swing aboard. Grabbing a boat hook, Michael swung it like a baseball bat and caught him across the cheekbone. Howling, the kid released the rope and touched his face. "Motherfucker!" he yelled. Then, sobbing, he pulled out his cell phone.

Michael peered inside the empty yacht. And then suddenly, Christophe was racing down the dock. "Mandragora! Let me explain."

Driven by the current, the boat was drifting back. The kid he'd hit was bleeding and cursing; regaining his senses. Voices filtered down from the château. He must go. Now.

Dashing from the stern, he flew downstairs passing white leather couches and a wooden galley decked out for a party. Sliding into one of the leather captain's chairs, he shoved the throttle lever forward, and the engine surged.

When Christophe appeared beside him, soaking wet, shivering, and garbling in French, Michael froze. *Damn him.*

"Mandragora!"

"Shut up." He couldn't think. Couldn't take his hands off the wheel, though he wanted to wring his bloody neck. Couldn't do a damn thing until he cleared the harbour. And then what? Cast his lover into the sea? He sure as hell couldn't take him along.

"Forgive, chéri, forgive. I thought—"

"Don't think, Christophe. Go...see if anyone else is on board."

"Oui, I will help."

Help? Help what? Help him escape the vampire? Michael had read plenty of vampire stories over the years. As a kid, he'd been obsessed.

Dracula, Salem's Lot, and Anne Rice's *Vampire Chronicles* kept him spellbound for hours. But they were just stories. Weren't they?

Could Diego *really* be a vampire, or was he simply a charade; an elaborate hoax created to entertain and defraud the rich and powerful? But myths had to come from somewhere. Was he cruel and heartless? Did he drink blood? Sire progeny? Fly like a bat? Could he drain humans of more than their assets? As he cleared the harbour, Michael searched the sky, wondering if some winged creature would descend suddenly, clutch him in its clawed talons, pierce his jugular, and transform him into something hideous.

Glancing over his shoulder, he saw Christophe emerge from the aft cabin, a white towel draped around his slender hips. With another, he was drying his long dark hair.

Angrily, he shoved the throttle full out and the yacht surged ahead. Steering into the darkness, he turned off the running lights and prayed there were no submerged rocks or deadheads in the channel. They would surely follow. A posse. He studied the map on the console. None of the names were familiar. He needed a place to hole up, a place to think. He'd just stolen a yacht easily worth a million dollars, possibly two. That was grand theft. Add to that the assault on the deckhand. If he didn't figure this out, he was going to jail. That's if *they* didn't catch him first. *Outlaw.* He switched off the radio and the GPS. Did the yacht have a tracking device? He was almost sure that if he did not activate a distress beacon the boat could not be tracked by satellite…almost sure.

When he felt Christophe's cool hands clutch his shoulders, Michael's stomach churned again.

"Chéri, I thought you wanted to be vampire. You crave the blood. I thought—"

"You thought wrong, Christophe. But don't worry about it. I'm not angry. You made a mistake, that's all." The error was not in thinking Michael wanted to become a vampire, but in the treachery, the betrayal. Procurer. Vampire pimp. What gratuities did Christophe receive for his services? How many men had the cloying Frenchman lured to their deaths with promises of *ultimate love?*

"Ah, chéri." Michael felt kisses on the back of his neck, fingers in his hair, tender caresses along his ears, his throat, his chest. "Je t'aime." *I love you.* Christophe wanted sex. He assumed that once past *that* barrier, forgiveness was assured, and all would be forgotten.

Michael pulled back on the throttle and let the boat idle. Catching Christophe's face in his hands, he kissed him deeply and passionately. Let the boy think he was safe, loved, forgiven.

Grasping the towel, he flung it aside and pressed hard against the naked body. Christophe kissed him, and then dropped to his knees, as Michael knew he would, undid his trousers, and let them fall. Aroused by the familiar touch, Michael gasped as hungry lips engulfed him; the suctioning force of a lover's desperation. Dark wet hair caressed his thighs, fingers flickered across his flesh, squeezing, probing. He let it build, caught the damp head in his hands and held it, moaned, and filled it. Then, reaching across to the champagne bucket on the nearby table, he yanked a full bottle out of the tinkling ice and brought it crashing down against the side of the head. Careening sideways, the body lay still.

Michael picked up the frail wrist and felt a faint pulse. He would live. He dragged Christophe's body into the first cabin and laid him on the bed; careful to place him on his side facing the wall. Recovery position. He didn't want the *procurer* to awaken with a concussion and choke to death on his own puke. No one deserved to die like that. Searching through the drawers, he discovered several scarves which he used to bind the limp wrists and ankles behind the body. He considered a gag, then decided against it. Even if Christophe screamed, there was no one to hear him. Finally, Michael ripped the blankets from another bed and covered him. In case of shock, keep the body warm. Managing a nightclub had taught him a few things, at least.

I don't hate you, Christophe, but you should have asked me, not just served me up like the main course at a dinner party. How dare you presume to know me like that? There is only one man who really knows me, and he would never do a thing like that.

~~~

Rachel Erskine-Steele could spin a charm better than any witch Estrada had ever known. For two days, the amorous pair had not left her sandstone flat, except to christen the moonlit patio. If any vestige of Alastair had lingered in those Scandinavian ethers, it had been exorcized by their coupling. Estrada's flesh was scraped raw, while sparks literally flew from his fingertips, amid whispered promises and intimate confessions. She'd never known love, she said, and now she couldn't live without it, without him. In his delirium, he confessed how much he wanted to marry and have a child of his own someday, surprising himself with shivers of truth. She wanted a child too. A dark-haired, dark-eyed child.

On Thursday afternoon, when Sorcha rang to remind him about their meeting in Oban that night at ten o'clock, he didn't even consider going alone. With Rachel on the back of his Harley, Estrada felt strong and complete, like a man cruising through the past, present, and future collapsed in a single breath. And he knew something else. They were on their way to saving Dylan. With Rachel, he felt renewed: fearless, unstoppable, and hopeful.

Estrada was in love…and two hours late.

They were hit by Sorcha's anger as they descended the stairs at Murphy's Irish Bar. Surging red rays shot across the room. In no mood to watch the two women do battle, he deflected with swirling turquoise waves created from memories of the cenoté, his childhood refuge. For a moment, Rachel hesitated, struck by the heat, and then recovering, she entwined her fingers in his, straightened, and walked tall beside him.

"Why did you bring *that* cunt?" She downed the glass of whiskey clenched in her fist and slammed it on the table. It was not her first.

Everyone turned to see the cunt in question, and Rachel cast a stone-cold glare at the red-haired archaeologist that left her spitting fire. You don't have to be Wiccan to be a witch. Rachel, he'd discovered was a natural at manipulating energy and power and she didn't mind the pejorative. To be called a cunt in this land, he'd learned, was not uncommon, not particularly obscene, and not restricted to women.

"Detective," acknowledged Dubh, nodding to Rachel. He perched on the edge of the bar stool, his short legs dangling above the floor, and grinned, whether apologetically, with nerves, or simple delight, Estrada could not tell.

"Call me Rachel, please. I'm not on duty, Mr. Dubh."

"We're all grateful for *that*, detective. You may call me Magus."

"A fucking word, Estrada," demanded Sorcha. She'd hopped off her stool and stood stiffly against the bar. Braless, and poured into a copper tank and black jeans, he suddenly realized the root of her fury. She'd dressed for him—had come expecting to extend that kiss they'd shared before Kai burst into her tent.

Estrada glanced at Rachel. She was flushed from the wind, and a quick brush up against an outside wall. After teasing him all the way from Glasgow, he couldn't help himself. In a tight white mini, ankle boots, and leather jacket, she sent him reeling. Her long platinum hair hung long and loose around her face, her lips burned red with kisses.

"Jesus, Mary, and Joseph. Is the cunt in charge now?"

Grasping Sorcha by the wrist, he led her across the bar and into a snug. Rachel could manage with Dubh.

"What the fuck is wrong with you? This," he said, gesturing towards Rachel, "is not your concern."

"Ah, but that's where you're wrong. Herself is married to the bastard your man is accused of killing *and* she's a fucking copper. We can't trust her, and if you're tied to her, we can't trust *you*."

"You think I don't know she's a cop? I haven't considered the implications?"

"Frankly. No. I think you're thinking with this. Reaching down, she grabbed his crotch. He caught her hand and held it. "Probably think you're in fucking love with—"

Releasing her hand, he lowered his voice. "Listen. Rachel can help us. She—"

"*She* has never helped anyone, but herself. Any idea what that bitch has done to Dubh over the years?"

He shrugged. Hadn't thought about that. He knew they'd met previously, but he never considered their history. Glancing across the bar, he saw the two of them sitting side by side at the bar ignoring each other. "They seem to have sorted it out."

She shook her head. "Did you at least consider your woman?"

"My woman?"

"Aye. Primrose. Our fourth. The love of your life. Have you forgotten her so soon?" The women had forged a bond that night at the ceremony. Conjuring magic in a closed circle could do that.

"Primrose won't mind. She told me to move on and find another woman because of the way things are. She'll be happy—"

"Shhhhh." Sorcha was staring at something over his shoulder. He turned. With a flick of his head, Dubh motioned to a woman who'd just come down the stairs. Medium build, her long black hair was cut in layers. She had full bangs, just as Dubh described, and overkill eyes. Slithering in a tight black dress, she looked like a cobra slipping out of a sack. Sitting back, he scanned her aura. A pale bluish haze whispered only of sadness. The woman was in pain, had been abused somehow. Perhaps Kai—

"Cleo," said Sorcha, under her breath.

"I'll talk to her," Estrada said, and tried to rise, but her hand came out, caught the edge of his belt and yanked him back down.

"Some detective you are. Never heard of surveillance? Let's see what she's up to. Perhaps, she's here to meet someone." He could see Sorcha's point, but the woman looked so sad, he thought if he spoke to her, maybe she'd tell him what she knew. Perhaps all she needed was a comforting touch and a gentle ear.

Dubh appeared, and scuttled into the snug beside Sorcha. "I thought it best to disappear, just in case she recognizes me."

"Ah Magus. Always thinking. Not like Romeo here." Finding an opportunity to ditch Sorcha and her foul mood, Estrada stood. "Just keep Juliet away from me," she said, as he walked away. "And remember how *that* play ended."

Rachel perched on the barstool, her long legs crossed at the knee. She was sipping a gin and tonic. Leaning against her back, he placed his hands over hers on the counter as he had that first day in the kitchen. The band kicked up: loud, meaty, and with a Celtic edge.

Leaning in close, he yelled in her ear: "Dubh pointed out the woman who came into his shop."

She turned, and he caught her mouth with his. God, she was gorgeous. No matter what Sorcha said. No matter what anyone said. He loved her.

With his eyes, he gestured towards Cleo.

She smiled. "Now what?"

"Watch and wait."

"Bathroom." Slipping her leather bag over her shoulder, she kissed him, and sauntered off; her departure followed by sundry hungry eyes.

Catching the bartender, Estrada ordered a pint of amber ale and a glass of whiskey. He chugged the whiskey as he watched Cleo navigate the room. It burned its way down his throat and he extinguished the fire by downing half the pint. Then he ordered another round of the same.

Why did Sorcha have to bring up Primrose? She had healed him and he would always love her. But Rachel? Surely, she was the woman Primrose alluded to, the one to settle with, to make babies with—

His thoughts were interrupted by the sight of the serpentine woman mounting the stairs with a man. He downed the rest of his ale, and followed. Rachel had not returned from the bathroom, but he couldn't let this chance go by. He had to see where they'd end up. Likely the back seat of a car, but perhaps not.

At street level, they turned right, and he saw the man reach down and grab her ass. Leaning into him, she laughed invitingly, and Estrada considered that she might just be a working girl. If so, she might have been hired. He needed to talk to her to find out who—

Brass knuckles caught him in the throat. Concentrating so acutely on the couple in front, he hadn't seen it coming from the side. The force of the blow knocked him into the wall. He gasped, and then a knee landed in his crotch. The voice, the laugh. In a daze, he recognized his assailant. Kai Roskilde.

"How do *you* like it?"

Frantic, Estrada tried to think past the pain, to prepare a defence. Doubled over, it was easy enough to reach into his right boot and extract the knife he'd hidden there for this very reason. The cold metal gave him courage. Consciously, he braced himself and found his balance. Then he began the upward spiral that would end in him stabbing the Viking bastard in the gut. Except it never happened.

In the periphery, Estrada glimpsed Rachel's spectral form, heard her scream. Fingers grasped her pale hair—a knife kissed her throat.

"Drop it," Kai growled. Estrada stood his ground. Did the son of a bitch have the guts? "Drop the knife or I'll cut her. You don't believe me?" With a grizzled smile, he drew the knife across her white skin. Blood burst along the blade and dripped down her neck. "Don't try it hero," he threatened, and slowly backed away, still clutching Rachel. Estrada stood helpless, unable to make a move without endangering his lover.

It wasn't until Kai stopped beside a campervan that he suddenly understood. The bastard was taking her with him.

"Too bad we don't have a set of your handcuffs, detective. It would save your lovely face." For a second, Estrada wondered what he meant, as did she; and then, still clutching her by the hair, the bastard cracked her head viciously against the side of the van.

"No," Estrada cried. The blow was enough to knock her senseless. He rushed him then, but yanking a pistol from inside his belt, Kai fired.

"Damn," he scoffed. "Missed."

But, he had *not* missed. The bullet pierced Estrada's thigh, and he hit the ground grasping his bloody leg, fighting pain that seared the edges of his brain. Where the hell were Sorcha and Dubh? Opening the back door of the campervan, Kai thrust Rachel inside, and slammed it shut.

"That's for fucking with a Viking too pissed to fight back."

"Don't take her—"

"The bitch is mine. You want her? Come and get her. That's if you can, and you still want what's left when I'm done." He opened the driver's door and swung one leg into the cab, then stopped, and came limping back. "I almost forgot," Kai said, then lifted his boot and planted the heel firmly in his face.

Estrada felt the bones in his nose break. "Fuck!" he cried, choking on the blood. Coughing and snorting, he came up, ready to block, but another boot to the side of the head, landed him on the pavement.

"Night, night, asshole."

Whether they were kicks or punches, Estrada did not know, but they rained down on him, and within seconds, he lost consciousness.

~~~

Fear. People talk about how humans fight, flee, or freeze when faced with fear, but there's another kind too; a slow monopolizing fear that trickles like syrup on a warm spring day. Sometimes, people feel it percolating, incapacitating, but don't know what it is. Some demean it by calling it stress. But, Dylan knew it for its true nature, and was no stranger to it. This fear was one reason he'd made Wicca his refuge.

Nights, as he lay shivering and sweating on his prison bunk at Greenock, he would remember those times he'd met Fear. It dogged him through childhood in the guise of bullies—boys who were bigger, stronger, and meaner. Boys who took his fair skin and high blush; his quiet nature and his love of music and books, to mean gay. Boys who called him homo or fag-bag, and who persisted in trying to stick things up his arse, and often did—claiming it was for his pleasure and not their own—if he wasn't fast enough, or if they caught him alone.

Home was no refuge either once his dad had been sucked down by the sea, taking his mother with him in an alcoholic spume. He'd loved his dad. Still did. Bobbie McBride, was a natural fisherman who'd crossed the Atlantic from old to new Scotland dreaming of a better life.

But, sometimes dreams mean nothing, and sometimes dreams are obscured, like the bloated bodies of foundered fishermen.

When the late spring storm took Bobbie's trawler down off the shore of Yarmouth, it left Dylan with one more fear. The sea. Over the years, living in the Maritimes with an alcoholic mother, his fear grew into a freakish phobia that sent him digging underground to rocks and stones for comfort, and skyward to Wicca for inspiration.

This fear rippled through him now, and no amount of meditation or calling for protection brought him peace. His psychic cries to Estrada unanswered, Dylan realized that it was just a matter of time before his childhood bully struck again.

Today was Friday, his cellmate's birthday, and there was nowhere to run. Wiley's revelation, that he was no rapist, provided little consolation. He wanted consensual sex. It would benefit them both, he explained, and if Dylan refused, there was always Big Zeke.

He smelled Wiley's fetid breath before opening his eyes.

"Wish me Happy Birthday, Dylan. I'm thirty today." A clammy hand meandered under the blanket. Scooting sideways, Dylan wedged his back against the wall. "Come on, boy. Let me have a pull."

He had no words for Wiley's desire, but blinked—afraid to close his eyes, afraid to keep them open. His insides burned and shook.

Wiley stepped back and dropped his boxers. "Observe Dylan McBride. In ready mode, it's no bigger than a bratwurst. 'Twas made for a novice, darling."

"Shut up."

"It will fit in any orifice you please. Front-side. Back-side. Top or bottom. What's your pleasure?"

Dylan leapt off the bunk. It was nothing he'd planned. Days of lurid looks and sickening innuendos and suddenly he was on the little weasel, his hands twisting the skinny throat and shaking and shaking, and the little prick hanging gurgling, his eyes bulging, and then his bad knee busting that scrawny naked sack.

Finally, he flung the body against the bars so hard it pissed as it fell. The guards were on him then, and he knew he was done for. After dragging him out, they locked him in an isolation cell. Neither of them said a word, but he saw the smirks on their faces as they turned.

~~~

"Rachel!" Every cell in his body screamed for her, demanding fusion, and it hurt like hell. Kissing her caused a cataclysmic pain through his head, face, and jaw. His balls throbbed. He couldn't move his legs. Couldn't make love, but had to. Still he held her: crawling through those grey eyes, searching for release. Held her until she broke apart—her body shattering into billions of particles. Disappearing...vanishing inside a whirling vortex.

"Rachel—"

"Estrada." A voice pierced the edges. "You're having a nightmare." Insistent shaking hastened her disappearance and heightened the painful sensations in his desperate body. He'd only just found her. He couldn't lose her now. "Estrada, wake up, man."

He couldn't focus. Rubbed his eyes. "Where—?" Raw throat. It hurt to talk. Rachel. All he could remember was her face striking the side of the van, that look of shock.

"You're in hospital. You've had surgery. I think you need more pain meds. I'll call the nurse."

"No. I need to think." He couldn't afford to addle his brain with drugs. Breathe through the pain. Rescue Rachel. That's all that mattered. He had to find her before Kai Roskilde—

"All you've been doing is thinking…thinking and talking and moaning." Estrada glanced at the edge of the bed. Magus Dubh stood there. "Your throat must be dry. Sip some water." He placed a straw at his lips and Estrada sipped. The water soothed his throat. "I'd ask how you were feeling, but I have a damn good idea already."

"Where—"

"You're in Oban, at Lorn and Islands District Hospital."

"Rachel. Where's Rachel?"

He shook his head. "Sorry, man. The polis are on it; in fact, there's one standing just outside the door."

"Am I under arrest?"

"Not yet, but you're something of a celebrity. Two polis. There's a DCI here from Glasgow. He brought along a sergeant to *protect* you."

"Protect *me*? They should be searching for *her*."

"They are. That's why they're here."

"I have to get out of here. Kai—"

"Listen to me. That big Viking bastard beat the daylights out of you: busted your nose, bruised your throat, cracked a couple of ribs, and shot you in the thigh. You can't go anywhere just yet."

Estrada sighed. "I'll kill him." Once he'd heard the extent of his injuries, everything throbbed. Sliding his hand down his leg he felt the bandages.

"You are one lucky son of a bitch. The bullet just nicked the femoral artery. You could have bled out. It missed the bone. I talked to the pretty nurse."

"Where were you, Dubh? You and Sorcha?"

"I'm sorry, Estrada. I really am. I was trying to calm her down. Neither of us noticed that the girl had disappeared or that you'd gone after her. We ran upstairs when we heard the shot. Roskilde was just taking off in the van, and you were—"

Estrada rolled his eyes. "Some fucking team."

"I am sorry. If there is anything I can do to make it up to you, I will do it. I already owe you my life."

"There is. I need an infusion of fey blood, so I can find Rachel and plant that Viking's head on a stick."

"That will be difficult with Sergeant Cruickshank posted right outside the door. Besides, how would we get the blood from me to you? It's the middle of the afternoon."

Estrada thought for a few seconds. Initially, Dubh's blood had entered his body through cuts in his hand and his calf. Blood to blood. Those wounds had healed almost overnight. But, with the extent of these injuries, he'd need more than a few drops. If they couldn't rig up a transfusion, he'd have to ingest it another way.

"Cut a vein. I'll suck it—"

"Like a vampire?"

"Mr. Estrada. I see you've regained consciousness." A nod and a flashing badge. They'd crept up on him and he didn't like it. "I'm Detective Chief Inspector Lyon, Glasgow CID. He nodded to the uniform beside him. "This is Sergeant Cruickshank."

It was the same racist pig who'd threatened him with deportation to Mexico the day he arrived at Glasgow airport. Why was *he* here now? Surely, Oban was out of his jurisdiction.

"We've met," said Estrada.

"That we have," crooned the sergeant. He'd traded his MP5 for a Taser, but Estrada still wanted to shove it up his ass.

"We have a few questions," said Lyon.

"Have you found her?"

"Off you go, now," said the sergeant, shooing Dubh out the door. "You can come back and visit your boyfriend later." *Racist and homophobic*, thought Estrada. *Charming.*

Dubh smiled and gave him the finger. "Oh, I will sergeant, and I'll bring something special for you when I do."

"Mr. Estrada—" The velvety bass voice belonged to Lyon. Dressed in a tan suit, white shirt, and chocolate striped tie, the man exuded competence, and Estrada was glad of it. His thick auburn hair, buzzed short on the sides, receded into a widow's peak. Catching his gaze with piercing brown eyes, he found it hard to look away. The man had a mesmerizing charm, was handsome, and Estrada supposed, young for a chief inspector. He must be either smart or connected, or both.

"It's just Estrada" he said, extending his hand. Lyon's handshake was strong, and he caught himself liking the man despite his profession.

"We've lost one of our own, Estrada, and we need your help to find her."

"I want what you want."

"Good. We understand each other. This is a complex situation, as you can probably imagine. It's perplexing, as some aspects don't make sense. For example, we are having a difficult time understanding what you were doing with a detective whose husband was so recently murdered, allegedly by *your* friend." He shook his head. "It's unusual; some might say, unethical. You understand our need for clarification."

"It confused me too, at first." Estrada wondered why they hadn't brought the question of this unethical tryst to Rachel. Of course, it had only just occurred, and she was still on leave.

"Could you explain your *relationship* with Detective Erskine-Steele?"

"Rachel and I met a couple of weeks ago, when she came to Kilmartin Glen investigating her husband's murder." He shrugged. "One thing led to another. We fell in love."

"In love?"

Cruickshank snorted.

"It happens, Inspector. Do you not believe in love at first sight?"

"Since Mrs. Lyon is not present, I can confess that no, I do not. But, that's neither here nor there. What were you two doing here in Oban at Murphy's Irish Bar last night? Out on a date?"

Estrada wondered just how much he could say without implicating Sorcha and Dubh. Of course, the police already knew that Dubh was connected—that's why he'd been banished from the room. So, he decided to tell the truth. Besides, they both wanted the same thing: Rachel's release.

"Sir, as you know, my good friend, Dylan McBride, is imprisoned at Greenock for killing Alastair Steele. I came here to help him."

"We warned him about that at the airport as you instructed, sir," said Cruickshank.

"Yes, I know, sergeant."

Choking up suddenly, Estrada coughed. It had been Lyon who'd given the order to threaten him that day on the phone.

"Easy now. Take your time." Picking up the glass of water from the bedside table, Lyon handed it to him. Estrada sucked on the straw and felt the cool water soothe his throat.

He nodded his appreciation and took a deep breath, while he scrambled to put together the right words to convey the least amount of information.

"You were just about to tell me why you and Detective Erskine-Steele were in Oban last night."

"Right. Magus Dubh remembered a woman who came into his shop to inquire about buyers for an artifact unearthed the day before Steele was killed. We though this woman might lead us to Steele's killer."

"Why the Irish bar?"

"Sir, you and I both know that a man of your intelligence already knows the answer to that one."

"Perhaps our thoughts differ."

"Steele was at Murphy's the night he was killed. He was interested in the artifact, and later, he ended up dead, close to the site where it was discovered." He left out the part about Sorcha's Black Spaniard. That would lead them down trails he would rather remain closed.

"Did you discover the identity of this woman?"

Estrada shook his head, then took another sip of water. "No, but she was there last night. I was following her when Roskilde attacked me." His throat ached almost as much as everything else. He needed Dubh's blood inside him, needed to heal enough to get out of this place and away from these people. He needed to find Rachel.

"And this Kai Roskilde...the man that assaulted you, and kidnapped Detective Erskine-Steele. How does he figure into this?"

"Just an asshole that hates me."

"Imagine that," said Cruickshank, sarcastically. He punctuated the close of his remark by sucking in his thin lips and releasing them with a pop. Estrada wanted to choke him with his checkered hat band. Instead, he winked. Cruickshank narrowed his eyes in response.

"I understand that Roskilde also works at the Kilmartin dig," said the Inspector. Estrada nodded. He was about to say that Kai didn't work there anymore because Sorcha fired him, but that would only generate more questions he did not want to answer. "Do you think he had anything to do with the theft of the artifact or Steele's death?"

Estrada shrugged. "Like I said, he's an asshole that hates me."

"You must have an opinion...suspicions."

"Since you're *in bed* with a police detective." Cruickshank grinned at his own bad joke.

Estrada ignored him. It was either that, or get into something he had no chance of winning. "Honestly Inspector, I don't know who's behind this, but if Kai Roskilde is Steele's killer, I'll be thrilled. For what he's done to Rachel, I hope you send him to prison for the rest of his life."

"Estrada, you've done nothing illegal. You're a victim in last night's debacle, and I encourage you to press charges. However, I must direct you to stay out of the investigation from here on in. You are *not* to go after Detective Erskine-Steele...not under any circumstances. You must leave the policing to us. Do you understand?"

Estrada nodded once.

"If you are contacted by Kai Roskilde or anyone else, you are to call me *immediately*." He took out his card and laid it on the table. "Otherwise, I will charge you with obstruction. We take abduction of our officers seriously. Be assured, we *will* find her and bring to justice *all* who are responsible."

"I hope so, sir."

"I've assigned Sergeant Cruickshank to guard you."

"You said, I wasn't under arrest."

"It's strictly for reasons of security."

Whose: his or theirs? Was this punishment for messing in things he was warned to stay out of? Estrada rolled his eyes. Police protection. Inspector Lyon was putting him under hospital arrest.

Cruickshank stroked his Taser. "My pleasure," he said, punctuating the finality of this statement with another one of his annoying pops.

Business concluded, Lyon nodded and left. Estrada knew his answers meant nothing to the man. This disingenuous interview was orchestrated to feel him out and warn him politely to mind his own business. It was something he had no intention of doing and they both knew it. Still he'd done his duty. Cruickshank was his guard dog…a dog he now needed to distract, so he could get that fey blood percolating in his system. He was still reflecting on this when Dubh walked back into the room.

Estrada's mind was inordinately fuzzy, a lingering effect of surgery, no doubt. He was plagued by fragments of last night's fiasco: Sorcha's rage, Dubh's mysterious woman, Kai's brass knuckles, his knife at Rachel's throat, her pale swanlike neck stained red with blood, her head crashing against the metal van. God, what had he done to her? What was he doing even now? And why? Was all of this just to get alone with him, so he could vent his insane jealousy? Or was there more to it?

"Sorcha just called," said Dubh. "She sends her love."

Cruickshank snorted and continued to hover by the door.

"Shouldn't you be standing on guard outside the door?" asked Estrada.

The cop sent him a scathing look and hunkered down in a chair just to piss him off.

"Sorcha says the Harley's safe," continued Dubh. "She rode it home last night, but she'll be along with it later—not that you're in any shape to ride."

"That could be remedied," Estrada murmured. The threads of a plan to distract Cruickshank were drawing together in his muddled mind. If his thoughts still ran through Dubh's mind, they just might pull it off. "I'm curious about something Dubh."

"What's that, Estrada?"

The comment intrigued the sergeant, who sat up straighter in his chair and tilted his head like a sheepdog. Stealth was not his forte.

"I'm curious why you came here with *me* last night when you could have gone back to Kilmartin Glen and spent the night with Sorcha." He winked. "I know how you like cuddling with your Irish queen."

"I do at that, but we Picts take our debts seriously, as I mentioned before."

"Is that the *only* reason?" Catching his glance, Estrada batted his eyelids flirtatiously. Picking up on it immediately, Dubh closed in on the bed.

"Ah, now you've found me out, I must confess." Laying his hand along Estrada's cheek, he brushed his lips with the edge of his thumb. "Sorcha was jealous of Rachel, but not nearly as jealous as myself. You are tantalizing, my sweet. Even when broken."

"Ah Jesus," scoffed Cruickshank. "Jobby jabbers. You make me sick."

"That sounds offensive, officer. Don't you have to undergo some kind of sensitivity training in Scotland?"

"Aye, but homosexuality is still disparaged by some Scots; men in particular. It was a criminal offence until 1980," stated Dubh. "They didn't pass a bill to outlaw gay discrimination until 2009, and we've only just allowed same sex marriage."

"Seriously?"

"Oh aye. Trust me. I know a wee bit about discrimination."

"I imagine you would. Perhaps, the sergeant here could use some sensitizing." Estrada patted the space beside him, and a second later, Dubh climbed on the bed and cuddled against his chest. "I have to admit; I've never been with anyone quite so—"

"Small?"

"I was going to say blue. I know that small is inaccurate. Sorcha told me about the mighty dragon."

"He's rather shy, but emerges on special occasions. You two should meet." Lifting his worn leather kilt, Dubh revealed his blue-scaled cock. "Spits molten fire, does the mighty dragon."

"Incredible? How painful was that?"

"Ah Jeez. Put that away," growled Cruickshank, his cheeks pulsing through his flush. "Don't be doing that in here!"

"Considering that this is *my* room, and homosexuality is no longer a criminal offence, we can do whatever we like in here. If you're offended by it, sergeant, I suggest you step outside." Estrada turned to Dubh. "I think he's a peeper, don't you?"

"Oh, aye. Likely watches gay porn with his hand on his Taser."

Cruickshank wavered for a moment, caught between disgust and duty. "This is a public place," he stated at last. "Ah, but you're not worth it." Then, shaking his head, he stepped outside the door and shut it.

"I wonder what he'd do if he saw what we're about to do now?" asked Dubh, and producing a pocketknife, he deftly slit a small vein in his wrist. "Stop when I say, and don't spill a drop."

Holding the wee man's blue-etched wrist to his mouth, Estrada took a deep breath and swallowed the precious faerie blood.

CHAPTER FOURTEEN

Monster, Monster

FOR THE PAST THREE HOURS, MICHAEL HAD DRIVEN from the flybridge atop the yacht. His eyes adjusted quickly to steering by moon and stars, after turning off everything that might betray his, not so stealthy, exit from the island. His plan was to find a city with an airport. He'd left his wallet aboard the sailing yacht, but he could call Nigel collect, get him to wire money, and book him a flight back to Vancouver. He travelled slowly, watching the compass and the shoreline, while fighting to stay alert to hazards. The quiet sough of the propeller was soothing, and combined with distance and the churning sea, drowned out Christophe's moans.

He was still contemplating the disposal of his lover. He did not relish complicating the situation, so murder was out of the question. Abandonment was not. Christophe's intentions may have been pure, but Michael felt deeply betrayed. This journey up the strait was no *ultimate gift*. Christophe intended him never to return; at least, not as the man he once was. And, wasn't that tantamount to murder?

Somehow, Michael had steered through the tangle of islands in the sound, and fought the westerlies through the passage into Johnstone Strait. When they'd sailed in, he'd been drunk and fighting with Christophe, begging to go home; yet, there were flashes of things he remembered: a village ruin; a logging operation; a rustic lodge; things once seen, he knew he'd passed before.

A *phoof* of exhaled breath roused him from his stupor. He turned as an enormous pod of orcas surfaced on his starboard side; their jagged white markings reflecting in the scant moonlight. Killer whales. Travelling west up the strait, they must be hunting salmon caught in the flood tide. He steered in a meandering sort of way, carried along by the tide like the salmon, skirting bouncing whales, and buoys that alerted him to the presence of submerged rocks.

An impenetrable wall of evergreens swathed the land on both sides, and behind him, in the northwest, massive roiling clouds obliterated the stars. Mountains loomed to the north, feeding a fear that he could follow the shoreline to the end of a blind inlet, break a prop, or hit a reef, and end up marooned.

He stared at the compass. He must continue sailing east, follow the strait and find the lighthouse on the point. From there, he could make his way to the more populated south coast. It had taken the better part of the day to travel from their last mooring to Le Chateau de Vampire, so the lighthouse was hours off. Still, he had a plan.

Michael shook his head and lit a cigarette. He'd been a fool. Just before they'd arrived, Christophe, the bastard, had the boys anchor in some bay, long enough to ply him with champagne, oysters, and sex…long enough to convince him that this really was the *ultimate gift*. He wanted him calm and receptive. Christophe's allegiance was to Diego, whoever or whatever *he* was, and he wanted no fights or scenes, nothing to mar his big surprise.

Huddled in the chair, Michael fumed. He'd never felt so cold and alone. Even after ransacking the cabins and appropriating a long-sleeved white T-shirt, he couldn't get the chill out of his bones. He checked the time—3:47 a.m. The witching hour, when the world folds in on itself. Anyone still conscious is either only aware of immediate concerns or mired in an introspective stupor. Even night creatures like himself. Dawn was imminent, though daylight would take some time to reach him as it was blocked by mountains. Still, with the sunrise, his greatest fear—that Diego would swoop down from the sky and snatch him up in taloned claws—might dissipate.

If the stories were true…

Captivated by the moon-slick sea, Michael's mind drifted back through time to a summer sixteen years ago. Though just a boy, that summer he'd driven a yacht like this one, but twice the size. He was grateful now that his grandfather had sent him away for several weeks to work aboard his godfather's yacht near Baja, California; though he'd never told Nigel, or anyone else, what happened out there.

Victor Carvello owned several nightclubs in California, a mediocre hotel in Vegas, and *The Deception,* a 120-foot yacht that exuded swank. No one ever boarded with someone they knew, unless it was the partner of someone they knew too well. In this floating circus of chicanery, strangers signed a pre-boarding contract that forbade them—under threat of death—from ever divulging anything about the experience. Carvello could back the threat, and had. Michael had once seen photographs. He boarded *The Deception* an innocent boy—not quite thirteen—and disembarked having experienced every possible decadence.

Carvello came for him that first night, took him to his cabin, and showed him what some men crave and will sell their souls to possess. And Michael learned what Carvello already knew: he was naturally gifted in the art of sensual pleasure. The boy wanted it all, and they all wanted the boy. He played no favourites—except for Carvello, of course—and he was no whore. He never took money, other than his crew wages, though tokens often appeared in his cabin after a stopover in port: chocolate, a fine bottle of wine or some exotic liqueur, a pair of butter soft leather boots or jacket, silky shirts and cashmere sweaters, designer jeans, and once an emerald the size of his thumbnail, that was said to match his eyes. Grown up gifts for a grown-up boy. Carvello called him *Peter Fucking Pan.* While his friends back home were playing video games, Michael was playing sex games, and winning. He became a chameleon, using what he learned to his advantage; just as he now used the knowledge of how to navigate and pilot a yacht.

After lighting another cigarette, he blew smoke at the cursed moon. Too bad Carvello wasn't here. He'd know what to do with his sweet French ex. He lingered over the last few puffs of Turkish tobacco, then finally tossed it overboard. *Coffee.* That's what he needed.

When he cut the engine, his ears rang with the silence. Quietly, he descended the stairs, and then just at the foot, he stopped. *Voices.* Christophe, the little bastard, was talking to someone, and that someone was talking back. *Diego.*

~~~

After several hours in solitary, the guards opened Dylan's cell, shackled his wrists, and led him down the hall. He did not know if it was day or night. He'd slept fitfully, silently crying out in vain for Estrada, even sending his spirit home to Tarbert. But the man was not there. Leastways, he couldn't rouse him. Couldn't rouse a soul. When the guards stopped in front of Big Zeke's cell, Dylan's lip trembled. It was over. He was being offered up to the devil.

~~~

Estrada's eyes were closed, but even before she spoke, he knew she was there. He could smell her. The feral scent of leather and sweat, damp earth and denim, the mint in her cheek, the green apples in her fiery hair, and something else: coffee and whiskey. He grinned, and her heartbeat quickened. Sorcha O'Hallorhan was ovulating and horny. *Well, well Dubh*. He laughed aloud.

"How's your Scottish sojourn been so far, man? Let's see. You've fallen in love with a copper who's been kidnapped; beaten a man near senseless; been beaten near senseless yourself; been punched, cut, and shot. Himself is still in the slammer, and you're no closer to solving the mystery of who murdered the cunt." Sorcha had the mouth of a whore and Estrada adored her. He opened his eyes, recalling the first time they'd met in the cemetery at Kilmartin Glen, when he'd touched her nipple and called her bluff.

When she slipped off her short leather jacket, her ivory skin shimmered with sweat. Her white tank was split almost to the buckle of her jeans.

"Must be hot out."

"Global fuckin' warming." Leaning over, she kissed him on the lips, opening her mouth, inviting him in. He accepted, sucked the mint off her tongue, and felt a stir. He was feeling infinitely better. She smiled. "I'm sorry, Estrada. I really am. Forgive me for being such a bitch."

"We're good," he said.

"I brought you an Irish coffee, made as my gran would have done. If it won't heal you, it will at least distract you."

"I must confess. Dubh had a go at me already and it's worked like a charm. Thanks for this," he said, accepting the coffee. "Did you make it with that Connemara peat?"

"Peat's what we burn in our fires, but you're close. It's the least I can do, since your entanglements with me have brought this misery down upon you. So, what's the craic?"

"Is that dick still outside the door?"

"Aye. Ginger-haired goon. Buff, but not lovely like you." Cruickshank was wiry and dark. They must have changed shifts. The news gave him some relief.

"There's something I need you to do, Sorcha."

"Name it, and it's yours."

"Go to Greenock Prison and see Dylan. I mean *see* him. I had a terrible dream earlier. I feel like he was trying to connect with me when I was unconscious. I think he's in trouble."

"You think he's been scrappin'?"

"Not willingly. And if someone's been *at him*—you'll be able to tell—go talk to the guards. Demand to see the warden if need be. He'd never tell them himself."

"Holy God. It was me that got him in there, and you in here. I'm worse than a fucking hex."

He shook his head. "No, you're not."

"Well, I'm here to make amends. I'll go tomorrow, and use my feminine wiles to get in and see your man."

"Remember that he loves you, Sorcha—and remember that you're not supposed to know."

"Aye sure. I'll be kind, and I won't let on. Anything else I can do for you while you're lying there in bed looking so helpless and alone?"

One thing he could say for Sorcha—she never gave up trying. "Yeah. Unwrap the dressing on my leg. I want to see how it's healing. Dubh gave me some of his magic juice, and I'm feeling mighty spry for someone who just took a bullet in the leg."

"Ah, jeez, Estrada. I'm sorry Kai's such an arse." He watched as she lifted the sheet and carefully removed the gauze. The skin, though pinkish, was almost healed. "That's amazing."

"Yeah, but how am I going to explain it?"

"Miracle? Holy Spirit? Perhaps, the Blessed Virgin Herself?"

"Or maybe, it would be best if I left now, before the nurse comes to change the dressing and Cruickshank returns."

"Cruickshank?"

"Yeah, you wouldn't much like him." He shook his head. "It's time this magician pulled a vanishing act."

"Are you feeling that good?"

"Good enough to sit on the back of a Harley."

While Sorcha worked her magic on the ginger cop, Estrada dressed, and then wrapped himself up in a blanket. She packed him into a wheelchair, and they started off down the corridor. Two nurses smiled as they passed by.

"What did you tell the cop?" he asked.

She pulled a card from the pocket of her jeans and flashed it before his eyes. "I promised to have you back in ten," she said, "and join him for coffee in fifteen."

Estrada laughed. "Vixen."

She continued to push him casually around the hallways until it seemed no one was paying them any attention, then slipped right out the door. It was late afternoon and he shielded his eyes from the bright July sunshine.

They'd almost reached the bike when Kelly Mackeras sauntered out of the parking lot. They saw him right about the same time he saw them, so there was no avoiding a conversation. He was flustered and embarrassed. His shaggy hair needed washing and dark smudges ringed his bloodshot eyes. The hollows of his cheeks had deepened as if he'd been starving himself. Still he was pretty, his blue eyes as intense as a summer sky.

Estrada wanted to hold him, to brighten the dreary slate clouds that shrouded his heart. He liked Kelly. He liked him a lot, and he pitied him. Kelly was trapped in a world that didn't understand him, didn't even try.

When all of this was over, he'd invite him to Vancouver, introduce him to Michael, and let nature take its course. Michael sought pleasure, but like himself, valued freedom above all else. He'd sort Kelly out in no time at all.

"Kelly, hey. What's the craic?"

"Sorcha. I didn't think I'd run into you here. Is that? Estrada, is that you?"

"Yeah man."

"He got into a scrap with Kai on Thursday night at Murphy's," explained Sorcha.

"Really?" He paused for a moment as if imagining the fight. "I'd like to have seen that. What does Kai look like? Worse, I hope, than you?"

"Afraid not. The bastard got the jump on me with a pair of brass knuckles and a gun."

"Gob-shite. If anyone deserves an arse-kicking, it's Kai."

"Well, Thursday night was payback for what I did to him last week." His lip curled into a half-smile.

"So, what brings you here, Kelly? Everything alright?" asked Sorcha. After seeing the sickly vibes streaming off him, Estrada hoped to avoid the question entirely. Leave it to her.

"It's my mum. She's taken a bad turn. The doctors admitted her yesterday into palliative."

"Sorry man."

"I'm staying here in Oban until..."

"If there's anything we can do, you'll call, yeah?" said Sorcha.

"Same goes for me. Call anytime. I've got Dylan's phone."

"Dylan," he mumbled, his voice breaking.

"I'm going to see him tomorrow," said Sorcha.

"Well, I should go back. The doctors say it's just days, maybe even hours. If I wasn't there…"

Kelly had one of the saddest smiles Estrada had ever seen. "Listen man, I'll see you back in Tarbert." He didn't want to talk about Rachel or what he was about to do. The kid had enough to worry about.

"Sure. Come for tea again." He smiled. "Wait—take this, Estrada." He reached into his pocket and pulled out a key. "Leave it under a flowerpot outside and use the flat whenever you like. You can even stay there. The net's working and my laptop's there. You should use it."

"Are you sure?"

"Aye, of course."

When Kelly turned to go, Estrada couldn't stop himself. He got out of the wheelchair, spun him around, and hugged him. Kelly rested his head on his shoulder, and sighed. Estrada could feel the beating of his heart through his breast, the quiet sough of his quivering breath against his neck. His hair smelled of whiskey and cigarettes. He was tired. Exhausted from weeks of caring for an ailing parent. Estrada stroked his hair, and when Kelly glanced up, he kissed him. His lips were soft and full, his mouth open and welcoming, the kiss lingering and affectionate.

"We'll talk in a few days, okay?"

Tears glazed his eyes as Kelly nodded. Then, he turned and walked on.

As they mounted the Harley, Sorcha whispered, "So, Kelly's gay, is he?"

"Gay. Straight. What does it fucking matter? Kelly needed that. We both needed that." He cleared his throat, and spit.

~~~

"Alright wee man?" Big Zeke had been staring at Dylan across the cell for several moments, and finally spoken, his voice as harsh as a bear after hibernation. "Heard ya play the pipes."

Dylan swallowed, and prepared to defend himself against whatever was coming. "Is that what you call it? Well, I don't—"

"Aye, you do. *Heard* ya...in Glasgow."

"In Glasgow?" Just how far did these sick rumours travel?

"Half dozen years back at the World Pipe Championships. You was just a kid. Competed against my brother, Jer. You won fair and square."

Dylan sat back on his heels. He hadn't thought of that day in ages. After living with his grandad in Tarbert for two years and playing the bagpipes for hours every day, he'd entered the competition and placed first. He was fourteen.

"Oh. The bagpipes." He took a long deep breath. "Your brother plays the bagpipes." A month ago, if a man had asked Dylan if he played the pipes, he would have known exactly what he meant. Strange, how fear could wipe a man's mind of all the saner thoughts.

The big man's muted weeping filled the small confined space and sparked a shiver. Dylan glanced at the floor, and waited.

"Played," he muttered at last.

"Oh. I'm sorry."

"That's why I'm here."

Not knowing how to respond, Dylan stared at the floor gobsmacked. Was Zeke in prison for killing his brother? Not a muscle moved in that grim chiselled face, and then one tear rolled down his cheek. Zeke wiped it away with the back of his fist. "You could be twins, and he was *like* you too." Dylan cocked his head, not understanding what he meant. "G A Y." He spelled it out.

"But, I'm not—"

"Listen, laddie. I don't care if you are, or you aren't. All I know is that you remind me of Jer, and he was killed for it." Gay bashing? Dylan had read plenty of news stories about gay bashing in the UK. Bullies everywhere concocted their own excuses. "So, that weasel is not touching you, McBride, unless... Unless it's what you want."

Dylan stared in disbelief and then shook his head. "It's not. I hate Wiley, and I'm not gay. It's not what I want at all."

"I couldn't protect Jer, but I *can* protect you."

"I don't know what to say."

"Say what ya want done with Wiley. Weasel tried to fuck with you. Someone should fuck with him. Guards are saying ya beat him. You're a fucking hero, laddie."

"Hero?" Suddenly the fear was gone, and with it, Dylan could think clearly again. "Wiley's just trying to survive, like the rest of us."

"Well, you're bunked in here with me now." He gestured to the empty upper bunk and Dylan raised his eyebrows. "No one will fuck with ya. No one fucks with me." Zeke's deep belly laugh broke the pressure in the room. "Hah. They'll think you're my bitch, when really you'll be my new wee brother."

Dylan smiled for the first time in weeks. He wished he could remember Jerry from all the pipers that competed at that championship years ago; wished he could say something wonderful about him; wished Jerry would have won that day instead of him. Dylan had his own thoughts on homosexuality. It wasn't his thing, but no one deserved to be harassed, beaten, or killed because of their sexual preferences or identity. He thought about the boys that used to assault him; and then about Estrada, his liberal lifestyle, and his advice.

"I'm sorry about your brother," he said, at last.

"Aye." Zeke sniffed, and rubbed his eyes with giant crusty mitts. "If we really were the prophets mum named us for, we'd have known. We could have stopped it."

"Prophets?"

"Ezekiel and Jeremiah."

"Aye, of course."

"If I'd known…" His voice drifted off, and Dylan didn't ask.

Now, for the first time in many days, he felt so relieved, he was overcome with the need to sleep.

~~~

How had Diego made it to the yacht undetected? Michael braced to turn, but before he had the chance, the vampire approached. He stood staring, astonished by what he saw. Dressed in a black cassock with red satin buttons, the vampire's bare feet floated several inches above the floor.

"You wonder why I wear the vestments of the Catholic church," he said, as if reading Michael's mind. He shrugged. "Comfort." His head sank to the right and one eye narrowed. "I took it from an English bishop, who condemned me to Hell right before I drained him of his life's blood." Smirking, he shook his head. "I never liked the English." His dark hair blew back from his face, and he pursed his lips. "Unfortunately, I overindulged and spilled. It left a small stain, right here. You see?"

Michael glanced at the red piping that trimmed the black cape falling from Diego's shoulders. He crossed his trembling hands across his chest. Couldn't swallow…couldn't breathe. A razor-edged fingernail caught the cleft of his chin and forced him to confront that mesmerizing gaze. Rancid breath, sallow skin, and eyes like smouldering coal.

"Be calm," he said. "It's not your time…not yet." He ran a fingernail through Michael's messy hair. "First, I must know *why*, Mandragora? Christophe never falls in love. I would have chosen you, if only for him."

"I don't want to be your *chosen* one." He whimpered, and hated himself for it.

"*That* is a lie. To be vampire excites you beyond any pornography you might conjure in that lurid mind of yours. For years, you have impersonated us, lived the romance. You taste the blood and dream. Yet now, when offered the chance to live your fantasy, you cower and run like a frightened girl, steal a yacht, *my* yacht, and assault my—"

"Pimp?"

"Agent…procurer." The clawed finger trailed down Michael's neck and chest, tracing blood rich veins, and came to rest upon his throbbing heart. Leaning in, Diego inhaled sharply, and the rasping air caught in his throat. Then, lifting the edge of his thin lip, he exposed a fang.

"He kindles my thirst, Christophe. The flesh smells French. Château Margaux. Is this what draws you to him?"

Michael had forgotten his lover. He emerged from the shadow of the cabin, dressed in a pair of skinny black tights that clung to his pelvis. His hair had dried as he slept, and hung straight and black, covering his ribcage. But his face was stained with tears, one side swollen and bruised from the bottle.

"I do not know why I love him, Padrino."

"Even *now* you love him? After his abuse, his insults?"

"Oui. Mandragora is my world." Michael trembled. When had his lover's fascination become an obsession? They'd only been seeing each other a few weeks.

"What would you have me do, Christophe?"

Michael stood staring; unable to speak, though words raged in his brain. Diego was preparing to bite him, perhaps drain him. If Christophe loved him, could he persuade the vampire to let him go unharmed? It was the only way out.

"Christophe, please," he whispered at last. "You know I love you. I just…I just—"

"I just…I just," mocked Diego. "Say what you mean, Mandragora. You want to be vampire, but on your own terms. What you cannot abide is losing control."

"No man should decide another man's fate," he said.

"There you see Christophe? It is neither you, nor vampire, that Mandragora spurns. He simply feels he was not given a choice. He worries that he is no longer in control of his destiny. Like other insolent children of his era, he must decide for himself, and if he cannot, he will have none of it. Such arrogant volatility is dangerous. Do you really want such a creature?"

"Christophe…please—" The slap hit his face like lightning, and spun him across the cabin. Crashing into a table, he fell to the floor.

"Enough theatrics. I grow weary."

But the hand that caught his arm and helped him rise was tender. Leaning against Christophe's shoulder, the coppery taste of his own blood filled his mouth. He watched Diego disappear into the cabin.

"Please help me," Michael whispered. "I'm sorry. I shouldn't have hit you and tied you up. I was just so angry and scared."

"I forgive you, chéri." Christophe kissed him gently on the lips. "This is the first time I have tasted your blood. Now we have sipped of each other."

Diego reappeared carrying a slim red oak coffin by its two brass handles. He set it down before the men. On the lid, a gold plate was engraved with a blossoming rose. In its centre, was a calligraphic *D*.

Michael's breath caught in his chest.

"It is almost sunrise," Diego stated. "It is time."

Michael exhaled. If Diego feared the sun he must retire to the coffin as the legends claimed. Surely, Christophe would choose him over this monster. And, when he slept, what couldn't he and his lover do to Diego? *A wooden stake? Fire?* He tried to remember all the ways to destroy a vampire.

"Christophe, you have served me faithfully. For your fidelity, I give you this *man*." He said the word with a twist of contempt. "Tonight you shall be joined."

"Oh, Padrino." Falling prostrate before the vampire, Christophe clasped his hand and kissed it.

Michael glowered. *Given? Joined? What new threat was this?*

"As you see by the insignia, this coffin belongs to my family. When my sons travel, they must rest by day, and so we store them on board. Now, Mandragora, you will experience another aspect of vampire. When Diego lifted the lid, Michael stared at the shimmering scarlet satin that lined the coffin. "Lie down."

"What? You want me to—"

"Lie down in the coffin. Am I so difficult to understand? You will rest. I, too, will rest. Christophe will pilot the yacht back to my palacio, and tonight we three shall meet again for the joining."

"Joining? What do you—?" But before he could say another word, the vampire scooped him up and flung him on his back in the coffin. The lid clamped down, and Michael could hear nothing save his own cries ringing in his ears. Pounding his fists against the lid, he begged and pleaded, but to no avail. The coffin lid stayed shut.

~~~

Christophe watched as Don Diego padlocked Mandragora's coffin and slipped the key into his inner suit pocket. "I will keep the key, so your obsession with this man does not cloud your judgment."

"Oui, Padrino."

Christophe hunched over and held his aching gut. He never intended for any of this to happen. His plan had been simple and perfect. Take Mandragora to the island, where Don Diego would choose him as his next son. He had confessed his love already to his patron and assurances had been made. Mandragora would be thrilled to live out his fantasy, and Christophe would become his personal blood doll, supplying his lover with all the pleasure he could ever desire.

Mandragora's melancholy would disappear, and once he lived in the palacio, he would forget this *Estrada* ever existed.

Never once did Christophe consider that Mandragora would refuse this coveted gift or steal his padrino's yacht. Though once he had, Christophe knew that Don Diego would come after him. Offended and dishonoured, he would pursue Mandragora until appeased. The vampire stood beside him now pointing to the sky. Dawn was mere minutes away, yet dense grey clouds obscured the heavens like a thick churning blanket.

"A storm threatens," he said. "Come inside. The yacht drifts in the flood."

Glancing up, Christophe noticed the moon had disappeared. He shivered, remembering how once, centuries ago, Don Diego had lost his only son to a storm at sea.

"You must not fear the storm, Christophe."

"But, I have never driven the yacht...and alone...and in a storm."

"Follow the coastline north. Keep as close to shore as possible. You look pale. If the storm breaks, unleash the anchor, and steer the bow into the wind. You will learn because you must. You will pilot the ship because you must. There is no one else."

Christophe glanced at the dark red coffin. "But, I'm frightened, Padrino."

"You must be brave, Christophe." A cold hand caressed his shoulder. "Tonight, I honour you."

"You honour *me*? Do you mean—?"

"Why do you look so shocked? Do you not believe yourself worthy of being the next Salvador?"

"But, you *never* choose me."

"Because I am greedy. The young men you bring to me are always perfect."

"And, I am not."

"You are wrong, my son. You surpass perfection. Both exquisite, and the best procurer I have known in two centuries. The others do not have your talents. Still, tonight I will reward your devotion. You are my son, and you will become my Salvador."

"Oh, Padrino."

"As for your lover," he said, pointing to the coffin. "I leave it to you to decide his fate. You may turn him. Or, you may keep him as a human captive; a blood slave to quench your desires. Mandragora is my gift to you. But now, I must depart, for though we cannot see the sun, I feel the tingling of its rays upon my skin."

Christophe stood on the deck, hair flying like Medusa's snakes in the burgeoning wind. First rain, and then hail, erupted from the black sky, decreasing visibility, and increasing his anxiety. He'd come outside to see just how close he was to the shoreline. Very close. Too close. On his way back, he passed the red oak coffin that imprisoned Mandragora.

Gripping the controls, he tried to manoeuvre the yacht away from the shoreline and into the oncoming wind. The problem was that the westerlies kept blowing it into shore, and he was driving so slowly the yacht could gain no momentum. Yet, he was afraid to drive any faster. Perhaps, he should stop and let down the anchor? The roaring of the wind and waves assaulted his ears. He trembled. Mandragora knew how to drive a yacht. If only Don Diego had not padlocked the coffin. A flash of lightning illuminated the vampire's coffin in the master cabin as if to say, *I know what you are thinking.* Could he perceive a man's thoughts even in his daily rest?

Suddenly the wind caught the yacht broadside. It lurched sideways and water surged over the deck. Christophe screamed. What to do? Was it dark enough in the cabin to open Don Diego's coffin and extract the key? Could he free Mandragora without hurting his Padrino? Liquor bottles hurtled from the bar smashing against walls and windows. Cupboards opened, casting out their contents, as glass and china shattered in the chaos. And then, the boat tilted.

Mandragora's coffin slid across the floor.

Running, clutching, Christophe sprawled across the red oak lid.

"I will get the key," he cried.

But getting there was impossible. The boat pitched so far sideways, he could only reach the cabin by grasping furniture and hauling his body up; and alas, Christophe had no upper body strength. When finally, he fought and won and hung against the doorway of the stateroom, he glanced back, only to see Mandragora's coffin afloat. The sliding door at the back of the yacht had come ajar and water gushed in. The posh salon was flooded.

When the realization struck him, he laughed at the absurdity of it. He was going to drown alone, while the two men he loved most in the world floated in sealed coffins.

After releasing the door frame, he staggered back across the salon through frigid seawater, and grasped the brass handles of Mandragora's coffin. Clinging to it with all his strength, his body trembled. The water was so cold, so deep. Laying his head against the wet wood, he heard the pounding fists, the terrified cries, but could do nothing.

"I will not leave you, chéri," he cried.

And then the boat flipped.

Everything was underwater. The will to live overcame his fear, and he swam and fought his way to the surface. He was so cold, so tired, fighting desperately to remain afloat in water that churned around him, when all he wanted was for it all to end. When a coffin hit him in the back, he used what little strength he had remaining to hoist himself on top and cling there; chest flat against the wood, heart slowing, numb fingers clutching the handles at either side, and drifting like so much flotsam and jetsam in the storm.

He would not leave his lover; would not abandon him to die alone.

It was an hour before Christophe realized that the coffin he clung to was black. Don Diego slept below him, not Mandragora. The man he loved was somewhere lost in the tempest. When the truth of this sunk into his heart, the young Frenchman bit through his lip until he tasted his own blood. And then, prying his stiff frozen fingers from the brass handles, he slid off the coffin and into the sea.

CHAPTER FIFTEEN

Pink Poppies

SUNDAY AFTERNOON. THREE DAYS AND NIGHTS had passed since Kai Roskilde kidnapped Rachel Erskine-Steele outside Murphy's Irish Bar, and Estrada had still not received a call. What game was the man playing? His words repeated over and over in his mind: The bitch is mine. You want her? Come and get her. That's if you can, and you still want what's left when I'm done. Rachel was a cop, but Roskilde was psychotic. He'd seen him bash her head against the door of that van. And, when you're dealing with insanity, as he'd learned last fall, sometimes you lose. The waiting was driving him mad.

He could have gone with Sorcha to Greenock, but he wanted Dylan to have some alone time with the woman he loved. He also wanted to give him time to mend from whatever had ensued. Estrada felt a sense of peace with him that he hadn't felt before, so he assumed the crisis had abated, at least for the moment. However, if he spent any time with Dylan, he'd know if he'd been raped, and Dylan would know that he knew, and that would devastate him. Having a secret shame is one thing; having it discovered is quite another. Let Sorcha go and distract him with her bawdy Irish charm. She owed him that, and for now at least, his friend deserved to dream.

He stretched out on the floor and obsessed about his beautiful white goddess. Determined that he would not allow another woman to die because a man was obsessed with *him*, Estrada attempted to call in divine guidance. If he could just focus, his spirit guides might show him where she was, or how she was; at least, proffer a clue. The one thing he knew was that she was still alive. Even though they'd only met a couple of weeks before, they'd bonded in the most intimate of ways. He could feel her energy, and like a candle flame, it flickered yet.

Roskilde was intensifying his sadistic game by making him wait. Of course, he did not know that Estrada was already healed. With the beating he'd inflicted, Kai would assume he'd be incapacitated for weeks, not days. He'd want his opponent weak, but healthy enough to break again. That's how bullies worked.

He closed his eyes and watched his breath. *Breathe in. Breathe out.* It was the simplest way to engage his mind. The technique, he'd learned years before from a Buddhist monk at a Vancouver temple. *Count each breath.* He'd put his own spin on it by adding visuals. *1 2 3.* He watched as gold numerical images formed on the black screen of his inner forehead. Shimmering. Calligraphic. *4 5 6.*

He switched to letters, using one for each breath in and out. *A B C.* He drew them in his mind, on blank vellum with a quill, imagining that he was some medieval monk, like those who penned the *Book of Kells. A B C. D D D.* He took a deep breath, concentrated, thought *E F G* and saw the letter *D.* Curling and glowing golden, it was surrounded by a rose.

When for seven successive breaths, nothing changed, he stood up, rubbed his eyes, and searched Dylan's desk for a piece of writing paper and a pencil. Sitting back down, he drew the vision from memory: a multi-petalled rose and in its centre a calligraphic *D.* This was a message, but what did it mean? Initial? Tattoo? Logo? *D,* but *D* for what?

He closed his eyes and the *D* reappeared; this time engraved on a gold metallic plate. He lifted the edges of the vision, zooming out to deepen and widen, but saw only a rich shade of vermillion beyond the gold borders. The sensation that enveloped him then, came not from Rachel or Dylan, but from Michael, and it chilled him like winter rain. Even in the July heat, he shivered. Michael was imprisoned somewhere so dark; he could see only the outline of his supine form.

"Michael!" When he called his name, his head moved slightly, as if in response. And, then the vision vanished.

Grabbing the upstairs phone, he tapped in Michael's number. *Answer. Come on.* But, even as he listened to it ring and ring, he sensed the futility.

After lighting candles in a circle around the room, he laid back down, took several breaths, and begged his guides for help. Swiftly, his mind swept into a swirling vortex of crashing waves and floating debris. Breathing calmly in and out, he waited. And then, within the waves he discerned a golden plate. It was attached to the lid of a dark red wooden coffin. *Jesus Christ. A coffin? Was Michael inside?*

Estrada called Nigel, knowing it was Sunday morning in Vancouver. He'd be irritated, but he'd be home. Sunday was the one day he dedicated to his wife, starting with breakfast.

He answered on the third ring. "This better be good."

"Nigel. It's Estrada."

"Sandolino. Are you back?" He was at least pleased to hear his voice.

"No, and I won't be for a while yet. But where's Michael? Have you seen him? He's not answering his phone."

"It's strange you should call. I haven't seen Michael since Monday morning. He went sailing in the Gulf Islands with a friend. I expected him back by Friday morning, and frankly, I'm concerned. He didn't show up for work, and that's not like him."

"I think you should call the police and the Coast Guard. I think he's been kidnapped."

"Kidnapped? Has someone contacted you? How could you—?"

"Please, Nigel. Just trust me. I know this will sound weird, but I think that Michael is locked in a coffin; floating somewhere in the sea."

"That's insane? Floating in a coffin? Why would someone—?"

"I don't know. I didn't want to believe it myself, but now that you tell me he went sailing in the Gulf Islands and he's not back—"

"God damn it." He paused and took a deep breath to regain his composure. Nigel was not a man to emote. "We had a vicious storm here last night. Gale force winds…damn near a hurricane."

"Nigel, he needs us."

"I know you're involved in some strange things, Sandolino, but how can I tell the police something like this?"

"Tell them he called you. Make something up. Call in a favour. Michael is in trouble."

"I'll call Mowbray, and I'll call you back at this number, as soon as I hear something."

Seconds later, Dylan's cell phone rang. It was Sorcha.

"I thought you'd want to hear the craic. Angus ran into Kelly last night in Oban. His mom's passed on."

"Damn. How's he taking it?"

"No one's heard from him. Can you go by the house? Him giving you a key and all?" He was sure the "and all" referred to the kiss they'd shared in the parking lot.

"Yeah, sure. I'll do that."

"Grand, and listen. About what you said, back there at the hospital. I want you to know—I've been with my share of fellas *and* girls. I wasn't judging Kelly. I was just surprised. Christ, I don't even know the people I'm working with. I mean, I saw him, but I didn't really *see* him. You know what I'm saying?"

"Sure.

"It pisses me off, yeah?"

"I get it."

"Oh. I almost forgot. I've a message for you from Dylan. He said to tell you that the Oak King came through."

"Really?"

"Aye, and it wasn't just for my fucking benefit either. Dylan looked grand today."

"Grand?"

"Aye. Relaxed, happy even. I was almost after applying for a conjugal visit."

"Well, if you do, make sure you mean it."

"You're one to talk about meaning it."

"Later Sorcha."

"Cheers."

Estrada expected to see Sergeant Cruickshank hunkered down outside in his patrol car when he left the McBride's house. He'd come calling last night to see what he was up to, so he'd put on a limp and grimace, and explained that he hated hospitals. Still, the sergeant remained outside for several hours, waiting and watching. It appeared he'd given up the chase, at least temporarily. He supposed they too were itchy. Rachel was one of their own. Still, he kept up the limp as he walked to Kelly's flat, just in case Cruickshank appeared out of nowhere. Cops had their own brand of magic.

An old woman was cutting flowers in the garden when he arrived.

"Good day, lad. Name's Mary Rose. Can I help you?"

"I'm just here to see Kelly."

She pulled out a hanky and dabbed her eyes. "Ach, he could use a friend right now. The poor lad is cursed. I've been renting this flat to Ann and Kelly for years. I just can't believe she's gone." She wandered as she talked. "That poor lad's endured tragedy upon tragedy. First, his father disappears, and then Ann gets sick with the cancer, and now she's gone too."

She'd trapped him in an awkward conversation that he couldn't politely disengage from, as she didn't stop talking long enough for him to get a word in.

"Ach, did he ever tell you about his father? I suppose he doesn't like to talk about it. The poor lad never knew him. Ann was still carrying him when it happened."

He raised his eyebrows involuntarily and she took this as sign to explain.

"It was during one of those terrible wars. I can never get those countries straight. Alan and Ann had just married. Well, they had no money so he joined the army. The next thing you know he's been shipped off to Africa." She shook her head. "Never came back, and there was the poor wee thing widowed and with child."

"That *is* tragic."

"Oh aye. That was almost twenty years ago, but I remember it like it was yesterday." She cut another flower. "Even as a bairn, wee Kelly was special."

"Special?"

"Ah, you know, he dressed like a girl, and such. Ann indulged it. She always wanted a girl. Bought him wee pumps and dresses at the thrift shop. Ah, he was such a sweet child with his lovely big brown eyes. And those curls!" She smiled. "I volunteered at the shop some days, and that's when she would come, on the sly-like, so no one would know."

A picture appeared in Estrada's mind of a pretty boy in a wig and heels who cruised the local bars leaving no one the wiser.

"Of course, they knew. You know how it is in a small town." He followed her around to the other side of the flower bed. "Some were right gobsmacked by it—Ann carrying on like that, pretending he was a girl. Well, Kelly'd had enough of it by the time he went to high school—you'd not get away with a thing like that around here—and then he trotted off to Edinburgh to become an actor. Well, he was a natural. Hadn't he been acting his whole life?"

He certainly had. Estrada had to smile at the ludicrous explanation Mrs. Rose created to explain Kelly's preferences. Remembering why he'd come, he asked again. "Is Kelly home? Have you seen him?"

"Aye sure. Poor lad came home late last night. I don't think he slept well though. I heard noises far into the night; you know, pacing, and furniture being shoved about. I was going to knock on the door and say something, but then I thought, *Mary Rose, the lad's just lost his mum. You let him be.* Must have been looking through her things, rummaging through memories. He's been quiet as a church mouse today. Must be exhausted. Shall I let you in?"

He nodded. "That would be great." There was no point telling her that Kelly had given him a key. That would just be one more bit of gossip to add to the tragic tale of Kelly Mackeras. After she unlocked the door, she handed him the bouquet she'd been collecting as they talked, and he felt a twinge of guilt for branding her an old busybody, even if that's what she was.

"Kelly likes daisies. Helped me plant these when he was just a lad. And poppies. Oh, he just loves the deep pinks. Of course, poppies don't last once you cut them. No matter," she said, and after cutting several pink poppies, she added them to the daisies already gathered. "Take these upstairs now, and tell him, if there's anything he needs Mrs. Rose is right downstairs."

"I'm sure he'll appreciate that. Thank you for your help."

When Estrada's foot touched the bottom step, his flesh broke out in shivers and his throat went dry. Something was wrong. With each creak of each step the sensations deepened. At the top of the stairs, he stood on the landing, faced the door, and touched the doorknob. He turned it slightly, and then stopped. Perhaps Kelly was asleep, and it was just unfathomable grief that weighed him down. He knocked and waited.

"Kelly," he called out, and knocked again. When there was still no answer, he turned the knob, and pushed open the door.

Jesus. Kelly. Hanging from a beam in the front room…tongue, swelled and purple, jutting from a face as pale as a lily…a noose wound tightly around his neck.

Estrada dropped the flowers and ran, righted the wooden chair, and stood on it. Lifting Kelly, he hugged his cold stiff body. Knew it was too late. Clung to him, unable to let go. His throat was aching with words unsaid, his nose streaming, the snot dampening Kelly's shirt.

Why? I know it's hard, but why? Your grief would have passed. You could have left this town, gone back to Edinburgh, gone anywhere in the world. Gone to a place where you could be yourself without hiding and live your life without fear. Jesus Christ, Kelly. You could have come to Vancouver with me. You could have been free.

After a while the rant ended. The shell that had held Kelly was empty and lifeless. He shivered to hold it. The boy was gone. He climbed down from the chair and took out his phone. He must call someone. But who? Sorcha. Sorcha would know.

She answered on the second ring, almost as if she'd been waiting. "What's wrong, Estrada?"

"It's Kelly. He's…"

"He's what? Say it, man."

"Dead. Hanging in the flat."

"Holy God. Are you there now? Have you called 999?"

"I'm here. I don't know who to call."

"I'll call. Have you checked his pulse? Are you sure?"

"He's gone. He's pale and cold and stiff and— Christ, he's been here a while, Sorcha."

"Right so. Just wait there. And don't touch a fucking thing."

"I can't leave him hanging here like this."

"Oh aye, you can. Go wait outside if you must. But, do *not* cut him down. They'll want to investigate."

"Sorcha, he looks so—"

"Estrada! Stop looking at him. Jesus Christ. Are you after having more trouble? Let the police handle it. Promise me you will not touch a thing!"

He turned his face away, closed his eyes, and took a deep breath. "You come too, eh?"

"Aye, I'm coming. Just wait there and—"

"I know. I know."

He ended the call and glanced around the room, looking at anything but the lifeless body dangling from the beam. And that's when he saw it. On the coffee table—where they'd sat and drank a cup of tea together only last week—an envelope with *his* name on it. He felt the key in his pocket and knew that Kelly planned this. He'd given *him* the key so *he* would be the one to find him. But, why?

Estrada sat down on the couch, picked up the envelope, and slid it open. He pulled out the letter. It was handwritten on plain white paper with a gel tip pen. The ink was smudged in several places.

Dear Estrada,

I'm sorry you found me like this, but when you read this letter you will understand. This morning I realized we were kindred spirits, and they are few in this world. More than a friend to me, you are a friend to Dylan. You must give this letter to the police, for it is my confession and Dylan's ticket to freedom. You might ask why I've waited so long and the answer is simple. I'm a selfish prick. I couldn't put mum through any more shame in this town. She protected me from the time I was born. It was my turn to protect her. But now she's gone and I can tell the truth.

I killed Alastair Steele.

What? Kelly killed Steele?

On Friday, June 30, I drove to Murphy's Irish Bar in Oban to meet up with Sorcha's team and celebrate her find. After Dylan went outside, I got my things from the car and changed, as I've done many times before. I've left everything I wore that night on my bed. The pink sweater in the plastic bag is stained with Steele's blood.

In Edinburgh, I started going out to bars dressed as a woman. I cannot tell you how good it felt to be myself in public. Once I returned to Tarbert to look after mum, things got tricky. Still I managed. Sometimes I even found men who didn't care what lurked beneath my skirt. By the time we got down to it, they were either drunk or wasted or willing to do anything to get it off. Many of them were thrilled by it too, though most wouldn't admit it.

Alastair Steele was not one of them. He was right keen on me as a woman, and wanted to know all about the Egyptian collar he'd heard about in the bar. I told him that I worked at the dig and could get my hands on it. Lord, that thrilled him. Thought he'd get it off and steal the artifact. So, we got in his van and started driving. He bragged about taking photos and a video of my boss sucking the bejesus out of some lad in the beer garden. When I saw them, and realized it was Dylan and Sorcha, I just thought, what an arsehole.

By the time we got to Dunchraigaig Cairn, Steele was so into me, I thought he wouldn't care. He kept saying he had a morbid fascination with cemeteries and dead things. It was his idea to crawl inside the tomb and do it there. So, we started up and Steele right away stuck his hand up my skirt. Well, he started cursing. Called me things I'd never heard before, described the horrible things he was going to do to me. I got scared. He ripped off my bra, yanked it so hard it cut clear across my back. And then he grabbed my balls. Said, he was going to get a knife and make me a girl. He spat on me. And then he said he was going to kill me, slow and painful-like because that's what fags deserved.

Sometimes it's just talk, but I heard the hate in his voice. He meant it. So, I reached out and grabbed a rock, and I hit him in the head as hard as I could. I just meant to knock him out, so I could get away, but he grabbed my throat and choked me. I hit him until he fell over and went quiet.

I never meant to kill him. You've got to believe me. Then I thought of Dylan and how those pictures would end up all over the Internet once his body was discovered, so I took the phone. I erased the photos and the video. His mobile is in the bag with my clothes.

Estrada stopped reading. Clearly, Kelly killed Steele in self-defence. The bastard had attacked and threatened to kill him. And what if he was transgender? Wouldn't his mother, of all people, have accepted that? She must have known. If he'd only said something. He looked at his body dangling from the rope. "Jesus, Kelly."

I'd just crawled out of the cairn and was heading towards the van when I heard a voice, and I knew that voice and despised it. Kai Roskilde. "Where do you think you're going? I saw you. I saw it all," he says. He grabbed my hair and my wig came off. Well, he laughed when he recognized me. Said he always knew I was a little fag and now I was a murdering little fag. Said he owned me. Said I'd do whatever he wanted from now on, and the first thing I was going to do was steal Sorcha's artifact and fence it for him. Said if I didn't, I was going to jail for murder. I couldn't refuse. It would have killed Mum, broke her heart. So, I said I'd do whatever he wanted.

I stole the collar from underneath Sorcha's cot. It was right where Kai said it would be. She was passed out and didn't hear a thing. Kai waited for me. We drove Steele's van back to Oban and left it near Murphy's. I got my car and drove us back to camp.

A few days later, he sent me to Glasgow to see that tattooed dwarf at The Blue Door and ask about buyers. I don't know where the collar is now, and I feel terrible for betraying Sorcha. Please tell her I'm sorry. I didn't have a choice.

When Dylan was arrested for Steele's murder, I didn't know what to do. I knew Mum was dying. I just couldn't tell the truth, not then. But now I have, and I beg forgiveness.

All my life I just wanted to be accepted for what I am, whatever that is, and you did that, Estrada. Thank you. I'm sorry you had to find me like this.

I ask the Crown to free Dylan McBride and make things right with him. He is innocent, the most innocent man I know. And I beg Dylan to forgive me for putting him through the hell that should have been my own. This is God's truth and I swear it on the Bible.
Kelvin Mackeras

Estrada folded the letter, slipped it back in the envelope, and dropped it on the table where he found it. Then, he considered a few things. Kelly might have hit Steele in the head with a rock to defend himself, but Kai Roskilde sat back and witnessed it; could have stopped it, and didn't. Instead, he blackmailed Kelly into stealing the collar. He wondered too, how much Kai had to do with framing Dylan for Steele's murder. In all his details, Kelly never mentioned stashing Dylan's bloody hanky. He suspected Roskilde was to blame for that, and if that was the case, he'd gone back to the cairn without Kelly to do it.

Kai Roskilde had Sorcha's Egyptian artifact stashed somewhere. And he had Rachel.

Estrada stood up and walked into the bedroom. There, on the white bedspread, was his wardrobe—dresses, wigs, shoes, lingerie, makeup—all neatly laid out on a garbage bag. And off to the side was a clear plastic freezer bag, inside of which was a cell phone and a bloodstained sweater—two pieces of evidence that would exonerate Dylan and free him from a life in prison.

He wandered over to the window and peered into the back garden. Mrs. Rose was gone, but someone else was there. A dark-haired woman, laughed and danced around the flower garden. He watched her pluck an armful of pink poppies and hold them out, and then, he shivered. Kelly stood in the middle of the garden. He took the poppies from his mother and tossed them high in the air. Then, laughing, they joined hands and danced in circles beneath the falling petals.

Once Estrada started sobbing he couldn't stop, not even when he heard sirens and the thud of police boots on the stairs.

CHAPTER SIXTEEN

Freedom

IRONICALLY, THOUGH MICHAEL STRYKER had played at being a vampire for several years at Club Pegasus, he did not believe in the existence of such creatures. Unlike Estrada, he was too practical for such romantic drivel. For him, vampire was an elaborate charade. As Michael, he was just a man, but as Mandragora, he was liberated, coveted, celebrated—a shadowy character who revelled in pleasure. Of course, he knew several eccentrics, like himself, who claimed to be sanguinarian because of their penchant for drinking blood. A nest of them, lived together in an East Vancouver basement, and frequented his club. It was there, he'd first seen bloodletting and tasting; tried it, and savoured it. Now, he mused, Christophe had been there too, lurking in the shadows, waiting and watching.

But, the undead—immortals who morphed from human to animal, who burned in sunlight and slept in coffins—in this, Michael could not believe. They were merely an erotic creature of myth and story. Even now. Especially now. For to believe in the existence of Don Diego, a Spaniard who'd sailed the Pacific with Quadra in the late 1700s, was to believe in his own imminent death, or something worse, eternal torment.

Still, it rattled him. How had Diego travelled unseen from the castle to the yacht? As much as he fought to deny it, as he laid locked in the coffin, Michael came to accept the truth.

When Diego had picked him up, as if he was a child, he'd seen the telltale canines, ocher-stained with age and blood in the reeking copper mouth, the flaring amber eyes, the pallid flesh. He'd seen it, and smelled it, and he knew. Diego was real. With acceptance, came a panic far greater than he'd felt when the lid closed over him, and it sent him into a paralytic stupor.

He laid shivering, wondering how he could escape what would surely be death, by one means or another. What had that vile creature said to Christophe? You decide? Surely, Christophe, who loved him desperately, would turn him into a vampire, rather than drain him dry in one orgasmic moment of exsanguination. Then what? As a vampire, would he lose all sense of morality? Become an evil murderer like Diego? Would he stalk Estrada one black night and bite him? Turn him into a monster too, so they could spend eternity driving each other mad like Louie and Lestat?

Despair descended like a linen sheath when he realized that Estrada was the only man he'd ever truly loved. There'd been an endless stream of lovers, but none of them ever mattered. Now his life was ending, and the last thing he'd said to the man he loved was something mean and petty. He'd thrown him out of his flat and refused to take his calls, and then he'd stopped calling. Now it was too late.

Wedged in his scarlet tomb, he imagined Estrada and remembered intimate moments, so rare he could count them on his fingers. Moments, when just the two of them made love, as if no one else existed. Crossing his hands on his chest, Michael felt the throbbing of his heart. He must cling to these fragments of humanity: this obsessive mind, this beating blood-soaked heart.

His intellect warned him to stay very still and ration the oxygen. It was black as soot. There were no air holes in this box. Somewhere, he'd read that a man buried alive in a coffin could live between one and two hours. What did the dead need with ventilation?

When the coffin shifted suddenly, his right shoulder crashed against the wood beneath the slick satin cover. Instinctively, he banged on the lid with the heel of his hand. "Christophe. You son of a bitch! Let me out!" And then, a shift back to the left, so fast his head hit. Wedging his arms and legs against the sides of the box, he tried to stop the jostling. What the hell was happening out there? He had to keep calm. The more excited a man became, the more oxygen he consumed and the faster he died. No. He would *not* die. They were just fucking with him, trying to scare him, punishing him for ruining their party. Christophe and that horrid creature. His head was throbbing. His neck a rigid rope of muscles. He needed a cigarette.

Sliding, Crashing. Battering. Bruising.

Suddenly the coffin was lifting and though the motion continued, it was different, cushioned somehow, the swaying still intense, but less aggressive. Chaos tossed his body against the side of the wooden box. His head pounded and nausea overtook him. Seasick. The coffin was floating. As the movement steadily worsened, he turned his head and puked. Then the box keeled over and down, thrusting all his weight against one end, wedging his head, and finally flipping several times.

Christ! The bastards had tossed him overboard.

"If I ever get out of here, I will kill you Christophe. I will slit your pretty throat."

~~~

It was late Sunday night before the cops released Estrada. DCI Lyon had been there with Cruickshank. It appeared, that anytime his name came up, this duo was summoned. They were thorough—he'd give them that. Had he said too much? Forgotten something key? He sat by the edge of the sea with the conversation playing over and over in his head.

Kelly worked at the Kilmartin Glen dig. He'd met him in the pharmacy in Tarbert two weeks ago, and Kelly had invited him home to use his computer because he knew he was a friend of Dylan's. Yesterday, he and Sorcha had run into him at the hospital and he'd told them his mother was dying. She'd called today, to say that his mom *had* died and asked Estrada to look in on him, which he did. Mrs. Rose, the landlady, had let him in. Everything was just as he'd found it, except that he'd opened and read the letter. His name was on it. Why was Kelly's suicide note addressed to him? Most likely because he knew that he was trying to find Steele's killer, so Dylan could go free. But, how did he know that Estrada would be the one to find him? He didn't, not for sure, but he'd invited him to come and use the computer again, so assumed he'd eventually appear. They'd taken the letter as evidence.

When Estrada returned to Piper's Dream, Dermot was waiting up, and they shared a bottle of scotch. Both men were overjoyed about Dylan's release, but also shocked and saddened by Kelly's suicide. Half-drunk and exhausted, he staggered upstairs to the shower.

Afterwards, when he scooped his jeans up off the floor, the key fell out of his pocket. He picked it up and held it in his hand. And, then the tears came. All Kelly wanted was the freedom to be himself, to fulfill his desires. Why must the cost be so high? Still clutching the key, he collapsed on the bed, and tried to erase the image from his mind.

He jumped, startled, when his cell phone rang, felt the surge of adrenalin through his body. It was well past midnight. He must have fallen asleep. When Rachel's number flashed across the screen, he bolted upright and answered.

"Rachel?"

"I just wanted to make sure you were still in the game, hero. Now that your boyfriend's getting out of jail."

Kai Roskilde. "Of course I am. But how do *you* know?"

"Blondie had her police radio in her purse." He coughed, then sniffed. "So, the little fag's confessed to murdering Steele." Kai was fishing. He wanted to know if Kelly had mentioned him in the confession. Estrada only cared about one thing.

"Let me talk to Rachel." He glanced at his trembling hand, was shaking from the inside out.

"She's busy. Let me put the phone down so you can hear—"

"Shut up, Kai. Put her on the phone." He heard her cry out as if he'd grabbed her.

"Estrada?"

"Rachel. Are you hurt?"

"Do what he says. Please." His mind flashed on the pain that crossed her face when Kai smashed it against the metal door.

"I love you, Rachel."

"I love you, Rachel," Kai mocked.

Estrada clenched his shaking fist around his rage. "Now what?"

"Now you wait."

"I've been waiting. Why—" The call ended. "You bastard."

What was Roskilde waiting for? Was it merely to torture him or did it involve the artifact? At least he knew one thing: Rachel was still alive.

~~~

Like a deadhead, Michael's red oak coffin careened through wave after wave, while all around him the tempest raged. The ungodly wail of the wind united with the continual driving rain on the wooden roof of his prison to create one deafening assault. And then some new horror amplified the cacophony: the cannon crash of surf against rock. He laid on his right side, wedged against the crimson satin, knees and chin drawn up to his chest, like some fetus in an ungodly womb; throat and gut aching from relentless vomiting.

Grasping the back of his neck to calm his throbbing head, he envisioned a mountain stream, a fountain, a backyard hose, a running tap, a tall glass of water, god, even a toilet. Dehydrated and suffering with oxygen deprivation, he licked his parched lips and wanted to die; and then, when he realized he *was* dying, wanted only to live.

The coffin had somehow righted itself in what he now realized was a storm, a hell of a storm. Percy Shelley's body washed ashore after his boat sank off the coast of Italy in a storm like this, and it was said that Byron could not look at his friend's decomposing body when they burned it on a beach pyre. Two years later, Byron himself died while a devilish storm raged over Greece. Had he thought of Shelley in those last few hours? Died broken-hearted? Too young. They were both too young. And he was too young.

How ironic that a fake vampire, a fraud, a pretender, should meet Death locked in a coffin. Still, it was prudent he should die alone this way. Had Don Diego or Christophe embraced him with a vampiric kiss, he would most surely have hunted Estrada and turned him too, because, honestly, he could not live in a world without him. He loved him and wanted more than anything to tell him so, to call him now and say with his last breath: I love *you* Estrada. I have always loved *you*."

But, without a phone, there would be no last words.

The first thrust came with such force he bit through his tongue and tasted blood—the vibration passing through his back teeth like a dentist's drill. Holding his breath, he waited as the coffin was drawn back by the waves, and then exhaled as it hurled forward again. A rhythmic crash of wood against rock. Understanding came in the next reprise. The coffin was caught in breakers. This was it, then. His body would be dashed on the rocks and wash up someday, somewhere, a pale bloated unrecognizable mass of beaten flesh.

With the third collision came the shriek of splintering wood. He batted his eyes to a narrow crack of light, rolled onto his back, braced himself, and waited.

The fourth slam widened the crack all the way to the hinges. With all his strength, he kicked at the lid with both feet—once, twice, three times, and then, success. The lid opened, and he raised his head just as the box hit the rocks for the fifth time. Icy water poured in. He turned and shifted to his knees with the outward ebb, pushed off the lid, and grasped the side.

A beach lay to the left. To the right was a wall of rock and crazy surf. Rain poured from the hoary sky overhead. Opening his mouth, he tasted and swallowed, sucking in its freshness, reviving his wilted flesh. Straightening, he stretched his cramped muscles.

And then the coffin launched forward again and slammed into the jagged rocks. He screamed, wrenched back his hand. *Stupid. Stupid.* The rock had shattered bone and flesh.

The coffin was breaking apart, the wood splintering. Another crash. He cradled his hand against his ribs. No time to wrap it. No time for anything. He had to jump into the sea and clear the surf, or it would catch him, and hurl him into the rocks, and his whole body would end up as mangled as his hand.

After sucking in one last deep breath, he jumped.

~~~

Wracked by conflicting emotions, Dylan perched on the edge of a bench. He was relieved to be going free, but at what cost? His lawyer had come first thing that morning with the news that Kelly Mackeras had written a letter confessing to the murder of Alastair Steele, and then hung himself. He hadn't even waited for his mother's funeral. Kelly. His mate. How had *he* got mixed up with a son of a bitch like Steele? Surely, it was self-defence. One thing he knew for sure was that Kelly didn't have a violent bone in his body.

To make matters worse, the last few days, Zeke had blathered on nonstop about how much he and Jerry were alike. They'd connected, but now he was leaving Greenock, and Zeke would be alone again…losing his brother for a second time. When the guards came to take Dylan away the big man cried. Bittersweet. That was the word.

Now, dressed in khakis and a navy-blue T-shirt, Dylan was about to walk out the door to freedom. The guard opened it, and nodded. He took his first breath of fresh air. And then he saw her. Recognized her from a photograph. Zeke's mum. She trudged up the sidewalk, a sad abstracted scowl on her face. He had to stop her. Had to say something.

"Excuse me, Mrs.—" He paused awkwardly, didn't know her name.

"Aye?"

"I wanted to say—" Another awkward pause. He stared at the sidewalk, could not meet her eyes. "Your son, Zeke. He and I—"

"Oh. You're Dylan McBride. I recognize you from the telly. I heard you was being released. You must be thrilled."

He shrugged. "I wanted to tell you that Zeke watched out for me in here. I don't know what would have happened if he hadn't."

"Ezekiel has good and bad bits like all of us. I'm glad you saw the good."

"I did. He remembered me from a bagpipe competition years ago."

She furrowed her brow. "Ezekiel's never been to a bagpipe competition. His younger brother, ach now, he could play the pipes."

"It was the National Championships in Glasgow, six years ago."

"He's dreamin', laddie." She shook her head. "Now that I look at you, though, I remember you myself."

Dylan surveyed her quizzically, the bleached blond hair and sad brown eyes. Wrinkles creased her pale neck and thin lips. Her uneven teeth were stained with nicotine. The stink of cigarette smoke wafted from her skin. She was maybe forty-five and looked sixty.

"You do?"

"Aye, sure. You played your heart out and won first place. But, Zeke? He wasn't there." She shook her head. "I'm sure of it. When Jeremiah won second at the Glasgow Championships, Ezekiel was locked up here in Greenock: two years for armed robbery and assault."

"But, he said—"

"He must have imagined it. Has a lively imagination, my Ezekiel does. Used to tell such stories when he was a bairn." She shrugged, then opened her purse and took out a package of cigarettes. After lighting one, she smoked for a moment in silence.

Hearing Zeke's laughter suddenly in his head, Dylan thought of the Oak King and their ceremony that night at the Ballymeanoch Stones.

"I'm sorry about your boys," he said. "I hope they find Jerry's killer so Zeke can be exonerated at last. It happens. It happened to me."

"Don't be daft, lad. They know who killed Jerry. There were a dozen witnesses. A whole crowd who watched my son get beaten to death by a gang of skinheads, and kept right on watching as Zeke ran up, pulled out a gun and shot them all dead. So many testified. Found their courage in the courtroom, after it was too late." Sniffing, she shook her head. "Ezekiel will never be free. Not while I'm alive at least."

"What?"

"The doctor says he blocked out the memory of killing those boys. I know, he just felt guilty. He'd never been around for Jeremiah, and he just couldn't take it. Seeing those boys beat up his brother like that, drove him mad."

She puffed on her smoke. "He was a homosexual, my Jerry. Ach, I was proud of him. And I'm proud of Ezekiel too, for taking revenge on those cunts. All those people just standin' there watchin' a gentle boy get beat to death, and the bloody polis never there when you need 'em."

"I...I'm sorry." Dylan heard his own stammering voice. Didn't know what else to say. The poor woman lost both her boys that night.

"Zeke mentioned you to me. Said you reminded him of Jerry. I can see it, the resemblance."

"He looked out for me like he would have done for his brother, and I know…I know he didn't mean—"

She touched his arm. "Write to Zeke sometimes, yeah?"

"Aye, sure. I can do that."

Then, she crushed out her cigarette and walked on. Dylan stood and watched her enter the prison for the thousandth time. Then, he turned, and walked away from Greenock and into the arms of his smiling grandad.

~~~

"I'm not up for a party. Not tonight," said Dylan. Estrada had parked the Harley in the lot across from Dunchraigaig Cairn. Dylan was feeling antsy after an awkward meal, where no one knew quite what to say. He needed to be on the move, and Estrada was glad to oblige. Though he didn't quite understand why he wanted to go back to the place he'd been apprehended.

"It wasn't my idea. You know Sorcha. She thinks you need to celebrate your freedom."

"My freedom?" Dylan pulled off the helmet and ran a hand through his hair. "I can't celebrate *my* freedom when it cost Kelly his life. Jesus Christ. He's been my mate since high school." Estrada took the helmet and stashed it in the saddlebag along with his own. "I just can't believe he killed a man…or that he was a tranny all this time."

"It was self-defence. And as for his sexual identity—people are masterminds at hiding who they really are. The world has made us that way."

Dylan shook his head. "I don't care what he was. I'm just shocked that I didn't know. We went to school together. Come on, Estrada, let's walk. I need to feel wind on my face and earth beneath my feet. That's how I want to celebrate my freedom."

They crossed the highway and strolled up the path towards the cairn. Estrada thought he was going to go exploring, but he veered left to give it a wide berth, and he watched with interest as Dylan avoided even stepping on the stones.

As if reading his mind, he said, "They'll show me. I can't handle seeing and feeling what went on in there that night."

Estrada nodded. Walking on, they passed the crazy trees that looked like giant brushes with their bushy heads and narrow trunks, turned at the farmer's gate, and wandered down the fenced path separating the fields.

Glancing at the moss-crested stones, Estrada thought of home for the first time in weeks—Sensara, their forest walks, and ceremonies at Buntzen Lake. It was almost August and the coven would be preparing for Lughnasadh. Was she training Yasu to take his place? He'd been so afraid of losing his position as High Priest of Hollystone Coven. Did it even matter now? Once he'd rescued Rachel from Roskilde, he planned to propose. Perhaps, they'd stay here in Scotland and make a baby. He smiled at the infinite possibilities.

Dylan seemed lost in his own world. Stopping quite suddenly, he sat on a stump and wiped tears from his flushed face using his fists. Estrada stretched out on the grass and gazed at the flawless sky.

"In jail—" Dylan began, and then paused. Estrada waited silently, wondering what his friend was about to disclose. This was as good a place as any to air confessions. "In jail, I met a man. His name was Ezekiel, like the prophet. They called him Big Zeke. The thing is, he saved me. If he hadn't, I don't know what would have happened. Wiley was—" Pausing, he pulled out a handful of grass and tossed it into the wind. "It was the magic, Estrada. It happened because of what you did here that night."

Estrada sat up. "So, the ritual worked."

"Aye, it worked. And the thing is, Zeke was...is my friend. He's in prison because he shot a gang of skinheads after they beat his brother to death in the street."

"Jesus."

"His brother was gay, and those skinheads— Well, it was a hate crime. Jerry was just walking down the street, and up comes a gang of thugs, and they beat him to death—*to death*—in front of a crowd of people. No one tried to stop them. And then along comes Zeke and catches them at it, and he goes mad. Shoots them. You know, they would have killed him too if they'd had the chance, and yet *he* ends up having to live the rest of his life in prison." He shook his head. "I just can't reconcile it."

"Some things can't be reconciled."

"And, what about Kelly? He could have ended up as dead as Jerry, and for the same reason. He fights back and still ends up dead. I just don't understand it." Shrugging, he took a deep breath and exhaled loudly. "I mean, some people do terrible things and nothing happens, and other people—"

"Kelly's dilemma left him with few choices. He didn't want to hurt his mum while she was sick, and yet he felt horrible for hurting you—"

"That's just it. He didn't hurt me. Nothing happened to me. And, I'm not innocent."

"Come on Dylan, you're the most innocent guy I know."

"But, you *don't* know. You don't know the real me. Just like, I didn't know Kelly, and no one knew Zeke, or his brother." He stood up and paced. "I'll tell you a story, and then you can decide how *innocent* I am."

Estrada stood and followed Dylan through the grassy field.

"When I was a kid in Nova Scotia, there were three boys who used to torment me something awful. It wasn't your regular kind of bullying—it was something else…something I can't say aloud, not now…maybe never.

"Anyway, I watched them all the time. I couldn't let my guard down, not for a second. I needed to know everything about them every minute of the day and night. I discovered that they had a hangout in this cove. It was an old fishing boat. They'd rigged it with an outboard motor, and they used to take it out in the bay.

"Well, one day, I stole a forty pounder of my mother's whiskey, and I left it down there in that boat in the cove. She hadn't even cracked it yet. I knew I'd get a thrashing later, but I didn't care. I hid behind some rocks and waited. And I watched those three boys drink so much booze they couldn't barely stand nor walk. And I waited and watched those drunken boys pile into that boat, just like I knew they would, and take her out in the bay. They didn't get far because there was a fair-sized submerged rock out there. I knew about that too. And, sure enough, they hit it dead on driving full tilt. Two of them drowned right then. I sat on shore and watched them go down. The third one made it home, but his dad put the boots to him so bad, he was never right in the head."

Estrada didn't know what to say.

"So, you see? I'm not innocent."

"That's a heavy cross to bear."

He stared at Estrada. "Aye." He sniffed and wiped his eyes. "How am I any different than Zeke or Kelly? I killed those boys just as sure as Zeke killed those skinheads, or Kelly killed Steele."

"I can't answer that, Dylan."

"Neither can I, but I keep asking."

"Vigilante justice, vengeance, self-defence. I've dragged my crosses too."

"I suspected so." Dylan winked, and for some odd reason, they both laughed.

"You know why they call it *doing time* right? All you have in there is *time*—time to think about all the things you did that got you there. You've got to let it go, man. Those boys chose to drink that booze. And that father chose to beat his son when he could have hugged him and been happy that he survived. And Kelly...he made a choice too—though I can think of so many other ways that could've gone. So did your man, Zeke. He didn't have to pull that trigger. The one thing I've learned from life is that it's all about making choices."

Dylan sighed. "What choice do I make now?"

"Let it go. Party and get wasted for once in your life. Maybe lose that *virgins rule* badge that you've been wearing ever since I've known you." He scoffed, but Estrada gestured across the pasture. "Now's your chance."

"Sorcha. Jesus." Dylan sniffed and wiped his face, then took a couple of deep breaths.

"You still bit?"

"Oh aye. She's all through me."

"There's your choice, man. Kai's out of the picture now. Take your shot. If you can handle what comes out of her mouth—"

"That's just it. I like it."

"You like being called a cunt?"

"Aye, sure. It's endearing. Besides, just look at her. She's spectacular." In her tight khaki shorts and spilling out of a lime green halter, she was that. She'd brushed her hair out and it flew burnished auburn in the sun like a lion's mane. Dylan knew he was in love. What he didn't know, was that Estrada had texted Sorcha from his phone about an hour before and asked her to meet him at Ballymeanoch. Sometimes, a man needed a little help to make the right choice.

"Well, you know what to do, man."

"I've got the general idea." He licked his lips. "Listen, thank you for everything. I couldn't have gotten through this—"

"We're not through it yet. We've still got a Viking to crucify.

CHAPTER SEVENTEEN

I Am Here for You

THANK GOD THE WATER WAS SHALLOW and Michael didn't have to swim. He'd never learned; preferring to remain indoors while others attempted to conquer the pool. Chlorine and other kids' piss and robust girls who yelled from the deck were not his style, even then. As he waded through the frigid waves, he was thankful to be wearing leather boots that saved his flesh from the cruelest rocks and barnacles.

On shore at last, he sank back against the sand and drank in the rain. If he hadn't been overcome by a fit of shivering that set his teeth jumping, he may have stayed that way, but the gale screeched and thrashed, slicing his flesh with its steely blades.

Sitting up, he examined his left hand. Crushed between coffin and rocks, it was bruised, swollen, bleeding, and most definitely broken. Already, he couldn't bend the last three fingers. Fragments of bone protruded just above the knuckles and all three nails were crushed. His little finger had sustained the worst damage. Nigel had insisted he keep up his first aid certification as club manager, so he knew it was a compound fracture. He'd need to clean it, splint it, and somehow wrap it; make a sling if possible. No antibiotics, and all he had to work with was his belt and the shirt on his back. Thank god, he was right-handed.

He padded his trouser pockets. Still had his lighter and cigarettes: one soggy uncracked pack; ten more in his gunmetal case and—Lord have mercy—six fat joints. He immediately peeled the paper from one and ate the pot. That should alleviate some of the pain.

Staring at the cigarettes, he thought: *nicotine withdrawal.* How long had it been? Hours? Days? They were too wet to smoke, but tobacco could dry out, if he could find some place to stash it out of the rain. He must find shelter.

He stood and looked around. The grey sea churned before him, but there was no sign of life. No boat. No lighthouse. Turning, he surveyed the shoreline. The small sandy beach was mainly cobblestone, strewn with shells, driftwood, seaweed, and a few bits of garbage. Flotsam and jetsam, cast up by the sea, like him. It was about thirty paces to the forest. Trees could provide some shelter, and if he was lucky, he might find a freshwater stream draining into the sea. Maybe someone even lived here, or had at one time.

How long had it been since he'd slept? Days? An extended party on the yacht, and then this crazy night of running and shaking and puking. His legs were stiff. His back aching. His hand throbbing. It must be mid-morning, though he wasn't sure. In the great roiling mass of grey clouds, he could find no sun. He shuddered to think that if Christophe had succeeded, this would have been his existence for eternity—misery and shadows, devoid of sun. Death-in-life.

As he stumbled across the beach, he picked up a driftwood branch, hooked on one end and knotted in the centre. A staff. His first gift from the island. Crooking it under his armpit, he picked and wandered his way along the wooded shoreline searching for water. The staff provided strength, stability, and oddly, comfort. Where there was no path a man must forge his own. Using the staff for balance he climbed over boulders, flung helter-skelter in the last ice age. The trees were bearded giants. Estrada would like this place. He'd be quoting poetry; was always talking about his nature treks and rituals in the woods.

An eagle's trill drew his eyes upwards, and he noticed that the sky was a shade lighter, the rain lessening, the storm ending. Exhaling, he staggered on.

The rippling voice of the stream called to him before he saw it and he followed its melodious song. Engorged by the rain, it flooded its banks. He fell to his knees and soaked his aching hand in the frigid water to numb the pain. It had swollen to twice its size, and the open fractures, riddled with debris, would soon become infected. He'd have to clean it well, wrap it, and sling it.

At last the rain had ended and the wind calmed. As he soaked his broken hand, he brought his mouth to the water and drank. Sweet and cold, it soothed his empty body and soul. Satiated, he sat up, took the soaked T-shirt and ripped it into strips as best he could. After rinsing off the worst of the mud, he hung bandages on branches to dry. Then, lying back, he cradled his head on a mossy log, and closed his eyes.

God, his hand was screaming! He'd get no rest this way. Then he remembered the pot. Grinning, he sat up, and gently shook out the gunmetal case. He set the cigarettes and five of the joints on the flat rock beside his cell phone. The last, he ripped in half and ate, one piece at a time, washing it down with another drink from the stream. Then he opened the sealed pack of cigarettes. They were damp, but he slipped one in his mouth and flicked his monogrammed lighter. Once. Twice. Three times. It burst into flame. Touching it to the end of his cigarette, he breathed in the precious tobacco and settled back against the moss. Thank you, god. He smoked it down to the filter, then jammed it in the dirt and closed his eyes.

When he awoke, the clouds had shifted and sun streaks were visible over the sea. He guessed it was perhaps six or seven o'clock. Had he slept the whole day away? The weed had worked well to dull the pain. The joints felt almost dry, so he lit one using his lighter and inhaled the smoke slowly and deeply; cupping his hands to suck in every bit. Then, he ate the roach. He sat a while staring at the shifting clouds, and then, grimacing, set about picking the worst of the debris from his injured fingers. Finally, he rinsed and wrapped his hand in the dried bandages. Fighting through the pain, he promised himself another cigarette when it was all over. Finally, he tied the two sleeves together to fashion a sling and slipped his hand through.

The falling temperature reminded him that he needed shelter: a camp and a fire. Even though it was mid-July, nights on the coast chilled considerably, and he had no protection, not even a shirt. With his hand bound and secured by the sling, he stood and slipped the staff under his right armpit. He could leave his cigarettes drying on the rock, but he'd need to mark it. Taking one of the unused bandages, he tied it to a branch beside the stream. At least, it was something to distinguish this place from others like it. He felt like he was finally taking control. Nature was harsh, but he could survive.

"All streams flow into the sea," he said aloud in a very British accent, then chuckled. Years ago, when he and Estrada first met, they spent one winter drinking brandy and smoking their version of pipe-weed, while reading *The Lord of the Rings* aloud in sundry accents. Estrada was charmed by Tolkien. Michael couldn't remember a time, he'd laughed more. "Ah. Not even one day alone in the woods and already I've turned into Gandalf."

"Gandalf didn't say that."

Michael glanced around.

"And, you're not alone, are you?"

"I thought I was." The husky male voice carried an odd accent. "Who are you? Show yourself."

When the branches parted, a tall man emerged, his half-naked body tattooed in spirals. His deep brown eyes were lined in kohl, his chin bearded, his lips painted deep gothic purple, and his face… It was no ordinary face: the nose long and angular, the ears pointed. A golden torque twisted around his neck like a coiled serpent and from his long braided chestnut hair sprung the velvety antlers of a stag.

"Narnia," said Michael. "This pot is spectacular. I've changed books."

"I am *not* a character from a book." The creature huffed, offended. "Neither a faun, nor a satyr, though they were fashioned from me."

"What are you, then?"

"Don't be impertinent," it thundered, and swaggered a few steps closer. "I am not a what. I am a *god*." Michael gasped, as the word echoed through the trees. And he saw at the end of the muscular legs, two cloven hooves. This statement was followed by another snort. "I believe, Michael Stryker, that you fall under my portfolio."

"I fall what—?" Michael sniffed and grimaced as a strange musky odour filled the air. "Under your portfolio?" He chuckled. "I'm game."

"Yes. Game to that bloodsucker that hunts you."

"What are you talking about?"

"Now, he floats in the sea. But once he rises and realizes that you are alive, he will come for you."

This was something Michael had not considered. Would Diego pursue a vendetta? "How do you know this?"

"Do you not listen? I am a god, and as I said, *you* fall under my portfolio. I've been tracking your activities since I was summoned."

"Summoned? By who?"

"The shaman...the magic one."

"The magic one?"

"Must you repeat everything I say?"

"Do you mean *Estrada*?"

When the creature winked and smiled, light spread in shimmering waves through the forest. "The shaman and I made a good deal." With one twist of his pelvis an enormous erection burst through the skins hanging from its hips.

"What the hell is that?"

"Have you never seen—"

"Yes, but why now? Did you and Estrada—?" Michael took a deep breath and exhaled loudly. This was getting stranger and stranger. "Is that for me?"

Narrowing his eyes, the creature turned his head reflectively.

Really, really good weed," breathed Michael.

"Follow me," said the creature. It looked annoyed then, like sufficient homage had not been paid. When it turned its back, a sough escaped Michael's lips. "What is it now?" It was irritated.

Michael shrugged. "It's just...your body is magnificent, as perfect as a Greek statue."

The creature rolled its eyes and spit. "Bloody Greeks...so overrated."

"Well, if you're not Greek, what are you?"

"I am the Horned God. I am life. I am death," he boomed.

"Do you have a name?" Riddles. Michael disliked riddles.

"Of course. How else could the shaman summon me?"

"Well, what is it?" A scathing glare sent a shiver rippling through Michael's flesh.

"A name is a power cache. It is not meant to be used casually or indiscriminately. Nor can it be demanded."

"Please, tell me. I promise to be respectful of your name. What can I call you?"

The creature reached one hand back offering it, as if in introduction. Long and slender, the skin was like supple leather, the dark nails sharp as hooks. For a moment, Michael hesitated, then remembering the vampire, he clasped the proffered hand.

Pulling back its mulberry-stained lips in a devilish smile, the creature pulled him close. Its dark eyes were much like Estrada's. Trembling, he breathed its musky scent.

"Very well, Michael Stryker. You may call me Cernunnos. For I am here for you."

~~~

The moon was full to bursting that July night. Dylan remembered that because it bathed the leafy valley in silvery shadow and merged with the fiery glow reflected in Sorcha's face to create perfection. He'd drunk just enough whiskey to feel its intoxicating effects without dulling his senses. Now, he was nursing a pale ale, so that later, when he'd taken her up on the offer she made him at Murphy's that night, he'd be feeling and remembering every detail. One thing this chaos had taught him was that life was short—too short to be clinging to romantic notions of forever love. She'd reaffirmed her offer this afternoon by the stones, and he'd accepted with a long slow kiss.

He was admiring her now from across the circle, listening to her voice harmonize with the others, watching her body sway to the rhythm of the guitars. It was all the foreplay he needed.

"Party wasn't such a bad idea, eh?" Estrada's question interrupted his reverie. Glancing up, he noticed that his eyes were as pink as his shirt. Bloodshot. He was wasted. Magus Dubh had brought along some strong pot and the two of them had been off smoking. Estrada reeked of it.

"Pure dead brilliant," he said, knowing it had been Sorcha's idea.

"Things worked out this afternoon then, between you and—"

"Aye. We went for a long walk. We talked."

"Talked? Is that all?"

"Aye."

"Sorcha's been a big help, you know. There were things I couldn't say while you were locked up; things I didn't want the authorities to know."

"I know."

"She introduced me to Dubh." He gestured at the wee man who slouched beside her on the blanket, begging for attention like a dog. "She helped me save his life, and later, he saved mine."

Dylan nodded. "I heard."

"What's going on, man?"

"Nothing."

"Something's going on. You've barely spoken to me all night." Dylan shrugged. "You think I *slept* with her. Is that what this is about? Listen, man. I did *not* sleep with her."

"You would have."

"Oh, I get it. She told you why Roskilde is so bent on ruining me, did she? Christ, Dylan. It was just a kiss."

"Just a kiss? What would have happened if Kai *hadn't* barged into her tent? I know you, Estrada. I know you would have—"

"No man, I wouldn't have. Believe me. Besides that, *she* kissed me." Dylan drained his beer and opened another. "It's true. *She* kissed me, and I was thinking about *you* the whole time—"

"Ach, don't make it worse! Stop talking."

"Come on, Dylan. You can't be mad at me for kissing her."

Dylan smiled at last. "Relax, man. I'm just taking the piss. I don't mind that you kissed her. I just want you to know, that I know." He'd laid claim to Sorcha, and he intended to defend it.

"She's gorgeous, man. Look at her."

"Oh, I'm looking. I've been looking all night."

"Well, what are you waiting for? Get your arse over there. Make your move."

"Ah, jeez, I can't. I don't know how to—"

"Dylan, listen. Go over there and kneel behind her on the blanket. Massage her neck and shoulders. Run your fingers through her hair, and when she leans back against you, which I guarantee she will, kiss the side of her neck, right below the earlobe."

"Is that one of your moves?"

Estrada winked. "Come in from behind, man. It's primal."

"Primal." Dylan stood and snorted. "Ach, fine." He sauntered around the outside of the circle, then knelt behind Sorcha and touched the tops of her shoulders. Immediately she turned.

"Finally! For a man who's been in prison for the past three weeks, you sure took your sweet time getting here." She pulled him down to the blanket beside her and sat on top of him. All Dylan could do was grin.

Then, holding the whiskey bottle high in the air, she yelled. "To Kelly Mackeras. Kelly, lad, you will be missed and always honoured in this camp."

She took a haul on the open bottle, while the echo of her tribute reverberated around the fire. "To Kelly Mackeras."

"And to Dylan McBride, his friend and ours, who survived three weeks in Greenock." He heard his name chanted amidst the cheers. "And, who I plan to ravage mercilessly." Whistles and whoops cut through his embarrassment. Clutching both sides of her face, he pulled her down and kissed her; mostly just to shut her up.

"Mercilessly," he whispered.

"Oh aye, McBride. I'll have you crying to the gods in no time."

"Me too," said Dubh, who'd suddenly appeared between them.

"Estrada's lonely," said Dylan, grinning. "He was just telling me how much he likes you, Magus Dubh. He said you saved his life and he wants to show you just how much he cares."

"Release the mighty dragon," giggled Sorcha.

"Aye, go on over. Creep up behind him and give him a peck on the back of the neck. It's primal."

~~~

"How do you know that Diego will come after me?" Cernunnos had led Michael to a small isolated beach where stood the ruins of a cabin. In the wreckage of a stone hearth, he'd helped him find enough dry wood and tinder to build a fire. Michael lounged on the sand with his back against a driftwood log and basked in the heat. Feeling the effects of another joint, he revelled in his hallucination, believing he'd created some strange apparition to allay his fears.

"The vampire has lost something of value. He holds you responsible."

"Something of value? The yacht?"

Cernunnos smirked. "It is no wonder your profane world hovers on the edge of oblivion."

"If not the yacht, then what?"

"Use your mind for something other than obsessing over sensual pleasure."

"There's no need to insult me. I'm injured and starving and—"

"The human," he growled, drawing out the words with his deep honeyed voice.

"The human? You mean Christophe? What happened? Is he...dead?"

Cernunnos nodded.

Michael hadn't thought about Christophe since he'd washed up on the beach. Now, the notion that he was being hunted by a vampire because of an ex-lover revolted him.

"How is that *my* fault? Did I *ask* to be taken to a vampire? Did I *ask* to be locked in a coffin? Did *I* conjure a gale to sink that bloody yacht?"

Cernunnos reached over suddenly and slapped a steely hand across Michael's mouth. "You will need your strength when he comes. I will release you only if you remain calm. Do you understand?"

Michael nodded, and the creature released his grip. He swaggered to the fire, took out a cigarette, and lit it from a flaming twig.

"When the boy thought you were lost, he gave himself to the sea. The vampire knows this, and will have his revenge."

"Suicide? Jesus, Christophe. Why did you do this to me?" Michael kicked the sand and a small explosion of debris landed on the creature.

Dusting himself off, Cernunnos shook his head. "You are nothing like the shaman."

"What do you mean by that?"

"His magic is great. He knows not *how* great. He uses only a fraction of the power he possesses, but, endeavours to benefit others."

"Oh, I see. I'm narcissistic, and Estrada's a fucking superhero."

"Would you give your life to save another? *He* will choose—" Cernunnos cocked his head slightly and sniffed, as if he had picked up a scent on the wind, and then, Diego descended.

Picking Michael up by the chin, the vampire hurled him against the stone hearth. He hung there confused, trying to remember what he was supposed to do. Finally, pulling a torch from the fire, he waved it in front of the vampire like a sword.

Diego laughed. "I thought to share my gift with you because *he* loved you, but you are nothing." Raising his lips, he revealed his fangs. "Insignificant. A mere aperitif."

"I could use a little backup here," Michael called out. Turning, he scanned the beach, but could see no sign of Cernunnos. Perhaps, he'd never been there at all—and yet, he was sure he'd just heard him say something about Estrada giving his life.

The vice-like grip on his wrist forced him to drop the torch. With one kick, it flew and landed in the sea. Holding him by the shoulders, the vampire stared into his eyes. Michael expected to see nothing but the cold eyes of a monster, yet saw something else. Grief.

"Did you love him?" Diego asked.

Inhaling the reeking carnivorous breath, Michael turned his face away and gagged. "No," he spat. There was something in that mesmerizing gaze that compelled him to tell the truth.

"I knew. I knew you did not love him." In his rage, the vampire squeezed. Michael felt the vicious claws dig into his biceps, saw the blood drip down. His right humerus cracked first—pain shot up and into his head. Dazed, he felt bile rise into his mouth. He coughed and spit. "Christophe was to be my next Salvador. You used him like a toy and abandoned him." The vampire's hand slid up his arm and bit into his shoulder. He swayed with the pain. "Ah, but what do you know of love? You have never loved anyone but yourself."

"That's not true," screamed Michael. "I love Estrada."

"Estrada?" The cackle was deafening. "A Spaniard? You love a *Spaniard?*"

"Yes, and there's nothing you can do to change that!" His only thought now was to die, before this filthy monster could turn him into something vile and monstrous.

Diego smirked and stroked his beard. "Ah, but there is, brainless boy." A cuff to the side of the head sent Michael reeling. It was only the creature's grip that kept him standing upright. "This Spaniard will become my progeny and then he will *drain you dry.*" Each of his final three words were punctuated by a stronger squeeze. Michael felt himself losing consciousness.

"Estrada will never do that," he muttered.

"The Spaniard will do as I command. He will have no choice." Diego caught the soft skin of Michael's neck with one of his fangs, ripped off a chunk of flesh, and spit it aside. Then he licked the blood like a dog.

"I will not drain you now," he said, wiping his mouth. "You will suffer as I suffer. Each time you look at your reflection in the mirror, you will see this scar, and remember," he breathed. "And you will tremble to know that one night I will come for him. I will take this man that you love, this *Estrada*, and he will belong to *me*...forever."

With a quick turn, he flung Michael across the beach and his head hit the rocks.

CHAPTER EIGHTEEN

Rachel

NOTHING MUCH HAPPENED FOR SEVERAL DAYS, as Estrada waited to hear from Kai Roskilde. If he'd harmed Rachel in any way, he would repay every hurt in triplicate. That was three-fold Wiccan Law. Kelly may have confessed to killing Alastair Steele, but Roskilde was just as guilty, and once Rachel was safely back in his arms, Estrada meant to bring the bastard to justice.

Healing from both his physical injuries and his grief over Kelly's suicide, he embraced village life, went for long silent walks in the countryside, and revelled in his heightened senses. Several afternoons, he sat on the sun-glazed hilltop by the ruin of Tarbert Castle, and read *The White Goddess* in the company of the stray goat. He was intrigued by Graves' divinely inspired words, and wondered if the Oak King himself had prompted the poet to write his story. Dylan believed that the Oak King had protected him in the guise of Big Zeke. Estrada hoped that his shield extended to Rachel and Michael, and continued to invoke both him and Cernunnos at nightly protection rituals.

And so, all remained quiet until the following Thursday when two events occurred, one right after the other.

Estrada was awakened at dawn by Dermot's insistent shaking. "Did you not hear the telephone ring, laddie?" He shook his head, hadn't heard a thing. "It's a man for you, a Nigel Stryker from Vancouver." He handed him the cordless. "He says it's urgent."

"Nigel?"

"Sandolino, I've just heard from the police. They found Michael. He's in a Coast Guard helicopter, on route to the hospital."

"Is he hurt? What happened?"

"Some kayakers discovered his camp on a small, secluded island off Johnson Strait. He was way the hell up the coast…injured and starving. But he'll recover."

"Thank god."

"Thank *you*, Sandolino. I don't know the whole story yet, but something happened on that yacht. It's a bloody miracle that he survived the storm, and that they found him. I'm going to see him in the morning and I'll make sure he calls you."

After Estrada hung up the phone, he turned to Dermot, who stood waiting. Throwing his arms around the old man, he hugged him. "My friend is safe. He was lost in a storm, but they found him."

"Oh, aye. Good," Dermot said awkwardly. "I'll just go and put the coffee on."

But, before he could leave, the phone rang again. It was Dylan calling from Kilmartin Glen, where he was shacked up with Sorcha. Dermot handed him the phone, nodded, and went downstairs.

"I just got a text from Rachel's cell phone. Kai wants to meet tonight at seven. He says to come alone. No cops or else. He sent coordinates."

"Coordinates? Like on a map?"

"Aye."

"Do you know where he is?"

"Scarba. It's an island in the Firth of Lorne."

"So, we'll need a boat."

"We? There's no *we*. I can't help you with this, Estrada. I wish I could, after all you've done for me. But, boats…I can't, man."

"Look Dylan. I've never driven a boat. Do you know someone—"

"*I'll* come," yelled Sorcha. "I can pilot a boat."

"Alright. I'll be there soon," he said, and hung up. If Dylan was that freaked out by boats, he must have his reasons. But, he refused to involve the police, and he knew nothing about boats. He'd have to take Sorcha. She could handle herself—that wasn't an issue. But, she despised Rachel, and that could be.

On the way to Kilmartin Glen, Estrada perseverated on Roskilde. Why call him out to an island? There was only one answer to that. He had murder on his mind. But why? Surely, his ego was not *so* fragile that one beating demanded death? He'd already beat him, broke his nose, *and* shot him. Even by Viking standards that should suffice for payback.

He drove the Harley through the fields and parked close to the camp. He hadn't seen Dylan since Monday night when he'd left him there after the party. The two of them were sitting outside drinking coffee, along with the others who worked the dig. Sorcha was mellower than he'd ever seen her, and Dylan looked different—like he'd been worked over by a wrestler, but won the fight. He was wearing a sleeveless T-shirt, shit-kicking boots, and his blue and green plaid kilt. That could only mean one thing. The last time he'd put on *that* kilt, they'd gone to rescue *Dylan's* girl. Now they were going to rescue his. Estrada wondered what had changed his mind.

"Hey handsome," said Sorcha. "Angus here's done some serious kayaking out around Scarba. He was just regaling us with facts about the island." She poured him a steaming mug of coffee and sat back in her battered lounge chair. "Better than fucking Google, aren't you Angus. Tell Estrada what you told us."

"Aye, sure. Scarba's part of a marine conservation area, so the folks you see out there are mainly kayakers, whale-watchers, photographers, eco-tourists, that lot. The island itself is in a treacherous location. The Strait of Grey Dogs at the north end is impassable, and the tides at the south end churn up the Corryvreckan whirlpools. They're considered some of the biggest, most treacherous whirlpools in the world."

"Jesus."

"Aye. Think of a funnel, but with tides from both east and west rushing through simultaneously. When they smash against the Old Hag—that's an underwater basalt pillar—the water is forced up to create a maelstrom. The currents can reach eight to ten knots, and that, along with contrary eddies, reefs and shoals. Well, it's a recipe for disaster."

"What's the island like?"

"Rocky. Patched in heather. It's part of the Slate Islands and the coastline is riddled with caves. At one time, there were keepers. Kilmory Lodge still stands in the northeast corner, but the island's uninhabited now. Except for ghosts and faeries, of course."

"Ah, ghosts and faeries, is it?" echoed Sorcha. "You've got a leg up there."

"Anywhere to land a boat?" Estrada asked.

Angus nodded. "There are plenty of sheltered bays with good anchorage, especially along the eastern shoreline. We sometimes put in at Bagh Gleann a'Mhaoil. There's a derelict cottage there. Just be sure you give Corryvreckan a wide berth."

"*Corryvreckan.* Even the name sounds treacherous," said Sorcha.

"It comes from the Gaelic: Bhreacain's Cauldron," explained Angus. "Bhreacain was a Norse king intent on winning the princess of the isles. To prove his bravery, he attempted to anchor his boat in the whirlpool. We learned that story in school. Remember Dylan?"

"Aye," replied Dylan. "But, King Bhreacain did not win the princess, did he? The poor man drowned."

"But his rope of virgin's hair lasted longer than the hemp or wool, he tied to the anchor," said Angus, "which just goes to show you—"

"Where can we rent a boat?" Estrada was eager to get going. Now he finally had Rachel in his sites, he wanted her back. Rested and fully healed, he was hungry for battle.

"I know a place," said Dylan.

"So, you're coming—?"

"We need to talk."

"Ah boys. Keep the broken bits to a minimum now. I'm tired of sponging up blood."

Estrada downed his coffee and followed Dylan up a trail that led away from the main camp. As he watched the plaid pleats sway with each step, he wondered again why he'd changed his mind.

"I see you're wearing your traditional hero gear."

"Aye." Dylan turned and stood with his hands on his hips, as stern and solid as a standing stone. "Sorcha will not be going on this caper. It's too dangerous, and it'll only piss Kai off." Estrada wondered who would be *more* pissed—her former lover, or her current.

"Have you told *her* yet?"

"No, but I will."

"Listen. I don't know what you have against boats, but I don't want to force you, man. Perhaps Dubh—"

"Don't be daft."

"Hey, the man's a Druid. He's powerful."

Dylan shook his head. "As I said before: there's things you don't know about me." Grasping the horizontal branch of a tree with both hands, he did a few chin-ups. When he saw Estrada admiring his bulging muscles, he said, "I worked out in Greenock. I like how it feels."

"I'm glad it did you *some* good being in there."

Dylan glanced away and would not meet his eyes. "I'm going to say this, and then we'll not talk about it ever again. Agreed?"

Estrada nodded once. "Agreed."

"My dad was a fisherman. He wanted me to be a fisherman too. Taught me everything he knew. He loved the sea and I did too. Then, one morning, he sailed out and the weather turned. They never found his body. I haven't been in a boat since that day. Christ. I haven't even eaten a fish."

"But, you're coming with me?"

"Aye. You came here to help me. It's only right."

Estrada nodded. "I'm sorry about your dad, man." Lost fathers. That was one more thing the two men shared.

Dylan shrugged. "There's another reason I'm coming. This all started when Sorcha unearthed Meritaten's broad collar. Kelly might have stolen it, but who's got it now? Kai." He ground his teeth, his anger seething like molten rock. "I want it back. I want it back for Sorcha."

"We'll get it back. Just promise me one thing."

"What's that?" asked Dylan.

"I get Roskilde. I owe that Viking bastard for taking Rachel."

"Sorry, man. I can't promise you that. But we *can* take turns."

Spray flew from the propeller as Dylan cranked up the power boat and they headed southwest through the Firth of Lorne. Estrada cleaned and repositioned his shades. The late afternoon sun glinting off the green water was near blinding. As they cleared the harbour, they passed a cluster of kayakers and several small pleasure craft. The place was a maze of rocky forested islands, much like the Pacific coast back home.

Sorcha had dropped them off without a fight, just a promise to stay in contact. Estrada was relieved that she would be on the mainland with her cell phone, just in case things got complicated. Angus had told them that the Police Marine Unit patrolled the shoreline. The problem was: there were five thousand square miles of coastal waters and only a dozen of them. If the police didn't know their exact location, they'd never find them. The boat they'd rented was a Viking river cruiser; something Estrada found ironic considering who they were hunting. It was about thirty years old and built for canals, but it was peak season and the only craft available.

Dylan drove from the cockpit in the flybridge, which was decked out in faded blue vinyl. Estrada hunkered down beside him. He wasn't much into boats either and his gut was aching. He pulled his new knife out of the sheath in his boot. It was a razor-sharp Bowie he'd just purchased at a rod and gun shop in Oban. He'd considered buying a pistol, but that required a Firearms Certificate, and there was no way he wanted his name attached to it; not with the police already on his case. Besides, he was much better with a knife. He'd used them all his life; even incorporated his throwing skills into his act.

Dylan glanced over as he hefted it. "That's a beauty. What are you planning to do with it?"

"Whatever it takes. I've met men like Kai Roskilde before. He's got a big mouth but I don't think he can back up his bullshit."

Dylan nodded. "Aye. Between us, we can take him."

"I'm glad you're confident. Too bad, you haven't got one of these stashed up your kilt."

Flipping up a corner of his plaid, Dylan revealed a small sheath knife belted around his right thigh. He grinned.

"Jesus, you're full of surprises. I assume you know how to *use* a knife."

"I know enough. Pull it out. Stick it in."

"Dylan, you—"

"Don't hesitate. Just do it."

"Only if you have to. If you're cornered and—"

"That's Scarba," Dylan said, gesturing with his chin at a distant rocky outcropping to the right. He'd outgrown his advice.

Estrada glanced at the waves, as they hummed along in silence, and thought about Rachel, prayed she was safe. He tried to pick up on her energy, but got nothing—it was jammed like a cell phone. This disturbed him. They'd only been together a few days, but he loved her. He should feel *something*. Unless, anxiety blocked him, or she was—

"We're close to those coordinates," Dylan said, at last. He slowed the engine, unrolled a chart and examined it.

"Estrada picked up a pair of binoculars and scanned all directions. "No boats. No one on shore either."

"The son of a bitch is out there watching us," said Dylan.

"Yeah. He won't appear until he knows he's safe. Didn't Angus say something about caves?"

"Aye."

"Maybe he stashed the boat in one of those sheltered coves and he's holed up in a cave? Stalking us from behind some rock like a snake."

Dylan scowled. "There's an easterly breeze and the tide's coming in fast. That's why he chose this time."

"I knew he wouldn't make it easy."

"We need to set an anchor. Have you ever done it?"

"Nope."

"There's a shallow bar off that point. I'll bring her in there."

"What should I do?"

"At the bow there"—he gestured to the front of the boat— "there's an anchor tied to a length of nylon rope. You'll need maybe thirty metres, maybe more. You never drop an anchor; just ease it slowly over the side, and hold it taught until you feel it hit the bottom."

"Okay." Estrada stood. "I can do that."

"Once it's set, you'll need to tie off the line around the bow cleat. Nothing fancy, just make sure your knot holds. I'll do the rest." Dylan sniffed and rubbed his nose. "And don't get caught up in the line."

"There," said Estrada. *Steele Away.* The name was painted in cobalt blue on the side of the sailing yacht. Rachel hadn't mentioned that they owned a yacht. How the hell did it end up in the hands of Kai Roskilde? Had the bastard bullied her into signing it over to him?

"Go below," he said to Dylan. "Call Sorcha, and stay hidden."

Rachel stood on the flybridge swaying like a silver willow, caught between Kai Roskilde and that bastard who'd cut Dubh. *They were partners.* The man stood slightly behind her. Had a gun jammed in her back. She called his name, then winced, as he pushed it a little deeper between her ribs. Her long platinum hair was flying free, her face healed. Draped in white, she looked perfect. His white goddess. He glanced at Roskilde and his adrenalin surged. If they'd raped her—

All three came down from the flybridge and stood on the deck.

"I don't believe you two have met, officially," Kai called out. "May I introduce Héctor Hassan?"

"What do you want, Roskilde?"

A corner of his lip flickered. "Come aboard. We'll talk."

"I don't want to talk. I came to—"

"Do you want her, or not?"

Roskilde hooked the gunwale of their craft, drew them together, and bound them. He had no choice. Estrada crossed over as the two craft bounced and bumped together in the current.

"Such heroic sacrifice…like something from a myth. I never could understand why a man would get his head kicked in for a woman."

"Are you forgetting Sorcha? If I remember, *you* took a beating—"

"Sit," said Kai, shoving him down on a stool.

Estrada didn't protest. He even allowed Kai to bind his wrists and ankles. A few punches should do it, and he could take that, if it meant Rachel would go free. Darkness had fallen, but she stood beneath a light and glowed. He admired her beauty, remembered those three frantic days and nights they'd spent together. She smiled…was relieved that he'd come for her.

Kai yanked him up and tied him to a pole, so he couldn't move his torso, arms, or legs. The coward was leaving nothing to chance.

"You have me. Let her go."

"Rachel, darling. Are you ready to leave us?" asked Kai.

She walked forward, grasped the back of Estrada's head, and kissed him; tenderly at first, and then she bit his bottom lip so hard, he tasted blood. Smirking, she backhanded him across the face. Estrada spat, hung there, and stared as she sashayed back and embraced Héctor.

"Gosh, I'm afraid she's not. As you can see, Rachel and Héctor have *bonded*. Oh, it's not Stockholm syndrome. These two have been at it for months." Cuddling up behind her, Héctor glared. "Keep watching, Estrada. It gets better. An audience really gets our detective wound up."

His jaw clenched. He couldn't swallow…couldn't believe…

"Ah, did you really think she was fucking you because she *loved* you? A man of the world like you?"

"Jesus, Rachel." His eyes itched, yet he dared not cry. Not now. Not in front of them.

"I warned you not to get involved," she said, coolly.

"Why? Why all the talk about relationships? About love?"

"Oh, did you pledge your love?" asked Roskilde, clutching his chest. "I think my heart is breaking."

"You wouldn't stop. I warned you. I threatened you…"

"Was it all lies? The Swedish mother? The cop father who died in the line of duty?"

She shrugged, then walked over and kissed him. He pulled away and spat in her face. She wiped it off with the back of her hand, then rolled her eyes. "It was three days, Estrada."

"Well, I hate to cut your reunion short kids, but we must go," said Roskilde. "Héctor, pop over to the cruiser and have a look around, will you? I smell a rat in the hold. Rachel darling, hoist their anchor."

The pair climbed aboard the river cruiser. "Perhaps, I can assist," said Kai, and taking out his cell phone, he keyed in a number. "Ah. The Proclaimers."

Estrada heard Héctor shout, and then he appeared on deck with Dylan in a headlock. With his other hand, he held his bleeding stomach. "Little prick stabbed me."

Roskilde climbed across and sucker-punched Dylan in the gut, then bound his hands and feet. Dylan cursed and struggled, until the two of them disabled him. Estrada hoped he'd got through to Sorcha. It was the only way they were going to get out of this.

"You realize, you've left us with no alternative," said Kai.

"The police are coming," shouted Dylan. "They know exactly where we are."

"Héctor, I'll finish up here with McBride. I'm sure you have something you want to say to Estrada for spending so much time with your woman."

As Héctor's swift fist connected with his face, pain sliced through Estrada's head. The blood dripping from his broken nose spurred the man on. After the beating, Héctor cut the rope that bound him to the pole, shoved him to the deck, and wound it around his legs. Then he tied it off with an anchor.

Estrada glanced over at Dylan. He too was trussed up and weighted down. The bastards were going to toss them both into the sea.

"He's done nothing," Estrada yelled. Blood dripped down the back of his throat. He coughed and spat on the deck.

"Oh, I disagree. Charlie informs me that he's been fucking Sorcha, and *she* is mine."

"Charlie?"

"My man in camp. Charlie is my eyes and ears, so to speak." He shrugged. "You boys really need to learn to keep your hands off women who don't belong to you."

Dylan was vibrating, but Estrada didn't know how to help him. And then, Roskilde let fly with a punch to Dylan's testicles that doubled him over in a heap. "That should do it." Hefting Dylan, he hurled him over the side of the boat.

"No," Estrada shouted, as he watched him sink beneath the cold dark waves.

"They should die together," said Rachel, in an icy monotone. She'd crossed back over and stood beside Héctor.

"I will kill you all," Estrada promised. Launching himself at Héctor's legs, he battered him with his head and shoulders. They laughed, then the two of them hoisted him up, and flung him into the sea.

The salt water stung his eyes, but he forced them open and searched frantically for Dylan. He remembered how he'd found Héctor that night in the alley. Heat imprints. Somehow, he had to do that again. Dylan's body would be warmer than the water. If he could find the trail, perhaps he could save him, or at the very least, not let him die alone.

When his vision adjusted, Estrada could see through the murky water. He searched for traces of colour, as he worked at the ropes that bound his hands. He'd never had a problem getting free of ropes. That was one of the first escapes he'd learned. But they didn't know that. He'd even performed Houdini's water escape a few times. If he remained calm, he could hold his breath for three minutes.

Within the first minute, he'd freed his hands, and then his feet, taken the knife from his boot, and cut the weight tied to his legs. Clinging to the anchor, he continued to sink.

Glancing up, he saw the two hulls of the boats drifting through the hazy water. Kai had used the anchor from the river cruiser to weigh Dylan down. Now they were towing it away. Even if the police were close, there would be no sign of them by the time they arrived. What should he do? Release the weight, swim to the surface, and tread water until the police boat came? Or keep sinking and searching? The answer came in a burst of scarlet mist seven metres below.

He dove towards it, holding the weight out in front of him and using his feet as propellers. Dylan was caught on a shoal, face down, snagged on a jagged rock. Estrada turned him over. If he wasn't dead already, he was damn close. He tried to ventilate with what little air he held in his lungs. It was no good. His face ached with broken bones and he had no oxygen left to give. He cut him free of the anchor and hauled him up. He couldn't leave him to decompose in the sea like his father.

Up, up, through the frigid water he struggled with Dylan's body. He was almost there. But, the body grew heavier as he grew dizzier. He could feel himself slipping into a place of darkness...couldn't do this alone...too tired.

And, then he glimpsed a man in the water. *Search and Rescue. They'd come.* He pushed Dylan's body into the man's arms and let go, praying he was still alive.

~~~

The face. Dylan knew the face. "Dad?"

"Aye, my boy. Cough up that water, now. Clear those lungs." Dylan felt his father's strong arms, holding him above the waves in the churning sea. His throat and nose burned from coughing up brine. He wiped his face, and stared into his father's brown eyes.

"But you drowned, daddy. You drowned when I was just a kid."

"Aye, laddie, but I never left. Always kept my eye on you. And, I'm damn proud of the man you've become."

"Am I drowned too?"

"No lad. It's not your time. That's why he saved you."

"Who?"

"Your mate."

"Where is he?" Dylan searched frantically. He could see nothing in the waves.

"There. Out in the channel."

At last, he saw Estrada's head bobbing in and out of the frothy waves where the tide poured into the strait.

"You've got to save him. He's caught in the current. It'll drag him into the whirlpool. He'll die."

"I can't son. I'm only here for you."

"Daddy. Please."

"He did his part. Saved your life. Brought you as far as he could and gave you to me."

"His part? Frantic tears streamed down Dylan's face. "Estrada doesn't deserve to die."

"I'm sorry, son—"

"But, we can't—"

"You've got to let him go, boy."

"We can't let him die."

"Look now. The police boat's coming for you."

"Please. I beg you." His anguished sobs were drowned out by the oncoming motor.

"You'll be fine, son."

"No. I won't. He's my best friend. He saved my life." He closed his eyes in desperation and when he opened them again, his father had vanished. Another hand clutched his arm. "Dad? Dad, please don't go."

With his ankles and wrists still bound by Kai's ropes, Dylan let them haul him into the police boat. "You've got to go after Estrada. He's there, caught in the currents. He's headed straight into Corryvreckan."

"The tide is at its peak, lad. We can't go in there now. It's not safe." The man shrugged. "I'm sorry."

"You can't just be sorry. It's your job to save people. You've got to try." He beat the officer on the chest, and then collapsed with his head in his hands, tears streaming down his face. "It's not fair. He saved my life. It's just not fair."

CHAPTER NINETEEN

Corryvreckan

OVER THE NEXT THREE DAYS, Dylan camped out with Sorcha at the dig, while the police searched the island of Scarba and surrounding coastline. They found nothing. Estrada had simply vanished. Sucked into the maelstrom, they believed his battered body had been dragged out to sea with the current. Nor was there any sign of Kai Roskilde, Rachel Erskine-Steele, or Héctor Hassan. Dylan spent hours with the police repeating all he had seen and heard. To no avail.

At first, the police prickled at the notion that a detective could be involved, but then a DCI Lyon arrived from Glasgow and changed everything. The Detective Chief Inspector had been watching Rachel Erskine-Steele for months because of her romantic liaison with Héctor Hassan, a suspected drug smuggler. According to Lyon, seventy percent of the cocaine coming into the United Kingdom originated from Columbia, then travelled through West Africa and Barcelona. Hassan was the Spanish connection, and Lyon was convinced they were using the yacht to smuggle it into Scotland.

Unfortunately, none of this helped assuage Dylan's grief over the loss of Estrada. And once the shock wore off, Sorcha was inconsolable. He'd never seen her so despondent.

"You're acting like you're somehow to blame for this. You're not," said Dylan.

"Kelly. Now Estrada. You're forgetting this all started when I found the artifact. I thought it was a blessing, but it's a curse."

"Ach, come on. You're a scientist. You don't believe in Egyptian curses. Besides, you didn't excavate a tomb and desecrate the dead. You only found her broad collar. Meritaten should be grateful."

"Dylan, it showed me things."

"What kind of things?"

"I saw herself. Meritaten. They hated her. The shaman tried to force her out of here. The cunt ripped off her collar and threw it in the pit. That's how it ended up in there. She's cursed it, she has. I know it."

Dylan remembered the scene he'd envisioned that night as he laid among the stones, her haughty demeanour and the shaman's chagrin. "Why didn't you say something before?"

"You'd have thought me mad."

"You're not mad, Sorcha."

"I know that now. I've seen crazier things since then. Hanging around Estrada—" She broke down then, and Dylan caught her in his arms.

"Listen. I have to call Michael Stryker," he said, once she'd calmed down. "I've been putting it off, hoping…" He shrugged.

"Who's Michael Stryker?"

"Estrada's mate. I don't know how to reach him though. I'll have to call the Club Pegasus. They'll know. And, I should call Sensara and Sylvia and Daphne. God, I just can't believe he's gone. He saved my life. Christ. If he'd just let me drown…"

~~~

Estrada awoke in a shadowy world of fractured rock and rumbling water. Had he sunk below the sea to some undiscovered Atlantean world? Or, been cast up onto one of the islands surrounding the maelstrom? One thing was certain: the salt-stained grotto in which he lay flooded intermittently. His body had been placed—he knew not by what magical force—on a ledge that projected from the side of the striated rock wall, mere inches above the waterline. Whether to be grateful or not, remained to be seen. He was barely alive, after having survived a violent trouncing by the Old Hag, and his recollections were scant. Choking. Panic. Thrashing. Defeat. What chance had a man—even a man with an ounce of faerie blood—against a primeval basalt pillar?

He licked his lips and tasted blood in his parched mouth. His flesh shuddered from the cold, and itched with dried salt. Battered and broken, his limbs were a mass of abrasions. He could not move them and feared paralysis. He dreaded to think the worst: that his back was broken beyond pain. If that was the case; his prognosis was death: a slow, malingering death. Dehydration. Delirium. Kidney failure. Coma.

In a fit of exasperation, he screamed long and hard; the thunderous breaking waves outside his cell beating against his brain like Thor's hammer. If he had such a tool and could lift his hand, he would use it to bash in his own skull. What was left but a lonely agonizing time in which to reflect upon his folly? For he was nothing but a fool.

Again, he'd let himself fall in love, only to be duped by a psychopath. For like Hamlet, Rachel Erskine-Steele was mad in craft. She'd played him since that moment in the underground, when she'd first invited him to her flat—her true motive to assure Héctor Hassan's escape. Taunting him with liquor and that tight white slip of a dress, she'd seduced him. Stopping him the first time he tried to make love to her, so he would ache to try again. And, when he didn't rush back fast enough, she came for him. He wasn't naïve enough to consider himself a victim. He was as much to blame as she was. He knew that she was crazy, but couldn't stop himself. Falling in love was like clasping a branch in an avalanche.

But what did it matter now? His only hope was that Dylan survived. He'd handed him off to a man in the water just before losing consciousness, and trusted that he was safely home. He could at least die knowing he'd accomplished what he came to this country to do.

Hours, or perhaps days, later, Estrada awoke to the warm rasping pressure of a tongue licking his face. The great pounding of Thor's hammer had lessened, though his head still ached incessantly. His weighted eyelids were swollen shut, and it took a great deal of effort to force them open.

When he did, he was confronted by the close furry face of a handsome black dog with copper-coloured eyes. A word emerged from childhood. *Perro.* As the dog stood staring, Estrada heard a voice: *do not be afraid.*

Truthfully, he *was* afraid. Not of this wolfish dog, with whom he felt an immediate bond, but of dying alone in a cave. Afraid that kayakers would stumble upon his rancid skeleton years from now and wonder who and what and why. After some time, the dog laid down beside him, and though he smelled bad, as wet dogs do, the warm familiarity of his body afforded some comfort. Again, he slept.

Awakening some time later, he felt a heavy weight on his chest and opened his eyes to Perro's wolfish head. The dog slept, muzzle pillowed on his breast. He lifted his hand from his side and stroked the damp black fur. It took several moments before he realized what had just occurred. *He'd moved his hand.* His shoulder ached, and he cried with joy to feel the pain. He assumed it was dislocated again—he'd suffered that agony before—but if he could move his hand, soon he could move other parts of his body. That meant, he could reset his shoulder. He'd done that before too. In pain, there was hope. If he could endure long enough, without water, he might eventually crawl out of this cave.

Sleeping and waking soon assumed a natural rhythm, as did the tide that ebbed and flowed in the cave. Had Perro found him here, or brought him here? Once during a slack tide, he awoke in the pristine silence of a chapel and laid listening to a soothing swirl of water at his back. Perhaps, some freshwater stream fed into the cave from above. He determined to move his legs, and after some time wiggled his toes. He laughed, then yelled: "Perro, I can move. I'm not paralyzed." The dog's answering whine reassured him that he understood.

Not long after that, he could move his hands and arms. In agony, he reached down, grasped his knee and pulled until he felt his shoulder slip back into place. Perro could not stand the violent swearing that accompanied this wrenching, and vanished. He often arrived just before the flood and slept on the ledge alongside him during high water, then left again during slack tide. Perhaps, he hunted or visited his family. A dog as friendly and healthy as Perro was no stray. He wondered why he'd not brought his humans to meet him and discussed this with him. The dog did not answer, but looked downcast, so Estrada never mentioned it again.

If the tide ebbed and flowed twice a day, he reckoned he'd been holed up in the cave for three days, when he investigated the source of the dripping. After easing his body off the ledge, he crawled on hands and knees into the dark recess of the cave. A tremendous headache prevented him from standing, but he knew time was running out. His heart beat rapidly and he was feverish. He must find fresh water or die.

Perro was absent when he began, but by the time he located the small slate crevasse at the base of a tiny waterfall, the dog was there beside him. They lapped up water together. Braced against the rock, Estrada drank for a very long time. When at last he felt satiated, he stuck his head under the icy waterfall and cleansed his salty skin. He discovered several gashes clotted with dried blood on his skull and determined that he'd likely suffered a concussion. If not for the faerie blood that flowed through his veins, he would most surely not have survived the Hag. He would like to have stayed lying on the cool smooth rocks by the waterfall, but he realized that during high tide this part of the cave flooded. After bathing as best he could, he crept back to his ledge and slept, while the sea claimed the cave once again.

As his pain and fever lessened, he obsessed about things, particularly food. Favourites paraded through his mind, especially the traditional foods his mother cooked when he was very young in Mexico: corn tortillas and guacamole, tamales, roast pork, hot chocolate and cinnamon, scrambled eggs and peppers, fresh fruit, goat cheese, chilies, and aged wine.

After the food came the people. Faces he'd not seen in far too long: grandparents and parents, sisters, aunts and uncles. Laughing faces from photographs and long misplaced memories.

And Michael, green eyes and long honey hair, his face all angles and seductive shadows. He touched the back of his hand to his chapped lips, closed his eyes, and kissed him. It was all he longed to do, and he slipped into sleep pressing his feverish mouth against Michael's.

Days later, after drinking his fill of water, he limped to the opening of the cave, sank to his knees, and peered out at the sea. The cave mouth was small, adequate for Perro, and just big enough for him to crawl through on hands and knees. Blinded momentarily by the harsh sunlight, he shielded his eyes.

Corryvreckan stood before him, bounded by a rock-strewn beach. Perro had not yet returned from his travels, but he knew the dog could find him if he chose to. He picked his way through the hag's rubble—

scattered shards of slate, slimy seaweed, and the skeletons of once sentient creatures—moving towards what appeared to be a climbable slope. Like some shipwrecked explorer, once at the top, Estrada could survey his kingdom.

~~~

"He's coming." Dylan tucked his mobile back in his pocket and managed a smile.

"Who?" asked Sorcha.

"Michael Stryker. He's furious that the police gave up the search for Estrada after only three days. Apparently, Michael's grandad, has connections here in the U.K. They're going to put the pressure on."

They were huddled around the campfire at Sorcha's rapidly diminishing camp. Charlie had been escorted out by two police officers. Dylan interrogated him until he admitted to being Kai's spy, but claimed he'd only done it because he'd been threatened. There seemed to be no end to the man's evil.

"Who is he, this Michael Stryker?" asked Sorcha.

"Estrada's best mate."

"As in…"

"As in what?"

"*You* know, Dylan. Are they just friends or something else?"

"I don't know. I don't ask things like that."

"You're lying, Dylan McBride."

"I am *not* lying."

"You're blushing, and you scratched your ear."

"So?"

"So, that's what you do when you're lying." Dylan scowled. "Oh, don't get your thong in a twist. I'm curious, is all. I saw himself kiss Kelly once."

"You did?"

"Aye. Right on the mouth. It was beautiful and sexy."

"Estrada's a free spirit, always has been. Do you think that he and Kelly—?"

"Oh, I don't know. I don't ask things like that," replied Sorcha, and punched him in the arm. The punch turned into a wrestling match on the grass and ended in a long leisurely kiss. "Don't distract me with sex, McBride. Tell me about this Michael Stryker. I'm curious what kind of man Estrada would choose."

"Honestly. I don't know him."

"Well, what's the craic? Come on, you must have *heard* things?"

"Just that he manages the Club Pegasus. It's a gothic nightclub in Vancouver. People dress up in costumes, party, get wasted—"

"Sounds cool."

"Estrada headlines there whenever he's in town."

"As a magician."

"Aye."

"What sort of magic does he do?"

"Theatrics, I think. Illusions, hypnotism, escapes...that sort of thing. Jeremy used to call him Houdini."

"Did he now? So, Estrada's an escape artist, is he?"

"Aye. I know he's good with straitjackets," he said, remembering their adventure last year.

Suddenly, Sorcha bolted upright and clasped his arm. "He's not dead, Dylan."

"What?"

"*Estrada is not dead.* A man like that does not drown in the sea off the coast of Scotland. I was there when he conjured up the old gods. I watched him hypnotize a man to save the life of Magus Dubh. And now, you tell me he's an escape artist. The cunt's not dead."

"I want to believe that," said Dylan.

"Believe it. The sooner this Michael Stryker gets here the better. We're chartering a yacht—one with a captain who knows his way around these islands. Estrada's out there, and we're going to find him."

~~~

Perhaps, he was still suffering the effects of dehydration or concussion, but anchored in a pale aqua bay below him, Estrada spied a yacht that looked remarkably like the *Steele Away*. There was no sign of activity or the murdering trio. Lying on his belly in the sun-warm grass, he leaned over the cliff and scrutinized the craft. A white and blue Sea Saga; she flew the Union Jack. They'd audaciously changed the name to *La Escapada*—Héctor's influence, no doubt—but it was the very same yacht, right down to the ropes they'd used to bind and weight him before tossing him in the sea.

Gingerly, he threaded his way down the rocky escarpment and around the bay, always keeping out of sight of the yacht. He intended a surprise reunion and, for once, he had the upper hand. They thought he was dead.

While passing a series of caves on his way towards the beach, he heard a peal of familiar laughter. Slipping inside the cavernous mouth, he crouched behind a boulder and surveyed the scene below.

Rachel Erskine-Steele and Héctor Hassan were packing a mountain of white powder into dry bags. Suddenly, the ruse made sense. It had nothing to do with jealousy—that was all peripheral; a sleight concocted to divert his attention away from the real trick. Rachel Erskine-Steele was a dirty cop, involved in a drug smuggling operation with Héctor Hassan and Kai Roskilde. The cocaine—at least, he assumed that's what it was—had been dumped, either on the island, or in the ocean, and these three were collecting it for distribution.

Had Alastair Steele discovered his wife's liaison with the Spanish smuggler, or her involvement in the operation? Kelly Mackeras assumed that he'd murdered Steele, but what if he hadn't? What if Steele was only unconscious when he walked away from the cave that night? Kai Roskilde had been there. What if he'd returned to murder Steele as he lay unconscious in the cairn, after sending Kelly to obtain the artifact?

These two were most likely armed. With this amount of dope to move, they'd have weapons to protect their investment. All he had was the knife in his boot. He was planning his approach when Rachel grew tired of the monotonous packing.

"This is boring," she whined. Pulling a small wooden box out of her pack, she slipped behind a rock.

"What are you up to, baby?" *Baby*. Estrada wanted to strangle Héctor Hassan just on principle. He was a proponent of sexual freedom, but what kind of man encouraged his woman to whore herself for the cause?

"Bow to your queen," Rachel ordered, sashaying from her hiding place. Naked, but for a sheer sarong knotted at the hip, she wore what could only be Meritaten's broad collar around her throat. Shaped like a crescent moon, the piece lay flat around her neck and shoulders. It was the first time Estrada had seen it, and for a moment, it took his breath away. Though Sorcha had explained that faience was only moulded and glazed ceramic created in the likeness of turquoise and lapis lazuli, the effect of the aqua interwoven with gold and precious jewels was startling. And, there was the knowledge of its antiquity...and Rachel.

Once, he had imagined her thus: long straight platinum hair falling across her cheeks, ornate jewels capping her creamy shoulders and that swanlike neck. Now, all he wanted to do was wring it.

"Down on your knees, slave," she commanded. Estrada wondered how far she would take this narcissistic drama. The bitch sure liked to play games.

"Yes, my queen. For you, I will do anything."

"Will you, Héctor? Will you really do *anything?*"

Héctor, who had dropped to his knees before her, loosed her sarong and let it fall to the ground. With hands and lips, he slowly explored the pale wasteland before him. "Oh yes, my queen."

"Would you die for me, Héctor?" she asked, gasping, as he found his mark.

"I would."

"And would you kill for me?"

He glanced up at her. "You know I would. I helped kill McBride and that interfering Mexican, and it's not my fault the dwarf survived." He smirked. "I would have killed your husband too, if *you* hadn't beaten me to it."

"What?" The word escaped Estrada's lips before he could stop it.

She shushed Héctor, and they paused in their play, listening. "Did you hear something?"

Estrada held his breath and waited. *Rachel.* It was her all along. No wonder she didn't want him to solve Steele's murder: *She* was the killer. She must have been there that night too, hiding in the dark by the cairn, waiting for her chance. This was the woman he'd first laid eyes on in the café at Kilmartin Glen: the cold and callous queen.

"It was only the sea," Héctor said, at last. He slipped out of his shorts and tossed them aside. Then, kneeling in front of Rachel, he kissed his way back down her belly. "I love how salty you taste after we swim, how the salt seeps into every crevasse."

It took everything Estrada had not to rush in and pummel them into the rocks. How many innocent people had to die for their pleasure? But, he needed to know the whole truth, to hear it all.

"Can you imagine how perfect life would be if *all* of this was ours, Héctor? I mean, just yours and mine? We could buy an Egyptian palace, and with this collar, we could start our own collection. Imagine it, Héctor. We could *be* Nefertiti and Akhenaten."

For several moments, the cave resounded with her escalating murmurs as Héctor continued to worship his queen. Then he stood, and scooped her up in his strong arms. Taking advantage of the moment, Estrada slipped behind them unobserved.

From this new vantage point, he scrutinized Héctor as a man does his nemesis. His skin was slick with sweat, and he was much stronger than Estrada expected. Biceps bulging, he held her airborne, exerting full control over each movement. His tall, sinewy body was lean and sculpted, and Estrada found himself impressed. Their cries crescendoed through the cave, until, at last, they collapsed on an empty dry bag.

"Consider it done, my love," said Héctor. "Once we've loaded the yacht, I'll take care of Roskilde. I hate the bastard. He's bossy, and he never shuts up."

"I couldn't agree more," Estrada said, sliding his knife against Héctor's warm quivering throat. Her scent, on his skin, was almost overpowering.

"Estrada," she cried. "How did you—?"

"Live?"

"I saw you—"

"Yes, you saw me bound and weighted and cast into the sea to drown. But, I didn't drown, did I?"

She stood staring, momentarily stunned by his resurrection.

"I know you're planning your new empire, Rachel, but I want that collar. Take it off and set it on the ground."

"No. It's mine."

He shook his head as he suddenly understood. "You told Héctor to kill Dubh just to ensure that Kai wouldn't sell it."

"Don't say anything," Héctor mumbled.

"Take it off, Rachel, or I'll cut your man. And I'll do it for real, not the way Kai cut you." He dragged the blade against Héctor's slick skin and watched the blood spurt.

"Stop," she said. Reaching behind her neck, she unhooked the collar and held it out. "It *is* exquisite, isn't it?"

He looked, and in that instant, she tossed it into a crevasse. Then Héctor jammed his elbow into Estrada's right leg, in precisely the place Kai had shot him; a place he'd just bruised during his fight with the Old Hag. Simultaneously, he struck his wrist with his left hand, snapping it back and extricating the knife, which fell to the rocks. Then, his fist broke Estrada's nose for the third time in as many weeks. Blood gushed.

"Jesus." Estrada went for him.

The sound of a pistol being cocked stopped them both. Héctor smirked. Rachel's first shot was naturally aimed at Estrada, but at the last second he dove behind Héctor. She moved involuntarily to avoid shooting her lover; the bullet ricocheted off a rock, and caught Héctor in the kidney. Clutching his bleeding back, he crashed to the ground. Still holding the gun, she ran to him, and stared at the wound in disbelief.

"Héctor. Get up," she ordered, crouching beside him. "You have to get up." He rolled his eyes and moaned. His blood was everywhere.

"I can help him, Rachel. Put down the gun and let me—"

"No," she screamed. "Stay away from him."

"Do you remember how fast my shoulder healed?" He ripped off his T-shirt. "Look. I don't even have a scar. And I survived the whirlpool. I can save him."

She pointed the gun at Estrada. "You ruined everything."

"If you shoot me now, he's a dead man. He's bleeding out—"

"I hate you," she spat, and squeezed the trigger. But, as she did, Perro launched from the shadows and hit her sideways, a muscular force of teeth and fur. His thick growls echoed through the cave mingling with her screams as she kicked and punched, desperate to break free. Estrada grabbed the gun and held it on her; while with open jaws, Perro wedged her down against the rocks, his teeth against her neck.

"Get it off me," she screamed.

"Perro. Let her go," he said. He had her in his sights and there would be no more trickery. Obeying, the black dog backed off and sat a few feet away, watching. A slow growl resounded in the cave.

"We're running out of time," Estrada said, kneeling by Héctor's back. "I'm going to help your boyfriend, so just stay there." He turned towards the dog. "Perro, watch her. If she moves, rip her throat out."

Estrada considered the implications, then taking his knife, he sliced across his left palm. Dropping the knife, he picked up the gun, just in case she couldn't keep still. Then, holding his bleeding palm over the bullet hole in Héctor's back he squeezed, and watched the precious fey blood drip into the wound.

"Rachel," moaned Héctor.

"He's scared. Let me hold him, please," she begged.

"How stupid do you think I—?"

Like a silver snake, she darted out, grasped the knife from the rocks, and lunged at Héctor. Estrada squeezed the trigger, just as Perro attacked. The bullet caught her in the shoulder, where only minutes before the faience beads had rested. She fell back and dropped the knife.

"You crazy heartless bitch. You'd kill him just to save yourself?" Estrada set the knife beside the dog, then balled up her shirt and shoved it against the bullet wound in her shoulder. "Sit here and hold this and don't you fucking move." Perro emitted a low steady growl as he stood watching, and Estrada knew he would not let either of them move again.

"You missed," she said.

"I intended to."

"Don't you hate me enough to—"

"Kill a cop? I may be a fool, but I'm not insane." Estrada shook his head. "Now, shut up, and let me finish this."

He turned to Héctor. "You have to stay alive, man, because you're going to tell the police what really happened to Alastair Steele." His nose was still gushing blood, so he took a handful and wiped it over the bullet hole. Then he folded Rachel's sarong and bound the wound tightly. He checked the man's pulse. It was barely beating. Héctor was in shock.

Taking the knife, Estrada made another cut in his palm beside the first and held it over Héctor's mouth.

The man licked his lips and grimaced. "What is that?"

"Elixir of the gods. Drink it. You're getting it just this once."

Then, placing both hands against his broken nose, Estrada set the bones. "Christ, that hurts. If you ever break my fucking nose again, I'll kill you." He wiped his bloody hands on his jeans and took a deep breath.

"Now, where's your phone?" Héctor glanced towards his shorts, which lay in a heap beside the bags of cocaine. "Don't pass out, man. You're going to call Roskilde and tell him to get his ass down here. Tell him you need help. Got it?"

The effect of the blood was startling; a miracle cure he had no intention of sharing with Rachel. Héctor nodded, and made the call. He was still weak, but the shock lessened as he regained his strength.

"Now tell me where the fuck we are."

"Jura."

"Is that an island?" Héctor nodded. Sweat drizzled down his face. "*Where* on Jura? What's this bay called?"

"Pigs. Bay of Pigs."

"Well, isn't that ironic?" Estrada pressed 0 for the operator and asked for the police. He needed Héctor alive. He needed him to tell the police that it was Rachel who killed Alastair Steele. It shouldn't be much of a problem since she'd just tried to kill him. He wanted the memory of Kelly Mackeras vindicated, and as much as he hated Rachel, he didn't want to be the one to take her life. He'd seen enough death. And, he was tired. Tired of loving. Tired of fighting. Tired of playing games.

Still, he had one last son of a bitch to reckon with before he slept. He bound both Rachel and Héctor, and left Perro to guard them. Then he walked outside into the sunshine.

On the beach, he chose a chunk of driftwood the size of a baseball bat, and hunkered down inside the mouth of the cave to wait.

CHAPTER TWENTY

PELLO

"DID YOU HEAR THAT?" asked Sorcha.

"What?" asked Dylan. "What's happening?"

"On the marine radio. The Coast Guard's just issued a mayday."

"Aye," said the young pilot of the charter yacht. "Someone's in need of police and emergency medical at Bagh Gleann nam Muc."

"Where?" asked Michael. He'd been resting, but hearing the excitement, suddenly appeared at the helm.

"*Bay of Pigs*. If we keep following this coastline, we'll be there in twenty minutes. Since, we're in the area, we're bound to respond."

"Do you think?" asked Sorcha. "Do you think it could be him?"

"It has to be him," said Michael.

He'd arrived in Paisley only that morning, looking frail, starved, and beaten. Dylan had picked him up at the airport. His left hand was in a cast, as was his right arm from shoulder to fingertips. His neck was bandaged, his skin cut and bruised. *There was no way, this Michael Stryker should be out of hospital,* thought Sorcha, *let alone flying halfway across the fucking world. So, this was the kind of man Estrada would choose.*

"But, what about Corryvreckan? Aren't we heading straight for it?" asked Dylan.

"Aye, but it's slack tide," said the pilot. "I've cruised by the Hag a couple of dozen times at slack tide with no problem. Best to sit down though, and stay clear of the side of the boat. I don't want you to bounce out if we get hit by a rogue wave. It could get rough."

The blood drained from Michael's face.

~~~

Estrada felt Kai Roskilde's erratic energy before the man entered the cave. Hovering at the right of the entrance, he hoisted the driftwood bat and whacked him across both shins as he stepped inside. Kai screamed, then went down gasping and gibbering; doubling over instinctively to protect his soft organs from further assaults.

Estrada stood over him and smirked. "Look up, Kai. Look up."

His head tilted, and when the hazy blue eyes connected, the blood drained from the Viking's face. "Surprized to see me? Sometimes, dead men *do* rise."

Kai grimaced and spat. "Coward."

"Yeah, I admit that was cowardly. I don't usually break a man's legs before a fight, but I'm tired. And that was payback for shooting me in the thigh." He rubbed his jaw. "This," he said, catching Kai underneath the chin with the bat and breaking the left side of his jaw, "is for the brass knuckles."

Kai fell forward holding his face, and moaned.

"Pain is excruciating, isn't it? Shoots right up into your brain." Kai's eyes burned with inner rage. "The police are on their way. Maybe, they'll give you something for the pain; maybe they won't. Better get used to it. This is just the beginning." In his eyes, Estrada saw the terror the man had instilled in others his whole life. "I owe you enough pain to last a lifetime, and I intend to settle that debt. Dylan owes you too. In fact, we debated who would get to beat you first. I guess I won that one, because...well, here we are."

Estrada paused, then cleared his throat and spit. "Now, you and your *friends* attempted to drown me, so I've been sitting here imagining how I could pay *that* back. Poetic justice, you know. I thought about dragging you down to the sea and holding your head under with my boot." Kai pulled back in terror. "And, I thought about shooting you somewhere inconvenient with Rachel's Glock," he said, pulling the gun from his pocket.

Kai snorted and mumbled. "Just try it."

"Broken jaw, and still talking?" Bringing up his right foot, Estrada balanced on his left. "I even thought about breaking your god-damned nose." Jamming the heel of his boot into Kai's face, he listened to the bones crack. Tears welled up in the man's eyes. "Oh, come on, man, you can't blame me for that."

Sitting down, Estrada leaned back against the rock wall with his hands behind his head, fondled the gun, and ignored the cursing and moaning. "Anyway, after all this reflection, I realized that Dylan owes you more than I do. You're the bastard that planted that bloody hanky and got him sent to prison. You even cleaned Kelly's prints off that bloody rock, and called the cops that morning to tell them that the killer was sleeping by the Ballymeanoch Stones."

"I did not," breathed Kai, through one side of his jaw.

"Héctor says you did," said Estrada, pulling a cell phone from his jacket pocket. "In fact, Héctor says that you planned it all. Listen to this." He hit play and a man's voice echoed through the cave.

Kai Roskilde phoned us real late Friday night. It was almost morning. We were asleep at my place in Ardfern. Steele had found out about the smuggling and wanted in. He threatened to turn in Rachel. Kai said, he had a way to get rid of Steele and get the Egyptian collar without getting us involved. He could blame a couple of kids. So, we drove to the cairn and found Steele unconscious just like Kai said he would be.

"Enough?" asked Estrada. "Or do you want to hear the part where he explains how you used Kelly Mackeras to steal the artifact and framed Dylan for murdering Steele?"

"No evidence," said Kai.

"Maybe not. I don't know. But I'm willing to testify to what happened on that fucking yacht. I'm sure there's still evidence there: fingerprints, blood spatter..." Kai's faced paled. "Attempted murder. Two counts: me and Dylan. That'll get you into Greenock."

Estrada glanced at the sky, distracted by the thunder of an incoming chopper. Kai's eyes closed. He was passing out.

"Wait. Wake up. Here's the part you don't want to miss," Estrada said. "Dylan made a great friend in Greenock Prison: a lifer who's in there for shooting a whole gang of skinheads because they murdered his gay brother. Can you imagine that? Big guy. Tough. Crazy as shit. How is Big Zeke going to feel when he finds out that you set Dylan up for…what? That mountain of blow in there? And then, you tied him to an anchor and tossed him in the sea? And Dylan fucking hates the ocean."

The police helicopter landed nimbly on the cliff above the cave.

"Anything else you want to say, Kai, because I'm about done and the cops are here?"

"Fuck off," he breathed.

"Yeah, that's what I thought you'd say."

When the police arrived, he gave them Rachel's Glock and Héctor's phone. Then, he went outside and leaned back against a rock. Closing his eyes, he took a moment to breathe and to ground. The violence had taken its toll. Now, all he wanted was peace.

"Excuse me. Is your name Estrada?"

He opened his eyes to an inquisitive young officer.

"It is."

"We've been looking for you. Heard you went down in the whirlpool. How'd you survive all this time?"

"What do you mean *all* this time? How long's it been?"

"Seven days."

"Seven days?"

"Aye. After three days, they called off the search, and then yesterday, it was on again. Someone cares enough about you not to give up."

"Aye, but not just someone. Everyone."

Estrada turned and scrambled up when he heard Dylan's voice. "Hey man. You *are* alive. I prayed that wasn't a dream. Thank god, they got you out."

"*You* got me out," Dylan replied, and the two men embraced.

"Estrada!" screamed Sorcha, grasping them both.

"Easy now," said Dylan. "He's likely broken."

"On the mend. But how did you—?" He stopped in mid-thought when he saw who was standing behind them. "Michael?" Shivers ran up and down Estrada's arms. Michael's right arm was in a cast from shoulder to fingertips. His neck bandaged. His left hand in a cast. He wore a baseball cap and sunglasses and tears dripped down his cheeks. "What the fuck are you doing here?"

"I knew we'd find you." He fell against Estrada's chest.

"Are you crying, man?"

"I thought I'd lost you, compadre. Christ, I thought I'd lost me."

Estrada held Michael, feeling things he couldn't put into words. And then, he too, was crying...holding Michael and sobbing into his shoulder.

Later that night, after hours spent conversing with the police, they huddled around the fire at Sorcha's camp, swapping wine and stories. It was July twenty-fifth—exactly one month since Estrada flew to Scotland. When he got to the part about Perro, Dylan burst out laughing and snorting; grasping his stomach until tears ran down his cheeks.

"What is *so* funny?" asked Estrada.

"Jeez, man. A thing like that couldn't happen to anyone but you."

"What do you mean?"

"Do you remember the story of Breachan, the Norwegian King who tried to conquer the whirlpool so he could win the hand of the island princess?"

"Yeah, the fool drowned."

"Aye, but we did not tell you the end. Breachan's body was pulled from the whirlpool by his faithful black dog and deposited in a cave on the north end of Jura."

"No way." Estrada skin rippled with goose bumps.

"Aye, it's true. The cave is called Uamb Breacain and it's right where you said you woke up."

"Holy Christ, Estrada. Dylan's right. Only *you* could be rescued by a ghost dog," said Sorcha.

Had the dog pulled his body from the whirlpool and dragged him to that ledge? But he couldn't have been a ghost. Rachel and Héctor had seen him too. When she tried to shoot him, he'd knocked her down.

"Perro saved my life," he muttered. "Twice."

"What happened to him?" asked Sorcha.

"He disappeared." Estrada shrugged. "He knew I didn't need him anymore."

"I hope they're locked away for life," said Dylan, suddenly serious. "All three of them."

"Hey, I almost forgot." Estrada pulled a box from his jacket pocket. "I have a gift for you, Ms. O'Hallorhan."

When she opened it, her eyes grew wide. "Hah! You found it. I thought herself had hidden it where no one ever would."

"She tried. Wanted to use it to build her empire." He scoffed. "But it came home. It belongs here with you."

"Ah, you're wrong there, Estrada. Meritaten's collar belongs to the Lord's Remembrancer; at least for the moment." Sorcha took the collar from the box, closed her eyes, and touched it to her heart.

"What the hell is that, anyway? The Lord's Remembrancer?"

"Ah, it's Scotland," said Dylan. "Tradition and all that."

"But, it's probably worth millions. Dubh could broker it. With that kind of money, you could do anything—"

"True enough," said Sorcha. "But this collar is both blessed and cursed. I'm sure you've heard of Egyptian curses. They're nothing to fuck with."

"Where *is* Dubh?" asked Estrada. "He should be here tonight."

"No idea," said Sorcha.

"Magus Dubh is someone you really should meet," Estrada said to Michael. "He is extraordinary in the truest sense of the word."

Dylan stood, and touched Estrada's arm. "Got a minute?"

"Sure." He rubbed Michael's uninjured shoulder. "I'll be right back." Michael had been quietly popping painkillers, but Estrada didn't think chemicals could touch what he was going through. Locked in a coffin, floating in the sea during a gale—that was traumatic enough. But, he suspected that something else happened out there on the coast. Something unspeakable. He'd tried to find the old Michael, but he'd vanished. This new man was a stranger, so tightly bound, if he pulled the wrong thread, he might come unravelled. Still, after the ordeal he'd been through, Michael had come all this way to find him, and that meant the world.

He followed Dylan out into the shadowy field. When they stopped at last, he looked deadly serious and Estrada felt a shiver of apprehension, wondering what was coming next.

Dylan took a deep breath. "I need to tell you something."

"I'm listening."

"After three days the police called off the search. They told us... They thought you were dead. I thought you were dead. I saw you caught in the current." He shrugged.

Estrada nodded. "It's okay, man. I thought I was dead too."

"Aye." He paused, gnawing his lip.

"What is it?"

"Well, I felt it was my duty to call home and tell them what happened. I called Club Pegasus and they put me in touch with Michael."

"Yeah, man. Thanks for doing that. I'm glad he's here."

Dylan shrugged. "Then, I called Sylvia. I thought the coven should know."

Estrada nodded. "Absolutely." He couldn't imagine what tragic news Dylan was building to. Had someone been hurt back home? Was Yasu now High Priest? Had Sensara ousted him in his absence?

"Sylvia told me something...something you should know."

"Just say it Dylan."

"It's about Sensara."

He held his breath. "Go on."

"She's pregnant."

"Pregnant?" He choked and coughed. Of all the things, he expected to hear, *that* was the furthest from his thoughts.

"Aye. Sensara's having a baby."

But, who was the father? Yasu? Things must be more serious with them than he suspected.

"Sylvia said, she's due the beginning of August."

"What? That's next week," said Estrada. His eyes narrowed in confusion.

"Aye."

"How did we not know something like that?"

"She's been hiding it all this time. She told the girls a few months back, but swore them to secrecy. Estrada, count back, man." He held up nine fingers. "The baby is yours."

"Mine?" He shook his head. "But, that's not possible. Sensara always made me—" His mind raced back to the previous fall, their brief affair, the last night they made love…in the hallway outside Michael's place. She'd been so desperate; she hadn't cared about protection.

Dylan smiled. "Estrada, you're going to be a father."

"A father." Somehow, he just couldn't imagine it. And yet, he knew in his heart, it was something he wanted. He remembered his conversations with Rachel, and with Primrose; especially what she prophesied that day in the forest at Taynish. *You'll be a father and a grand one.*

"Jesus, Dylan. I'm just…I'm amazed."

"Ach, there's not a man I know would make a better dad than you, Estrada. You saved my life, and I'll never forget that, but you also made me a better person. And, that's what dads do. That's what you'll do for your child."

"*My* child," echoed Estrada. He was going to be a father, and life would never be the same again.

EPILOGUE

THINGS HAD BEEN QUIET AROUND SORCHA'S CAMP since the sensation died down, the paparazzi disappeared, and most of her crew returned to their respective jobs and universities. That included Dylan, who'd just completed another year of study in Vancouver. He wanted to return to Kilmartin Glen, but she was ready to pull up stakes. She didn't know why she'd stayed so long. It was time.

She'd written and published her paper on Meritaten, the Egyptian Princess who visited the Hebrides and left behind her broad collar in 1350 B.C. And, she'd lectured at several universities. But Sorcha's mind kept returning to that night, last July, when she stood naked by the standing stones and promised herself to the horned god.

It seemed like a dream, and yet, on moonlit nights, she wandered the fields, calling his name. *Cernunnos*. It was derived from the Greek word *carn* meaning horn. He was as old as humanity, the spirit of the hunt. Christ, he'd inspired the word *horny*. After his image was painted on a cave wall at Caverne de Trois-Frères in France, during the Paleolithic, he'd drifted through prehistory, surviving until Christians turned him into Satan.

She'd traced the appearance of the horned god through a myriad of cultures, times, and locales: beginning with Pashupati from the Indus Valley, into Minoan Crete and what was once Thrace; through the Danube Valley, Northern Italy, and into Gaul; where his name and image was etched on a pillar beneath Notre Dame Cathedral in Paris.

She'd even travelled to the British Museum to see the original Gundestrup Cauldron. Crafted by multiple silversmiths and gilded in gold during the Iron Age, this ritual cauldron depicts the horned god seated as a yogi. He holds a Celtic torque and a serpent in each hand, and is surrounded by lions, deer, and gryphons. The cauldron's origins are debated, yet Sorcha knew if she could only touch it, hold it in her hands, she would know the truth.

And she wanted to know, needed to know.

Cernunnos. With those primordial hands, he had touched her, and left her longing to be touched again.

It was the first of May. Beltane. She was sleeping when his scent wafted over her, infused with everything in nature she relished most—the odour of fecund earth after a spring rain, musky wild horses, and puppy's ears, ripe peaches soaked in honeyed spices—and something else, some pheromone that awakened her desire.

Sitting up, she turned on the torch beside her bed and shone it around the carpeted walls of her tent. Seeing nothing, she emerged, and opened the partition, feeling her pulse quicken as the scent intensified. He was near, but where? She poured herself a large shot of whiskey and downed it, then drew a soft white cotton robe around her naked body and slipped outside barefoot. It was around three in the morning, thank god, so the few volunteers in her sparse camp were asleep. She followed a sheep trail through the damp grass, down through the meadow, towards the stream.

When he touched the back of her neck, she gasped, lost her balance and fell to the ground. Reaching down, he offered his hand. His touch made her weep.

"I don't know why I'm crying."

"To find that which you seek can be overwhelming." Sweeping her into his arms, he held her against his chest. "Do you fear me, Sorcha O'Hallorhan?"

"Certainly not."

"Good. I will not hurt or force you, though my desire for you is immense."

"Aye," she smiled. "I can feel it."

"It has been a very long time since I coupled with a woman on Beltane…over two millennia."

"Really? But, why now? Why me?"

"The shaman summoned me, and you…you offered yourself. *You believe.* How could I not accept such an offer?" The touch of his dark lips against her neck sent a shiver spiralling down her spine, and she gasped again. "I know you, Sorcha O'Hallorhan. I know your desires and your dreams, and I can give you the answers you seek."

"What do you mean?"

"You long to live in the past, to experience what exists no more."

"That's true."

"Then I shall take you there." His dark eyes, so mesmerizing, caught and held her. Laying his palm against her cheek, he touched her warm lips with his thumb. "Anywhere in this world, to any time or culture you desire. It is your choice."

Impulses flooded her body, fantastic sensations, building like the force of a sensual current when the cavern walls close in. "I can't think. I can't—"

"Close your eyes." As his mouth opened to hers, their breath and flesh merged, sensations deepened, rippling through every cell of her body culminating, at last, in an orgasmic peak.

"Did we just—?"

"You did."

"From a kiss?"

When he smiled, a torch burned in his dark eyes. "It was needed to balance your equilibrium."

"Cernunnos." Reaching up, she touched his horn. "I'm still feeling a little unbalanced."

Smiling, he brushed her lips with his. "Have you decided?"

"How can I? There are so many cultures, so many moments in time I've studied and dreamed of experiencing."

"Close your eyes, breathe, and envision this place of your dreams."

Nestled in his arms, her mind drifted through a theatre of stars and came at last to rest. "It's incredible. But, I don't know where I am."

"I do, Sorcha O'Hallorhan. For I am here for you.

Series Characters

The Witches of Hollystone Coven (British Columbia, Canada):

- Sensara Narado: High Priestess. Therapist/psychic, she created the coven, makes and enforces the rules.
- Sandolino Estrada: High Priest. Estrada is a magician who performs weekly at Club Pegasus in Vancouver when he's not performing at other venues, or out solving crimes.
- Dylan McBride: Canadian archaeology student, raised by his grandfather in Tarbert, Scotland. Dylan travels the world playing bagpipes with the university pipe band.
- Daphne Sky: landscaper gardener and earth mother
- Raine Carrera: a journalist for an alternative press who recently joined the coven. Raine and Daphne are partners.
- Dr. Sylvia Black: Welsh university professor who publishes books on Celtic Studies. When Dylan arrived from Scotland, Sylvia became his foster mother and introduced him to the witches of Hollystone Coven.
- Jeremy Jones: an exceptional costume designer who specializes in medieval clothing, ritual tools, and paraphernalia. He sells through his online shop, Regalia.
- Maggie Taylor: Canadian girl who joins the coven in *To Charm a Killer* and later moves to Ireland.

Others:

- Nigel Stryker: entrepreneur and owner of the Club Pegasus in Vancouver, Canada
- Michael Stryker/Mandragora: Hedonistic manager of Club Pegasus, Michael is Estrada's best friend. He believes himself the reincarnation of Lord Byron and likes to play vampire.
- Magus Dubh (Dove): the tattooed half-fey dwarf who deals in antiquities through his Glasgow shop, The Blue Door

Acknowledgements

The archaeological story in this book is derived from the work of Egyptologist Lorraine Evans in her book *Kingdom of the Ark: The Startling Story of how the Ancient British Race is Descended from the Pharaohs* (London: Pocket Books, 2001).

The story is set in Kilmartin Glen, Scotland, an area rich in megaliths. I would especially like to acknowledge Rachel Butter's book, *Kilmartin: An Introduction and Guide*, with photography by David Lyons (Kilmartin House Trust, 1999). When I created Dylan McBride with his unique ability to speak with stones, I knew he lived in Argyll and discovered his talent there. Later, I found this helpful book, while visiting. For more information, visit the Kilmartin Museum online. Thanks to Kat McCarthy at Aeternum Designs for creating a beautiful cover from my random thoughts.

Special thanks to Jackie, my travelling companion in Scotland. Without Jackie's keen eye, I would never have found Ballymeanoch, where Dylan sleeps with the stones. A big thank you to Andrew MacDiarmid, proprietor of The Moorings Bed and Breakfast in Tarbert, Scotland. When Jackie and I arrived in the village late one night we were fortunate to discover that Andrew had one room left "obviously meant for us".

Thank you to Marina at the Archives in Lochgilphead for her answers to my email queries regarding police and legal proceedings in Argyll, Scotland. Errors are my own. I've taken liberties and apologize to Police Scotland, who I'm sure are a sensitive, respectful, and dedicated force. Thank you, also to Kenny Turner, my Scottish friend, for invaluable insight into the appropriate use of slang; particularly Sorcha O'Hallorhan's more colourful vocabulary.

I'm also grateful to my beta-reader Eman Ferdaoussi of abooknation.com who provided valuable commentary. And, as always, special thanks to my very first reader, Tara Patrice.

Finally, I must acknowledge poet Robert Graves, who authored *The White Goddess: A Historical Grammar of Poetic Myth*. (UK: Faber and Faber, 1999). Without Graves' intuitive insights, I'm afraid that Estrada would never have really understood the Oak King. Permission to discuss Graves' work obtained through Carcanet Press, Manchester, UK.

While the characters in this story are fictional, many of the places are real, and most I have visited. Buntzen Lake, where the witches of Hollystone Coven perform their Sabbat ceremonies, is in British Columbia. Most settings in Scotland exist, including Dunchraigaig Cairn in Kilmartin Glen, and Her Majesty's Prison Greenock. If you're curious about the Corryvreckan Whirlpool, you can find more information at Whirpool Scotland and watch a fantastic video of this unique landscape. Scotland is a beautiful and magical land; a place to be explored time and again.

WL Hawkin
March 2017

Author Bio

WL Hawkin completed a BA in Indigenous Studies at Trent University, and PBDs in Humanities at Simon Fraser University, Canada. Fascinated by her Celtic and Tuscarora ancestry, she explores history, myth, and spirituality in her work. She is passionate about literature, nature, and writing, and is happiest wandering by water. Born in Toronto, Canada, she currently lives in British Columbia, but dreams of living in Ireland.

Thank you for reading *To Sleep with Stones*. If you enjoyed it, you might like *To Charm a Killer* (Book One in the Hollystone Mysteries series). Please consider taking a moment to leave a review with your favourite retailer. For comments or questions, contact me at bluehavenpress.com. Follow me on Twitter @ladyhawke1003 or Facebook@wlhawkin ~Blessings, Wendy

CPSIA information can be obtained
at www.ICGtesting.com
Printed in the USA
LVOW12s1125150317

527276LV00001B/2/P